THEY ARE THE WE OF ME.

"Yesterday, and all the twelve years of her life, she had only been Frankie. She was an I person who had to walk around and do things by herself. All other people had a we to claim, all other except her. . . .

"Now all this was suddenly over with and changed. There was her brother and the bride, and it was as though when first she saw them something she had known inside of her: They are the we of me. . . ."

Carson McCullers's first novel, The Heart Is a Lonely Hunter, which became a literary sensation for the twenty-three-year-old author, was followed by Reflections in a Golden Eye, The Ballad of the Sad Café and Clock without Hands. The Member of the Wedding was a prize-winning Broadway play and a motion picture.

The Member of the Wedding

by Carson McCullers

BANTAM BOOKS

NEW YORK • TORONTO • LONDON • SYDNEY • AUCKLAND

The characters in this book
are fictitious; any resemblance to
real persons is wholly accidental
and unintentional

*This edition contains the complete text
of the original hardcover edition.*
NOT ONE WORD HAS BEEN OMITTED.

RL 6, IL age 12 and up

THE MEMBER OF THE WEDDING
*A Bantam Book / published by arrangement with
Houghton Mifflin Company*

PRINTING HISTORY
Houghton Mifflin edition published March 1946
New Houghton Mifflin edition published September 1961
Excerpt appeared in HARPER'S BAZAAR *January 1946*
Bantam edition / October 1950
New Bantam edition / March 1958

ISBN 0-553-25051-5

Published simultaneously in the United States and Canada

*Bantam Books are published by Bantam Books, a division of Bantam Doubleday
Dell Publishing Group, Inc. Its trademark, consisting of the words "Bantam Books"
and the portrayal of a rooster, is Registered in U.S. Patent and Trademark Office and
in other countries. Marca Registrada. Bantam Books, 666 Fifth Avenue, New York,
New York 10103.*

PRINTED IN THE UNITED STATES OF AMERICA

RAD   50 49 48 47 46 45 44 43 42 41

Part One

It HAPPENED that green and crazy summer when Frankie was twelve years old. This was the summer when for a long time she had not been a member. She belonged to no club and was a member of nothing in the world. Frankie had become an unjoined person who hung around in doorways, and she was afraid. In June the trees were bright dizzy green, but later the leaves darkened, and the town turned black and shrunken under the glare of the sun. At first Frankie walked around doing one thing and another. The sidewalks of the town were gray in the early morning and at night, but the noon sun put a glaze on them, so that the cement burned and glittered like glass. The sidewalks finally became too hot for Frankie's feet, and also she got herself in trouble. She was in so much secret trouble that she thought it was better to stay at home—and at home there was only Berenice Sadie Brown and John Henry West. The three of them sat at the kitchen table, saying the same things over and over, so that by August the words began to rhyme with each other and sound strange. The world seemed to die each afternoon and nothing moved any longer. At last the summer was like a green sick dream, or like a silent crazy jungle under glass. And then, on the last Friday of August, all this was changed: it was so sudden that Frankie puzzled the whole blank afternoon, and still she did not understand.

1

"It is so very queer," she said. "The way it all just happened."

"Happened? Happened?" said Berenice.

John Henry listened and watched them quietly.

"I have never been so puzzled."

"But puzzled about what?"

"The whole thing," Frankie said.

And Berenice remarked: "I believe the sun has fried your brains."

"Me too," John Henry whispered.

Frankie herself almost admitted maybe so. It was four o'clock in the afternoon and the kitchen was square and gray and quiet. Frankie sat at the table with her eyes half closed, and she thought about a wedding. She saw a silent church, a strange snow slanting down against the colored windows. The groom in this wedding was her brother, and there was a brightness where his face should be. The bride was there in a long white train, and the bride also was faceless. There was something about this wedding that gave Frankie a feeling she could not name.

"Look here at me," said Berenice. "You jealous?"

"Jealous?"

"Jealous because your brother going to be married?"

"No," said Frankie. "I just never saw any two people like them. When they walked in the house today it was so queer."

"You jealous," said Berenice. "Go and behold yourself in the mirror. I can see from the color in your eye."

There was a watery kitchen mirror hanging above the sink. Frankie looked, but her eyes were gray as they always were. This summer she was grown so tall that she was almost a big freak, and her shoulders were narrow, her legs too long. She wore a pair of blue black shorts, a B.V.D. undervest, and she was barefooted. Her hair had been cut like a boy's, but it had not been cut for a long time and was now not even parted. The reflection in the glass was warped and crooked, but Frankie knew well what she looked like; she drew up her left shoulder and turned her head aside.

"Oh," she said. "They were the two prettiest people I ever saw. I just can't understand how it happened."

"But what, Foolish?" said Berenice. "Your brother come home with the girl he means to marry and took dinner today with you and your Daddy. They intend to marry at her home in Winter Hill this coming Sunday. You and your Daddy are going to the wedding. And that is the A and the Z of the matter. So whatever ails you?"

"I don't know," said Frankie. "I bet they have a good time every minute of the day."

"Less us have a good time," John Henry said.

"Us have a good time?" Frankie asked. "Us?"

The three of them sat at the table again and Berenice dealt the cards for three-handed bridge. Berenice had been the cook since Frankie could remember. She was very black and broad-shouldered and short. She always said that she was thirty-five years old, but she had been saying that at least three years. Her hair was parted, plaited, and greased close to the skull, and she had a flat and quiet face. There was only one thing wrong about Berenice— her left eye was bright blue glass. It stared out fixed and wild from her quiet, colored face, and why she had wanted a blue eye nobody human would ever know. Her right eye was dark and sad. Berenice dealt slowly, licking her thumb when the sweaty cards stuck together. John Henry watched each card as it was being dealt. His chest was white and wet and naked, and he wore around his neck a tiny lead donkey tied by a string. He was blood kin to Frankie, first cousin, and all summer he would eat dinner and spend the day with her, or eat supper and spend the night; and she could not make him go home. He was small to be six years old, but he had the largest knees that Frankie had ever seen, and on one of them there was always a scab or a bandage where he had fallen down and skinned himself. John Henry had a little screwed white face and he wore tiny gold-rimmed glasses. He watched all of the cards very carefully, because he was in debt; he owed Berenice more than five million dollars.

"I bid one heart," said Berenice.

"A spade," said Frankie.

"I want to bid spades," said John Henry. "That's what I was going to bid."

"Well, that's your tough luck. I bid them first."

"Oh, you fool jackass!" he said. "It's not fair!"

"Hush quarreling," said Berenice. "To tell the truth, I don't think either one of you got such a grand hand to fight over the bid about. I bid two hearts."

"I don't give a durn about it," Frankie said. "It is immaterial with me."

As a matter of fact this was so: she played bridge that afternoon like John Henry, just putting down any card that suddenly occurred to her. They sat together in the kitchen, and the kitchen was a sad and ugly room. John Henry had covered the walls with queer, child drawings, as far up as his arm would reach. This gave the kitchen a crazy look, like that of a room in the crazy-house. And now the old kitchen made Frankie sick. The name for what had happened to her Frankie did not know, but she could feel her squeezed heart beating against the table edge.

"The world is certainy a small place," she said.

"What makes you say that?"

"I mean sudden," said Frankie. "The world is certainy a sudden place."

"Well, I don't know," said Berenice. "Sometimes sudden and sometimes slow."

Frankie's eyes were half closed, and to her own ears her voice sounded ragged, far away:

"To me it is sudden."

For only yesterday Frankie had never thought seriously about a wedding. She knew that her only brother, Jarvis, was to be married. He had become engaged to a girl in Winter Hill just before he went to Alaska. Jarvis was a corporal in the army and he had spent almost two years in Alaska. Frankie had not seen her brother for a long, long time, and his face had become masked and changing, like a face seen under water. But Alaska! Frankie had dreamed of it constantly, and especially this summer it was very real. She saw the snow and frozen sea and ice glaciers. Esquimau igloos and polar bears and the beautiful Northern lights. When Jarvis had first gone to Alaska, she had sent him a box of homemade fudge, packing it carefully and wrapping each piece separately in waxed paper. It had thrilled her to think that her fudge would be eaten in Alaska, and she had a vision of her brother passing it around to furry Esquimaux. Three months later, a thank-you letter had come from Jarvis with a five-dollar bill enclosed. For a while she mailed candy almost every week, sometimes divinity instead of fudge, but Jarvis did not send her another bill, except at Christmas time. Sometimes his short letters to her father disturbed her a little. For instance, this summer he mentioned once that he had been in swimming and that the mosquitoes were something fierce. This letter jarred upon her dream, but after a few days of bewilderment, she returned to her frozen seas and snow. When Jarvis had come back from Alaska, he had gone straight to Winter Hill. The bride was named Janice Evans and the plans for the wedding were like this: her brother had wired that he and the bride were coming this Friday to spend the day, then on the following Sunday there was to be the wedding at Winter Hill. Frankie and her father were going to the wedding, traveling nearly a hundred miles to Winter Hill, and Frankie had already packed a suitcase. She looked forward to the time her brother and the bride should come, but she did not picture them to herself, and did not think about the wedding. So on the day before the visit she only commented to Berenice:

"I think it's a curious coincidence that Jarvis would get to go to Alaska and that the very bride he picked to marry would come from a place called Winter Hill. Winter Hill," she repeated slowly, her eyes closed, and the name blended with dreams of Alaska and cold snow. "I wish tomorrow was Sunday instead of Friday. I wish I had already left town."

"Sunday will come," said Berenice.

"I doubt it," said Frankie. "I've been ready to leave this town so long. I wish I didn't have to come back here after the wedding. I wish I was going somewhere for good.

I wish I had a hundred dollars and could just light out and never see this town again."

"It seems to me you wish for a lot of things," said Berenice.

"I wish I was somebody else except me."

So the afternoon before it happened was like the other August afternoons. Frankie had hung around the kitchen, then toward dark she had gone out into the yard. The scuppernong arbor behind the house was purple and dark in the twilight. She walked slowly. John Henry West was sitting beneath the August arbor in a wicker chair, his legs crossed and his hands in his pockets.

"What are you doing?" she asked.

"I'm thinking."

"About what?"

He did not answer.

Frankie was too tall this summer to walk beneath the arbor as she had always done before. Other twelve-year-old people could still walk around inside, give shows, and have a good time. Even small grown ladies could walk underneath the arbor. And already Frankie was too big; this year she had to hang around and pick from the edges like the grown people. She stared into the tangle of dark vines, and there was the smell of crushed scuppernongs and dust. Standing beside the arbor, with dark coming on, Frankie was afraid. She did not know what caused this fear, but she was afraid.

"I tell you what," she said. "Suppose you eat supper and spend the night with me."

John Henry took his dollar watch from his pocket and looked at it as though the time would decide whether or not he would come, but it was too dark under the arbor for him to read the numbers.

"Go on home and tell Aunt Pet. I'll meet you in the kitchen."

"All right."

She was afraid. The evening sky was pale and empty and the light from the kitchen window made a yellow square reflection in the darkening yard. She remembered that when she was a little girl she believed that three ghosts were living in the coal house, and one of the ghosts wore a silver ring.

She ran up the back steps and said: "I just now invited John Henry to eat supper and spend the night with me."

Berenice was kneading a lump of biscuit dough, and she dropped it on the flour-dusted table. "I thought you were sick and tired of him."

"I am sick and tired of him," said Frankie. "But it seemed to me he looked scared."

"Scared of what?"

Frankie shook her head. "Maybe I mean lonesome," she said finally.

"Well, I'll save him a scrap of dough."

After the darkening yard the kitchen was hot and bright and queer. The walls of the kitchen bothered Frankie—the queer drawings of Christmas trees, airplanes, freak soldiers, flowers. John Henry had started the first pictures one long afternoon in June, and having already ruined the wall, he went on and drew whenever he wished. Sometimes Frankie had drawn also. At first her father had been furious about the walls, but later he said for them to draw all the pictures out of their systems, and he would have the kitchen painted in the fall. But as the summer lasted, and would not end, the walls had begun to bother Frankie. That evening the kitchen looked strange to her, and she was afraid.

She stood in the doorway and said: "I just thought I might as well invite him."

So at dark John Henry came to the back door with a little week-end bag. He was dressed in his white recital suit and had put on shoes and socks. There was a dagger buckled to his belt. John Henry had seen snow. Although he was only six years old, he had gone to Birmingham last winter and there he had seen snow. Frankie had never seen snow.

"I'll take the week-end bag," said Frankie. "You can start right in making a biscuit man."

"O.K."

John Henry did not play with the dough; he worked on the biscuit man as though it were a very serious business.

Now and then he stopped off, settled his glasses with his little hand, and studied what he had done. He was like a tiny watchmaker, and he drew up a chair and knelt on it so that he could get directly over the work. When Berenice gave him some raisins, he did not stick them all around as any other human child would do; he used only two for the eyes; but immediately he realized they were too large—so he divided one raisin carefully and put in eyes, two specks for the nose, and a little grinning raisin mouth. When he had finished, he wiped his hands on the seat of his shorts, and there was a little biscuit man with separate fingers, a hat on, and even walking stick. John Henry had worked so hard that the dough was now gray and wet. But it was a perfect little biscuit man, and, as a matter of fact, it reminded Frankie of John Henry himself.

"I better entertain you now," she said.

They ate supper at the kitchen table with Berenice, since her father had telephoned that he was working late at his jewelry store. When Berenice brought the biscuit man from the oven, they saw that it looked exactly like any biscuit man ever made by a child—it had swelled so that all the work of John Henry had been cooked out, the fingers were run together, and the walking stick resembled a sort of tail. But John Henry just looked at it through his glasses, wiped it with his napkin, and buttered the left foot.

It was a dark, hot August night. The radio in the dining room was playing a mixture of many stations: a war voice crossed with the gabble of an advertiser, and underneath there was the sleazy music of a sweet band. The radio had stayed on all the summer long, so finally it was a sound that as a rule they did not notice. Sometimes, when the noise became so loud that they could not hear their own ears, Frankie would turn it down a little. Otherwise, music and voices came and went and crossed and twisted with each other, and by August they did not listen any more.

"What do you want to do?" asked Frankie. "Would you like for me to read to you out of Hans Brinker or would you rather do something else?"

"I rather do something else," he said.

"What?"

"Less play out."

"I don't want to," Frankie said.

"There's a big crowd going to play out tonight."

"You got ears," Frankie said. "You heard me."

John Henry stood with his big knees locked, then finally he said: "I think I better go home."

"Why, you haven't spent the night! You can't eat supper and just go on off like that."

"I know it," he said quietly. Along with the radio they could hear the voices of the children playing in the night. "But less go out, Frankie. They sound like they having a mighty good time."

"No they're not," she said. "Just a lot of ugly silly children. Running and hollering and running and hollering. Nothing to it. We'll go upstairs and unpack your week-end bag."

Frankie's room was an elevated sleeping porch which had been built onto the house, with a stairway leading up from the kitchen. The room was furnished with an iron bed, a bureau, and a desk. Also Frankie had a motor which could be turned on and off; the motor could sharpen knives, and, if they were long enough, it could be used for filing down your fingernails. Against the wall was the suitcase packed and ready for the trip to Winter Hill. On the desk there was a very old typewriter, and Frankie sat down before it, trying to think of any letters she could write: but there was nobody for her to write to, as every possible letter had already been answered, and answered even several times. So she covered the typewriter with a raincoat and pushed it aside.

"Honestly," John Henry said, "don't you think I better go home?"

"No," she answered, without looking around at him. "You sit there in the corner and play with the motor."

Before Frankie there were now two objects—a lavender seashell and a glass globe with snow inside that could be shaken into a snowstorm. When she held the seashell to her ear, she could hear the warm wash of the Gulf of Mexico, and think of a green palm island far away. And she could hold the snow globe to her narrowed eyes and watch the whirling white flakes fall until they blinded her. She dreamed of Alaska. She walked up a cold white hill and looked on a snowy wasteland far below. She watched the sun make colors in the ice, and heard dream voices, saw dream things. And everywhere there was the cold white gentle snow.

"Look," John Henry said, and he was staring out of the window. "I think those big girls are having a party in their clubhouse."

"Hush!" Frankie screamed suddenly. "Don't mention those crooks to me."

There was in the neighborhood a clubhouse, and Frankie was not a member. The members of the club were girls who were thirteen and fourteen and even fifteen years old. They had parties with boys on Saturday night. Frankie knew all of the club members, and until this summer she had been like a younger member of their crowd, but now they had this club and she was not a member. They had said she was too young and mean. On Saturday night she could hear the terrible music and see from far away their light. Sometimes she went around to the alley behind the clubhouse and stood near a honeysuckle fence. She stood in the alley and watched and listened. They were very long, those parties.

"Maybe they will change their mind and invite you," John Henry said.

"The son-of-a-bitches."

Frankie sniffled and wiped her nose in the crook of her arm. She sat down on the edge of the bed, her shoulders slumped and her elbows resting on her knees. "I think they have been spreading it all over town that I smell bad," she said. "When I had those boils and that black bitter smelling ointment, old Helen Fletcher asked what was that funny smell I had. Oh, I could shoot every one of them with a pistol."

She heard John Henry walking up to the bed, and then she felt his hand patting her neck with tiny little pats. "I don't think you smell so bad," he said. "You smell sweet."

"The son-of-a-bitches," she said again. "And there was

something else. They were talking nasty lies about married people. When I think of Aunt Pet and Uncle Ustace. And my own father! The nasty lies! I don't know what kind of fool they take me for."

"I can smell you the minute you walk in the house without even looking to see if it is you. Like a hundred flowers."

"I don't care," she said. "I just don't care."

"Like a thousand flowers," said John Henry, and still he was patting his sticky hand on the back of her bent neck.

Frankie sat up, licked the tears from around her mouth, and wiped off her face with her shirttail. She sat still, her nose widened, smelling herself. Then she went to her suitcase and took out a bottle of Sweet Serenade. She rubbed some on the top of her head and poured some more down inside the neck of her shirt.

"Want some on you?"

John Henry was squatting beside her open suitcase and he gave a little shiver when she poured the perfume over him. He wanted to meddle in her traveling suitcase and look carefully at every thing she owned. But Frankie only wanted him to get a general impression, and not count and know just what she had and what she did not have. So she strapped the suitcase and pushed it back against the wall. "Boy!" she said. "I bet I use more perfume than anybody in this town."

The house was quiet except for the low rumble of the radio in the dining room downstairs. Long ago her father had come home and Berenice had closed the back door and gone away. There was no longer the sound of children's voices in the summer night.

"I guess we ought to have a good time," said Frankie.

But there was nothing to do. John Henry stood, his knees locked and his hands clasped behind his back, in the middle of the room. There were moths at the window —pale green moths and yellow moths that fluttered and spread their wings against the screen.

"Those beautiful butterflies," he said. "They are trying to get in."

Frankie watched the soft moths tremble and press against the window screen. The moths came every evening when the lamp on her desk was lighted. They came from out of the August night and fluttered and clung against the screen.

"To me it is the irony of fate," she said. "The way they come here. Those moths could fly anywhere. Yet they keep hanging around the windows of this house."

John Henry touched the gold rim of his glasses to settle them on his nose and Frankie studied his flat little freckled face.

"Take off those glasses," she said suddenly.

John Henry took them off and blew on them. She looked through the glasses and the room was loose and crooked. Then she pushed back her chair and stared at John Henry. There were two damp white circles around his eyes.

"I bet you don't need those glasses," she said. She put her hand down on the typewriter, "What is this?"

"The typewriter," he said.

Frankie picked up the shell. "And this?"

"The shell from the Bay."

"What is that little thing crawling there on the floor?"

"Where?" he asked, looking around him.

"That little thing crawling along near your feet."

"Oh," he said. He squatted down. "Why, it's an ant. I wonder how it got up here."

Frankie titled back in her chair and crossed her bare feet on her desk. "If I were you I'd just throw those glasses away," she said. "You can see good as anybody."

John Henry did not answer.

"They don't look becoming."

She handed the folded glasses to John Henry and he wiped them with his pink flannel glasses rag. He put them back on and did not answer.

"O.K." she said. "Suit yourself. I was only telling you for your own good."

They went to bed. They undressed with their backs turned to each other and then Frankie switched off the motor and the light. John Henry knelt down to say his prayers and he prayed for a long time, not saying the words aloud. Then he lay down beside her.

"Good night," she said.

"Good night."

Frankie stared up into the dark. "You know it is still hard for me to realize that the world turns around at the rate of about a thousand miles an hour."

"I know it," he said.

"And to understand why it is that when you jump up in the air you don't come down in Fairview or Selma or somewhere fifty miles away."

John Henry turned over and made a sleepy sound.

"Or Winter Hill," she said. "I wish I was starting for Winter Hill right now."

Already John Henry was asleep. She heard him breathe in the darkness, and now she had what she had wanted so many nights that summer; there was somebody sleeping in the bed with her. She lay in the dark and listened to him breathe, then after a while she raised herself on her elbow. He lay freckled and small in the moonlight, his chest white and naked, and one foot hanging from the edge of the bed. Carefully she put her hand on his stomach and moved closer; it felt as though a little clock was ticking inside him and he smelled of sweat and Sweet Serenade. He smelled like a sour little rose. Frankie leaned down and licked him behind the ear. Then she breathed deeply, settled herself with her chin on his sharp damp shoulder, and closed her eyes: for now, with somebody sleeping in the dark with her, she was not so much afraid.

The sun woke them early the next morning, the white August sun. Frankie could not make John Henry go home. He saw the ham Berenice was cooking, and that the special company dinner was going to be good. Frankie's father read the paper in the living room, then went downtown to wind the watches at his jewelry store.

"If that brother of mine don't bring me a present from Alaska, I will be seriously mad," said Frankie.

"Me too," agreed John Henry.

And what were they doing that August morning when her brother and the bride came home? They were sitting in the arbor shade and talking about Christmas. The glare was hard and bright, the sun-drunk bluejays screamed and murdered among themselves. They talked, and their voices tired down into a little tune and they said the same things over and over. They just drowsed in the dark shade of the arbor, and Frankie was a person who had never thought about a wedding. That was the way they were that August morning when her brother and the bride walked in the house.

"Oh, Jesus!" Frankie said. The cards on the table were greasy and the late sun slanted across the yard. "The world is certainy a sudden place."

"Well, stop commenting about it," said Berenice. "You don't have your mind on the game."

Frankie, however, had some of her mind on the game. She played the queen of spades, which were trumps, and John Henry threw off a little two of diamonds. She looked at him. He was staring at the back of her hand as though what he wanted and needed was angled eyesight that could cut around corners and read people's cards.

"You got a spade," said Frankie.

John Henry put his donkey necklace in his mouth and looked away.

"Cheater," she said.

"Go on and play your spade," said Berenice.

Then he argued: "It was hid behind the other card."

"Cheater."

But still he would not play. He sat there sad and holding up the game.

"Make haste," said Berenice.

"I can't," he said finally. "It's a jack. The only spade I got is a jack. I don't want to play my jack down under Frankie's queen. I'm not going to do it either."

Frankie threw her cards down on the table. "See!" she said to Berenice. "He don't even follow the first beginning laws! He's a child! It is hopeless! Hopeless! Hopeless!"

"Maybe so," said Berenice.

"Oh," Frankie said, "I am sick unto death."

She sat with her bare feet on the rungs of the chair, her eyes closed, and her chest against the table edge. The red greasy cards were messed together on the table, and the sight of them made Frankie sick. They had played cards after dinner every single afternoon; if you would eat those old cards, they would taste like a combination of all the dinners of that August, together with a sweaty-handed nasty taste. Frankie swept the cards from the table. The wedding was bright and beautiful as snow and the heart in her was mashed. She got up from the table.

"It is a known truth that gray-eyed people are jealous."

"I told you I wasn't jealous," Frankie said, and she was walking fast around the room. "I couldn't be jealous of one of them without being jealous of them both. I sociate the two of them together."

"Well, I were jealous when my foster brother married," said Berenice. "I admit that when John married Clorina I sent a warning I would tear the ears off her head. But you see I didn't. Clorina got ears like anybody else. And now I love her."

"J A," said Frankie. "Janice and Jarvis. Isn't that the strangest thing?"

"What?"

"J A," she said. "Both their names begin with J A."

"And? What about it?"

Frankie walked round and round the kitchen table. "If only my name was Jane," she said. "Jane or Jasmine."

"I don't follow your frame of mind," said Berenice.

"Jarvis and Janice and Jasmine. See?"

"No," said Berenice. "By the way, I heard this morning on the radio that the French people are chasing the Germans out of Paris."

"Paris," Frankie repeated in a hollow tone. "I wonder if it is against the law to change your name. Or to add to it."

"Naturally. It is against the law."

"Well, I don't care," she said. "F. Jasmine Addams."

On the staircase leading to her room there was a doll, and John Henry brought it to the table and sat rocking it in his arms. "You serious when you gave me this," he said. He pulled up the doll's dress and fingered the real panties and body-waist. "I will name her Belle."

Frankie stared at the doll for a minute. "I don't know what went on in Jarvis's mind when he brought me that doll. Imagine bringing me a doll! And Janice tried to explain that she had pictured me as a little girl. I had counted on Jarvis bringing me something from Alaska."

"Your face when you unwrapped the package was a study," said Berenice.

It was a large doll with red hair and china eyes that opened and closed, and yellow eyelashes. John Henry held her in a lying-down position, so that the eyes were shut, and he was now trying to open them by pulling up the eyelashes.

"Don't do that! It makes me nervous. In fact, take that doll somewhere out of my sight."

John Henry took it to the back porch where he could pick it up when he went home.

"Her name is Lily Belle," he said.

The clock ticked very slowly on the shelf above the stove, and it was only quarter to six. The glare outside the window was still hard and yellow and bright. In the back yard the shade beneath the arbor was black and solid. Nothing moved. From somewhere far away came the sound of whistling, and it was a grieving August song that did not end. The minutes were very long.

Frankie went again to the kitchen mirror and stared at her own face. "The big mistake I made was to get this close crew-cut. For the wedding I ought to have long bright yellow hair. Don't you think so?"

She stood before the mirror and she was afraid. It was the summer of fear, for Frankie, and there was one fear that could be figured in arithmetic with paper and a pencil at the table. This August she was twelve and five-sixths years old. She was five feet five and three quarter inches tall, and she wore a number seven shoe. In the past year she had grown four inches, or at least that was what she judged. Already the hateful little summer children hollered to her: "Is it cold up there?" And the comments of grown people make Frankie shrivel on her heels. If she reached her height on her eighteenth birthday, she had five and one-sixth growing years ahead of her. Therefore, according to mathematics and unless she could somehow stop herself, she would grow to be over nine feet tall. And what would be a lady who is over nine feet high? She would be a Freak.

In the early autumn of every year the Chattahoochee Exposition came to town. For a whole October week the fair went on down at the fairgrounds. There was the Ferris Wheel, the Flying Jinney, the Palace of Mirrors—and there, too, was the House of the Freaks. The House of the Freaks was a long pavilion which was lined on the inside with a row of booths. It cost a quarter to go into the general tent, and you could look at each Freak in his booth. Then there were special private exhibitions farther back in the tent which cost a dime apiece. Frankie had seen all of the members of the Freak House last October:

> The Giant
> The Fat Lady
> The Midget
> The Wild Nigger
> The Pin Head
> The Alligator Boy
> The Half-Man Half-Woman

The Giant was more than eight feet high, with huge loose hands and a hang-jaw face. The Fat Lady sat in a chair, and the fat on her was like loose-powdered dough which she kept slapping and working with her hands—next was the squeezed Midget who minced around in little trick evening clothes. The Wild Nigger came from a savage island. He squatted in his booth among the dusty bones and palm leaves and he ate raw living rats. The fair gave a free admission to his show to all who brought rats of the right size, and so children carried them down in strong sacks and shoe boxes. The Wild Nigger knocked the rat's head over his squatted knee and ripped off the fur and crunched and gobbled and flashed his greedy Wild Nigger eyes. Some said that he was not a genuine Wild Nigger, but a crazy colored man from Selma. Anyway, Frankie did not like to watch him very long. She pushed through the crowd to the Pin Head booth, where John Henry had stood all afternoon. The little Pin Head skipped and giggled and sassed around, with a shrunken head no larger than an orange, which was shaved except for one lock tied with a pink bow at the top. The last booth was always very crowded, for it was the booth of the Half-Man Half-Woman, a morphidite and a miracle of science. This Freak was divided completely in half—the left side was a man and the right side a woman. The costume on the left was a leopard skin and on the right side a brassiere and a spangled skirt. Half the face was dark bearded and the other half bright glazed with paint. Both eyes were strange. Frankie had wandered around the tent and looked at every booth. She was afraid of all the Freaks, for it seemed to her that they had looked at her in a secret way and tried to connect their eyes with hers, as though to say: we know you. She was afraid of their long Freak eyes. And all the years she had remembered them, until this day.

"I doubt if they ever get married or go to a wedding," she said. "Those Freaks."

"What freaks you talking about?" said Berenice.

"At the fair," said Frankie. "The ones we saw there last October."

"Oh, those folks."

"I wonder if they make a big salary," she said.

And Berenice answered: "How would I know?"

John Henry held out an imaginary skirt and, touching his finger to the top of his big head, he skipped and danced like the Pin Head around the kitchen table.

Then he said: "She was the cutest little girl I ever saw. I never saw anything so cute in my whole life. Did you, Frankie?"

"No," she said. "I didn't think she was cute."

"Me and you both," said Berenice.

"Shoo!" John Henry argued. "She was, too."

"If you want my candy opinion," said Berenice, "that whole crowd of folks down yonder at the fair just give me the creeps. Ever last one of them."

Frankie watched Berenice through the mirror, and finally she asked in a slow voice. "Do *I* give you the creeps?"

"You?" asked Berenice.

"Do you think I will grow into a Freak?" Frankie whispered.

"You?" said Berenice again. "Why, certainy not, I trust Jesus."

Frankie felt better. She looked sidewise at herself in the mirror. The clock ticked six slow times, and then she said: "Well, do you think I will be pretty?"

"Maybe. If you file down them horns a inch or two."

Frankie stood with her weight resting on her left leg, and she slowly shuffled the ball of her right foot on the floor. She felt a splinter go beneath the skin. "Seriously," she said.

"I think when you fill out you will do very well. If you behave."

"But by Sunday," Frankie said. "I want to do something to improve myself before the wedding."

"Get clean for a change. Scrub your elbows and fix yourself nice. You will do very well."

Frankie looked for a last time at herself in the mirror, and then she turned away. She thought about her brother and the bride, and there was a tightness in her that would not break.

"I don't know what to do. I just wish I would die."

"Well, die then!" said Berenice.

And: "Die," John Henry echoed in a whisper.

The world stopped.

"Go home," said Frankie to John Henry.

He stood with his big knees locked, his dirty little hand on the edge of the white table, and he did not move.

"You heard me," Frankie said. She made a terrible face at him and grabbed the frying pan that hung above the stove. She chased him three times around the table, then up through the front hall and out of the door. She locked the front door and called again: "Go home."

"Now what makes you act like that?" said Berenice. "You are too mean to live."

Frankie opened the door to the stairway that led up to her room, and sat down on one of the lower steps. The kitchen was silent and crazy and sad.

"I know it," she said. "I intend to sit still by myself and think over everything for a while."

This was the summer when Frankie was sick and tired

of being Frankie. She hated herself, and had become a loafer and a big no-good who hung around the summer kitchen: dirty and greedy and mean and sad. Besides being too mean to live, she was a criminal. If the Law knew about her, she could be tried in the courthouse and locked up in the jail. Yet Frankie had not always been a criminal and a big no-good. Until the April of that year, and all the years of her life before, she had been like other people. She belonged to a club and was in the seventh grade at school. She worked for her father on Saturday morning and went to the show every Saturday afternoon. She was not the kind of person ever to think of being afraid. At night she slept in the bed with her father, but not because she was scared of the dark.

Then the spring of that year had been a long queer season. Things began to change and Frankie did not understand this change. After the plain gray winter the March winds banged on the windowpanes, and clouds were shirred and white on the blue sky. April that year came sudden and still, and the green of the trees was a wild bright green. The pale wistarias bloomed all over town, and silently the blossoms shattered. There was something about the green trees and the flowers of April that made Frankie sad. She did not know why she was sad, but because of this peculiar sadness, she began to realize she ought to leave the town. She read the war news and thought about the world and packed her suitcase to go away; but she did not know where she should go.

It was the year when Frankie thought about the world. And she did not see it as a round school globe, with the countries neat and different-colored. She thought of the world as huge and cracked and loose and turning a thousand miles an hour. The geography book at school was out of date; the countries of the world had changed. Frankie read the war news in the paper, but there were so many foreign places, and the war was happening so fast, that sometimes she did not understand. It was the summer when Patton was chasing the Germans across France. And they were fighting, too, in Russia and Saipan. She saw the battles, and the soldiers. But there were too many different battles, and she could not see in her mind the millions and millions of soldiers all at once. She saw one Russian soldier, dark and frozen with a frozen gun, in Russian snow. The single Jap with slanted eyes on a jungle island gliding among green vines. Europe and the people hung in trees and the battleships on the blue oceans. Four-motor planes and burning cities and a soldier in a steel war helmet, laughing. Sometimes these pictures of the war, the world, whirled in her mind and she was dizzy. A long time ago she had predicted that it would take two months to win the whole war, but now she did not know. She wanted to be a boy and go to the war as a Marine. She thought about flying aeroplanes and winning gold medals for bravery. But she could not join the war, and this made her sometimes feel restless and blue. She decided to donate blood to the Red Cross; she wanted to donate a quart a week and her blood would be in the veins of Australians and Fighting French and Chinese, all over the whole world, and it would be as though she were close kin to all of these people. She could hear the army doctors saying that the blood of Frankie Addams was the reddest and the strongest blood that they had ever known. And she could picture ahead, in the years after the war, meeting the soldiers who had her blood, and they would say that they owed their life to her; and they would not call her Frankie—they would call her Addams. But this plan for donating her blood to the war did not come true. The Red Cross would not take her blood. She was too young. Frankie felt mad with the Red Cross, and left out of everything. The war and the world were too fast and big and strange. To think about the world for very long made her afraid. She was not afraid of Germans or bombs or Japanese. She was afraid because in the war they would not include her, and because the world seemed somehow separate from herself.

So she knew she ought to leave the town and go to some place far away. For the late spring, that year, was lazy and too sweet. The long afternoons flowered and lasted and the green sweetness sickened her. The town began to hurt Frankie. Sad and terrible happenings had never made

Frankie cry, but this season many things made Frankie
suddenly wish to cry. Very early in the morning she would
sometimes go out into the yard and stand for a long time
looking at the sunrise sky. And it was as though a question
came into her heart, and the sky did not answer. Things
she had never noticed much before began to hurt her:
home lights watched from the evening sidewalks, an unknown voice from an alley. She would stare at the lights
and listen to the voice, and something inside her stiffened
and waited. But the lights would darken, the voice fall
silent, and though she waited, that was all. She was afraid
of these things that made her suddenly wonder who she
was, and what she was going to be in the world, and why
she was standing at that minute, seeing a light, or listening,
or staring up into the sky: alone. She was afraid, and there
was a queer tightness in her chest.

One night in April, when she and her father were going
to bed, he looked at her and said, all of a sudden: "Who
is this great big long-legged twelve-year-old blunderbuss
who still wants to sleep with her old Papa." And she was
too big to sleep with her father any more. She had to sleep
in her upstairs room alone. She began to have a grudge
against her father and they looked at each other in a slant-
eyed way. She did not like to stay at home.

She went around town, and the things she saw and
heard seemed to be left somehow unfinished, and there
was the tightness in her that would not break. She would
hurry to do something, but what she did was always
wrong. She would call her best friend, Evelyn Owen, who
owned a football suit and a Spanish shawl, and one would
dress in the football suit and the other in the Spanish shawl
and they would go down to the ten-cent store together. But
that was a wrong thing and not what Frankie wanted. Or
after the pale spring twilights, with the smell of dust and
flowers sweet and bitter in the air, evenings of lighted
windows and the long drawn calls at supper time, when
the chimney swifts had gathered and whirled above the
town and flown off somewhere to their home together,
leaving the sky empty and wide; after the long twilights

of this season, when Frankie had walked around the side-walks of the town, a jazz sadness quivered her nerves and her heart stiffened and almost stopped.

Because she could not break this tightness gathering within her, she would hurry to do something. She would go home and put the coal scuttle on her head, like a crazy person's hat, and walk around the kitchen table. She would do anything that suddenly occurred to her—but whatever she did was always wrong, and not at all what she had wanted. Then, having done these wrong and silly things, she would stand, sick-ened and empty, in the kitchen door and say:

"I just wish I could tear down this whole town."

"Well, tear it down, then. But quit hanging around here with that gloomy face. Do something."

And finally the troubles started.

She did things and she got herself in trouble. She broke the law. And having once become a criminal, she broke the law again, and then again. She took the pistol from her father's bureau drawer and carried it all over town and shot up the cartridges in a vacant lot. She changed into a robber and stole a three-way knife from the Sears and Roebuck Store. One Saturday afternoon she commit-ted a secret and unknown sin. In the MacKeans' garage, with Barney MacKean, they committed a queer sin, and how bad it was she did not know. The sin made a shrivel-ing sickness in her stomach, and she dreaded the eyes of everyone. She hated Barney and wanted to kill him. Some-times alone in the bed at night she planned to shoot him with the pistol or throw a knife between his eyes.

Her best friend, Evelyn Owen, moved away to Florida, and Frankie did not play with anybody any more. The long and flowering spring was over and the summer in the town was ugly and lonesome and very hot. Every day she wanted more and more to leave the town: to light out for South America or Hollywood or New York City. But al-though she packed her suitcase many times, she could never decide to which of these places she ought to go, or how she would get there by herself.

So she stayed home and hung around the kitchen, and

the summer did not end. By dog days she was five feet five and three-quarter inches tall, a great big greedy loafer who was too mean to live. She was afraid, but not as she had been before. There was only the fear of Barney, her father, and the Law. But even these fears were finally gone; after a long time the sin in the MacKeans' garage became far from her and was remembered only in her dreams. And she would not think of her father or the Law. She stuck close in the kitchen with John Henry and Berenice. She did not think about the war, the world. Nothing hurt her any longer; she did not care. She never stood alone in the back yard in order to stare up at the sky. She paid no attention to sounds and summer voices, and did not walk the streets of town at night. She would not let things make her sad and she would not care. She ate and wrote shows and practiced throwing knives against the side of the garage and played bridge at the kitchen table. Each day was like the day before, except that it was longer, and nothing hurt her any more.

So that Sunday when it happened, when her brother and the bride came to the house, Frankie knew that everything was changed; but why this was so, and what would happen to her next, she did not know. And though she tried to talk with Berenice, Berenice did not know either.

"It gives me this kind of a pain," she said, "to think about them."

"Well, don't," said Berenice. "You done nothing but think and carry on about them all this afternoon."

Frankie sat on the bottom step of the stairs to her room, staring into the kitchen. But although it gave her a kind of a pain, she had to think about the wedding. She remembered the way her brother and the bride had looked when she walked into the living room, that morning at eleven o'clock. There had been in the house a sudden silence, for Jarvis had turned off the radio when they came in; after the long summer, when the radio had gone on day and night, so that no one heard it any more, the curious silence had startled Frankie. She stood in the doorway, coming from the hall, and the first sight of her brother and the bride had shocked her heart. Together they made in her this feeling that she could not name. But it was like the feelings of the spring, only more sudden and more sharp. There was the same tightness and in the same queer way she was afraid. Frankie thought until her mind was dizzy and her foot had gone to sleep.

Then she asked Berenice: "How old were you when you married your first husband?"

While Frankie was thinking, Berenice had changed into her Sunday clothes, and now she sat reading a magazine. She was waiting for the people who were due to meet her at six o'clock, Honey and T. T. Williams; the three of them were going to eat supper at the New Metropolitan Tea Room and sashay together around the town. As Berenice read, she moved her lips to shape each word. Her dark eye looked up as Frankie spoke, but, since Berenice did not raise her head, the blue glass eye seemed to go on reading the magazine. This two-sighted expression bothered Frankie.

"I were thirteen years old," said Berenice.

"What made you get married so young for?"

"Because I wanted to," said Berenice. "I were thirteen years old and I haven't growed a inch since."

Berenice was very short, and Frankie looked hard at her and asked: "Does marrying really stop your growth?"

"It certainy do," said Berenice.

"I didn't know that," Frankie said.

Berenice had been married four different times. Her first husband was Ludie Freeman, a brickmason, and the favorite and best one of the four; he gave Berenice her fox fur, and once they had gone to Cincinnati and seen snow. Berenice and Ludie Freeman had seen a whole winter of Northern snow. They loved each other and were married for nine years, until the November he was sick and died. The other three husbands were all bad, each one worse than the one before, and it made Frankie blue just to hear about them. The first was a sorry old liquor-drinker. The next went crazy on Berenice: he did crazy things, had eating dreams in the night and swallowed a corner of the sheet; and what with one thing and another he distracted Berenice so much that finally she had to quit him. The last husband was terrible. He gouged out Berenice's eye and stole her furniture away from her. She had to call the Law on him.

"Did you marry with a veil every time?" asked Frankie.

"Two times with a veil," said Berenice.

Frankie could not keep still. She walked around the kitchen, although there was a splinter in her right foot and she was limping, her thumbs hooked in the belt of her shorts and her undershirt clinging and wet.

Finally she opened the drawer of the kitchen table and selected a long sharp butcher knife. Then she sat down and rested the ankle of her sore foot on her left knee. The sole of her foot was long and narrow, pitted with ragged whitish scars, as every summer Frankie stepped on many nails; Frankie had the toughest feet in town. She could slice off waxy yellow rinds from the bottoms of her feet, and it did not hurt her very much, although it would hurt other people. But she did not chisel for the splinter immediately —she just sat there, her ankle on her knee and the knife in her right hand, looking across the table at Berenice.

"Tell me," she said. "Tell me exactly how it was."

"You know!" said Berenice. "You seen them."

"But tell me," Frankie said.

"I will discuss it for the last time," said Berenice. "Your brother and the bride come late this morning and you and John Henry hurried in from the back yard to see them. The next thing I realize you busted back through the kitchen and run up to your room. You came down with your organdie dress on and lipstick an inch thick from one ear to the next. Then you all just sat around in the living room. It was hot. Jarvis had brought Mr. Addams a bottle of whiskey and they had liquor drinks and you and John Henry had lemonade. Then after dinner your brother and the bride took the three-o'clock train back to Winter Hill. The wedding will be this coming Sunday. And that is all. Now, is you satisfied?"

"I am so disappointed they couldn't stay longer—at least spend the night. After Jarvis being away so long. But I guess they want to be together as long as they can. Jarvis said he had some army papers to fill out at Winter Hill."

She took a deep breath. "I wonder where they will go after the wedding."

"On their honeymoon. Your brother will have a few days' leave."

"I wonder where that honeymoon will be."

"Well, I'm sure I don't know."

"Tell me," Frankie said again. "Exactly what did they look like?"

"Look like?" said Berenice. "Why, they looked natural. Your brother is a good-looking blond white boy. And the girl is kind of brunette and small and pretty. They make a nice white couple. You seen them, Foolish."

Frankie closed her eyes, and, though she did not see them as a picture, she could feel them leaving her. She could feel the two of them together on the train, riding and riding away from her. They were them, and leaving her, and she was her, and sitting left all by herself there at the kitchen table. But a part of her was with them, and she could feel this part of her own self going away, and farther away; farther and farther, so that a drawn-out sickness came in her, going away and farther away, so that the kitchen Frankie was an old hull left there at the table.

"It is so queer," she said.

She bent over the sole of her foot, and there was something wet, like tears or sweat drops on her face; she sniffled and began to cut for the splinter.

"Don't that hurt you none?" asked Berenice.

Frankie shook her head and did not answer. Then after a moment she said: "Have you ever seen any people that afterward you remembered more like a feeling than a picture?"

"How you mean?"

"I mean this," said Frankie slowly. "I saw them O.K. Janice had on a green dress and green high-heel dainty shoes. Her hair was done up in a knot. Dark hair and a little piece of it was loose. Jarvis sat by her on the sofa. He had on his brown uniform and he was sunburned and very clean. They were the two prettiest people I ever saw. Yet it was like I couldn't see all of them I wanted to see. My brains couldn't gather together quick enough and take it all in. And then they were gone. You see what I mean?"

"You hurting yourself," said Berenice. "What you need is a needle."

"I don't care anything about my old feet," Frankie said.

It was only half-past six, and the minutes of the afternoon were like bright mirrors. From outside there was no longer the sound of whistling and in the kitchen nothing moved. Frankie sat facing the door that opened onto the back porch. There was a square cat-hole cut in a corner of the back door, and near-by a saucer of lavender sour milk. In the beginning of dog days Frankie's cat had gone away. And the season of dog days is like this: it is the time at the end of the summer when as a rule nothing can happen—but if a change does come about, that change remains until dog days are over. Things that are done are not undone and a mistake once made is not corrected.

That August Berenice scratched a mosquito bite under her right arm and it became a sore: that sore would never heal until dog days were over. Two little families of August gnats picked out the corner of John Henry's eyes to settle down in, and though he often shook himself and blinked, those gnats were there to stay. Then Charles disappeared. Frankie did not see him leave the house and walk away, but on the fourteenth of August, when she called him to his supper, he did not come, and he was gone. She looked for him everywhere and sent John Henry wailing out his name through all the streets of town. But it was the season of dog days and Charles did not come back again. Every afternoon Frankie said exactly the same words to Berenice, and the answers of Berenice were always the same. So that now the words were like an ugly little tune they sang by heart.

"If only I just knew where he has gone."

"Quit worrying yourself about that old alley cat. I done told you he ain't coming back."

"Charles is not alley. He is almost pure Persian."

"Persian as I is," Berenice would say. "You seen the last of that old tom cat. He gone off to hunt a friend."

"To hunt a friend?"

"Why, certainy. He roamed off to find himself a lady-friend."

"You really think so?"

"Naturally."

"Well, why don't he bring his friend home with him. He ought to know I would be only too glad to have a whole family of cats."

"You seen the last of that old alley cat."

"If only I just knew where he is gone."

And so each gloomy afternoon their voices sawed against each other, saying the same words, which finally reminded Frankie of a raggedy rhyme said by two crazies. She would end by telling Berenice: "It looks to me like everything has just walked off and left me." And she would put her head down on the table and feel afraid.

But this afternoon Frankie suddenly changed all this. An idea came to her, and she put down the knife and got up from the table.

"I know what I ought to do," she suddenly said. "Listen."

"I can hear."

"I ought to notify the police force. They will find Charles."

"I wouldn't do that," said Berenice.

Frankie went to the hall telephone and explained to the Law about her cat. "He is almost pure Persian," she said. "But with short hair. A very lovely color of gray and with a little white spot on his throat. He answers to the name of *Charles,* but if he don't answer to that, he might come if you call *Charlina.* My name is Miss F. Jasmine Addams and the address is 124 Grove Street."

Berenice was giggling when she came back, a soft high giggle. "Whew! They going to send around here and tie you up and drag you off to Milledgeville. Them fat blue police chasing tomcats around alleys and hollering: *Oh Charles, Oh come here, Charlina!* Sweet Jesus!"

"Aw, shut up," Frankie said.

Berenice was sitting at the table; she had stopped giggling and her dark eye roved in a teasing way as she sloshed coffee into a white china saucer to cool.

"At the same time," she said, "I can't see how it is such

a wise idea to trifle around with the Law. No matter for what reason."

"I'm not trifling with the Law."

"You just now set there and spelled them out your name and your house number. Where they can lay hold of you if ever they take the notion."

"Well, let them!" said Frankie angrily. "I don't care! I don't care!" And suddenly she did not care if anybody knew she was a criminal or not. "Let them come get me for all I care."

"I was just teasing you," said Berenice. "The trouble with you is that you don't have no sense of humor any more."

"Maybe I'd be better off in jail."

Frankie walked around the table and she could feel them going away. The train was traveling to the North. Mile after mile they went away, farther and farther away from the town, and as they traveled to the North, a coolness came into the air and dark was falling like the evening dark of wintertime. The train was winding up into the hills, the whistle wailing in a winter tone, and mile after mile they went away. They passed among themselves a box of bought store candy, with chocolates set in dainty, pleated shells, and watched the winter miles pass by the window. Now they had gone a long, long way from town and soon would be in Winter Hill.

"Sit down," said Berenice. "You make me nervous."

Suddenly Frankie began to laugh. She wiped her face with the back of her hand and went back to the table. "Did you hear what Jarvis said?"

"What?"

Frankie laughed and laughed.

"They were talking about whether to vote for C. P. MacDonald. And Jarvis said: *Why, I wouldn't vote for that scoundrel if he was running to be the dog-catcher.* I never heard anything so witty in my life."

Berenice did not laugh. Her dark eye glanced down in a corner, quickly saw the joke, and then looked back at Frankie. Berenice wore her pink crepe dress and her hat with the pink plume was on the table. The blue glass eye made the sweat on her dark face look bluish also. Berenice was stroking the hat plume with her hand.

"And you know what Janice remarked?" asked Frankie. "When Papa mentioned about how much I've grown, she said she didn't think I looked so terribly big. She said she got the major portion of her growth before she was thirteen. She did, Berenice!"

"O.K.! All right."

"She said she thought I was a lovely size and would probably not grow any taller. She said all fashion models and movie stars——"

"She did not," said Berenice. "I heard her. She only remarked that you probably had already got your growth. But she didn't go on and on like that. To hear you tell it, anybody would think she took her text on the subject."

"She said——"

"This is a serious fault with you, Frankie. Somebody just makes a loose remark and then you cozen it in your mind until nobody would recognize it. Your Aunt Pet happened to mention to Clorina that you had sweet manners and Clorina passed it on to you. For what it was worth. Then next thing I know you are going all around and bragging how Mrs. West thought you had the finest manners in town and ought to go to Hollywood, and I don't know what all you didn't say. You keep building on to any little compliment you hear about yourself. Or, if it is a bad thing, you do the same. You cozen and change things too much in your own mind. And that is a serious fault."

"Quit preaching at me," Frankie said.

"I ain't preaching. It is the solemn truth."

"I admit it a little," said Frankie finally. She closed her eyes and the kitchen was very quiet. She could feel the beating of her heart, and when she spoke her voice was a whisper. "What I need to know is this. Do you think I made a good impression?"

"Impression? Impression?"

"Yes," said Frankie, her eyes still closed.

"Well, how would I know?" said Berenice.

"I mean how did I act? What did I do?"

"Why, you didn't do anything."

"Nothing?" asked Frankie.

"No. You just watched the pair of them like they was ghosts. Then, when they talked about the wedding, them ears of yours stiffened out the size of cabbage leaves——"

Frankie raised her hand to her left ear. "They didn't," she said bitterly. Then after a while she added. "Some day you going to look down and find that big fat tongue of yours pulled out by the roots and laying there before you on the table. Then how do you think you will feel?"

"Quit talking so rude," said Berenice.

Frankie scowled down at the splinter in her foot. She finished cutting it out with the knife and said, "That would have hurt anybody else but me." Then she was walking round and round the room again. "I am so scared I didn't make a good impression."

"What of it?" said Berenice. "I wish Honey and T. T. would come on. You make me nervous."

Frankie drew up her left shoulder and bit her lower lip. Then suddenly she sat down and banged her forehead on the table.

"Come on," said Berenice. "Don't act like that."

But Frankie sat stiff, her face in the crook of her elbow and her fists clenched tight. Her voice had a ragged and strangled sound. "They were so pretty," she was saying. "They must have such a good time. And they went away and left me."

"Sit up," said Berenice. "Behave yourself."

"They came and went away," she said. "They went away and left me with this feeling."

"Hooee!" said Berenice finally. "I bet I know something."

The kitchen was silent and she tapped four times with her heel: one, two, three—*bang!* Her live eye was dark and teasing and she tapped with her heel, then took up the beating with a dark jazz voice that was like a song.

> Frankie got a crush!
> Frankie got a crush!
> Frankie got a crush!
> On the *Wedd*-ing!

"Quit," said Frankie.

Frankie got a crush!
Frankie got a crush!

Berenice went on and on, and her voice was jazzed like the heart that beats in your head when you have fever. Frankie was dizzy, and she picked up the knife from the kitchen table.

"You better quit!"

Berenice stopped very suddenly. The kitchen was suddenly shrunken and quiet.

"You lay down that knife."

"Make me."

She steadied the end of the handle against her palm and bent the blade slowly. The knife was limber, sharp, and long.

"Lay it down, DEVIL!"

But Frankie stood up and took careful aim. Her eyes were narrowed and the feel of the knife made her hands stop trembling.

"Just throw it!" said Berenice. "You just!"

All the house was very quiet. The empty house seemed to be waiting. And then there was the knife whistle in the air and the sound the blade made when it struck. The knife hit the middle of the stairway door and shivered there. She watched the knife until it did not shiver any longer.

"I am the best knife-thrower in this town," she said.

Berenice, who stood behind her, did not speak.

"If they would have a contest I would win."

Frankie pulled the knife from the door and laid it on the kitchen table. Then she spat on her palm and rubbed her hands together.

Berenice said finally: "Frances Addams, you going to do that once too often."

"I never miss outside of a few inches."

"You know what your father said about knife-throwing in this house."

"I warned you to quit picking with me."

"You are not fit to live in a house," said Berenice.

"I won't be living in this one much longer. I'm going to run away from home."

"And a good riddance to a big old bad rubbage," said Berenice.

"You wait and see. I'm leaving town."

"And where you think you are going?"

Frankie looked at all the corners of the room, and then said, "I don't know."

"I do," said Berenice. "You going crazy. That's where you going."

"No," said Frankie. She stood very still, looking around the queerly pictured wall, and then she closed her eyes. "I'm going to Winter Hill. I'm going to the wedding. And I swear to Jesus by my two eyes I'm never coming back here any more."

She had not been sure that she would throw the knife until it struck and shivered on the stairway door. And she had not known that she would say these words until already they were spoken. The swear was like the sudden knife; she felt it strike in her and tremble. Then when the words were quiet, she said again:

"After the wedding I'm not coming back."

Berenice pushed back the damp bangs of Frankie's hair and finally she asked: "Sugar? You serious?"

"Of course!" said Frankie. "Do you think I would stand here and swear that swear and tell a story? Sometimes, Berenice, I think it takes you longer to realize a fact than it does anybody who ever lived."

"But," said Berenice, "you say you don't know where you're going. You going, but you don't know where. That don't make no sense to me."

Frankie stood looking up and down the four walls of the room. She thought of the world, and it was fast and loose and turning, faster and looser and bigger than ever it had been before. The pictures of the War sprang out and clashed together in her mind. She saw bright flowered islands and a land by the northern sea with the gray waves on the shore. Bombed eyes and the shuffle of soldiers' feet. Tanks and a plane, wing broken, burning and downward-falling in a desert sky. The world was cracked by the loud battles and turning a thousand miles a minute. The names of places spun in Frankie's mind: China, Peachville, New Zealand, Paris, Cincinnati, Rome. She thought of the huge and turning world until her legs began to tremble and there was sweat on the palms of her hands. But still she did not know where she should go. Finally she stopped looking around the four kitchen walls and said to Berenice:

"I feel just exactly like somebody has peeled all the skin off me. I wish I had some cold good chocolate ice cream."

Berenice had her hands on Frankie's shoulders and was shaking her head and staring with the live eye narrowed into Frankie's face.

"But every word I told you was the solemn truth," she said. "I'm not coming back here after the wedding."

There was a sound, and when they turned they saw that Honey and T. T. Williams were standing in the doorway. Honey, though he was her foster brother, did not resemble Berenice—and it was almost as though he came from some foreign country, like Cuba or Mexico. He was lightskinned, almost lavender in color, with quiet narrow eyes like oil, and a limber body. Behind the two of them stood T. T. Williams, and he was very big and black; he was gray-haired, older even than Berenice, and he wore a church suit with a red badge in the buttonhole. T. T. Williams was a beau of Berenice, a well-off colored man who owned a colored restaurant. Honey was a sick-loose person. The army would not include him, and he had shoveled in a gravel pit until he broke one of his insides and could not do heavy work any more. They stood, the three of them, dark and grouped together in the door.

"What you all creep up like that for?" asked Berenice. "I didn't even hear you."

"You and Frankie too busy discussing something," said T. T.

"I am ready to go," said Berenice. "I been ready. But do you wish a small little quickie before we start?"

T. T. Williams looked at Frankie and shuffled his feet. He was very proper, and he liked to please everybody, and he always wanted to do the right thing.

"Frankie ain't no tattle-tale," said Berenice. "Is you?"

Frankie would not even answer such a question. Honey wore a dark red rayon slack suit and she said: "That sure is a cute suit you got on, Honey. Where did you get it?"

Honey could talk like a white school-teacher; his lavender lips could move as quick and light as butterflies. But he only answered with a colored word, a dark sound from the throat that can mean anything. "Ahhnnh," he said.

The glasses were before them on the table, and the hair-straightening bottle that held gin, but they did not drink. Berenice said something about Paris and Frankie had the extra feeling that they were waiting for her to leave. She stood in the door and looked at them. She did not want to go away.

"You wish water in yours, T. T.?" asked Berenice.

They were together around the table and Frankie stood extra in the door alone. "So long, you all," she said.

" 'Bye, Sugar," said Berenice. "You forget all that foolishness we was discussing. And if Mr. Addams don't come home by dark, you go on over to the Wests. Go play with John Henry."

"Since when have I been scared of the dark?" said Frankie. "So long."

"So long," they said.

She closed the door, but behind her she could hear their voices. With her head against the kitchen door she could hear the murmuring dark sounds that rose and fell in a gentle way. Ayee—ayee. And then Honey spoke above the idle wash of voices and he asked: "What was it between you and Frankie when we come in the house?" She waited, her ear pressed close against the door, to hear what Berenice would say. And finally the words were: "Just foolishness. Frankie was carrying on with foolishness." She listened until at last she heard them go away.

The empty house was darkening. She and her father were alone at night, as Berenice went to her own home directly after supper. Once they had rented the front bedroom. It was the year after her grandmother died, when Frankie was nine. They rented the front bedroom to Mr. and Mrs. Marlowe. The only thing Frankie remembered about them was the remark said at the last, that they were common people. Yet for the season they were there, Frankie was fascinated by Mr. and Mrs. Marlowe and the front room. She loved to go in when they were away and carefully, lightly meddle with their things—with Mrs. Marlowe's atomizer which skeeted perfume, the gray-pink powder puff, the wooden shoe-trees of Mr. Marlowe. They left mysteriously after an afternoon that Frankie did not understand. It was a summer Sunday and the hall door of the Marlowes' room was open. She could see only a portion of the room, part of the dresser and only the footpiece of the bed with Mrs. Marlowe's corset on it. But there was a sound in the quiet room she could not place, and when she stepped over the threshold she was startled by a sight that, after a single glance, sent her running to the kitchen, crying: Mr. Marlowe is having a fit! Berenice had hurried through the hall, but when she looked into the front room, she merely bunched her lips and banged the door. And evidently told her father, for that evening he said the Marlowes would have to leave. Frankie had tried to question Berenice and find out what was the matter. But Berenice had only said that they were common people and added that with a certain party in the house they ought at least to know enough to shut a door. Though Frankie knew she was the certain party, still she did not understand. What kind of a fit was it? she asked. But Berenice would only answer: Baby, just a common fit. And Frankie knew from the voice's tones that there was more to it than she was told. Later she only remembered the Marlowes as common people, and being common they owned common things—so that long after she had ceased to think about the Marlowes or fits, remembering merely the name and the fact that once they had rented the front bedroom, she associated common people with gray-pink powder puffs and perfume atomizers. The front bedroom had not been rented since.

Frankie went to the hall hatrack and put on one of her father's hats. She looked at her dark ugly mug in the mirror. The conversation about the wedding had somehow been wrong. The questions she had asked that afternoon had all been the wrong questions, and Berenice had an-

swered her with jokes. She could not name the feeling in
her, and she stood there until dark shadows made her
think of ghosts.

Frankie went out to the street before the house and
looked up into the sky. She stood staring with her fist on
her hip and her mouth open. The sky was lavender and
slowly darkening. She heard in the neighborhood the
sound of evening voices and noticed the light fresh smell
of watered grass. This was the time of the early evening
when, since the kitchen was too hot, she would go for a
little while outdoors. She practiced knife-throwing, or sat
before the cold-drink store in the front yard. Or she would
go around to the back yard, and there the arbor was cool
and dark. She wrote shows, although she had outgrown all
of her costumes, and was too big to act in them beneath
the arbor; this summer she had written very cold shows—
shows about Esquimaux and frozen explorers. Then when
night had come she would go again back in the house.

But this evening Frankie did not have her mind on
knives or cold-drink stores or shows. Nor did she want to
stand there staring up into the sky; for her heart asked the
old questions, and in the old way of the spring she was
afraid.

She felt she needed to think about something ugly and
plain, so she turned from the evening sky and stared at
her own house. Frankie lived in the ugliest house in town,
but now she knew that she would not be living there much
longer. The house was empty, dark. Frankie turned and
walked to the end of the block, and around the corner,
and down the sidewalk to the Wests'. John Henry was leaning against the banisters of his front porch, with a lighted
window behind him, so that he looked like a little black
paper doll on a piece of yellow paper.

"Hey," she said. "I wonder when that Papa of mine is
coming home from town."

John Henry did not answer.

"I don't want to go back in that dark old ugly house
all by myself."

She stood on the sidewalk, looking at John Henry, and

the smart political remark came back to her. She hooked her thumb in the pockets of her pants and asked: "If you were going to vote in an election, who would you vote for?"

John Henry's voice was bright and high in the summer night. "I don't know," he said.

"For instance, would you cast your vote for C. P. Mac-Donald to be mayor of this town?"

John Henry did not answer.

"Would you?"

But she could not get him to talk. There were times when John Henry would not answer anything you said to him. So she had to remark without an argument behind her, and all by herself like that it did not sound so very smart: "Why, I wouldn't vote for him if he was running to be dog-catcher."

The darkening town was very quiet. For a long time now her brother and the bride had been at Winter Hill. They had left the town a hundred miles behind them, and now were in a city far away. They were them and in Winter Hill, together, while she was her and in the same old town all by herself. The long hundred miles did not make her sadder and make her feel more far away than the knowing that they were them and both together and she was only her and parted from them, by herself. And as she sickened with this feeling a thought and explanation suddenly came to her, so that she knew and almost said aloud: *They are the we of me.* Yesterday, and all the twelve years of her life, she had only been Frankie. She was an *I* person who had to walk around and do things by herself. All other people had a *we* to claim, all other except her. When Berenice said *we,* she meant Honey and Big Mama, her lodge, or her church. The *we* of her father was the store. All members of clubs have a *we* to belong to and talk about. The soldiers in the army can say *we,* and even the criminals on chain-gangs. But the old Frankie had had no *we* to claim, unless it would be the terrible summer *we* of her and John Henry and Berenice— and that was the last *we* in the world she wanted. Now all this was suddenly over with and changed. There was her brother and the bride, and it was as though when first she saw them something she had known inside of her: *They are the we of me.* And that was why it made her feel so queer, for them to be away in Winter Hill while she was left all by herself; the hull of the old Frankie left there in the town alone.

"Why are you all bent over like that?" John Henry called.

"I think I have a kind of pain," said Frankie. "I must have ate something."

John Henry was still standing on the banisters, holding to the post.

"Listen," she said finally. "Suppose you come on over and eat supper and spend the night with me."

"I can't," he answered.

"Why?"

John Henry walked across the banisters, holding out his arms for balance, so that he was like a little blackbird against the yellow window light. He did not answer until he safely reached the other post.

"Just because."

"Because why?"

He did not say anything, and so she added: "I thought maybe me and you could put up my Indian tepee and sleep out in the back yard. And have a good time."

Still John Henry did not speak.

"We're blood first cousins. I entertain you all the time. I've given you so many presents."

Quietly, lightly, John Henry walked back across the banisters and then stood looking out at her with his arm around the post again.

"Sure enough," she called. "Why can't you come?"

At last he said. "Because, Frankie, I don't want to."

"Fool jackass!" she screamed. "I only asked you because I thought you looked so ugly and so lonesome."

Lightly John Henry jumped down from the banisters. And his voice as he called back to her was a clear child's voice.

"Why, I'm not a bit lonesome."

Frankie rubbed the wet palms of her hands along the sides of her shorts and said in her mind: Now turn around and take yourself on home. But in spite of this order, she was somehow unable to turn around and go. It was not yet night. Houses along the street were dark, lights showed in windows. Darkness had gathered in the thick-leaved trees and shapes in the distance were ragged and gray. But the night was not yet in the sky.

"I think something is wrong," she said. "It is too quiet. I have a peculiar warning in my bones. I bet you a hundred dollars it's going to storm."

John Henry watched her from behind the banister.

"A terrible terrible dog day storm. Or maybe even a cyclone."

Frankie stood waiting for the night. And just at that moment a horn began to play. Somewhere in the town, not far away, a horn began a blues tune. The tune was grieving and low. It was the sad horn of some colored boy, but who he was she did not know. Frankie stood stiff, her head bent and her eyes closed, listening. There was something about the tune that brought back to her all of the spring: flowers, the eyes of strangers, rain.

The tune was low and dark and sad. Then all at once, as Frankie listened, the horn danced into a wild jazz spangle that zigzagged upward. At the end of the jazz spangle the music rattled thin and far away. Then the tune returned to the first blues song, and it was like the telling of that long season of trouble. She stood there on the dark sidewalk and the drawn tightness of her heart made her knees lock and her throat feel stiffened. Then, without warning, the thing happened that at first Frankie could not believe. Just at the time when the tune should be laid, the music finished, the horn broke off. All of a sudden the horn stopped playing. For a moment Frankie could not take it in, she felt so lost.

She whispered finally to John Henry West: "He has stopped to bang the spit out of his horn. In a second he will finish."

But the music did not come again. The tune was left broken, unfinished. And the drawn tightness she could no longer stand. She felt she must do something wild and sudden that never had been done before. She hit herself on the head with her fist, but that did not help any at all. And she began to talk aloud, although at first she paid no attention to her own words and did not know in advance what she would say.

"I told Berenice that I was leaving town for good and she did not believe me. Sometimes I honestly think she is the biggest fool that ever drew breath." She complained aloud, and her voice was fringed and sharp like the edge of a saw. She talked and did not know from one word to the next what she would say. She listened to her own voice, but the words she heard did not make much sense. "You try to impress something on a big fool like that and it's just like talking to a block of cement. I kept on telling and telling and telling her. I told her I had to leave this town for good because it is inevitable."

She was not talking to John Henry. She did not see him any more. He had moved from the lighted window; but he was still listening from the porch, and after a little while he asked her:

"Where?"

Frankie did not answer. She was suddenly very still and quiet. For a new feeling had come to her. The sudden feeling was that she knew deep in her where she would go. She knew, and in another minute the name of the place would come to her. Frankie bit the knuckles of her fist and waited: but she did not hunt for the name of the place and did not think about the turning world. She saw in her mind her brother and the bride, and the heart in her was squeezed so hard that Frankie almost felt it break.

John Henry was asking in his high child voice: "You want me to eat supper and sleep in the tepee with you?"

She answered: "No."

"You just a little while ago invited me!"

But she could not argue with John Henry West or answer anything he said. For it was just at that moment that Frankie understood. She knew who she was and how she was going into the world. Her squeezed heart suddenly opened and divided. Her heart divided like two wings. And when she spoke her voice was sure.

"I know where I'm going," she said.

He asked her: "Where?"

"I'm going to Winter Hill," she said. "I'm going to the wedding."

She waited, to give him a chance to say: "I already knew that, anyhow." Then finally she spoke the sudden truth aloud.

"I'm going with them. After the wedding at Winter Hill, I'm going off with the two of them to whatever place that they will ever go. I'm going with them."

He did not answer.

"I love the two of them so much. We'll go to every place together. It's like I've known it all my life, that I belong to be with them. I love the two of them so much."

And having said this, she did not need to wonder and puzzle any more. She opened her eyes, and it was night. The lavender sky had at last grown dark and there was slanted starlight and twisted shade. Her heart had divided like two wings and she had never seen a night so beautiful.

Frankie stood looking into the sky. For when the old question came to her—the who she was and what she would be in the world, and why she was standing there that minute—when the old question came to her, she did not feel hurt and unanswered. At last she knew just who she was and understood where she was going. She loved her brother and the bride and she was a member of the wedding. The three of them would go into the world and they would always be together. And finally, after the scared spring and the crazy summer, she was no more afraid.

Part Two

1

THE DAY before the wedding was not like any day that F. Jasmine had ever known. It was the Saturday she went into the town, and suddenly, after the closed blank summer, the town opened before her and in a new way she belonged. Because of the wedding, F. Jasmine felt connected with all she saw, and it was as a sudden member that on this Saturday she went around the town. She walked the streets entitled as a queen and mingled everywhere. It was the day when, from the beginning, the world seemed no longer separate from herself and when all at once she felt included. Therefore, many things began to happen—nothing that came about surprised F. Jasmine and, until the last at least, all was natural in a magic way.

At the country house of an uncle of John Henry, Uncle Charles, she had seen old blindered mules going round and round in the same circle, grinding juice from the sugar cane for syrup. In the sameness of her tracks that summer, the old Frankie had somehow resembled that country mule; in town she browsed around the counters of the ten-cent store, or sat on the front row of the Palace show, or hung around her father's store, or stood on street corners watching soldiers. Now this morning was altogether different. She went into places she had never dreamed of entering until that day. For one thing, F. Jasmine went to a hotel—it was not the finest hotel in the town, or even the next to the finest, but nevertheless it was a hotel and F. Jasmine was there. Furthermore, she was there with a soldier, and that, too, was an unforeseen event, as she had never in her life laid eyes on him until that day. Only yesterday, if the old Frankie had glimpsed a box-like vision of this scene, as a view seen through a wizard's periscope, she would have bunched her mouth with unbelief. But it was a morning when many things occurred, and a curious fact about this day was a twisted sense of the astonishing; the unexpected did not make her wonder, and only the long known, the familiar, struck her with a strange surprise.

The day began when she waked up at dawn, and it was as though her brother and the bride had, in the night, slept on the bottom of her heart, so that the first instant she recognized the wedding. Next, and immediately, she thought about the town. Now that she was leaving home she felt in a curious way as though on this last day the town called to her and was now waiting. The windows of her room were cool dawn-blue. The old cock at the Mac-Keans' was crowing. Quickly she got up and turned on the bed-lamp and the motor.

It was the old Frankie of yesterday who had been puzzled, but F. Jasmine did not wonder any more; already she felt familiar with the wedding for a long, long time. The black dividing night has something to do with this. In the twelve years before, whenever a sudden change had come about there was a certain doubt during the time when it was happening; but after sleeping through a night, and on the very next day, the change did not seem so sudden after all. Two summers past, when she had traveled with the Wests to Port Saint Peter on the bay, the first sea evening with the scalloped gray ocean and empty sand was to her like a foreign place, and she had gone around with slanted eyes and put her hands on things in doubt. But after the first night, as soon as she awoke next day, it was as though she had known Port Saint Peter all her life. Now it was likewise with the wedding. No longer questioning, she turned to other things.

She sat at her desk wearing only the blue-and-white striped trousers of her pajamas which were rolled up above the knees, vibrating her right foot on the ball of her bare foot, and considering all that she must do on this last day. Some of these things she could name to herself, but there were other things that could not be counted on her fingers or made into a list with words. To start with, she decided to make herself some visiting cards with *Miss F. Jasmine Addams, Esq.*, engraved with squinted letters on a tiny card. So she put on her green visor eyeshade, cut up some cardboard, and fitted ink pens behind both ears. But her mind was restless and zigzagged to other things, and soon she began to get ready for town. She dressed carefully that morning in her most grown and best, the pink organdie, and put on lipstick and Sweet Serenade. Her father, a very early riser, was stirring in the kitchen when she went downstairs.

"Good morning, Papa."

Her father was Royal Quincy Addams and he owned a jewelry store just off the main street of the town. He answered her with a kind of grunt, for he was a grown person who liked to drink three cups of coffee before he started conversation for the day; he deserved a little peace and quiet before he put his nose down to the grindstone. F. Jasmine had heard him bungling about his room when once she waked up to drink water in the night, and his face was pale as cheese this morning, his eyes had a pink and ragged look. It was a morning when he despised a saucer because his cup would rattle against it and not fit, so he put his cup down on the table or stove top until brown circles were left all over everywhere and flies settled in quiet rings. There was some sugar spilt on the floor, and each time his step made a gritty sound his face shivered. This morning he wore a pair of saggy-kneed gray trousers and a blue shirt unfastened at the collar and with the tie loose. Since June she had had this secret grudge against him that almost she did not admit—since the night he had asked who was the great big blunderbuss who still wanted to sleep with her old Papa—but now she had this grudge no longer. All of a sudden it seemed to F. Jasmine that she saw her father for the first time, and she did not see him only as he was at that one minute, but pictures of the old days swirled in her mind and crossed each other. Remembrance, changing and fast, made F. Jasmine stop very still and stand with her head cocked, watching him both in the actual room and from somewhere inside her. But there were things that must be said, and when she spoke her voice was not unnatural.

"Papa, I think I ought to tell you now. I'm not coming back here after the wedding."

He had ears to hear with, loose large ears with lavender rims, but he did not listen. He was a widowman, for her mother had died the very day that she was born—and, as a widowman, set in his ways. Sometimes, especially in the early morning, he did not listen to things she said or new suggestions. So she sharpened her voice and chiseled the words into his head.

"I have to buy a wedding dress and some wedding shoes and a pair of pink, sheer stockings."

He heard and, after a consideration, gave her a permission nod. The grits boiled slowly with blue gluey bubbles, and as she set the table, she watched him and remembered. There were the winter mornings with frost flowers on the windowpanes and the roaring stove and the look of his brown crusty hand as he leaned over her shoulder to help with a hard part of the last-minute arithmetic that she was working at the table, his voice explaining. Blue long spring evenings, she saw also, and her father on the dark front porch with his feet propped on the banisters, drinking the frosted bottles of beer he had sent her to bring home from Finny's Place. She saw him bent over the workbench down at the store, dipping a tiny spring in gasoline, or whistling and peering with his round jeweler's glass into a watch. Remembrances came sudden and swirled, each colored with its own season, and for the first time she looked back on all the twelve years of her life and thought of them from a distance as a whole.

"Papa," she said, "I will write you letters."

Now he walked the dawn-stale kitchen like a person who has lost something, but has forgotten what it is that he has lost. Watching him, the old grudge was forgotten, and she felt sorry. He would miss her in the house all by himself when she was gone. He would be lonesome. She wanted to speak some sorry words and love her father, but just at that moment he cleared his throat in the special way he used when he was going to lay down the law to her and said:

"Will you please tell me what has become of the monkey-wrench and screw-driver that were in my tool chest on the back porch?"

"The monkey-wrench and screw-driver——" F. Jasmine stood with her shoulders hunched, her left foot drawn up to the calf of the right leg. "I borrowed them, Papa."

"Where are they now?"

F. Jasmine considered. "Over at the Wests'."

"Now pay attention and listen to me," her father said, holding the spoon that had been stirring the grits, and shaking it to mark the words. "If you don't have the sense and judgment to leave things alone——" He stared at her in a long and threatening way, and finished: "You'll have to be taught. From now on you walk the chalkline. Or you'll have to be taught." He sniffed suddenly. "Is that toast burning?"

It was still early in the morning when F. Jasmine left the house that day. The soft gray of the dawn had lightened and the sky was the wet pale blue of a watercolor sky just painted and not yet dried. There was a freshness in the bright air and cool dew on the burnt brown grass. From a back yard down the street, F. Jasmine could hear children's voices. She heard the calling voices of the neighborhood children who were trying to dig a swimming pool. They were all sizes and ages, members of nothing, and in the summers before, the old Frankie had been like leader or president of the swimming-pool diggers in that part of town—but now that she was twelve years old, she knew in advance that, though they would work and dig in vari-

ous yards, not doubting to the very last the cool clear swimming pool of water, it would all end in a big wide ditch of
shallow mud.

Now, as F. Jasmine crossed her yard, she saw in her
mind's eye the swarming children and heard from down
the street their chanting cries—and this morning, for the
first time in her life, she heard a sweetness in these sounds,
and she was touched. And, strange to say, her own home
yard which she had hated touched her a little too; she felt
she had not seen it for a long time. There, under the elm
tree was her old cold-drink store, a light packing case that
could be dragged around according to the shade, with a
sign reading, DEW DROP INN. It was the time of morn-
ning when, the lemonade in a bucket underneath the store,
she used to settle herself with her bare feet on the counter
and the Mexican hat tilted down over her face—her eyes
closed, smelling the strong smell of sun-warmed straw,
waiting. And sometimes there would be customers, and
she would send John Henry to the A. & P. to buy some
candy, but other times the Tempter Satan got the best of
her and she drank up all the stock instead. But now this
morning the store looked very small and staggered, and
she knew that she would never run it any more. F. Jasmine
thought of the whole idea as something over and done
with that had happened long ago. A sudden plan came to
her: after tomorrow, when she was with Janice and Jarvis,
in the far place where they would be, she would look back
on the old days and— But this was a plan F. Jasmine did
not finish, for, as the names lingered in her mind, the glad-
ness of the wedding rose up inside her and, although the
day was an August day, she shivered.

The main street, too, seemed to F. Jasmine like a street
returned to after many years, although she had walked up
and down it only Wednesday. There were the same brick
stores, about four blocks of them, the big white bank, and
in the distance the many-windowed cotton mill. The wide
street was divided by a narrow aisle of grass on either side
of which the cars drove slowly in a browsing way. The
glittering gray sidewalks and passing people, the striped
awning over the stores, all was the same—yet, as she

walked the street that morning, she felt free as a traveler who had never seen the town before.

And that was not all; she had no sooner walked down the left side of the main street and up again on the right sidewalk, when she realized a further happening. It had to do with various people, some known to her and others strangers, she met and passed along the street. An old colored man, stiff and proud on his rattling wagon seat, drove a sad blindered mule down toward the Saturday market. F. Jasmine looked at him, he looked at her, and to the outward appearance that was all. But in that glance, F. Jasmine felt between his eyes and her own eyes a new unnamable connection, as though they were known to each other—and there even came an instant vision of his home field and country roads and quiet dark pine trees as the wagon rattled past her on the paved town street. And she wanted him to know her, too—about the wedding.

Now the same thing happened again and again on those four blocks: with a lady going into MacDougal's store, with a small man waiting for the bus before the big First National Bank, with a friend of her father's called Tut Ryan. It was a feeling impossible to explain in words—and later when she tried to tell of it at home Berenice raised up her eyebrows and dragged the word in a mocking way: Connection? Connection? But nevertheless it was there, this feeling—a connection close as answers to calls. Furthermore, on the sidewalk before the First National Bank she found a dime and any other day that would have been a grand surprise, but now this morning she only paused to shine the dime on her dress front and put it in her pink pocketbook. Under the fresh blue early sky the feeling as she walked along was one of newly risen lightness, power, entitlement.

It was in a place called the Blue Moon that she first told about the wedding, and she came to the Blue Moon in a roundabout way, as it was not on the main street, but on the street called Front Avenue which bordered the river. She was in this neighborhood because she had heard the organ of the monkey and the monkey-man and had set out immediately to find them. She had not seen the monkey and the monkey-man through the whole summer and it seemed a sign to her that she should run across them on this last day in town. She had not seen them for so long that sometimes she thought the pair of them might even be dead. They did not go around the streets in wintertime, for the cold wind made them sick; they went South in October to Florida and came back to the town in warm late spring.

They, the monkey and the monkey-man, wandered to other towns also—but the old Frankie would come across them on various shaded streets through all the summers she could remember, except this one. He was a darling little monkey, and the monkey-man was nice also; the old Frankie had always loved them, and now she was dying to tell her plans and let them know about the wedding. So, when she first heard the broken-sounding, faint organ, she went at once in search of it, and the music seemed to come from near the river on Front Avenue. So she turned from the main street and hurried down the side street, but just before she reached Front Avenue the organ stopped, and when she gazed up and down the avenue she could not see the monkey or the monkey-man and all was silent and they were nowhere in sight. They had stopped, maybe, in a doorway or a shop—so F. Jasmine walked slowly with a watchful air.

Front Avenue was a street that had always drawn her, although it had the sorriest, smallest stores in town. On the left side of the street there were warehouses, and in between were glimpses of brown river and green trees. On the right side there was a place with a sign reading Prophylactic Military, the business of which had often puzzled her, then other various places: a smelly fish shop with the shocked eyes of a single fish staring from some crushed ice in the window, a pawnshop, a second-hand clothing store with out-of-style garments hanging from the narrow entrance and a row of broken shoes lined up on the sidewalk outside. Then finally there was the place called the Blue Moon. The street itself was cobbled with brick and angry-looking in the glare, and along the gutter she passed some eggshells and rotten lemon peels. It was not a fine street, but nevertheless the old Frankie had liked to come here now and then at certain times.

The street was quiet in the mornings and on the weekday afternoons. But toward evening, or on holidays, the street would fill up with the soldiers who came from the camp nine miles away. They seemed to prefer Front Avenue to almost any other street, and sometimes the pavement resembled a flowing river of brown soldiers. They came to town on holidays and went around in glad, loud gangs together, or walked the sidewalks with grown girls. And the old Frankie had always watched them with a jealous heart; they came from all over the whole country and were soon going all over the world. They went around in gangs together, those lasting twilights of the summertime —while the old Frankie dressed in her khaki shorts and Mexican hat, watched from a distance by herself. Noises and weathers of distant places seemed to hover about them in the air. She imagined the many cities that these soldiers came from, and thought of the countries where they would go—while she was stuck there in the town forever. And stealing jealousy sickened her heart. But now this morning her heart was occupied with one intention: to tell of the wedding and her plans. So, after walking down the burning pavement, hunting for the monkey and the monkey-man, she came to the Blue Moon and it occurred to her that maybe they were there.

The Blue Moon was a place at the end of Front Avenue, and often the old Frankie had stood out on the sidewalk with her palms and nose pressed flat against the screen door, watching all that went on there. Customers, most of them soldiers, sat at the boothed tables, or stood at the counter having drinks, or crowded around the jukebox. Here sometimes there were sudden commotions. Late one afternoon when she passed the Blue Moon, she heard wild angry voices and a sound like a bottle being thrown, and as she stood there a policeman came out on the sidewalk pushing and jerking a torn-looking man with wobbly legs. The man was crying, shouting; there was blood on his ripped shirt and dirty tears dripped down his face. It

was an April afternoon of rainbow showers, and by and
by the Black Maria screamed down the street, and the poor,
arrested criminal was thrown into the prisoners' cage and
carried off down to the jail. The old Frankie knew the
Blue Moon well, although she had never been inside.
There was no written law to keep her out, no lock and
chain on the screen door. But she had known in an unworded way that it was a forbidden place to children. The
Blue Moon was a place for holiday soldiers and the
grown and free. The old Frankie had known she had no
valid right to enter there, so she had only hung around the
edges and never once had she gone inside. But now this
morning before the wedding all of this was changed. The
old laws she had known before meant nothing to F. Jasmine, and without a second thought she left the street and
went inside.

There in the Blue Moon was the red-headed soldier who
was to weave in such an unexpected way through all that
day before the wedding. F. Jasmine, however, did not notice him at first; she looked for the monkey-man, but he
was not there. Aside from the soldier the only other person in the room was the Blue Moon owner, a Portuguese,
who stood behind the counter. This was the person F. Jasmine picked to be the first to hear about the wedding, and
he was chosen simply because he was the one most likely
and near.

After the fresh brightness of the street, the Blue Moon
seemed dark. Blue neon lights burned over the dim mirror
behind the counter, tinting the faces in the place pale
green, and an electric fan turned slowly so that the room
was scalloped with warm stale waves of breeze. At that
early morning hour the place was very quiet. There were
booth tables across the room, all empty. At the back of
the Blue Moon a lighted wooden stairway led up to the
second floor. The place smelled of dead beer and morning coffee. F. Jasmine ordered coffee from the owner behind the counter, and after he brought it to her, he sat
down on a stool across from her. He was a sad, pale man
with a very flat face. He wore a long white apron and,
hunched on the stool with his feet on the rungs, he was

reading a romance magazine. The telling of the wedding gathered inside her, and when it was so ready she could no longer resist, she hunted in her mind a good opening remark—something grown and off-hand, to start between them the conversation. She said in a voice that trembled a little: "It certainly has been an unseasonable summer, hasn't it?"

The Portuguese at first did not seem to hear her and went on reading the romance magazine. So she repeated her remark, and when his eyes were turned to hers and his attention caught, she went on in a higher voice: "Tomorrow this brother of mine and his bride are marrying at Winter Hill." She went straight to the story, as a circus dog breaks through the paper hoop, and as she talked, her voice became clearer, more definite, and sure. She told her plans in a way that made them sound completely settled, and not in the least open to question. The Portuguese listened with his head cocked to one side, his dark eyes ringed with ash-gray circles, and now and then he wiped his damp veined dead-white hands on his stained apron. She told about the wedding and her plans and he did not dispute with her or doubt.

It is far easier, it came to her as she remembered Berenice, to convince strangers of the coming to pass of dearest wants than those in your own home kitchen. The thrill of speaking certain words—Jarvis and Janice, wedding and Winter Hill—was such that F. Jasmine, when she had finished, wanted to start all over again. The Portuguese took from behind his ear a cigarette which he tapped on the counter but did not light. In the unnatural neon glow his face looked startled and when she had finished he did not speak. With the telling of the wedding still sounding inside her, as the last chord of a guitar murmurs a long time after the strings are struck, F. Jasmine turned toward the entrance and the framed blazing street beyond the door: dark people passed along the sidewalk and footsteps echoed in the Blue Moon.

"It gives me a funny feeling," she said. "After living in this town all my whole life, to know that after tomorrow I'll never be back here any more."

It was then she noticed him for the first time, the soldier who at the very end would twist so strangely that last, long day. Later, on thinking back, she tried to recall some warning hint of future craziness—but at the time he looked to her like any other soldier standing at a counter drinking beer. He was not tall, nor short, nor fat, nor thin—except for the red hair there was nothing at all unusual about him. He was one of the thousands of soldiers who came to the town from the camp near-by. But as she looked into this soldier's eyes, in the dim light of the Blue Moon, she realized that she gazed at him in a new way.

That morning, for the first time, F. Jasmine was not jealous. He might have come from New York or California—but she did not envy him. He might be on his way to England or India—she was not jealous. In the restless spring and crazy summer, she had watched the soldiers with a sickened heart, for they were the ones who came and went, while she was stuck there in the town forever. But now, on this day before the wedding, all this was changed; her eyes as she looked into the soldier's eyes were clear of jealousy and want. Not only did she feel that unexplainable connection she was to feel between herself and other total strangers that day, there was another sense of recognition: it seemed to F. Jasmine they exchanged the special look of friendly, free travelers who meet for a moment at some stop along the way. The look was long. And with the lifting of the jealous weight, F. Jasmine felt at peace. It was quiet in the Blue Moon, and the telling of the wedding seemed still to murmur in the room. After this long gaze of fellow travelers, it was the soldier who finally turned his face away.

"Yes," said F. Jasmine, after a moment and to no one in particular, "it gives me a mighty funny feeling. In a way it's like I ought to do all things I would have done if I was staying in the town forever. Instead of this one day. So I guess I better get a move on. Adios." She spoke the last word to the Portuguese, and at the same time her hand reached automatically to lift the Mexican hat she had worn all summer until that day, but, finding nothing, the gesture withered and her hand felt shamed. Quickly she scratched her head, and with a last glance at the soldier, left the Blue Moon.

It was the morning different from all other mornings she had ever known because of several reasons. First, of course, there was the telling of the wedding. Once, and a long time ago, the old Frankie had liked to go around the town playing a game. She had walked all around— through the north side of town with the grass-lawned houses and the sad mills section and colored Sugarville— wearing her Mexican hat and the high-laced boots and a cowboy rope tied round her waist, she had gone around pretending to be Mexican. Me no speak English—Adios Buenos Noches—abla pokie peekie poo, she had jabbered in mock Mexican. Sometimes a little crowd of children gathered and the old Frankie would swell up with pride and trickery—but when the game was over, and she was home, there would come over her a cheated discontent. Now this morning reminded her of those old days of the Mexican game. She went to the same places, and the people, mostly strangers to her, were the same. But this morning she was not trying to trick people and pretend; far from it, she wanted only to be recognized for her true self. It was a need so strong, this want to be known and recognized, that F. Jasmine forgot the wild hard glare and choking dust and miles (it must have been at least five miles) of wandering all over town.

A second fact about that day was the forgotten music that sprang suddenly into her mind—snatches of orchestra minuets, march tunes and waltzes, and the jazz horn of Honey Brown—so that her feet in the patent-leather shoes stepped always according to a tune. A last difference about that morning was the way her world seemed layered in three different parts, all the twelve years of the old Frankie, the present day itself, and the future ahead when the J A three of them would be together in all the many distant places.

As she walked along, it seemed as though the ghost of the old Frankie, dirty and hungry-eyed, trudged silently along nor far from her, and the thought of the future, after the wedding, was constant as the very sky. That day alone seemed equally important as both the long past and the bright future—as a hinge is important to a swinging door. And since it was the day when past and future mingled, F. Jasmine did not wonder that it was strange and long. So these were the main reasons why F. Jasmine felt, in an unworded way, that this was a morning different from all mornings she had ever known. And of all these facts and feelings the strongest of all was the need to be known for her true self and recognized.

Along the shaded sidewalks on the north side of the town, near the main street, she passed a row of lace-curtained boarding houses with empty chairs behind the banisters until she came upon a lady sweeping her front porch. To this lady, after the opening remark about the weather, F. Jasmine told her plans and, as with the Portuguese in the Blue Moon café and all the other people she was to meet that day, the telling of the wedding had an end and a beginning, a shape like a song.

First, just at the moment she commenced, a sudden hush came in her heart; then, as the names were named and the plan unfolded, there was a wild rising lightness and at the end content. The lady meanwhile leaned on the broom, listening. Behind her there was a dark open hall, with a bare stairway, and to the left a table for letters, and from this dark hall came the strong hot smell of cooking turnip greens. The strong waves of smell and the dark hall seemed to mingle with F. Jasmine's joy, and when she looked into the lady's eyes, she loved her, though she did not even know her name.

The lady neither argued nor accused. She did not say anything. Until at the very end, just as F. Jasmine turned to go, she said: "Well, I declare." But already F. Jasmine, a quick gay band tune marching her feet, was hurrying on her way again.

In a neighborhood of shaded summer lawns she turned down a side street and met some men mending the road. The sharp smell of melted tar and hot gravel and the loud tractor filled the air with noisy excitement. It was the tractor-man F. Jasmine chose to hear her plans—running beside him, her head thrown back to watch his sunburned face, she had to cup her hands around her mouth to make her voice heard. Even so it was uncertain if he understood, for when she stopped, he laughed and yelled back to her something she could not quite catch. Here, among the racket and excitement, was the place F. Jasmine saw the ghost of the old Frankie plainest of all—hovering close to the commotion, chewing a great big lump of tar, hanging around at noon to watch the lunch-pails being opened. There was a fine big motorcycle parked near the street-menders, and before going on F. Jasmine looked at it admiringly, then spat on the broad leather seat and shined it carefully with her fist. She was in a very nice neighborhood near the edge of town, a place of new brick houses with flower-bordered sidewalks and cars parked in paved driveways; but the finer the neighborhood, the fewer people are about, so F. Jasmine turned back toward the center of the town. The sun burned like an iron lid on her head and her slip was stuck wet to her chest, and even the organdie dress was wet and clinging in spots also. The march tune had softened to a dreaming song on a violin that slowed her footsteps to a wander. To this kind of music she crossed to the opposite side of the town, beyond the main street and the mill, to the gray crooked streets of the mill section, where, among the choking dust and sad gray rotten shacks, there were more listeners to tell about the wedding.

(From time to time, as she went around, a little conversation buzzed on the bottom of her mind. It was the voice of Berenice when later she would know about this morning. And you just roamed around, the voice said, taking up with total strangers! I never heard of such a thing in all my life! So the Berenice voice sounded, heard but unnoticed like the buzzing of a fly.)

From the sad alleys and crooked streets of the mill section she crossed the unseen line dividing Sugarville from the white people's town. Here were the same two-room shacks and rotted privies, as in the mill section, but round thick chinaberry trees cast solid shade and often cool ferns grew in pots upon the porches. This was a part of town well known to her, and as she walked along she found herself remembering these familiar lanes in long-past times and other weathers—the ice-pale mornings in the wintertime when even the orange fires under the black iron pots of wash-women seemed to be shivering, the windy autumn nights.

Meanwhile, the glare was dizzy bright and she met and talked to many people, some known to her by sight and name, some strangers. The plans about the wedding stiffened and fixed with each new telling and finally came unchangeable. By eleven-thirty she was very tired, and even the tunes dragged with exhaustion; the need to be recognized for her true self was for the time being satisfied. So she went back to the place from which she started —to the main street where the glittering sidewalks were baked and half-deserted in the white glare.

Always she went by her father's store whenever she came to town. Her father's store was on the same block as the Blue Moon, but two doors from the main street and in a much better location. It was a narrow store with precious jewels in velvet boxes placed in the window. Beyond the window was her father's workbench, and when you walked along the sidewalk you could see her father working there, his head bent over the tiny watches, and his big brown hands hovered as carefully as butterflies. You could see her father like a public person in the town, well known to all by sight and name. But her father was not proud and did not even look up at those who stopped and gazed at him. This morning, however, he was not at his bench, but behind the counter rolling down his shirtsleeves as though making ready to put on his coat and go outside.

The long glass showcase was bright with jewels and watches and silverware and the store smelled of watch-fixing kerosene. Her father wiped the sweat from his long upper lip with his forefinger and rubbed his nose in a troubled way.

"Where in the world have you been all morning? Berenice has called here twice trying to locate you."

"I've been all over the whole town," she said.

But he did not listen. "I'm going around to your Aunt

Pet's," he said. "She's had a sad piece of news today."

"What sad piece of news?" F. Jasmine asked.

"Uncle Charles is dead."

Uncle Charles was the great-uncle of John Henry West, but though she and John Henry were first cousins, Uncle Charles was not blood kin to her. He lived twenty-one miles out on the Renfroe Road in a shaded wooden country house surrounded by red cotton fields. An old, old man, he had been sick a long time; it was said he had one foot in the grave—and he always wore bedroom slippers. Now he was dead. But that had nothing to do with the wedding, and so F. Jasmine only said: "Poor Uncle Charles. That certainy is a pity."

Her father went back behind the gray sour velvet curtain that divided the store into two parts, the larger public part in front and behind a small dusty private part. Behind the curtain was the water cooler, some shelves of boxes, and the big iron safe where diamond rings were locked away from robbers in the night. F. Jasmine heard her Papa moving around back there, and she settled herself carefully at the workbench before the front window. A watch, already taken apart, was laid out on the green blotter.

There was a strong streak of watchmaker's blood in her and always the old Frankie had loved to sit at her father's bench. She would put on her father's glasses with the jeweler's loupe attached and, scowling busily, dip them in gasoline. She worked with the lathe, too. Sometimes a little crowd of sidewalk lazies would collect to watch her from the street and she would imagine how they said: "Frankie Addams works for her father and makes fifteen dollars a week. She fixes the hardest watches in the store and goes to the Woodmen of the World Club with her father. Look at her. She is a credit to the family and a big credit to the whole town." So she would imagine these conversations, as she scowled with a busy expression at a watch. But now today she looked down at the watch spread out on the blotter, and did not put on the jeweler's loupe. There was something more she ought to say about the death of Uncle Charles.

When her father returned to the front of the store, she said: "At one time Uncle Charles was one of the leading citizens. It will be a loss to the whole county."

The words did not seem to impress her father. "You had better go on home. Berenice has been phoning to locate you."

"Well, remember you said I could get a wedding dress. And stockings and shoes."

"Charge them at MacDougal's."

"I don't see why we always have to trade at MacDougal's just because it's a local store," she grumbled as she went out of the door. "Where I am going there will be stores a hundred times bigger than MacDougal's."

The clock in the tower of the First Baptist Church clanged twelve, the mill whistle wailed. There was a drowsing quietness about the street, and even the very cars, parked slantwise with their noses toward the center aisle of grass, were like exhausted cars that have all gone to sleep. The few people out at the noon hour kept close beneath the blunt shade of the awnings. The sun took the color from the sky and the brick stores seemed shrunken, dark, beneath the glare—one building had an overhanging cornice at the top which, from a distance, gave it a queer look of a brick building that has begun to melt. In this noon quietness, she heard again the organ of the monkey-man, the sound that always magnetized her footsteps so that she automatically went toward it. This time she would find them and tell them good-bye.

As F. Jasmine hurried down the street, she saw the two of them in her mind's eye—and wondered if they would remember her. The old Frankie had always loved the monkey and the monkey-man. They resembled each other —they both had an anxious, questioning expression, as though they wondered every minute if what they did was wrong. The monkey, in fact, was nearly always wrong; after he danced to the organ tune, he was supposed to take off his darling little cap and pass it around to the audience, but likely as not he would get mixed up and bow and reach out his cap to the monkey-man, and not the audience. And the monkey-man would plead with him, and finally begin to chatter and fuss. When he would make as if to slap the monkey, the monkey would cringe down and chatter also—and they would look at each other with the same scared exasperation, their wrinkled faces very sad. After watching them a long time, the old Frankie, fascinated, began to take on the same expression as she followed them around. And now F. Jasmine was eager to see them.

She could hear the broken-sounding organ plainly, although they were not on the main street, but up further and probably just around the corner of the next block. So F. Jasmine hurried toward them. As she neared the corner, she heard other sounds that puzzled her curiosity so that she listened and stopped. Above the music of the organ there was the sound of a man's voice quarreling and the excited higher fussing of the monkey-man. She could hear the monkey chattering also. Then suddenly the organ stopped and the two different voices were loud and mad. F. Jasmine had reached the corner, and it was the corner by the Sears and Roebuck store; she passed the store slowly, then turned and faced a curious sight.

It was a narrow street that went downhill toward Front Avenue, blinding bright in the wild glare. There on the sidewalk was the monkey, the monkey-man, and a soldier holding out a whole fistful of dollar bills—it looked at the first glance like a hundred dollars. The soldier looked angry, and the monkey-man was pale and excited also. Their voices were quarreling and F. Jasmine gathered that the soldier was trying to buy the monkey. The monkey himself was crouched and shivering down on the sidewalk close to the brick wall of the Sears and Roebuck store. In spite of the hot day, he had on his little red coat with silver buttons and his little face, scared and desperate, had the look of someone who is just about to sneeze. Shivering and pitiful, he kept bowing at nobody and offering his cap into the air. He knew the furious voices were about him and he felt blamed.

F. Jasmine was standing near-by, trying to take in the commotion, listening and still. Then suddenly the soldier grabbed at the monkey's chain, but the monkey screamed, and before she knew what it was all about, the monkey had skittered up her leg and body and was huddled on her shoulder with his little monkey hands around her head. It happened in a flash, and she was so shocked she could not move. The voices stopped and, except for the monkey's jibbered scream, the street was silent. The soldier stood slack-jawed, surprised, still holding out the handful of dollar bills.

The monkey-man was the first to recover; he spoke to the monkey in a gentle voice, and in another second the monkey sprang from off her shoulder and landed on the organ which the monkey-man was carrying on his back. The two of them went away. They quickly hurried around the corner and at the last second, just as they turned, they both looked back with the same expression—reproaching and sly. F. Jasmine leaned against the brick wall, and she still felt the monkey on her shoulder and smelt his dusty, sour smell; she shivered. The soldier muttered until the pair of them were out of sight, and F. Jasmine noticed then that he was red-haired and the same soldier who had been in the Blue Moon. He stuffed the bills in his side pocket.

"He certainy is a darling monkey," F. Jasmine said. "But it gave me a mighty funny feeling to have him run up me like that."

The soldier seemed to realize her for the first time. The look on his face changed slowly, and the angry expression went away. He was looking at F. Jasmine from the top of her head, down the organdie best dress, and to the black pumps she was wearing.

"I guess you must have wanted the monkey a whole lot," she said. "I've always wanted a monkey, too."

"What?" he asked. Then he remarked in a muffled voice, as if his tongue were made of felt or a very thick piece of blotting paper, "Which way are we going?" the soldier said. "Are you going my way or am I going yours?"

F. Jasmine had not expected this. The soldier was joining with her like a traveler who meets another traveler in a tourist town. For a second, it occurred to her that she had heard this remark before, perhaps in a picture show—that furthermore it was a set remark requiring a set answer.

Not knowing the ready-made reply, she answered carefully.

"Which way are you going?"

"Hook on," he said, sticking out his elbow.

They walked down the side street, on their shrunken noontime shadows. The soldier was the only person during that day who spoke first to F. Jasmine and invited her to join with him. But, when she began to tell about the wedding, something seemed lacking. Perhaps it was because she had already told her plans to so many people all over town that now she could rest satisfied. Or perhaps it was because she felt the soldier was not really listening. He looked at the pink organdie dress from the corner of his eye, and there was a half-smile on his mouth. F. Jasmine could not match her steps to his, although she tried, for his legs seemed loosely fastened to his body so that he walked in a rambling way.

"What state do you come from, if I may ask?" she said politely.

In that second that passed before his answer there was time for her skimming mind to picture Hollywood, New York, and Maine. The soldier answered: "Arkansas."

Now of all the forty-eight states in the Union, Arkansas was one of the very few that had never especially appealed to her—but her imagination, balked, immediately turned the opposite way so that she asked:

"Do you have any idea where you will be going?"

"Just banging around," the soldier said. "I'm out loose on a three-day pass."

He had mistaken the meaning of her question, for she had asked it to him as a soldier liable to be sent to any foreign country in the world, but, before she could explain what she had meant, he said:

"There's a kind of hotel around the corner I'm staying at." Then, still looking at the pleated collar of her dress, he added: "It seems like I've seen you somewhere before. Do you ever go dancing at the Idle Hour?"

They walked down Front Avenue, and now the street was beginning to have the air of Saturday afternoon. A lady was drying her yellow hair in the window of the second floor above the fish store, and she called down to two soldiers who passed along the street. A street preacher, a known town character, was preaching on a corner to a group of warehouse colored boys and scraggly children. But F. Jasmine did not have her mind on what was going on around her. The soldier's mention of dancing and the Idle Hour touched like a story-tale wand upon her mind. She realized for the first time that she was walking with a soldier, with one of the groups of loud, glad gangs that roamed around the streets together or walked with the grown girls. They danced at the Idle Hour and had a good time, while the old Frankie was asleep. And she had never danced with anybody, excepting Evelyn Owen, and had never put foot in the Idle Hour.

And now F. Jasmine walked with a soldier who in his mind included her in such unknown pleasures. But she was not altogether proud. There was an uneasy doubt that she could not quite place or name. The noon air was thick and sticky as hot syrup, and there was the stifling smell of the dye-rooms from the cotton mill. She heard the organ-grinder sounding faintly from the main street.

The soldier stopped: "This is the hotel," he said.

They were before the Blue Moon and F. Jasmine was surprised to hear it spoken of as a hotel, as she had thought it was only a café. When the soldier held the screen door open for her, she noticed that he swayed a little. Her eyes saw blinding red, then black, after the glare, and it took them a minute to get used to the blue light. She followed the soldier to one of the booths on the right.

"Care for a beer," he said, not in an asking voice, but as though he took her reply for granted.

F. Jasmine did not enjoy the taste of beer; once or twice she had sneaked swallows from her father's glass and it was sour. But the soldier had not left her any choice. "I would be delighted," she said. "Thank you."

Never had she been in a hotel, although she had often thought about them and written about them in her shows. Her father had stayed in hotels several times, and once, from Montgomery, he had brought her two little tiny cakes of hotel soap which she had saved. She looked around the

Blue Moon with new curiosity. All of a sudden she felt very proper. On seating herself at the booth table, she carefully smoothed down her dress, as she did when at a party or in church, so as not to sit the pleats out of the skirt. She sat up straight and on her face there was a proper expression. But the Blue Moon still seemed to her more like a kind of café than a real hotel. She did not see the sad, pale Portuguese, and a laughing fat lady with a golden tooth poured beer for the soldier at the counter. The stairway at the back led probably to the hotel rooms upstairs, and the steps were lighted by a blue neon bulb and covered with a runner of linoleum. A sassy chorus on the radio was singing an advertisement: Denteen Chewing Gum! Denteen Chewing Gum! Denteen! The beery air reminded her of a room where a rat has died behind a wall. The soldier walked back to the booth, carrying two glasses of the beer; he licked some foam that had spilled over his hand and wiped the hand on his trousers seat. When he was settled in the booth, F. Jasmine said, in a voice that was absolutely new to her—a high voice spoken through the nose, dainty and dignified:

"Don't you think it is mighty exciting? Here we are sitting here at this table and in a month from now there's no telling where on earth we'll be. Maybe tomorrow the army will send you to Alaska like they sent my brother. Or to France or Africa or Burma. And I don't have any idea where I will be. I'd like for us to go to Alaska for a while, and then go somewhere else. They say that Paris has been liberated. In my opinion the war will be over next month."

The soldier raised his glass, and threw back his head to gulp the beer. F. Jasmine took a few swallows also, although it tasted nasty to her. Today she did not see the world as loose and cracked and turning a thousand miles an hour, so that the spinning views of war and distant lands made her mind dizzy. The world had never been so close to her. Sitting across from the soldier at that booth in the Blue Moon, she suddenly saw the three of them—herself, her brother, and the bride—walking beneath a cold Alaskan sky, along the sea where green ice waves lay frozen and folded on the shore; they climbed a sunny glacier shot through with pale cold colors and a rope tied the three of them together, and friends from another glacier called in Alaskan their J A names. She saw them next in Africa, where, with a crowd of sheeted Arabs, they galloped on camels in the sandy wind. Burma was jungle-dark, and she had seen pictures in *Life* magazine. Because of the wedding, these distant lands, the world, seemed altogether possible and near: as close to Winter Hill as Winter Hill was to the town. It was the actual present, in fact, that seemed to F. Jasmine a little bit unreal.

"Yes, it's mighty exciting," she said again.

The soldier, his beer finished, wiped his wet mouth with the back of his freckled hand. His face, although not fat, seemed swollen, and it was glossy in the neon light. He had a thousand little freckles, and the only thing that seemed to her pretty was his bright, red curly hair. His eyes were blue, set close together, and the whites were raw. He was staring at her with a peculiar expression, not as one traveler gazes at another, but as a person who shares a secret scheme. For several minutes he did not talk. Then, when at last he spoke, the words did not make sense to her and she did not understand. It seemed to her the soldier said:

"Who is a cute dish?"

There were no dishes on the table and she had the uneasy feeling he had begun to talk a kind of double-talk. She tried to turn the conversation.

"I told you my brother is a Member of the Armed Forces."

But the soldier did not seem to listen. "I could of sworn I'd run into you some place before."

The doubt in F. Jasmine deepened. She realized now that the soldier thought she was much older than she was, but her pleasure in this was somehow uncertain. To make conversation she remarked:

"Some people are not partial to red hair. But to me it's my favorite color." She added, remembering her brother and the bride. "Except dark brown and yellow. I always think it's a pity for the Lord to waste curly hair on boys. When so many girls are going around with hair as straight as pokers."

The soldier leaned over the booth table and, still staring at her, he began to walk his fingers, the second and third fingers of both hands, across the table toward her. The fingers were dirty, with rinds of black beneath the nails. F. Jasmine had the sense that something strange was going to happen, when just at the moment there was a sudden racket and commotion and three or four soldiers shoved each other into the hotel. There was a babble of voices and the screen door banged. The soldier's fingers stopped walking across the table and, when he glanced at the other soldiers, the peculiar expression was scattered from his eyes.

"That certainy is a darling little monkey," she said.

"What monkey?"

The doubt deepened to the feeling that something was wrong. "Why, the monkey you tried to buy a few minutes ago. What's the matter with you?"

Something was wrong and the soldier put his fists up to his head. His body limpened and he leaned back in the seat of the booth, as though collapsed. "Oh, that monkey!" he said in his slurred voice. "The walk in the sun after all those beers. I was slamming around all night." He sighed, and his hands were open loose upon the table. "I guess maybe I'm just about beat."

For the first time F. Jasmine began to wonder what she was doing there and if she ought not to take herself on home. The other soldiers had crowded around a table near the stairway, and the lady with the golden tooth was busy behind the counter. F. Jasmine had finished her beer and a lace of creamy foam lined the inside of the empty glass. The hot, close smell in the hotel suddenly made her feel a little queer.

"I have to go home now. Thank you for treating me."

She got up from the booth, but the soldier reached out toward her and caught a piece of her dress. "Hey!" he said. "Don't just walk off like that. Let's fix up something for this evening. How bout a date for nine o'clock?"

"A date?" F. Jasmine felt as though her head was big and loose. The beer made her legs feel peculiar, too, almost as though she had four legs to manage instead of two. On any other day than this it would have seemed almost impossible that anyone, much less a soldier, would have invited her to a date. The very word, *date,* was a grown word used by older girls. But here again there was a blight upon her pleasure. If he knew she was not yet thirteen, he would never have invited her, or probably never joined with her at all. There was a troubled sense, a light uneasiness. "I don't know—"

"Sure," he urged. "Suppose we link up here at nine o'clock. We can go to the Idle Hour or something. That suit you all right? Here at nine o'clock."

"O.K." she said finally. "I will be delighted."

Again she was on the burning sidewalks, where passing walkers looked dark and shrunken in the angry glare. It took her a little while to come back to the wedding feeling of that morning, for the half-hour in the hotel had slightly distracted her frame of mind. But it did not take her very long, and by the time she reached the main street, the wedding feeling was recovered. She met a little girl, two grades below her at the school, and stopped her on the street to tell her her plans. She told her also that a soldier had invited her to have a date, and now she told it in a bragging tone. The girl went with her to buy the wedding clothes, which took an hour and meant the trying-on of more than a dozen beautiful dresses.

But the main thing that brought back the wedding frame of mind was an accident that occurred on the way home. It was a mysterious trick of sight and the imagination. She was walking home when all at once there was a shock in her as though a thrown knife struck and shivered in her chest. F. Jasmine stopped dead in her tracks, one foot still raised, and at first she could not take it in just what had happened. There was something sideways and behind her that had flashed across the very corner edge of her left eye; she had half-seen something, a dark double shape, in the alley she had just that moment passed. And because of this half-seen object, the quick flash in the corner of her eye, there had sprung up in her the sudden picture of her brother and the bride. Ragged and bright as lightning she saw the two of them as they had been when, for a moment, they stood together before the living-room mantelpiece, his arm around her shoulders. So strong was this picture that F. Jasmine felt suddenly that Jarvis and Janice were there behind her in the alley, and she had caught a glimpse of them—although she knew, and well enough, that they were in Winter Hill, almost a hundred miles away.

F. Jasmine lowered her raised foot to the pavement and slowly turned to look around. The alley lay between two grocery stores: a narrow alley, dark in the glare. She did not look at it directly, for somehow it was as though she was almost afraid. Her eyes stole slowly down the brick wall and she glimpsed again the dark double shapes. And what was there? F. Jasmine was stunned. There in the alley were only two colored boys, one taller than the other and with his arm resting on the shorter boy's shoulder. That was all—but something about the angle or the way they stood, or the pose of their shapes, had reflected the sudden picture of her brother and the bride that had so shocked her. And with this vision of them plain and exact the morning ended, and she was home by two o'clock.

2

The afternoon was like the center of the cake that Berenice had baked last Monday, a cake which failed. The old Frankie had been glad the cake had failed, not out of spite, but because she loved these fallen cakes the best. She enjoyed the damp, gummy richness near the center, and did not understand why grown people thought such cakes a failure. It was a loaf cake, that last Monday, with the edges risen light and high and the middle moist and altogether fallen—after the bright, high morning the afternoon was dense and solid as the center of that cake. And because it was the last of all the afternoons, F. Jasmine found an unfamiliar sweetness in the known old kitchen ways and tones. At two o'clock, when she came in, Berenice was pressing clothes. John Henry sat at the table blowing soapbubbles with a spool, and he gave her a long, green, secret look.

"Where in the world have you been?" asked Berenice.

"We know something you don't know," John Henry said. "Do you know what?"

"What?"

"Berenice and me are going to the wedding."

F. Jasmine was taking off her organdie dress, and his words startled her.

"Uncle Charles is dead."

"I heard that, but——"

"Yes," said Berenice. "The poor old soul passed on this morning. They're taking the body to the family grave-yard in Opelika. And John Henry is to stay with us for several days."

Now that she knew the death of Uncle Charles would in a sense affect the wedding, she made room for it in her thoughts. While Berenice finished pressing clothes, F. Jasmine sat in her petticoat on the stairs leading up to her room; she closed her eyes. Uncle Charles lived in a shady wooden house out in the country, and he was too old to eat corn on the cob. In June of this summer he took sick, and ever since he had been critical. He lay in the bed, shrunken and brown and very old. He complained that the pictures were hung crooked on the wall, and they took down all the framed pictures—it was not that. He complained that his bed was placed in a wrong corner, and so they moved the bed—it was not that. Then his voice failed, and when he tried to talk, it was as though his throat had filled with glue, and they could not understand the words. One Sunday the Wests had gone out to see him and taken Frankie with them; she had tiptoed to the open door of the back bedroom. He looked like an old man carved in brown wood and covered with a sheet. Only his eyes had moved, and they were like blue jelly, and she had felt they might come out from the sockets and roll like blue wet jelly down his stiff face. She had stood in the doorway staring at him— then tiptoed away, afraid. They finally made out that he complained the sun shone the wrong way through the window, but that was not the thing that hurt him so. And it was death.

F. Jasmine opened her eyes and stretched herself.

"It is a terrible thing to be dead!" she said.

"Well," said Berenice. "The old man suffered a lot and he had lived up his span. The Lord appointed the time for him."

"I know. But at the same time it seems mighty queer that he would have to die the very day before the wedding. And why on earth do you and John Henry have to go tagging to the wedding? Seems to me like you would just stay home."

"Frankie Addams," said Berenice, and she suddenly put her arms akimbo, "you are the most selfish human being that ever breathed. We all been cooped up in this kitchen and——"

"Don't call me Frankie!" she said. "I don't wish to have to remind you any more."

It was the time of early afternoon when in the old days a sweet band would be playing. Now with the radio turned off, the kitchen was solemn and silent and there were sounds from far away. A colored voice called from the sidewalk, calling the names of vegetables in a dark slurred tone, a long unwinding hollering in which there were no words. Somewhere, near in the neighborhood, there was the sound of a hammer and each stroke left a round echo.

"You would be mighty surprised if you knew whereall I've been today. I was all over this whole town. I saw the monkey and the monkey-man. There was this soldier who was trying to buy the monkey and holding a hundred dollars in his hand. Have you ever seen anybody try to buy a monkey on the street?"

"No. Was he drunk?"

"Drunk?" F. Jasmine said.

"Oh," said John Henry. "The monkey and the monkey-man!"

Berenice's question had disturbed F. Jasmine, and she took a minute to consider. "I don't think he was drunk. People don't get drunk in broad daylight." She had meant to tell Berenice about the soldier, but now she hesitated. "All the same there was something——" Her voice trailed at the end, and she watched a rainbow soapbubble floating in silence across the room. Here in the kitchen, barefooted and wearing only her petticoat, it was hard to realize and judge the soldier. About the promise for that evening she felt double-minded. The indecision bothered her, and so she changed the subject. "I hope you washed and ironed everything good of mine today. I have to take them to Winter Hill."

"What for?" said Berenice. "You only going to be there just one day."

"You heard me," F. Jasmine said. "I told you I wasn't coming back here after the wedding."

"Fool's hill. You have a whole lot less of sense than I was giving you credit for. What makes you think they want to take you along with them? Two is company and three is a crowd. And that is the main thing about a wedding. Two is company and three is a crowd."

F. Jasmine always found it hard to argue with a known saying. She loved to use them in her shows and in her conversation, but they were very hard to argue with, and so she said:

"You wait and see."

"Remember back to the time of the flood? Remember Noah and the ark?"

"And what has that got to do with it?" she asked.

"Remember the way he admitted them creatures."

"Oh, hush up your big old mouth," she said.

"Two by two," said Berenice. "He admitted them creatures two by two."

The argument that afternoon was, from the beginning to the end, about the wedding. Berenice refused to follow F. Jasmine's frame of mind. From the first it was as though she tried to catch F. Jasmine by the collar, like the Law catches a no-good in the wrong, and jerk her back where she had started—back to the sad and crazy summer that now seemed to F. Jasmine like a time remembered from long ago. But F. Jasmine was stubborn and not to be caught. Berenice had flaws to find in all of her ideas, and from the first word to the last she did her terrible, level best to try and deny the wedding. But F. Jasmine would not let it be denied.

"Look," F. Jasmine said, and she picked up the pink

organdie dress that she had just taken off. "Remember when I bought this dress the collar had teeny little pleats. But you have been ironing the collar like it was supposed to be ruffled. Now we got to set those little pleats like they ought to be."

"And who is going to do it?" said Berenice. She picked up the dress and judged the collar. "I got more to do with my time and trouble."

"Well, it's got to be done," F. Jasmine argued. "It's the way the collar is supposed to be. And besides, I might be wearing it out somewhere this evening."

"And where, pray tell me?" said Berenice. "Answer the question I asked when you came in. Where in the world have you been all morning?"

It was exactly as F. Jasmine had known it would be— the way Berenice refused to understand. And, since it was more a matter of feelings than of words or facts, she found it difficult to explain. When she spoke of connections, Berenice gave her a long, uncomprehending stare—and, when she went on to the Blue Moon and the many people, the broad, flat nose of Berenice widened and she shook her head. F. Jasmine did not mention the soldier; although she was on the verge of speaking of him several times, something warned her not to.

When she had finished, Berenice said:

"Frankie, I honestly believe you have turned crazy on us. Walking around all over town and telling total strangers this big tale. You know in your soul this mania of yours is pure foolishness."

"You wait and see," F. Jasmine said. "They will take me."

"And if they don't?"

F. Jasmine picked up the shoe box with the silver slippers and the wrapped box with the wedding dress. "These are my wedding clothes. I'll show them to you later."

"And if they don't?"

F. Jasmine had already started up the stairs, but she stopped and turned back toward the kitchen. The room was silent.

"If they don't, I will kill myself," she said. "But they will."

"Kill yourself how?" asked Berenice.

"I will shoot myself in the side of the head with a pistol."

"Which pistol?"

"The pistol that Papa keeps under his handkerchiefs along with Mother's picture in the right-hand bureau drawer."

Berenice did not answer for a minute and her face was a puzzle. "You heard what Mr. Addams told you about playing with that pistol. Go on upstairs now. Dinner will be ready in a little while."

It was a late dinner, this last meal that the three of them would ever eat together at the kitchen table. On Saturdays they were not regular about the times of meals, and they began the dinner at four o'clock, when already the August sun was slanting long and stale across the yard. It was the time of afternoon when the bars of sunlight crossed the back yard like the bars of a bright strange jail. The two fig trees were green and flat, the arbor sun-crossed and casting solid shade. The sun in the afternoon did not slant through the back windows of the house, so that the kitchen was gray. The three of them began their dinner at four o'clock, and the dinner lasted until twilight. There was hopping-john cooked with the ham bone, and as they ate they began to talk of love. It was a subject F. Jasmine had never talked about in all her life. In the first place, she had never believed in love and had never put any of it in her shows. But this afternoon when Berenice began this conversation, F. Jasmine did not stop up both her ears, but as she quietly ate the peas and rice and pot-liquor she listened.

"I have heard of many a queer thing," said Berenice. "I have knew mens to fall in love with girls so ugly that you wonder if their eyes is straight. I have seen some of the most peculiar weddings anybody could conjecture. Once I knew a boy with his whole face burned off so that——"

"Who?" asked John Henry.

Berenice swallowed a piece of cornbread and wiped her mouth with the back of her hand. "I have knew womens to love veritable Satans and thank Jesus when they put their split hooves over the threshold. I have knew boys to take it into their heads to fall in love with other boys. You know Lily Mae Jenkins?"

F. Jasmine thought a minute, and then answered: "I'm not sure."

"Well, you either know him or you don't know him. He prisses around with a pink satin blouse and one arm akimbo. Now this Lily Mae fell in love with a man name Juney Jones. A man, mind you. And Lily Mae turned into a girl. He changed his nature and his sex and turned into a girl."

"Honest?" F. Jasmine asked. "Did he really?"

"He did," said Berenice. "To all intents and purposes."

F. Jasmine scratched behind her ear and said: "It's funny I can't think who you are talking about. I used to think I knew so many people."

"Well, you don't need to know Lily Mae Jenkins. You can live without knowing him."

"Anyway, I don't believe you," F. Jasmine said.

"Well, I ain't arguing with you," said Berenice. "What was it we was speaking about?"

"About peculiar things."

"Oh, yes."

They stopped off a few minutes to get on with the dinner. F. Jasmine ate with her elbows on the table and her bare heels hooked on the rungs of the chair. She and Berenice sat opposite each other, and John Henry faced the window. Now hopping-john was F. Jasmine's very favorite food. She had always warned them to wave a plate of rice and peas before her nose when she was in her coffin, to make certain there was no mistake; for if a breath of life was left in her, she would sit up and eat, but if she smelled the hopping-john, and did not stir, then they could just nail down the coffin and be certain she was truly dead. Now Berenice had chosen for her death-test a piece of fried fresh-water trout, and for John Henry it was divinity fudge. But though F. Jasmine loved the hopping-john the very best, the others also liked it well enough, and all three of them enjoyed the dinner that day: the ham knuckle, the hopping-john, cornbread, hot baked sweet potatoes, and the buttermilk. And as they ate, they carried on the conversation.

"Yes, as I was just now telling you," said Berenice. "I have seen many a peculiar thing in my day. But one thing I never knew and never heard tell about. No siree, I never did."

Berenice stopped talking and sat there shaking her head, waiting for them to question her. But F. Jasmine would not speak. And it was John Henry who raised his curious face from his plate and asked: "What, Berenice?"

"No," said Berenice. "I never before in all my days heard of anybody falling in love with a wedding. I have knew many peculiar things, but I have never heard of that before."

F. Jasmine grumbled something.

"So I have been thinking it over and have come to a conclusion."

"How?" John Henry suddenly asked. "How did that boy change into a girl?"

Berenice glanced at him and straightened the napkin tied around his neck. "It was just one of them things, Candy Lamb. I don't know."

"Don't listen at her," F. Jasmine said.

"So I have been thinking it over in my mind and come to this conclusion. What you ought to begin thinking about is a beau."

"What?" Jasmine asked.

"You heard me," said Berenice. "A beau. A nice little white boy beau."

F. Jasmine put down her fork and sat with her head turned to one side. "I don't want any beau. What would I do with one?"

"Do, Foolish?" asked Berenice. "Why, make him treat you to the picture show. For one thing."

F. Jasmine pulled the bangs of her hair down over her forehead and slid her feet across the rung of the chair.

"Now you belong to change from being so rough and greedy and big," said Berenice. "You ought to fix yourself up nice in your dresses. And speak sweetly and act sly."

F. Jasmine said in a low voice: "I'm not rough and greedy any more. I already changed that way."

"Well, excellent," said Berenice. "Now catch you a beau."

F. Jasmine wanted to tell Berenice about the soldier, the hotel, and the invitation for the evening date. But something checked her, and she hinted around the edges of the subject: "What kind of a beau? Do you mean something like——" F. Jasmine paused, for at home in the kitchen that last afternoon, the soldier seemed unreal.

"Now that I cannot advise," said Berenice. "You got to decide for yourself."

"Something like a soldier who would maybe take me dancing at the Idle Hour?" She did not look at Berenice.

"Who is talking about soldiers and dancing? I'm talking about a nice little white boy beau your own age. How about that little old Barney?"

"Barney MacKean?"

"Why, certainy. He would do very well to begin with. You could make out with him until somebody else comes along. He would do."

"That mean nasty Barney!" The garage had been dark, with thin needling sunlight coming through the cracks of the closed door, and with the smell of dust. But she did not let herself remember the unknown sin that he had showed her, that later made her want to throw a knife between his eyes. Instead, she shook herself hard and began mashing peas and rice together on her plate. "You are the biggest crazy in this town."

"The crazy calls the sane the crazy."

So they began to eat again, all except John Henry. F. Jasmine was busy slicing open cornbread and spreading it with butter and mashing her hopping-john and drinking milk. Berenice ate more slowly, peeling off bits of ham from the knuckle in a dainty way. John Henry looked from one of them to the other, and after listening to their talk he had stopped eating to think for a little while. Then after a minute he asked:

"How many of them did you catch? Them beaus."

"How many?" said Berenice. "Lamb, how many hairs is in these plaits? You talking to Berenice Sadie Brown."

So Berenice was started, and her voice went on and on. And when she had begun this way, on a long and serious subject, the words flowed one into the other and her voice began to sing. In the gray of the kitchen on summer afternoons the tone of her voice was golden and quiet, and you could listen to the color and the singing of her voice and not follow the words. F. Jasmine let the long tones linger and spin inside her ears, but her mind did not stamp the voice with sense or sentences. She sat there listening at the table, and now and then she thought of a fact that all her life had seemed to her most curious: Berenice always spoke of herself as though she was somebody very beautiful. Almost on this one subject, Berenice was really not in her right mind. F. Jasmine listened to the voice and stared at Berenice across the table: the dark face with the wild blue eye, the eleven greased plaits that fitted her head like a skull-cap, the wide flat nose that quivered as she spoke. And whatever else Berenice might be, she was not beautiful. It seemed to her she ought to give Berenice advice. So she said at the next pause:

"I think you ought to quit worrying about beaus and be content with T. T. I bet you are forty years old. It is time for you to settle down."

Berenice bunched up her lips and stared at F. Jasmine with the dark live eye. "Wisemouth," she said. "How do you know so much? I got as much right as anybody else to continue to have a good time so long as I can. And as far as that goes, I'm not so old as some peoples would try and make out. I can still ministrate. And I got many a long year ahead of me before I resign myself to a corner."

"Well, I didn't mean go into a corner," F. Jasmine said.

"I heard what you meant," said Berenice.

John Henry had been watching and listening, and there was a little crust of pot-liquor around his mouth. A big blue lazy fly was hovering around him and trying to light on his sticky face, so that from time to time John Henry waved his hand to shoo the fly away.

"Did they all treat you to the picture show?" he asked. "All those beaus."

"To the show, or to one thing or another," she answered.

"You mean you never pay your own way?" John Henry asked.

"That's what I'm telling you," said Berenice. "Not when I go out with a beau. Now if I was to go somewhere with a crowd of womens, I would have to pay my way. But I'm not the kind of person to go around with crowds of womens."

"When you all took the trip to Fairview——" F. Jasmine said—for one Sunday that last spring there had been a colored pilot who took up colored people in his aeroplane. "Who paid the way?"

"Now let me see," said Berenice. "Honey and Clorina took care of their expenses, except I loaned Honey one dollar and forty cents. Cape Clyde paid his own way. And T. T. paid for himself and for me."

"Then T. T. treated you to the aeroplane ride?"

"That's what I'm telling you. He paid the bus tickets to and from Fairview and the aeroplane ride and the refreshments. The complete trip. Why, naturally he paid the way. How else do you think I could afford to fly around in an aeroplane? Me making six dollars a week."

"I didn't realize that," F. Jasmine admitted finally. "I wonder where T. T. got all of his money."

"Earned it," said Berenice. "John Henry, wipe off your mouth."

So they rested at the table, for the way they ate their meals, this summer, was in rounds: they would eat awhile and then let the food have a chance to spread out and settle inside their stomachs, and a little later they would start in again. F. Jasmine crossed her knife and fork on her empty plate, and began to question Berenice about a matter that had bothered her.

"Tell me. Is it just us who call this hopping-john? Or is it known by that name through all the country. It seems a strange name somehow."

"Well, I have heard it called various things," said Berenice.

"What?"

"Well, I have heard it called peas and rice. Or rice and peas and pot-liquor. Or hopping-john. You can vary and take your pick."

"But I'm not talking about this town," F. Jasmine said. "I mean in other places. I mean through all the world. I wonder what the French call it."

"Oh," said Berenice. "Well, you ask me a question I cannot answer."

"Merci a la parlez," F. Jasmine said.

They sat at the table and did not speak. F. Jasmine was tilted back in her chair, her head turned toward the window and the sun-crossed empty yard. The town was silent and the kitchen was silent except for the clock. F. Jasmine could not feel the world go round, and nothing moved.

"Now a funny thing has happened to me," F. Jasmine began. "I don't hardly know how to tell just what I mean. It was one of those strange things you can't exactly explain."

"What, Frankie?" John Henry asked.

F. Jasmine turned from the window, but before she could speak again there was the sound. In the silence of the kitchen they heard the tone shaft quietly across the room, then again the same note was repeated. A piano scale slanted across the August afternoon. A chord was struck. Then in a dreaming way a chain of chords climbed slowly upward like a flight of castle stairs: but just at the end, when the eighth chord should have sounded and the scale made complete, there was a stop. This next to the last chord was repeated. The seventh chord, which seems to echo all of the unfinished scale, struck and insisted again and again. And finally there was a silence. F. Jasmine and John Henry and Berenice looked at each other. Somewhere in the neighborhood an August piano was being tuned.

"Jesus!" said Berenice. "I seriously believe this will be the last straw."

John Henry shivered. "Me too," he said.

F. Jasmine sat perfectly still before the table crowded with plates and dinner dishes. The gray of the kitchen was a stale gray and the room was too flat and too square. After the silence another note was sounded, and then repeated an octave higher. F. Jasmine raised her eyes each time the tone climbed higher, as though she watched the note move from one part of the kitchen to another; at the highest point her eyes had reached a ceiling corner, then, when a long scale slid downward, her head turned slowly as her eyes crossed from the ceiling corner to the floor corner at the opposite side of the room. The bottom bass note was struck six times, and F. Jasmine was left staring at an old pair of bedroom slippers and an empty beer bottle which were in that corner of the room. Finally she shut her eyes, and shook herself, and got up from the table.

"It makes me sad," F. Jasmine said. "And jittery too." She began to walk around the room. "They tell me that when they want to punish them over in Milledgeville, they tie them up and make them listen to piano-tuning." She walked three times around the table. "There's something I want to ask you. Suppose you ran into somebody who seemed to you terribly peculiar, but you didn't know the reason why."

"In what ways peculiar?"

F. Jasmine thought of the soldier, but she could not further explain. "Say you might meet somebody you think he almost might be a *drunk*, but you're not sure about anything. And he wanted you to join with him and go to a big party or dance. What would you do?"

"Well, on the face of it, I don't know. It would depend on how I feel. I might go with him to the big party and meet up with somebody that suited me better." The live eye of Berenice suddenly narrowed, and she looked hard at F. Jasmine. "But why do you ask that?"

The quietness in the room stretched out until F. Jasmine could hear the drip-drop from the faucet of the sink. She was trying to frame a way to tell Berenice about the soldier. Then all at once the telephone rang. F. Jasmine jumped up and, turning over her empty milk glass, dashed to the hall—but John Henry, who was nearer, reached the telephone first. He knelt on the telephone chair and smiled into the mouthpiece before he said hello. Then he kept on saying hello until F. Jasmine took the receiver from him and repeated the hellos at least two dozen times before she finally hung up.

"Anything like that makes me so mad," she said when they had gone back to the kitchen. "Or when the express truck stops before the door and the man peers at our number and then takes the box somewhere else. I look on those things as a kind of sign." She raked her fingers through her crew-cut blond hair. "You know I'm really going to get my fortune told before I leave home in the morning. It's something I've been meaning to do for a long time."

Berenice said: "Changing the subject, when are you going to show me the new dress? I'm anxious to see what you selected."

So F. Jasmine went up to get the dress. Her room was what was known as a hotbox; the heat from the rest of the house rose up to her room and stayed there. In the afternoon the air seemed to make a buzzing sound, so it was a good idea to keep the motor running. F. Jasmine turned on the motor and opened the closet door. Until this day before the wedding she had always kept her six costumes hung in a row on coat-hangers, and she just threw her ordinary clothes up on the shelf or kicked them into a corner. But when she had come home this afternoon, she had changed this: the costumes were thrown up on the shelf and the wedding dress hung alone in the closet on a coat-hanger. The silver slippers were placed carefully on the floor beneath the dress with the toes pointed north, toward Winter Hill. For some reason F. Jasmine tiptoed around the room as she began to dress.

"Shut your eyes!" she called. "Don't watch me coming down the stairs. Don't open your eyes until I tell you."

It was as though the four walls of the kitchen watched her, and the skillet hanging on the wall was a watching round black eye. The piano-tuning was for a minute silent. Berenice sat with her head bowed, as though she was in church. And John Henry had his head bowed also, but he was peeking. F. Jasmine stood at the foot of the stairs and placed her left hand on her hip.

"Oh, how pretty!" John Henry said.

Berenice raised her head, and when she saw F. Jasmine her face was a study. The dark eye looked from the silver hair ribbon to the soles of the silver slippers. She said nothing.

"Now tell me your honest opinion," F. Jasmine said.

But Berenice looked at the orange satin evening dress and shook her head and did not comment. At first she shook her head with short little turns, but the longer she stared, the longer these shakes became, until at the last shake F. Jasmine heard her neck crack.

"What's the matter?" F. Jasmine asked.

"I thought you was going to get a pink dress."

"But when I got in the store I changed my mind. What is wrong with this dress? Don't you like it, Berenice?"

"No," said Berenice. "It don't do."

"What do you mean? It don't do."

"Exactly that. It just don't do."

F. Jasmine turned to look in the mirror, and she still thought the dress was beautiful. But Berenice had a sour and stubborn look on her face, an expression like that of an old long-eared mule, and F. Jasmine could not understand.

"But I don't see what you mean," she complained. "What is wrong?"

Berenice folded her arms over her chest and said: "Well, if you don't see it I can't explain it to you. Look there at your head, to begin with."

F. Jasmine looked at her head in the mirror.

"You had all your hair shaved off like a convict, and now you tie a silver ribbon around this head without any hair. It just looks peculiar."

"Oh, but I'm washing my hair tonight and going to try to curl it," F. Jasmine said.

"And look at them elbows," Berenice continued. "Here you got on this grown woman's evening dress. Orange satin. And that brown crust on your elbows. The two things just don't mix."

F. Jasmine hunched her shoulders and covered her rusty elbows with her hands.

Berenice gave her head another quick wide shake, then bunched her lips in judgment. "Take it back down to the store."

"But I can't!" said F. Jasmine. "It's bargain basement. They don't take back."

Berenice always had two mottoes. One was the known saying that you can't make a silk purse out of a sow's ear. And the other was the motto that you have to cut your suit according to the cloth, and make the best of what you have. So F. Jasmine was not certain if it was the last of these mottoes that made Berenice change her mind, or if she really began to improve her feelings about the dress. Anyway, Berenice stared for several seconds with her head to one side, and finally said:

"Come here. We'll make it fit better at the waist and see what we can do."

"I think you're just not accustomed to seeing anybody dressed up," F. Jasmine said.

"I'm not accustomed to human Christmas trees in August."

So Berenice took off the sash and patted and pulled the dress in various places. F. Jasmine stood stiff like a hat-rack and let her work with the dress. John Henry had got up from his chair and was watching, with the napkin still tied around his neck.

"Frankie's dress looks like a Christmas tree," he said.

"Two-faced Judas!" F. Jasmine said. "You just now said it was pretty. Old double-faced Judas!"

The piano tuned. Whose piano it was F. Jasmine did not know, but the sound of the tuning was solemn and insistent in the kitchen, and it came from somewhere not so far away. The piano-tuner would sometimes fling out a rattling little tune, and then he would go back to one note. And repeat. And bang the same note in a solemn and crazy way. And repeat. And bang. The name of the piano-tuner in the town was Mr. Schwarzenbaum. The sound was enough to shiver the gizzards of musicians and make all listeners feel queer.

"It almost makes me wonder if he does that just to torment us," F. Jasmine said.

But Berenice said no: "They tune pianos the same way in Cincinnati and the world over. It is just the way they do it. Less turn on the radio in the dining room and drown him out."

F. Jasmine shook her head. "No," she said. "I can't explain why. But I don't want to have that radio turned on again. It reminds me too much of this summer."

"Step back a little now," said Berenice.

She had pinned the waist higher and done one thing and another to the dress. F. Jasmine looked in the mirror over the sink. She could only see herself from the chest up, so after admiring this top part of herself, she stood on a chair and looked at the middle section. Then she began to clear away a corner of the table so she could climb up and see in the mirror the silver shoes, but Berenice prevented her.

"Don't you honestly think it is pretty?" F. Jasmine said. "I think so. Seriously, Berenice. Give me your candy opinion."

But Berenice rared up and spoke in an accusing voice: "I never knew somebody so unreasonable! You ask me my candy opinion, and I give it to you. Then you ask me again, and I give it to you. But what you want is not my honest opinion, but my good opinion on something I know is wrong. Now what kind of way is that to act?"

"All right," F. Jasmine said. "I only want to look good."

"Well, you look very well," said Berenice. "Pretty is as pretty does. You look well enough for anybody's wedding. Excepting your own. And then, pray Jesus, we will be in a position to do better. What I have to do now is get John Henry a fresh suit and figure about the outfit I'm going to wear myself."

"Uncle Charles is dead," John Henry said. "And we are going to the wedding."

"Yes, Baby," said Berenice. And from the sudden dreaming quietness of her, F. Jasmine felt that Berenice was carried back to all the other dead people she knew. The dead were walking in her heart, and she was remembering back to Ludie Freeman and the long-gone time of Cincinnati and the snow.

F. Jasmine thought back to the other seven dead people she knew. Her mother had died the very day that she was born, so she could not count her. There was a picture of her mother in the right-hand drawer of her father's bureau: and the face looked timid and sorry, shut up with the cold folded handkerchiefs in the drawer. Then there was her grandmother who had died when Frankie was nine years old, and F. Jasmine remembered her very well—but with crooked little pictures that were sunken far back in her mind. A soldier from that town called William Boyd had been killed that year in Italy, and she had known him both by sight and name. Mrs. Selway, two blocks away, had died; and F. Jasmine had watched the funeral from the sidewalk, but she was not invited. The solemn grown men stood around out on the front porch and it had rained, there was a gray silk ribbon on the door. She knew Lon Baker, and he was dead also. Lon Baker was a colored boy and he was murdered in the alley out behind her father's store. On an April afternoon his throat was slashed with a razor blade, and all the alley people disappeared in back doorways, and later it was said his cut throat opened like a crazy shivering mouth that spoke ghost words into the April sun. Lon Baker was dead and Frankie knew him. She knew, but only in a chancing kind of way, Mr. Pitkin at Brawer's Shoe Shop, Miss Birdie Grimes, and a man who had climbed poles for the telephone company: all dead.

"Do you think very frequently about Ludie?" F. Jasmine asked.

"You know I do," said Berenice. "I think about the years when me and Ludie was together, and about all the bad times I seen since. Ludie would never have let me be lonesome so that I took up with all kinds of no-good men. Me and Ludie," she said. "Ludie and me."

F. Jasmine sat vibrating her leg and thinking of Ludie and Cincinnati. Of all the dead people out of the world, Ludie Freeman was the one F. Jasmine knew the best, although she had never laid eyes on him, and was not even born when he had died. She knew Ludie and the city of

Cincinnati, and the winter when Ludie and Berenice had gone together to the North and seen the snow. A thousand times they had talked of all these things, and it was a conversation that Berenice talked slowly, making each sentence like a song. And the old Frankie used to ask and question about Cincinnati. What exactly they would eat in Cincinnati and how wide would be the Cincinnati streets? And in a chanting kind of voice they talked about the Cincinnati fish, the parlor in the Cincinnati house on Myrtle Street, the Cincinnati picture shows. And Ludie Freeman was a brickmason, making a grand and a regular salary, and he was the man of all her husbands that Berenice had loved.

"Sometimes I almost wish I had never knew Ludie at all," said Berenice. "It spoils you too much. It leaves you too lonesome afterward. When you walk home in the evening on the way from work, it makes a little lonesome quinch come in you. And you take up with too many sorry men to try to get over the feeling."

"I know it," F. Jasmine said. "But T. T. Williams is not sorry."

"I wasn't referring to T. T. He and me is just good friends."

"Don't you think you will marry him?" F. Jasmine asked.

"Well, T. T. is a fine upstanding colored gentleman," said Berenice. "You never hear tell of T. T. raring around like a lot of other mens. If I was to marry T. T., I could get out of this kitchen and stand behind the cash register at the restaurant and pat my foot. Furthermore, I respect T. T. sincerely. He has walked in a state of grace all of his life."

"Well, when are you going to marry him?" she asked. "He is crazy about you."

Berenice said: "I ain't going to marry him."

"But you just now was saying—" said F. Jasmine.

"I was saying how sincerely I respect T. T. and sincerely regard him."

"Well, then—?" F. Jasmine said.

"I respect and regard him highly," said Berenice. Her

dark eye was quiet and sober and her flat nose widened as she spoke. "But he don't make me shiver none."

After a moment F. Jasmine said: "To think about the wedding makes me shiver."

"Well, it's a pity," said Berenice.

"It makes me shiver, too, to think about how many dead people I already know. Seven in all," she said. "And now Uncle Charles."

F. Jasmine put her fingers in her ears and closed her eyes, but it was not death. She could feel the heat from the stove and smell the dinner. She could feel a rumble in her stomach and the beating of her heart. And the dead feel nothing, hear nothing, see nothing: only black.

"It would be terrible to be dead," she said, and in the wedding dress she began to walk around the room.

There was a rubber ball on the shelf, and she threw it against the hall door and caught it on the rebound.

"Put that down," said Berenice. "Go take off the dress before you dirty it. Go do something. Go turn on the radio."

"I told you I don't want that radio on."

And she was walking around the room, and Berenice had said to go do something, but she did not know what to do. She walked in the wedding dress, with her hand on her hip. The silver slippers had squeezed her feet so that the toes felt swollen and mashed like ten big sore cauliflowers.

"But I advise you to keep the radio on when you come back," F. Jasmine said suddenly. "Some day very likely you will hear us speaking over the radio."

"What's that?"

"I say very likely we might be asked to speak over the radio some day."

"Speak about what, pray tell me," said Berenice.

"I don't know exactly what about," F. Jasmine said. "But probably some eye-witness account about something. We will be asked to speak."

"I don't follow you," said Berenice. "What are we going to eye-witness? And who will ask us to speak?"

F. Jasmine whirled around and, putting both fists on her

hips, she set herself in a staring position. "Did you think I meant you and John Henry and me? Why, I have never heard of anything so funny in my whole life."

John Henry's voice was high and excited. "What, Frankie? Who is speaking on the radio?"

"When I said *we,* you thought I meant you and me and John Henry West. To speak over the world radio. I have never heard of anything so funny since I was born."

John Henry had climbed up to kneel on the seat of his chair and the blue veins showed in his forehead and you could see the strained chords of his neck. "Who?" he hollered. "What?"

"Ha ha ha!" she said, and then she burst out laughing; she went banging around the room and hitting things with her fist. "Ho ho ho!"

And John Henry wailed and F. Jasmine banged around the kitchen in the wedding dress and Berenice got up from the table and raised her right hand for peace. Then suddenly they all stopped at once. F. Jasmine stood absolutely still before the window, and John Henry hurried to the window also and watched on tiptoe with his hands to the sill. Berenice turned her head to see what had happened. And at that moment the piano was quiet.

"Oh!" F. Jasmine whispered.

Four girls were crossing the back yard. They were girls of fourteen and fifteen years old, and they were the club members. First came Helen Fletcher, and then the others walking slowly in single file. They had cut across from the O'Neils' back yard and were passing slowly before the arbor. The long gold sun slanted down on them and made their skin look golden also, and they were dressed in clean, fresh dresses. When they had passed the arbor, their single shadows stretched out long and gangling across the yard. Soon they would be gone. F. Jasmine stood motionless. In the old days that summer she would have waited in the hope that they might call her and tell her she had been elected to the club—and only at the very last, when it was plain that they were only passing, she would have shouted in angry loudness that they were not to cut across her yard. But now she watched them quietly, without jealousy. At the last there came an urge to call out to them about the wedding, but before the words could be formed and spoken, the club of girls was gone. There was only the arbor and the spinning sun.

"Now I wonder—" F. Jasmine said finally. But Berenice cut her short:

"Nothing, Curiosity," she said. "Curiosity, nothing."

When they began the second round of that last dinner, it was past five o'clock, and nearing twilight. It was the time of afternoon when in the old days, sitting with the red cards at the table, they would sometimes begin to criticize the Creator. They would judge the work of God, and mention the ways how they would improve the world. And Holy Lord God John Henry's voice would rise up happy and high and strange, and his world was a mixture of delicious and freak, and he did not think in global terms: the sudden long arm that could stretch from here to California, chocolate dirt and rains of lemonade, the extra eye seeing a thousand miles, a hinged tail that could be let down as a kind of prop to sit on when you wished to rest, the candy flowers.

But the world of the Holy Lord God Berenice Sadie Brown was a different world, and it was round and just and reasonable. First, there would be no separate colored people in the world, but all human beings would be light brown color with blue eyes and black hair. There would be no colored people and no white people to make the colored people feel cheap and sorry all through their lives. No colored people, but all human men and ladies and children as one loving family on the earth. And when Berenice spoke of this first principle her voice was a strong deep song that soared and sang in beautiful dark tones leaving an echo in the corners of the room that trembled for a long time until silence.

No war, said Berenice. No stiff corpses hanging from the Europe trees and no Jews murdered anywhere. No war, and the young boys leaving home in army suits, and no wild cruel Germans and Japanese. No war in the whole world, but peace in all countries everywhere. Also, no

starving. To begin with, the real Lord God had made free
air and free rain and free dirt for the benefit of all. There
would be free food for every human mouth, free meals
and two pounds of fatback a week, and after that each
able-bodied person would work for whatever else he
wished to eat or own. No killed Jews and no hurt colored
people. No war and no hunger in the world. And, finally,
Ludie Freeman would be alive.

The world of Berenice was a round world, and the old
Frankie would listen to the strong deep singing voice, and
she would agree with Berenice. But the old Frankie's
world was the best of the three worlds. She agreed with
Berenice about the main laws of her creation, but she
added many things: an aeroplane and a motorcycle to
each person, a world club with certificates and badges,
and a better law of gravity. She did not completely agree
with Berenice about the war; and sometimes she said she
would have one War Island in the world where those who
wanted to could go, and fight or donate blood, and she
might go for a while as a WAC in the Air Corps. She also
changed the seasons, leaving out summer altogether, and
adding much snow. She planned it so that people could instantly change back and forth from boys to girls, which
ever way they felt like and wanted. But Berenice would
argue with her about this, insisting that the law of human
sex was exactly right just as it was and could in no way be
improved. And then John Henry West would very likely
add his two cents' worth about this time, and think that
people ought to be half boy and half girl, and when the
old Frankie threatened to take him to the Fair and sell
him to the Freak Pavilion, he would only close his eyes and
smile.

So the three of them would sit there at the kitchen table
and criticize the Creator and the work of God. Sometimes
their voices crossed and the three worlds twisted. The Holy
Lord God John Henry West. The Holy Lord God Berenice Sadie Brown. The Holy Lord God Frankie Addams.
The Worlds at the end of the long stale afternoons.

But this was a different day. They were not loafing or
playing cards, but still eating dinner. F. Jasmine had taken

off the wedding dress and was barefooted and comfortable in her petticoat once more. The brown gravy of the peas had stiffened, the food was neither hot nor cold, and the butter had melted. They started in on second helpings, passing the dishes back and forth among themselves, and they did not talk of the ordinary subjects that usually they thought about this time of the afternoon. Instead, there began a strange conversation, and it came about in this way:

"Frankie," said Berenice, "Awhile back you started to say something. And we veered off from the subject. It was about something unnatural, I think."

"Oh, yes," F. Jasmine said. "I was going to tell you about something peculiar that happened to me today that I don't hardly realize. Now I don't exactly know how to explain just what I mean."

F. Jasmine broke open a sweet potato and tilted back in her chair. She began to try to tell Berenice what had happened when she had been walking home and suddenly seen something from the tail of her eye, and when she turned to look, it was the two colored boys back at the end of the alley. As she talked, F. Jasmine stopped now and then to pull her lower lip and study just for the right words to tell of a feeling that she had never heard named before. Occasionally she glanced at Berenice, to see if she was following her, and a remarkable look was breaking on Berenice's face: the glass blue eye was bright and astonished, as always, and at first her dark eye was astonished also; then a queer and conniving look changed her expression, and from time to time she turned her head with short little jerks, as though to listen from different earpoints and make sure that what she heard was true.

Before F. Jasmine finished, Berenice had pushed back her plate and reached into her bosom for her cigarettes. She smoked home-rolled cigarettes, but she carried them in a Chesterfield package, so that from the outward appearance she was smoking store Chesterfields. She twisted off a ragged fringe of loose tobacco and raised back her head when she held the match, so that the flame would not go up her nose. A blue layer of smoke hung over the three

of them at the table. Berenice held the cigarette between
her thumb and forefinger; her hand had been drawn and
stiffened by a winter rheumatism so that the last two fingers could not be straightened out. She sat listening and
smoking, and when F. Jasmine had finished, there was a
long pause, then Berenice leaned forward and asked suddenly:

"Listen to me! Can you see through them bones in my
forehead? Have you, Frankie Addams, been reading my
mind?"

F. Jasmine did not know what to answer.

"This is one of the queerest things I ever heard of,"
Berenice went on. "I cannot get over it."

"What I mean—" F. Jasmine started again.

"I know what you mean," said Berenice. "Right here
in this very corner of the eye." She pointed to the red-
webbed outside corner of the dark eye. "You suddenly
catch something there. And this cold shiver run all the way
down you. And you whirl around. And then you stand
facing Jesus knows what. But not Ludie and not who you
want. And for a minute you feel like you been dropped
down a well."

"Yes," F. Jasmine said. "That is it."

"Well, this is mighty remarkable," said Berenice. "This
is a thing been happening to me all my life. Yet just now
is the first time I ever heard it put into words."

F. Jasmine covered her nose and her mouth with her
hand, so that it would not be noticed that she was pleased
about being so remarkable, and her eyes were closed in a
modest way.

"Yes, that is the way when you are in love," said Berenice. "Invariably. A thing known and not spoken."

So that was how the queer conversation began at quarter to six on the last afternoon. It was the first time ever
they had talked about love, with F. Jasmine included in
the conversation as a person who understood and had
worthwhile opinions. The old Frankie had laughed at love,
maintained it was a big fake, and did not believe in it.
She never put any of it in her shows, and never went to
love shows at the Palace. The old Frankie had always gone

to the Saturday matinee, when the shows were crook shows, war shows, or cowboy shows. And who was it who had caused the confusion at the Palace that last May, when the movie had run an old show on Saturday called *Camille?* The old Frankie. She had been in her seat on the second row and she stamped and put two fingers in her mouth and began to whistle. And the other half-fare people in the first three rows began to whistle and stamp also, and the longer the love picture lasted, the louder they became. So that finally the manager came down with a flashlight and rooted the whole crowd of them out of their seats and marched them up the aisle and left them standing on the sidewalk: done out of their dimes, and disgusted.

The old Frankie had never admitted love. Yet here F. Jasmine was sitting at the table with her knees crossed, and now and then she patted her bare foot on the floor in an accustomed way, and nodded at what Berenice was saying. Furthermore, when she reached out quietly toward the Chesterfield package beside the saucer of melted butter, Berenice did not slap her hand away, and F. Jasmine took herself a cigarette. She and Berenice were two grown people smoking at the dinner table. And John Henry West had his big child head hunched close to his shoulder, watching and listening to all that went on.

"Now I will tell you a story," said Berenice. "And it is to be a warning to you. You hear me, John Henry? You hear me, Frankie?"

"Yes," John Henry whispered. He pointed with his gray little forefinger. "Frankie is smoking."

Berenice sat up straight, her shoulders square, and her dark twisted hands folded before her on the table. She raised her chin and drew in her breath in the way of a singer who is beginning a song. The piano tuned and insisted, but when Berenice began to speak, her dark gold voice rang in the kitchen and they did not listen to the piano notes. But to start this warning Berenice began with the old same story that they had heard many times before. The story of her and Ludie Freeman. A long time ago.

"Now I am here to tell you I was happy. There was no human woman in all the world more happy than I was in them days," she said. "And that includes everybody. You listening to me, John Henry? It includes all queens and millionaires and first ladies of the land. And I mean it includes people of all color. You hear me, Frankie? No human woman in all the world was happier than Berenice Sadie Brown."

She had started with the old story of Ludie. And it began an afternoon in late October almost twenty years ago. The story started at the place where first they met each other, in front of Camp Campbell's Filling Station outside of the city limits of the town. It was the time of the year when the leaves were turning and the countryside was smoky and autumn gray and gold. And the story went on from that first meeting to the wedding at the Welcome Ascension Church in Sugarville. And then on through the years with the two of them together. The house with the brick front steps and the glass windows on the corner of Barrow Street. The Christmas of the fox fur, and the June of the fish fry thrown for twenty-eight invited relatives and guests. The years with Berenice cooking dinner and sewing Ludie's suits and shirts on the machine and the two of them always having a good time. And the nine months they lived up North, in the city of Cincinnati, where there was snow. Then Sugarville again, and days merging one into another, and the weeks, the months, the years together. And the pair of them always had a good time, yet it was not so much the happenings she mentioned as the way she told about these happenings that made F. Jasmine understand.

Berenice spoke in an unwinding kind of voice, and she had said that she was happier than a queen. As she told the story, it seemed to F. Jasmine that Berenice resembled a strange queen, if a queen can be colored and sitting at a kitchen table. She unwound the story of her and Ludie like a colored queen unwinding a bolt of cloth of gold—and at the end, when the story was over, her expression was always the same: the dark eye staring straight ahead, her flat nose widened and trembling, her mouth finished and sad and quiet. As a rule, when the story was over, they would sit for a moment and then suddenly get busy doing something in a hurry: start a hand of cards, or make milk-shakes, or just stir around the kitchen with no particular purpose. But this afternoon they did not move or speak for a long time after Berenice had finished, until finally F. Jasmine asked:

"What exactly did Ludie die of?"

"It was something similar to pneumonia," said Berenice. "November the year 1931."

"The very year and the very month I was born," F. Jasmine said.

"The coldest November I ever seen. Every morning there was frost and puddles were crusted with ice. The sunshine was pale yellow like it is in wintertime. Sounds carried far away, and I remember a hound dog that used to howl toward sundown. I kept a fire in the hearth going day and night, and in the evening when I walk around the room there was this shaking shadow following alongside of me on the wall. And everything I seen come to me as a kind of sign."

"I think it is a kind of sign I was born the same year and the same month he died," F. Jasmine said. "Only the dates are different."

"And then it was a Thursday toward six o'clock in the afternoon. About this time of day. Only November. I remember I went to the passage and opened the front door. We were living that year at 233 Prince Street. Dark was coming on, the old hound was howling far away. And I go back in the room and lay down on Ludie's bed. I lay myself down over Ludie with my arms spread out and my face on his face. And I pray that the Lord would contage my strenth to him. And I ask the Lord let it be anybody, but not let it be Ludie. And I lay there and pray for a long time. Until night."

"How?" John Henry asked. It was a question that did not mean anything, but he repeated it in a higher, wailing voice: "How, Berenice?"

"That night he died," she said. She spoke in a sharp tone, as though they had disputed with her. "I tell you he died. Ludie! Ludie Freeman! Ludie Maxwell Freeman died!"

She was finished, and they sat there at the table. Nobody moved. John Henry stared at Berenice, and the fly that had been hovering above him lighted on the left rim of his glasses; the fly walked slowly across the left lens, and over the nosepiece, and across the right lens. It was only when the fly had flown away that John Henry blinked and waved his hand.

"One thing," F. Jasmine said finally. "There is Uncle Charles laying there dead right now. Yet somehow I can't cry. I know I ought to feel sad. Yet I feel sadder about Ludie than I do about Uncle Charles. Although I never laid eyes on Ludie. And I knew Uncle Charles all my life and he was blood kin to blood kin of mine. Maybe it's because I was born so soon after Ludie died."

"Maybe so," said Berenice.

It seemed to F. Jasmine that they might just sit there the rest of the afternoon, without moving or speaking, when suddenly she remembered something.

"You were starting out to tell a different story," she said. "It was some kind of warning."

Berenice looked puzzled for a moment, then she jerked her head up and said: "Oh, yes! I was going to tell you how this thing we was talking about applies to me. And what happened with them other husbands. Now you perk your ears."

But the story of the other three husbands was an old story also. As Berenice began to talk, F. Jasmine went to the refrigerator and brought back to the table some sweetened condensed milk to pour on crackers as a dessert. At first she did not listen very carefully.

"It was the April of the following year that I went one Sunday to the Fork Falls Church. And you ask what I was doing out there and I tell you. I was visiting that Jackson branch of my foster cousins who live out there and we had gone to their church. So there I was praying in this church where the congregation was strangers to me. I had my forehead down on the top of the pew in front of me, and my eyes were open—not gazing around in secret, mind you, but just open. When suddenly this shiver run all the way through me. I had caught sight of something from the corner of my eye. And I looked slowly to the left. And guess what I seen there? There on the pew, just six inches from my eye, was this *thumb*."

"What thumb?" F. Jasmine asked.

"Now I'm telling you," said Berenice. "To understand this, you have to know that there was only one little portion of Ludie Freeman which was not pretty. Every other part about him was handsome and pretty as anyone would ever wish. All except his right thumb, which had been mashed in a hinge. This one thumb had a mashed chewed appearance that was not pretty. You understand?"

"You mean you suddenly saw Ludie's thumb when you were praying?"

"I mean I seen *this* thumb. And as I kneel there a shiver run from my head to my heels. I just kneel there staring at this thumb, and before I looked any further, to find out whose thumb it might be, I begun to pray in earnest. I prayed out loud: Lord, manifest! Lord, manifest!"

"And did He?" F. Jasmine asked. "Manifest?"

Berenice turned aside and made a sound like spitting. "Manifest, my foot!" she said. "You know who that thumb belonged to?"

"Who?"

"Why Jamie Beale," said Berenice. "That big old no-good Jamie Beale. It was the first time I ever laid eyes on him."

"Is that why you married him?" F. Jasmine asked, for Jamie Beale was the name of the sorry old liquor-drinker, who was the second husband. "Because he had a mashed thumb like Ludie's?"

"Jesus knows," said Berenice. "I don't. I felt drawn to him on account of the thumb. And then one thing led to another. First thing I knew I had married him."

"Well, I think that was silly," F. Jasmine said. "To marry him just because of that thumb."

"Me too," said Berenice. "I'm not trying to dispute with you. I'm just telling you what happened. And the very same thing occurred in the case of Henry Johnson."

Henry Johnson was the third husband, the one who had gone crazy on Berenice. He was all right for three weeks after they had married, but then he went crazy, and he behaved in such a crazy way that finally she had to quit him.

"You mean to sit there and tell me Henry Johnson had one of those mashed thumbs too?"

"No," said Berenice. "It was not the thumb that time. It was the coat."

F. Jasmine and John Henry looked at each other, for what she was saying did not seem to make much sense. But Berenice's dark eye was sober and certain, and she nodded to them in a definite way.

"To understand this, you have to know what happened after Ludie died. He had a policy due to pay off two hundred and fifty dollars. I won't go into the whole business, but what happened was that I was cheated by them policy people out of fifty dollars. And in two days I had to scour around and raise the fifty dollars to make out for the funeral. Because I couldn't let Ludie be put away cheap. I pawned everything I could lay hands on. And I sold my coat and Ludie's coat. To that second-hand clothing store on Front Avenue."

"Oh!" F. Jasmine said. "Then you mean Henry Johnson bought Ludie's coat and you married him because of it."

"Not exactly," said Berenice. "I was walking down that street alongside of the City Hall one evening when I suddenly seen this shape before me. Now the shape of this boy ahead of me was so similar to Ludie through the shoulders and the back of the head that I almost dropped dead there on the sidewalk. I followed and run behind him. It was Henry Johnson, and that was the first time I ever saw him also, since he lived in the country and didn't come much into town. But he had chanced to buy Ludie's coat and he was built on the same shape as Ludie. And from the back view it looked like he was Ludie's ghost or Ludie's twin. But how I married him I don't exactly know, for to begin with it was clear that he did not have his share of sense. But you let a boy hang around and you get fond of him. Anyway, that's how I married Henry Johnson."

"People certainy do curious things."

"You telling me," said Berenice. She glanced at F. Jasmine, who was pouring a slow ribbon of condensed milk over a soda cracker, to finish her dinner with a sweet sandwich.

"I swear, Frankie! I believe you got a tate worm. I am perfectly serious. Your father looks over them big grocery bills and he naturally suspicions that I carry things off."

"You do," F. Jasmine said. "Sometimes."

"He reads over them grocery bills and he complains to me, Berenice, what in the name of holy creation did we do with six cans of condensed milk and forty-leven dozen eggs and eight boxes of marshmallows in one week. And I have to admit to him: Frankie eat them. I have to say to him: Mr. Addams, you think you feeding something human back here in your kitchen. That's what you think. I have to say to him: Yes, you imagine it is something human."

"After today I'm not going to be greedy any more," F. Jasmine said. "But I don't understand the point of what you was telling. I don't see how that about Jamie Beale and Henry Johnson applies to me."

"It applies to everybody and it is a warning."

"But how?"

"Why, don't you see what I was doing?" asked Berenice. "I loved Ludie and he was the first man I loved. Therefore, I had to go and copy myself forever afterward. What I did was to marry off little pieces of Ludie whenever I come across them. It was just my misfortune they all turned out to be the wrong pieces. My intention was to repeat me and Ludie. Now don't you see?"

"I see what you're driving at," F. Jasmine said. "But I don't see how it is a warning applied to me."

"Then do I have to tell you?" asked Berenice.

F. Jasmine did not nod or answer, for she felt that Berenice had laid a trap for her, and was going to make remarks she did not want to hear. Berenice stopped to light herself another cigarette and two blue slow scrolls of smoke came from her nostrils and lazed above the dirty dishes on the table. Mr. Schwarzenbaum was playing an arpeggio. F. Jasmine waited and it seemed a long time.

"You and that wedding at Winter Hill," Berenice said finally. "That is what I am warning about. I can see right through them two gray eyes of yours like they was glass. And what I see is the saddest piece of foolishness I ever knew."

"Gray eyes is glass," Johny Henry whispered.

But F. Jasmine would not let herself be seen through and outstared; she hardened and tensed her eyes and did not look away from Berenice.

"I see what you have in your mind. Don't think I don't. You see something unheard of at Winter Hill tomorrow, and you right in the center. You think you going to march down the center of the aisle right in between your brother and the bride. You think you going to break into that wedding, and then Jesus knows what else."

"No," F. Jasmine said. "I don't see myself walking down the center of the aisle between them."

"I see through them eyes," said Berenice. "Don't argue with me."

John Henry said again, but softer: "Gray eyes is glass."

"But what I'm warning is this," said Berenice. "If you start out falling in love with some unheard-of thing like that, what is going to happen to you? If you take a mania like this, it won't be the last time and of that you can be sure. So what will become of you? Will you be trying to break into weddings the rest of your days? And what kind of life would that be?"

"It makes me sick to listen at people who don't have any sense," F. Jasmine said, and she put her two fingers in her ears, but she did not push in the fingers very tight and she could still hear Berenice.

"You just laying yourself this fancy trap to catch yourself in trouble," Berenice went on. "And you know it. You been through the B section of the seventh grade and you are already twelve years old."

F. Jasmine did not speak of the wedding, but her argument passed over it, and she said: "They will take me. You wait and see."

"And when they don't?"

"I told you," F. Jasmine said. "I will shoot myself with Papa's pistol. But they will take me. And we're never coming back to this part of the country again."

"Well, I been trying to reason seriously," said Berenice. "But I see it is no use. You determined to suffer."

"Who said I was going to suffer?" F. Jasmine said.

"I know you," said Berenice. "You will suffer."

"You are just jealous," F. Jasmine said. "You are just trying to deprive me of all the pleasure of leaving town. And kill the joy of it."

"I am just trying to head this off," said Berenice. "But I see it is no use."

John Henry whispered for the last time: "Gray eyes is glass."

It was past six o'clock, and the slow old afternoon began slowly to die. F. Jasmine took her fingers from her ears and breathed a long tired sigh. When she had sighed, John Henry sighed also, and Berenice concluded with the longest sigh of all. Mr. Schwarzenbaum had played a ragged little waltz; but the piano was not yet tuned to suit him, and he began to harp and insist on another note. Again he played the scale up until the seventh note, and again he stuck there and did not finish. F. Jasmine was no longer watching the music with her eyes; but John Henry was watching, and when the piano stuck on the last note F. Jasmine could see him harden his behind and sit there stiff in the chair, his eyes raised, waiting.

"It is that last note," F. Jasmine said. "If you start with A and go on up to G, there is a curious thing that seems to make the difference between G and A all the difference in the world. Twice as much difference as between any other two notes in the scale. Yet they are side by side there on the piano just as close together as the other notes. Do ray mee fa sol la tee. Tee. Tee. Tee. It could drive you wild!"

John Henry was grinning with his snaggle teeth and giggling softly. "Tee-tee," he said, and he pulled at Berenice's sleeve. "Did you hear what Frankie said? Tee-tee."

"Shut your trap," F. Jasmine said. "Quit always being so evil-minded." She got up from the table, but she did not know where to go. "You didn't say anything about Willis Rhodes. Did he have a mashed thumb or a coat or something?"

"Lord!" said Berenice, and her voice was so sudden and

shocked that F. Jasmine turned and went back to the table.
"Now that is a story would make the hair rise on your head.
You mean to say I never told you about what happened
with me and Willis Rhodes?"

"No," F. Jasmine said. Willis Rhodes was the last and
the worst of the four husbands, and he was so terrible that
Berenice had had to call the Law on him. "What?"

"Well, imagine this!" said Berenice. "Imagine a cold
bitter January night. And me laying all by myself in the
big parlor bed. Alone in the house, because everybody else
had gone for the Saturday night to Forks Falls. Me, mind
you, who hates to sleep in a empty old bed all by myself
and is nervous in a house alone. Past twelve o'clock on this
cold bitter January night. Can you remember wintertime,
John Henry?"

John Henry nodded.

"Now imagine this!" said Berenice again. She had begun
stacking the dishes so that three dirty plates were piled
before her on the table. Her dark eye circled around the
table, roping in F. Jasmine and John Henry as her audience. F. Jasmine leaned forward, her mouth open and her
hands holding the table edge. John Henry shivered down
in his chair and he watched Berenice through his glasses
without batting his eyes. Berenice had started in a low and
creepy voice, then suddenly she stopped and sat there looking at the two of them.

"So what?" F. Jasmine urged, leaning closer across the
table. "What happened?"

But Berenice did not speak. She looked from one of
them to the other, and shook her head slowly. Then when
she spoke again her voice was completely changed, and she
said: "Why, I wish you would look yonder. I wish you
would look."

F. Jasmine glanced quickly behind her, but there was
only the stove, the wall, the empty stair.

"What?" she asked. "What happened?"

"I wish you would look," Berenice repeated. "Them two
little pitchers and them four big ears." She got up suddenly
from the table. "Come on, less wash the dishes. Then we

going to make some cup cakes to take tomorrow on the trip."

There was nothing F. Jasmine could do to show Berenice how she felt. After a long time, when the table before her was already cleared and Berenice stood washing dishes at the sink, she only said:

"If it's anything I mortally despise it's a person who starts out to tell something and works up people's interest and then stops."

"I admit it," said Berenice. "And I am sorry. But it was just one of them things I suddenly realize I couldn't tell you and John Henry."

John Henry was skipping and scuttling back and forth across the kitchen, from the stairway to the back porch door. "Cup cakes!" he sang. "Cup cakes! Cup cakes!"

"You could have sent him out of the room," F. Jasmine said. "And told me. But don't think I care. I don't care a particle what happened. I just wish Willis Rhodes had come in about that time and slit your throat."

"That is a ugly way to talk," said Berenice. "Especially since I got a surprise for you. Go out on the back porch and look in the wicker basket covered with a newspaper."

F. Jasmine got up, but grudgingly, and she walked in a crippled way to the back porch. Then she stood in the doorway holding the pink organdie dress. Contrary to all that Berenice had maintained, the collar was pleated with tiny little pleats, as it was meant to be. She must have done it before dinner when F. Jasmine was upstairs.

"Well, this is mighty nice of you," she said. "I appreciate it."

She would have liked for her expression to be split into two parts, so that one eye stared at Berenice in an accusing way, and the other eye thanked her with a grateful look. But the human face does not divide like this, and the two expressions canceled out each other.

"Cheer up," said Berenice. "Who can tell what will happen? You might dress up in that fresh pink dress tomorrow and meet the cutest little white boy in Winter Hill you ever seen. It's just on such trips as these that you run into beaus."

"But that's not what I'm talking about," F. Jasmine said. Then, after a while, still leaning against the doorway, she added: "Somehow we got off on the wrong kind of conversation."

The twilight was white, and it lasted for a long while. Time in August could be divided into four parts: morning, afternoon, twilight, and dark. At twilight the sky became a curious blue-green which soon faded to white. The air was soft gray, and the arbor and trees were slowly darkening. It was the hour when sparrows gathered and whirled above the rooftops of the town, and when in the darkened elms along the street there was the August sound of the cicadas. Noises at twilight had a blurred sound, and they lingered: the slam of a screen door down the street, voices of children, the whir of a lawnmower from a yard somewhere. F. Jasmine brought in the evening newspaper, and dark was coming in the kitchen. The corners in the room at first were dark, then the drawings on the wall faded. The three of them watched the dark come on in silence.

"The army is now in Paris."

"That's good."

They were quiet awhile and then F. Jasmine said: "I have a lot of things to do. I ought to start out now."

But although she stood ready in the doorway, she did not go. On this last evening, the last time with the three of them together in the kitchen, she felt there was some final thing she ought to say or do before she went away. For many months she had been ready to leave this kitchen, never to return again; but now that the time had come, she stood there with her head and shoulder leaning against the door jamb, somehow unready. It was the darkening hour when the remarks they made had a sad and beautiful sound, although there would be nothing sad or beautiful about the meanings of the words.

F. Jasmine said quietly: "I intend to take two baths tonight. One long soaking bath and scrub with a brush. I'm going to try to scrape this brown crust off my elbows. Then let out the dirty water and take a second bath."

"That's a good idea," said Berenice. "I will be glad to see you clean."

"I will take another bath," John Henry said. His voice was thin and sad; she could not see him in the darkening room, since he stood in the corner by the stove. At seven Berenice had bathed him and dressed him in his shorts again. She heard him shuffle carefully across the room, for after the bath he had put on Berenice's hat and was trying to walk in Berenice's high-heeled shoes. Again he asked a question which by itself meant nothing. "Why?" he asked.

"Why what, Baby?" said Berenice.

He did not answer, and it was F. Jasmine who finally said: "Why is it against the law to change your name?"

Berenice sat in a chair against the pale white light of the window. She held the newspaper open before her, and her head was twisted down and to one side as she strained to see what was printed there. When F. Jasmine spoke, she folded the paper and put it away on the table.

"You can figure that out," she said. "Just because. Think of the confusion."

"I don't see why," F. Jasmine said.

"What is that on your neck?" said Berenice. "I thought it was a head you carried on that neck. Just think. Suppose I would suddenly up and call myself Mrs. Eleanor Roosevelt. And you would begin naming yourself Joe Louis. And John Henry would try to pass off as Henry Ford. Now what kind of confusion do you think that would cause?"

"Don't talk childish," F. Jasmine said. "That is not the kind of changing I mean. I mean from a name that doesn't suit you to a name you prefer. Like I changed from Frankie to F. Jasmine."

"But still it would be a confusion," Berenice insisted. "Suppose we all suddenly changed to entirely different names. Nobody would ever know who anybody was talking about. The whole world would go crazy."

"I don't see——"

"Because things accumulate around your name," said Berenice. "You have a name and one thing after another happens to you, and you behave in various ways and do things, so that soon the name begins to have a meaning. Things have accumulated around the name. If it is bad and you have a bad reputation, then you just can't jump out of your name and escape like that. And if it is good and you have a good reputation, then you should be content and satisfied."

"But what had accumulated around my old name?" F. Jasmine asked. Then, when Berenice did not reply at once, F. Jasmine answered her own question. "Nothing! See? My name just didn't mean anything."

"Well, that's not exactly so," said Berenice. "People think of Frankie Addams and it brings to mind that Frankie is finished with the B section of the seventh grade. And Frankie found the golden egg at the Baptist Easter Hunt. And Frankie lives on Grove Street and——"

"But those things are nothing," F. Jasmine said. "See? They're not worth while. Nothing ever happened to me."

"But it will," said Berenice. "Things will happen."

"What?" F. Jasmine asked.

Berenice sighed and reached for the Chesterfield package inside her bosom. "You pin me down like that and I can't tell you truthfully. If I could I would be a wizard. I wouldn't be sitting here in this kitchen right now, but making a fine living on Wall Street as a wizard. All I can say is that things will happen. Just what, I don't know."

"By the way," F. Jasmine said after a while. "I thought I would go around to your house and see Big Mama. I don't believe in those fortunes, or anything like that, but I thought I might as well."

"Suit yourself. However, I don't think it is necessary."

"I suppose I ought to leave now," F. Jasmine said.

But still she waited in the darkening door and did not go away. The sounds of the summer twilight crossed within the silence of the kitchen. Mr. Schwarzenbaum had finished tuning the piano, and for the past quarter of an hour he had been playing little pieces. He played music memorized by note, and he was a nervous spry old man who reminded F. Jasmine of a silver spider. His music was spry and stiff also, and he played faint jerking waltzes and nervous lullabies. Farther down the block a solemn radio announced something they could not hear. In the O'Neils' back yard, next door, children were calling and swatting a ball. The sounds of evening canceled out each other, and they were faded in the darkening twilight air. The kitchen itself was very quiet.

"Listen," F. Jasmine said. "What I've been trying to say is this. Doesn't it strike you as strange that I am I, and you are you? I am F. Jasmine Addams. And you are Berenice Sadie Brown. And we can look at each other, and touch each other, and stay together year in and year out in the same room. Yet always I am I, and you are you. And I can't ever be anything else but me, and you can't ever be anything else but you. Have you ever thought of that? And does it seem to you strange?"

Berenice had been rocking slightly in the chair. She was not sitting in a rocking chair, but she had been tilting back in the straight chair, then letting the front legs hit the floor with little taps, her dark stiff hand held to the table edge for balance. She stopped rocking herself when F. Jasmine spoke. And finally she said: "I have thought of it occasionally."

It was the hour when the shapes in the kitchen darkened and voices bloomed. They spoke softly and their voices bloomed like flowers—if sounds can be like flowers and voices bloom. F. Jasmine stood with her hands clasped behind her head, facing the darkening room. She had the feeling that unknown words were in her throat, and she was ready to speak them. Strange words were flowering in her throat and now was the time for her to name them.

"This," she said. "I see a green tree. And to me it is green. And you would call the tree green also. And we would agree on this. But is the color you see as green the same color I see as green? Or say we both call a color black. But how do we know that what you see as black is the same color I see as black?"

Berenice said after a moment: "Those things we just cannot prove."

F. Jasmine scraped her head against the door, and put her hand up to her throat. Her voice shattered and died. "That's not what I meant to say, anyway."

The smoke of Berenice's cigarette lay bitter and warm and stagnant in the room. John Henry shuffled in the high-heeled shoes from the stove to the table and back again. A rat rattled behind the wall.

"This is what I mean," F. Jasmine said. "You are walking down a street and you meet somebody. Anybody. And you look at each other. And you are you. And he is him. Yet when you look at each other, the eyes make a connection. Then you go off one way. And he goes off another way. You go off into different parts of town, and maybe you never see each other again. Not in your whole life. Do you see what I mean?"

"Not exactly," said Berenice.

"I'm talking about this town," F. Jasmine said in a higher voice. "There are all these people here I don't even know by sight or name. And we pass alongside each other and don't have any connection. And they don't know me and I don't know them. And now I'm leaving town and there are all these people I will never know."

"But who do you want to know?" asked Berenice.

F. Jasmine answered: "Everybody. In the world. Everybody in the world."

"Why, I wish you would listen to that," said Berenice. "How about people like Willis Rhodes? How about them Germans? Them Japanese?"

F. Jasmine knocked her head against the door jamb and looked up at the dark ceiling. Her voice broke, and again she said: "That's not what I mean. That's not what I'm talking about."

"Well, what *is* you talking about?" asked Berenice.

F. Jasmine shook her head, almost as though she did not know. Her heart was dark and silent, and from her heart the unknown words flowered and bloomed and she waited to name them. From next door there was the evening sound of children's baseball and the long call: "Batteruup! Batteruup! Then the hollow pock of a ball and the clatter of a thrown bat and running footsteps and wild voices. The window was a rectangle of pale clear light and a child ran across the yard and under the dark arbor after the ball. The child was quick as a shadow and F. Jasmine did not

see his face—his white shirttails flapped loose behind him
like queer wings. Beyond the window the twilight was lasting and pale and still.

"Less play out, Frankie," John Henry whispered. "They
sound like they having a mighty good time."

"No," F. Jasmine said. "You go."

Berenice stirred in her chair and said: "I suppose we
could turn on the light."

But they did not turn on the light. F. Jasmine felt the
unsaid words stick in her throat and a choked sickness
made her groan and knock her head against the door jamb.
Finally she said again in a high ragged voice:

"This:"

Bernice waited, and when she did not speak again, she
asked: "What on earth is wrong with you?"

F. Jasmine could not speak the unknown words, so after
a minute she knocked her head a last time on the door and
then began to walk around the kitchen table. She walked
in a stiff-legged delicate way, as she felt sick, and did not
wish to joggle the different foods that she had eaten and
mix them up inside her stomach. She began to talk in a
high fast voice, but they were the wrong words, and not
what she had meant to say.

"Boyoman! Manoboy!" she said. "When we leave Winter Hill we're going to more places than you ever thought
about or even knew existed. Just where we will go first I
don't know, and it don't matter. Because after we go to
that place we're going on to another. We mean to keep
moving, the three of us. Here today and gone tomorrow.
Alaska, China, Iceland, South America. Traveling on
trains. Letting her rip on motorcycles. Flying around all
over the world in aeroplanes. Here today and gone tomorrow. All over the world. It's the damn truth. Boyoman!"

F. Jasmine jerked open the drawer of the table and fumbled inside for the butcher knife. She did not need the
butcher knife, but she wanted something to grasp in her
hand and wave about as she hurried around the table.

"And talking of things happening," she said. "Things
will happen so fast we won't hardly have time to realize
them. Captain Jarvis Addams sinks twelve Jap battleships

and decorated by the President. Miss F. Jasmine Addams breaks all records. Mrs. Janice Addams elected Miss United Nations in beauty contest. One thing after another happening so fast we don't hardly notice them."

"Hold still, Fool," said Berenice. "And lay down that knife."

"And we will meet them. Everybody. We will just walk up to people and know them right away. We will be walking down a dark road and see a lighted house and knock on the door and strangers will rush to meet us and say: Come in! Come in! We will know decorated aviators and New York people and movie stars. We will have thousands of friends, thousands and thousands and thousands of friends. We will belong to so many clubs that we can't even keep track of all of them. We will be members of the whole world. Boyoman! Manoboy!"

Berenice had a very strong long right arm, and when F. Jasmine passed her the next time as she was running around the table, this arm reached out and snatched her by the petticoat so quickly that she was caught up with a jerk that made her bones crack and her teeth rattle.

"*Is* you gone raving wild?" she asked. The long arm pulled F. Jasmine closer and wrapped around her waist. "You sweating like a mule. Lean down and let me feel your forehead. Is you got a fever?"

F. Jasmine pulled one of Berenice's plaits and pretended she was going to saw it off with the knife.

"You trembling," said Berenice. "I truly believe you took a fever walking around in that sun today. Baby, you sure you ain't sick?"

"Sick?" asked F. Jasmine. "Who, me?"

"Set here in my lap," said Berenice. "And rest a minute."

F. Jasmine put the knife on the table and settled down on Berenice's lap. She leaned back and put her face against Berenice's neck; her face was sweaty and Berenice's neck was sweaty also, and they both smelled salty and sour and sharp. Her right leg was flung across Berenice's knee, and it was trembling—but when she steadied her toes on the floor, her leg did not tremble any more. John Henry shuffled toward them in the high-heeled shoes and crowded up jealous and close to Berenice. He put his arm around Berenice's head and held on to her ear. Then after a moment he tried to push F. Jasmine out of her lap, and he pinched F. Jasmine with a mean and tiny little pinch.

"Leave Frankie alone," said Berenice. "She ain't bothered you."

He made a fretting sound: "I'm sick."

"Now no, you ain't. Be quiet and don't grudge your cousin a little bit of love."

"Old mean bossy Frankie," he complained in a high sad voice.

"What she doing so mean right now? She just laying here wore out."

F. Jasmine rolled her head and rested her face against Berenice's shoulder. She could feel Berenice's soft big ninnas against her back, and her soft wide stomach, her warm solid legs. She had been breathing very fast, but after a minute her breath slowed down so that she breathed in time with Berenice; the two of them were close together as one body, and Berenice's stiffened hands were clasped around F. Jasmine's chest. Their backs were to the window, and before them the kitchen was now almost dark. It was Berenice who finally sighed and started the conclusion of that last queer conversation.

"I think I have a vague idea what you were driving at," she said. "We all of us somehow caught. We born this way or that way and we don't know why. But we caught anyhow. I born Berenice. You born Frankie. John Henry born John Henry. And maybe we wants to widen and bust free. But no matter what we do we still caught. Me is me and you is you and he is he. We each one of us somehow caught all by ourself. Is that what you was trying to say?"

"I don't know," F. Jasmine said. "But I don't want to be caught."

"Me neither," said Berenice. "Don't none of us. I'm caught worse than you is."

F. Jasmine understood why she had said this, and it was John Henry who asked in his child voice: "Why?"

"Because I am black," said Berenice. "Because I am colored. Everybody is caught one way or another. But they done drawn completely extra bounds around all colored people. They done squeezed us off in one corner by ourself. So we caught that firstway I was telling you, as all human beings is caught. And we caught as colored people also. Sometimes a boy like Honey feel like he just can't breathe no more. He feel like he got to break something or break himself. Sometimes it just about more than we can stand."

"I know it," F. Jasmine said. "I wish Honey could do something."

"He just feels desperate like."

"Yes," F. Jasmine said. "Sometimes I feel like I want to break something, too. I feel like I wish I could just tear down the whole town."

"So I have heard you mention," said Berenice. "But that won't help none. The point is that we all caught. And we try in one way or another to widen ourself free. For instance, me and Ludie. When I was with Ludie, I didn't feel so caught. But then Ludie died. We go around trying one thing or another, but we caught anyhow."

The conversation made F. Jasmine almost afraid. She lay there close to Berenice and they were breathing very slowly. She could not see John Henry, but she could feel him; he had climbed up on the back rungs of the chair and was hugging Bernice's head. He was holding her ears, for in a moment Berenice said: "Candy, don't wrench my ears like that. Me and Frankie ain't going to float up through the ceiling and leave you."

Water dropped slowly in the kitchen sink and the rat was knocking behind the wall.

"I believe I realize what you were saying," F. Jasmine said. "Yet at the same time you almost might use the word loose instead of caught. Although they are two opposite words. I mean you walk around and you see all the people. And to me they look loose."

"Wild, you mean?"

"Oh, no!" she said. "I mean you don't see what joins them up together. You don't know where they all came from, or where they're going to. For instance, what made anybody ever come to this town in the first place? Where did all these people come from and what are they going to do? Think of all those soldiers."

"They were born," said Berenice. "And they going to die."

F. Jasmine's voice was thin and high. "I know," she said. "But what is it all about? People loose and at the same time caught. Caught and loose. All these people and you don't know what joins them up. There's bound to be some sort of reason and connection. Yet somehow I can't seem to name it. I don't know."

"If you did you would be God," said Berenice. "Didn't you know that?"

"Maybe so."

"We just know so much. Then beyond that we don't know no more."

"But I wish I did." Her back was cramped and she stirred and stretched herself on Berenice's lap, her long legs sprawling out beneath the kitchen table. "Anyway, after we leave Winter Hill I won't have to worry about things any more."

"You don't have to now. Nobody requires you to solve the riddles of the world." Berenice took a deep meaning breath and said: "Frankie, you got the sharpest set of human bones I ever felt."

This was a strong hint for F. Jasmine to stand up. She would turn on the light, then take one of the cup cakes from the stove, and go out to finish her business in the town. But for a moment longer she lay there with her face pressed close to Berenice's shoulder. The sounds of the summer evening were mingled and long-drawn.

"I never did say just what I was talking about," she said finally. "But there's this. I wonder if you have ever thought about this. Here we are—right now. This very minute. Now. But while we're talking right now, this minute is passing. And it will never come again. Never in all the world. When it is gone it is gone. No power on earth could bring it back again. It is gone. Have you ever thought about that?"

Berenice did not answer, and the kitchen was now dark. The three of them sat silent, close together, and they could

feel and hear each other's breaths. Then suddenly it
started, though why and how they did not know; the three
of them began to cry. They started at exactly the same
moment, in the way that often on these summer evenings
they would suddenly start a song. Often in the dark, that
August, they would all at once begin to sing a Christmas
carol, or a song like the Slitbelly Blues. Sometimes they
knew in advance that they would sing, and they would
agree on the tune among themselves.

Or again, they would disagree and start off on three different songs at once, until at last the tunes began to merge
and they sang a special music that the three of them made
up together. John Henry sang in a high wailing voice, and
no matter what he named his tune, it sounded always just
the same: one high trembling note that hung like a musi-
cal ceiling over the rest of the song. Berenice's voice was
dark and definite and deep, and she rapped the offbeats
with her heel. The old Frankie sang up and down the middle space between John Henry and Berenice, so that their
three voices were joined, and the parts of the song were
woven together.

Often they would sing like this and their tunes were
sweet and queer in the August kitchen after it was dark.
But never before had they suddenly begun to cry; and
though their reasons were three different reasons, yet they
started at the same instant as though they had agreed together. John Henry was crying because he was jealous,
though later he tried to say he cried because of the rat behind the wall. Berenice was crying because of their talk
about colored people, or because of Ludie, or perhaps because F. Jasmine's bones were really sharp. F. Jasmine
did not know why she cried, but the reason she named was
the crew-cut and the fact that her elbows were so rusty.
They cried in the dark for about a minute. Then they
stopped as suddenly as they had begun. The unaccustomed
sound had quieted the rat behind the wall.

"Get up from there," said Berenice. They stood around
the kitchen table and F. Jasmine turned on the light. Berenice scratched her head and sniffled a little. "We certainy
is a gloomy crowd. Now I wonder what started that."

The light was sudden and sharp after the darkness. F. Jasmine ran the faucet of the sink and put her head beneath the stream of water. And Berenice wiped off her face with a dishrag and patted her plaits before the mirror. John Henry stood like a little old woman dwarf, wearing the pink hat with the plume, and the high-heel shoes. The walls of the kitchen were crazy drawn and very bright. The three of them blinked at each other in the light as though they were three strangers or three ghosts. Then the front door opened and F. Jasmine heard her father trudging slowly down the hall. Already the moths were at the window, flattening their wings against the screen, and the final kitchen afternoon was over at last.

3

Early that evening F. Jasmine passed before the jail; she was on her way to Sugarville to have her fortune told and, though the jail was not directly on the way, she had wanted to have one final look at it before she left the town forever. For the jail had scared and haunted her that spring and summer. It was an old brick jail, three stories high, and surrounded by a cyclone fence topped with barbed wire. Inside were thieves, robbers, and murderers. The criminals were caged in stone cells with iron bars before the windows, and though they might beat on the stone walls or wrench at the iron bars, they could never get out. They wore striped jail clothes and ate cold peas with cockroaches cooked in them and cold cornbread.

F. Jasmine knew some people who had been locked up in jail, all of them colored—a boy called Cape, and a friend of Berenice who was accused by the white lady she worked for of stealing a sweater and a pair of shoes. When you were arrested, the Black Maria screamed to your house and a crowd of policemen burst in the door to haul you off down to the jail. After she took the three-bladed knife from the Sears and Roebuck Store, the jail had drawn the old Frankie—and sometimes on those late spring afternoons she would come to the street across from the jail, a place known as Jail-Widow's Walk, and stare for a long time. Often some criminals would be hanging to the bars; it seemed to her that their eyes, like the long eyes of the Freaks at the fair, had called to her as though to say: We know you. Occasionally, on Saturday afternoon, there would be wild yells and singing and hollering from the big cell known as the Bull Pen. But now this evening the jail was quiet—but from a lighted cell there was one criminal, or rather the outline of his head and his two fists around the bars. The brick jail was gloomy dark, although the yard and some cells were lighted.

"What are you locked up for?" John Henry called. He stood a little distance from F. Jasmine and he was wearing the jonquil dress, as F. Jasmine had given him all the costumes. She had not wished to take him with her; but he had pleaded and pleaded, and finally followed at a distance, anyway. When the criminal did not answer, he called again in a thin, high voice. "Are you going to be hung?"

"Hush up!" F. Jasmine said. The jail did not frighten her this evening, for this time tomorrow she would be far away. She gave the jail a last glance and then walked on. "How would you like for somebody to holler something like that to you if you were in jail?"

It was past eight o'clock when she reached Sugarville. The evening was dusty and lavender. Doors of the crowded houses on either side were open, and from some parlors there was the quavered flutter of oil lamps, lighting up the front-room beds and decorated mantelpieces. Voices sounded slurred and from a distance came the jazz of a piano and horn. Children played in alleyways, leaving whorled footsteps in the dust. The people were dressed for Saturday night, and on a corner she passed a group of jesting colored boys and girls in shining evening dresses. There was a party air about the street that reminded her that she, also, could go that very evening to a date at the Blue Moon. She spoke to people on the street and felt again the unexplainable connection between her eyes and other eyes. Mixed with the bitter dust, and smells of privies and suppertime, the smell of a clematis vine threaded the evening air. The house where Berenice lived was on the corner of Chinaberry Street—a two-room house with a tiny front yard bordered by shards and bottle-caps. A bench on the front porch held pots of cool, dark ferns. The door was only partly open and F. Jasmine could see the gold-gray flutters of the lamplight inside.

"You stay out here," she said to John Henry.

There was the murmuring of a strong, cracked voice behind the door, and when F. Jasmine knocked, the voice was quiet a second and then asked:

"Who that? Who is it?"

"Me," she said, for if she answered her true name, Big Mama would not recognize it. "Frankie."

The room was close, although the wooden shutter stood open, and there was the smell of sickness and fish. The crowded parlor was neat. One bed stood against the right wall, and on the opposite side of the room were a sewing machine and a pump organ. Over the hearth hung a photograph of Ludie Freeman; the mantelpiece was decorated with fancy calendars, fair prizes, souvenirs. Big Mama lay in the bed against the wall next to the door, so that in the daytime she could look out through the front window onto the ferny porch and street outside. She was an old colored woman, shriveled and with bones like broomsticks; on the left side of her face and neck the skin was the color of tallow, so that part of her face was almost white and the rest copper-colored. The old Frankie used to think that Big Mama was slowly turning to a white person, but Berenice had said it was a skin disease that sometimes happened to colored people. Big Mama had done fancy washing and fluted curtains until the year the misery had stiffened her back so that she took to bed. But she had not lost any faculties; instead, she suddenly found second-sight. The old Frankie had always thought she was uncanny, and when she was a little girl Big Mama was connected in her mind with the three ghosts who lived inside the coalhouse. And even now, a child no longer, she still had an eerie feeling about Big Mama. She was lying on three feather pillows, the covers of which were bordered with crochet, and over her bony legs there was a many-colored quilt. The parlor table with the lamp was pulled up close beside the bed so that she could reach the objects on it: a dream-book, a white saucer, a workbasket, a jellyglass of water, a Bible, and other things. Big Mama had been talking to herself before F. Jasmine came in, as she had the constant habit of telling herself just who she was and what she was doing and what she intended to do as she lay there in the bed. There were three mirrors on the wall which reflected the wavelike light from the lamp that fluttered gold-gray in the room and cast giant shadows; the lampwick needed trimming. Someone was walking in the back room.

"I came to get my fortune told," F. Jasmine said.

While Big Mama talked to herself when alone, she could be very silent at other times. She stared at F. Jasmine for several seconds before she answered: "Very well. Draw up that stool before the organ."

F. Jasmine brought the stool close to the bed, and leaning forward, stretched out her palm. But Big Mama did not take her palm. She examined F. Jasmine's face, then spat the wad of snuff into a chamberpot which she pulled from underneath the bed, and finally put on her glasses. She waited so long that it occurred to F. Jasmine that she was trying to read her mind, and this made her uneasy. The walking in the back room stopped and there was no sound in the house.

"Cast back your mind and remember," she said finally. "Tell me the revelation of your last dream."

F. Jasmine tried to cast back her mind, but she did not dream often. Then finally she remembered a dream she had had that summer: "I dreamed there was a door," she said. "I was just looking at it and while I watched, it began slowly to open. And it made me feel funny and I woke up."

"Was there a hand in the dream?"

F. Jasmine thought. "I don't think so."

"Was there a cockroach on that door?"

"Why—I don't think so."

"It signifies as follows." Big Mama slowly closed and opened her eyes. "There going to be a change in your life."

Next she took F. Jasmine's palm and studied it for quite a while. "I see here where you going to marry a boy with blue eyes and light hair. You will live to be your three-score and ten, but you must act careful about water. I see here a red-clay ditch and a bale of cotton."

F. Jasmine thought to herself that there was nothing to it, only a pure waste of money and time. "What does that signify?"

But suddenly the old woman raised her head and the cords of her neck stiffened as she called: "You, Satan!"

She was looking at the wall between the parlor and the kitchen, and F. Jasmine turned to look over her shoulder also.

"Yessum," a voice replied from the back room, and it sounded like Honey.

"How many times is I got to tell you to take them big feets off the kitchen table!"

"Yessum." Honey said again. His voice was meek as Moses, and F. Jasmine could hear him put his feet down on the floor.

"Your nose is going to grow into that book, Honey Brown. Put it down and finish up your supper."

F. Jasmine shivered. Had Big Mama looked clear through the wall and seen Honey reading with his feet up on the table? Could those eyes pierce through a pure blank wall? It seemed as though it would behoove her to listen carefully to every word.

"I see here a sum of money. A sum of money. And I see a wedding."

F. Jasmine's outstretched hand trembled a little. "That!" she said. "Tell me about that!"

"The wedding or the money?"

"The wedding."

The lamplight made an enormous shadow of them on the bare boards of the wall. "It's the wedding of a near relation. And I foresee a trip ahead."

"A trip?" she asked. "What kind of a trip? A long trip?"

Big Mama's hands were crooked, spotted with freckly pale blots, and the palms were like melted pink birthday candles. "A short trip," she said.

"But how—?" F. Jasmine began.

"I see a going and a coming back. A departure and a return."

There was nothing to it, for surely Berenice had told her about the trip to Winter Hill and the wedding. But if she could see straight through a wall—"Are you sure?"

"Well—" This time the old cracked voice was not so certain. "I see a departure and a return, but it may not be for *now*. I can't guarantee. For at the same time I see roads, trains, and a sum of money."

"Oh!" F. Jasmine said.

There was the sound of footsteps, and Honey Camden Brown stood on the threshold between the kitchen and the parlor. He wore tonight a yellow shirt with a bow tie, for he was usually a natty dresser—but his dark eyes were sad, and his long face still as stone. F. Jasmine knew what Big Mama had said about Honey Brown. She said he was a boy God had not finished. The Creator had withdrawn His hand from him too soon. God had not finished him, and so he had to go around doing one thing and then another to finish himself up. When she had first heard this remark, the old Frankie did not understand the hidden meaning. Such a remark put her in mind of a peculiar half-boy—one arm, one leg, half a face—a half-person hopping in the gloomy summer sun around the corners of the town. But later she understood it a little better. Honey played the horn, and had been first in his studies at the colored high school. He ordered a French book from Atlanta and learned himself some French. At the same time he would suddenly run hog-wild all over Sugarville and tear around for several days, until his friends would bring him home more dead than living. His lips could move as light as butterflies and he could talk as well as any human she had ever heard—but other times he would answer with a collored jumble that even his own family could not follow. The Creator, Big Mama said, had withdrawn His hand from him too soon, so that he was left eternally unsatisfied. Now he stood there leaning against the door jamb, bony and limp, and although the sweat showed on his face he somehow looked cold.

"Do you wish anything before I go?" he asked.

There was something about Honey that evening that struck F. Jasmine; it was as though, on looking into his sad, still eyes, she felt she had something to say to him. His skin in the lamplight was the color of dark wistaria and the lips were quiet and blue.

"Did Berenice tell you about the wedding?" F. Jasmine asked. But, for once, it was not about the wedding that she felt she had to speak.

"Aaannh," he answered.

"There's nothing I wish now. T. T. is due here in a minute to visit with me for a while and meet up with Berenice. Where you off to, boy?"

"I'm going over to Forks Falls."

"Well, Mr. Up and Sudden, when you done decide that?"

Honey stood leaning against the door jamb, stubborn and quiet.

"Why can't you act like everybody else?" Big Mama said.

"I'll just stay over through Sunday and come back Monday morning."

The feeling that she had something to say to Honey Brown still troubled F. Jasmine. She said to Big Mama: "You were telling me about the wedding."

"Yes." She was not looking at F. Jasmine's palm, but at the organdie dress and the silk hose and the new silver slippers. "I told you you would marry a light-haired boy with blue eyes. Later on."

"But that's not what I'm talking about. I mean the other wedding. And the trip and what you saw about the roads and trains."

"Exactly," said Big Mama, but F. Jasmine had the feeling she was no longer paying much mind to her, although she looked again at her palm. "I foresee a trip with a departure and a return and later a sum of money, roads and trains. Your lucky number is six, although thirteen is sometimes lucky for you too."

F. Jasmine wanted to protest and argue, but how could you argue with a fortune-teller? She wanted at least to understand the fortune better, for the trip with the return did not fit in with the foreseeing of roads and trains.

But as she was about to question further, there were

footsteps on the front porch, a door knock, and T. T. came into the parlor. He was very proper, scraping his feet, and bringing Big Mama a carton of ice cream. Berenice had said he did not make her shiver, and it was true he was nobody's pretty man; his stomach was like a watermelon underneath his vest and there were rolls of fat on the back of his neck. He brought in with him the stir of company that she had always loved and envied about this two-room house. Always it had seemed to the old Frankie, when she could come here hunting Berenice, that there would be many people in the room—the family, various cousins, friends. In the wintertime they would sit by the hearth around the draughty, shivering fire and talk with woven voices. On clear autumn nights they were always the first to have sugar cane and Berenice would hack the joints of the slick, purple cane and they would throw the chewed, twisted pieces, marked with their teethprints, on a newspaper spread upon the floor. The lamplight gave the room a special look, a special smell.

Now, with the coming of T. T., there was the old sense of company and commotion. The fortune was evidently over, and F. Jasmine put a dime in the white china saucer on the parlor table—for, although there was no fixed price, the future-anxious folks who came to Big Mama usually paid what they felt due.

"I declare I never did see anybody grow like you do, Frankie," Big Mama remarked. "What you ought to do is tie a brickbat to your head." F. Jasmine shriveled on her heels, her knees bent slightly, and her shoulders hunched. "That's a sweet dress you got on. And them silver shoes! And silk stockings! You look like a regular grown girl."

F. Jasmine and Honey left the house at the same time, and she was still fretted by the feeling that she had something to say to him. John Henry, who had been waiting in the lane, rushed toward them, but Honey did not pick him up and swing him around as he sometimes did. There was a cold sadness about Honey this evening. The moonlight was white.

"What are you going to do in Forks Falls?"

"Just mess around."

"Do you put any faith in those fortunes?" When Honey did not answer, she went on: "You remember when she hollered back to you to take your feet off the table. Gave me a shock. How did she know your feet were on the table?"

"The mirror," Honey said. "She has a mirror by the door so she can see what goes on in the kitchen."

"Oh," she said. "I never have believed in fortunes."

John Henry was holding Honey's hand and looking up into his face. "What are horsepowers?"

F. Jasmine felt the power of the wedding; it was as though, on this last evening, she ought to order and advise. There was something she ought to tell Honey, a warning or some wise advice. And as she fumbled in her mind, an idea came to her. It was so new, so unexpected, that she stopped walking and stood absolutely still.

"I know what you ought to do. You ought to go to Cuba or Mexico."

Honey had walked on a few steps farther, but when she spoke he stopped also. John Henry was midway between them, and as he looked from one to the other, his face in the white moonlight had a mysterious expression.

"Sure enough. I'm perfectly serious. It don't do you any good to mess around between Forks Falls and this town. I've seen a whole lot of pictures of Cubans and Mexicans. They have a good time." She paused. "This is what I'm trying to discuss. I don't think you will ever be happy in this town. I think you ought to go to Cuba. You are so light-skinned and you even have a kind of Cuban expression. You could go there and change into a Cuban. You could learn to speak the foreign language and none of those Cubans would ever know you are a colored boy. Don't you see what I mean?"

Honey was still as a dark statue, and as silent.

"What?" John Henry asked again. "What do they look like—them horsepowers?"

With a jerk Honey turned and went on down the lane. "It is fantastic."

"No, it is not!" Pleased that Honey had used the word fantastic to her, she said it quietly to herself before she went on to insist. "It's not a particle fantastic. You mark my words. It's the best thing you can do."

But Honey only laughed and turned off at the next alley. "So long."

The streets in the middle of the town reminded F. Jasmine of a carnival fair. There was the same air of holiday freedom; and, as in the early morning, she felt herself a part of everything, included and gay. On a Main Street corner a man was selling mechanical mice, and an armless beggar, with a tin cup in his lap, sat cross-legged on the sidewalk, watching. She had never seen Front Avenue at night before, for in the evening she was supposed to play in the neighborhood close to home. The warehouses across the street were black, but the square mill at the far end of the avenue was lighted in all its many windows and there was a faint mill humming and the smell of dyeing vats. Most of the businesses were open, and the neon signs made a mingling of varied lights that gave to the avenue a watery look. There were soldiers on corners, and other soldiers strolling along with grown date girls. The sounds were slurred late-summer sounds—footsteps, laughter, and above the shuffled noises, the voices of someone calling from an upper story down into the summer street. The buildings smelled of sunbaked brick and the sidewalk was warm beneath the soles of her new silver shoes. F. Jasmine stopped on the corner across from the Blue Moon. It seemed a long time since that morning when she had joined up with the soldier; the long kitchen afternoon had come between, and the soldier had somehow faded. The date, that afternoon, had seemed so very far away. And now that it was almost nine o'clock, she hesitated. She had the unexplainable feeling that there was a mistake.

"Where are we going?" John Henry asked. "I think it's high time we went home."

His voice startled her, as she had almost forgotten him. He stood there with his knees locked, big-eyed and drabbled in the old tarletan costume. "I have business in town. You go home." He stared up at her and took the bubble gum he had been chewing from his mouth—he tried to park the gum behind his ear, but sweat had made his ear too slippery, so finally he put the gum back in his mouth again. "You know the way home as well as I do. So do what I tell you." For a wonder, John Henry minded her; but, as she watched him going away from her down the crowded street, she felt a hollow sorriness—he looked so babyish and pitiful in the costume.

The change from the street to the inside of the Blue Moon was like the change that comes on leaving the open fairway and entering a booth. Blue lights and moving faces, noise. The counter and tables were crowded with soldiers, and men, and bright-faced ladies. The soldier she had promised to meet was playing the slot machine in a far corner, putting in nickel after nickel, but winning none.

"Oh, it's you," he said when he noticed her standing at his elbow. For a second his eyes had the blank look of eyes that are peering back into the brain to recollect—but only for a second. "I was scared you had stood me up." After putting in a final nickel, he banged the slot machine with his fist. "Let's find a place."

They sat at a table between the counter and the slot machine, and, though by the clock the time was not long, it seemed to F. Jasmine endless. Not that the soldier was not nice to her. He was nice, but their two conversations would not join together, and underneath there was a layer of queerness she could not place and understand. The soldier had washed, and his swollen face, his ears and hands, were clean; his red hair was darkened from wetting and ridged with a comb. He said he had slept that afternoon, he was gay and his talk was sassy. But although she liked gay people and sassy talk, she could not think of any answers. It was again as though the soldier talked a kind of double-talk that, try as she would, she could not follow—yet it was not so much the actual remarks as the tone underneath she failed to understand.

The soldier brought two drinks to the table; after a swallow F. Jasmine suspected there was liquor in them and, although a child no longer, she was shocked. It was a sin and against the law for people under eighteen to drink real liquor, and she pushed the glass away. The soldier was both nice and gay, but after he had had two other drinks

she wondered if he could be drunk. To make conversation
she remarked that her brother had been swimming in Alaska, but this did not seem to impress him very much. Nor
would he talk about the war, nor foreign countries and the
world. To his joking remarks she could never find replies
that fitted, although she tried. Like a nightmare pupil in a
recital who has to play a duet to a piece she does not know,
F. Jasmine did her best to catch the tune and follow. But
soon she broke down and grinned until her mouth felt
wooden. The blue lights in the crowded room, the smoke
and noisy commotion, confused her also.

"You're a funny kind of girl," the soldier said finally.

"Patton," she said. "I bet he will win the war in two
weeks."

The soldier was quiet now and his face had a heavy
look. His eyes gazed at her with the same strange expression she had noticed that day at noon, a look she had never
seen on anyone before and could not place. After a while
he said, and his voice was softened, blurred:

"What did you say your name is, Beautiful?"

F. Jasmine did not know whether or not to like the way
he called her, and she spoke her name in a proper voice.

"Well, Jasmine, how bout going on upstairs?" His tone
was asking, but when she did not answer at once, he stood
up from the table. "I've got a room here."

"Why, I thought we were going to the Idle Hour. Or
dancing or something."

"What's the rush?" he said. "The band don't hardly tune
up until eleven o'clock."

F. Jasmine did not want to go upstairs, but she did not
know how to refuse. It was like going into a fair booth,
or fair ride, that once having entered you cannot leave
until the exhibition or the ride is finished. Now it was the
same with this soldier, this date. She could not leave until
it ended. The soldier was waiting at the foot of the stairs
and, unable to refuse, she followed after him. They went
up two flights, and then along a narrow hall that smelled
of wee-wee and linoleum. But every footstep F. Jasmine
took, she felt somehow was wrong.

"This sure is a funny hotel," she said.

It was the silence in the hotel room that warned and frightened her, a silence she noticed as soon as the door was closed. In the light of the bare electric bulb that hung down from the ceiling, the room looked hard and very ugly. The flaked iron bed had been slept in and a suitcase of jumbled soldier's clothes lay open in the middle of the floor. On the light oak bureau there was a glass pitcher full of water and a half-eaten package of cinnamon rolls covered with blue-white icing and fat flies. The screenless window was open and the sleazy voile curtains had been tied at the top in a knot together to let in air. There was a lavatory in the corner and, cupping his hands, the soldier dashed cold water to his face—the soap was only a bar of ordinary soap, already used, and over the lavatory a sign read: STRICTLY WASHING. Although the soldier's footsteps sounded, and the water made a trickling noise, the sense of silence somehow remained.

F. Jasmine went to the window which overlooked a narrow alley and a brick wall; a rickety fire-escape led to the ground and light shafted from the two lower stories. Outside there was the August evening sounds of voices and a radio, and in the room there were sounds also—so how could the silence be explained? The soldier sat on the bed, and now she was seeing him altogether as a single person, not as a member of the loud free gangs who for a season roamed the streets of town and then went out into the world together. In the silent room he seemed to her unjoined and ugly. She could not see him any more in Burma, Africa, or Iceland, or even for that matter in Arkansas. She saw him only as he sat there in the room. His light blue eyes, set close together, were staring at her with the peculiar look— with a filmed softness, like eyes that have been washed with milk.

The silence in the room was like that silence in the kitchen when, on a drowsy afternoon, the ticking of the clock would stop—and there would steal over her a mysterious uneasiness that lasted until she realized what was wrong. A few times before she had known such silence— once in the Sears and Roebuck store the moment before she suddenly became a thief, and again that April after-

noon in the MacKeans' garage. It was the forewarning hush
that comes before an unknown trouble, a silence caused,
not by lack of sounds, but by a waiting, a suspense. The
soldier did not take those strange eyes from her and she
was scared.

"Come on, Jasmine," he said, in an unnatural voice,
broken and low, as he reached out his hand, palm upward,
toward her. "Let's quit this stalling."

The next minute was like a minute in the fair Crazy-
House, or real Milledgeville. Already F. Jasmine had
started for the door, for she could no longer stand the silence. But as she passed the soldier, he grasped her skirt
and, limpened by fright, she was pulled down beside him
on the bed. The next minute happened, but it was too crazy
to be realized. She felt his arms around her and smelled his
sweaty shirt. He was not rough, but it was crazier than if
he had been rough—and in a second she was paralyzed by
horror. She could not push away, but she bit down with all
her might upon what must have been the crazy soldier's
tongue—so that he screamed out and she was free. Then
he was coming toward her with an amazed pained face,
and her hand reached the glass pitcher and brought it down
upon his head. He swayed a second, then slowly his legs
began to crumple, and slowly he sank sprawling to the
floor. The sound was hollow like the hammer on a coconut,
and with it the silence was broken at last. He lay there still,
with the amazed expression on his freckled face that was
now pale, and a froth of blood showed on his mouth. But
his head was not broken, or even cracked, and whether he
was dead or not she did not know.

The silence was over, and it was like those kitchen times
when, after the first uncanny moments, she realized the
reason for her uneasiness and knew that the ticking of the
clock had stopped—but now there was no clock to shake
and hold for a minute to her ear before she wound it, feeling relieved. There slanted across her mind twisted remembrances of a common fit in the front room, basement
remarks, and nasty Barney; but she did not let these separate glimpses fall together, and the word she repeated was
"crazy." There was water on the walls which had been

slung out from the pitcher and the soldier had a broken look in the strewn room. F. Jasmine told herself: Get out! And after first starting toward the door, she turned and climbed out on the fire-escape and quickly reached the alley ground.

She ran like a chased person fleeing from the crazy-house at Milledgeville, looking neither to the right nor left, and when she reached the corner of her own home block, she was glad to see John Henry West. He was out looking for bats around the street light, and the familiar sight of him calmed her a little.

"Uncle Royal has been calling you," he said. "What makes you shake like that for, Frankie?"

"I just now brained a crazy man," she told him when she could get her breath. "I brained him and I don't know if he is dead. He was a crazy man."

John Henry stared without surprise. "How did he act like?" And when she did not answer all at once, he went on: "Did he crawl on the ground and moan and slobber?" For that was what the old Frankie had done one day to try to fool Berenice and create some excitement. Berenice had not been fooled. "Did he?"

"No," F. Jasmine said. "He—" But as she looked into those cold, child eyes she knew that she could not explain. John Henry would not understand, and his green eyes gave her a funny feeling. Sometimes his mind was like the pictures he drew with crayons on tablet paper. The other day he had drawn such a one and showed it to her. It was a picture of a telephone man on a telephone pole. The telephone man was leaning against his safety belt, and the picture was complete down to his climbing shoes. It was a careful picture, but after she had looked at it uneasiness had lingered in her mind. She looked at the picture again until she realized what was wrong. The telephone man was drawn in side-view profile, yet this profile had two eyes—one eye just above the nose bridge and another drawn just below. And it was no hurried mistake; both eyes had careful lashes, pupils, and lids. Those two eyes drawn in a side-view face gave her a funny feeling. But reason with John Henry, argue with him? You might as well argue with ce-

ment. Why did he do it? Why? Because it was a telephone man. What? Because he was climbing the pole. It
was impossible to understand his point of view. And he did
not understand her either.

"Forget what I just now told you," she said. But after
saying it, she realized that was the worst remark she could
have said, for he would be sure not to forget. So she took
him by the shoulders and shook him slightly. "Swear you
won't tell. Swear this: If I tell I hope God will sew up my
mouth and sew down my eyes and cut off my ears with the
scissors."

But John Henry would not swear; he only hunched his
big head down near his shoulders and answered, very
quietly: "Shoo."

She tried again. "If you tell anybody I might be put in
jail and we couldn't go to the wedding."

"I ain't going to tell," John Henry said. Sometimes he
could be trusted, and other times not. "I'm not a tattle-
tale."

Once inside the house, F. Jasmine locked the front door
before she went into the living room. Her father was reading the evening paper, in his sock feet, on the sofa. F. Jasmine was glad to have her father between her and the front
door. She was afraid of the Black Maria and listened anxiously.

"I wish we were going to the wedding right this minute,"
she said. "I think that would be the best thing to do."

She went back to the icebox and ate six tablespoons of
sweetened condensed milk, and the disgust in her mouth
began to go away. The waiting made her feel restless. She
gathered up the library books, and stacked them on the
living-room table. On one of them, a book from the grown
sections which she had not read, she wrote in the front with
pencil: *If you want to read something that will shock you,
turn to page 66.* On page 66 she wrote: *Electricity. Ha!
Ha!* By and by her anxiousness was eased; close to her
father she felt less afraid.

"These books belong to go back to the library."

Her father, who was forty-one, looked at the clock: "It's
time for everybody under forty-one to get to bed. Quick,

march, and without any argument. We have to be up at five o'clock."

F. Jasmine stood in the doorway, unable to leave. "Papa," she said, after a minute, "if somebody hits somebody with a glass pitcher and he falls out cold, do you think he is dead?"

She had to repeat the question, feeling a bitter grudge against him because he did not take her seriously, so that her questions must be asked twice.

"Why, come to think about it, I never hit anybody with a pitcher," he said. "Did you?"

F. Jasmine knew he asked this as a joke, so she only said as she went away: "I'll never be so glad to get to any place in all my life as Winter Hill tomorrow. I will be so thankful when the wedding is over and we have gone away. I will be so thankful."

Upstairs she and John Henry undressed, and after the motor and the light were off, they lay down on the bed together—although she said she could not sleep a wink. But nevertheless she closed her eyes, and when she opened them again a voice was calling and the room was early gray.

Part Three

SHE SAID: "Farewell, old ugly house," as, wearing a dotted Swiss dress and carrying the suitcase, she passed through the hall at quarter to six. The wedding dress was in the suitcase, ready to be put on when she reached Winter Hill. At that still hour the sky was the dim silver of a mirror, and beneath it the gray town looked, not like a real town, but like an exact reflection of itself, and to this unreal town she also said farewell. The bus left the station at ten past six—and she sat proud, like an accustomed traveler, apart from her father, John Henry, and Berenice. But after a while a serious doubt came in her, which even the answers of the bus-driver could not quite satisfy. They were supposed to be traveling north, but it seemed to her rather that the bus was going south instead. The sky turned burning pale and the day blazed. They passed the fields of windless corn that had a blue look in the glare, red-furrowed cotton land, stretches of black pine woods. And mile by mile the countryside became more southern. The towns they passed—New City, Leeville, Cheehaw—each town seemed smaller than the one before, until at nine o'clock they reached the ugliest place of all, where they changed busses, called Flowering Branch. Despite its name there were no flowers and no branch—only a solitary country store, with a sad old shredded circus poster on the clapboard wall and a chinaberry tree beneath which stood an empty wagon and a sleeping mule. There they waited for the bus to Sweet Well, and, still doubting anxiously, Frances did not despise the box of lunch that had so shamed her at the first, because it made them look like family people who do not travel very much. The bus left at ten o'clock, and they were in Sweet Well by eleven. The next hours were unexplainable. The wedding was like a dream, for all that came about occurred in a world beyond her power; from the moment when, sedate and proper, she shook hands with the grown people until the time, the wrecked wedding over, when she watched the car with the two of them driving away from her, and flinging herself down in the sizzling dust, she cried out for the last time: "Take me! Take me!" —from the beginning to the end the wedding was unmanaged as a nightmare. By mid-afternoon it was all finished and the return bus left at four o'clock.

"The show is over and the monkey's dead," John Henry quoted, as he settled himself in the next to the last bus seat beside her father. "Now we go home and go to bed."

Frances wanted the whole world to die. She sat on the back seat, between the window and Berenice, and, though she was no longer sobbing, the tears were like two little brooks, and also her nose ran water. Her shoulders were hunched over her swollen heart and she no longer wore the wedding dress. She was sitting next to Berenice, back with the colored people, and when she thought of it she used the mean word she had never used before, nigger—for now she hated everyone and wanted only to spite and shame. For John Henry West the wedding had only been a great big show, and he had enjoyed her misery at the end as he had enjoyed the angel cake. She mortally despised him, dressed in his best white suit, now stained with strawberry ice cream. Berenice she hated also, for to her it had only meant a pleasure trip to Winter Hill. Her father, who had said that he would attend to her when they got home, she would like to kill. She was against every single person, even strangers in the crowded bus, though she only saw them blurred by tears—and she wished the bus would fall in a river or run into a train. Herself she hated the worst of all, and she wanted the whole world to die.

"Cheer up," said Berenice. "Wipe your face and blow your nose and things will look better by and by."

Berenice had a blue party handkerchief, to match her blue best dress and blue kid shoes—and this she offered to Frances, although it was made of fine georgette and not, of course, due to be blown on. She would not notice it. In the seat between them there were three wet handkerchiefs of her father's, and Berenice began to dry the tears with one, but Frances did not move or budge.

"They put old Frankie out of the wedding." John Henry's big head bobbed over the back of his seat, smiling and snaggled-toothed. Her father cleared his throat and said: "That's sufficient, John Henry. Leave Frankie alone." And Berenice added: "Sit down in that seat now and behave."

The bus rode for a long time, and now direction made no difference to her; she did not care. From the beginning the wedding had been queer like the card games in the kitchen the first week last June. In those bridge games they played and played for many days, but nobody ever drew a good hand, the cards were all sorry, and no high bids made —until finally Berenice suspicioned, saying: "Less us get busy and count these old cards." And they got busy and counted the old cards, and it turned out the jacks and the queens were missing. John Henry at last admitted that he had cut out the jacks and then the queens to keep them company and, after hiding the clipped scraps in the stove, had secretly taken the pictures home. So the fault of the card game was discovered. But how could the failure of the wedding be explained?

The wedding was all wrong, although she could not point out single faults. The house was a neat brick house out near the limits of the small, baked town, and when she first put foot inside, it was as though her eyeballs had been slightly stirred; there were mixed impressions of pink roses, the smell of floor wax, mints and nuts in silver trays. Everybody was lovely to her. Mrs. Williams wore a lace dress, and she asked F. Jasmine two times what grade she was in at school. But she asked, also, if she would like to play out on the swing before the wedding, in the tone grown people use when speaking to a child. Mr. Williams was nice to her, too. He was a sallow man with folds in his cheeks and the skin beneath his eyes was the grain and color of an old apple core. Mr. Williams also asked her what grade she was in at school; in fact, that was the main question asked her at the wedding.

She wanted to speak to her brother and the bride, to talk to them and tell them of her plans, the three of them alone together. But they were never once alone; Jarvis was out checking the car someone was lending for the honeymoon, while Janice dressed in the front bedroom among a crowd of beautiful grown girls. She wandered from one to the other of them, unable to explain. And once Janice put her arms around her, and said she was so glad to have a little sister—and when Janice kissed her, F. Jasmine felt an aching in her throat and could not speak. Jarvis, when she went to find him in the yard, lifted her up in a roughhouse way and said: Frankie the lankie the alaga fankie, the tee-legged, toe-legged bow-legged Frankie. And he gave her a dollar.

She stood in the corner of the bride's room, wanting to say: I love the two of you so much and you are the we of me. Please take me with you from the wedding, for we belong to be together. Or even if she could have said: May I trouble you to step into the next room, as I have something to reveal to you and Jarvis? And get the three of them in a room alone together and somehow manage to explain. If only she had written it down on the typewriter in advance, so that she could hand it to them and they would read! But this she had not thought to do, and her tongue was heavy in her mouth and dumb. She could only speak in a voice that shook a little—to ask where was the veil?

"I can feel in the atmosphere a storm is brewing," said Berenice. "These two crooked joints can always tell."

There was no veil except a little veil that came down from the wedding hat, and nobody was wearing fancy clothes. The bride was wearing a daytime suit. The only mercy of it was that she had not worn her wedding dress on the bus, as she had first intended, and found it out in time. She stood in a corner of the bride's room until the piano played the first notes of the wedding march. They were all lovely to her at Winter Hill, except that they called her Frankie and treated her too young. It was so unlike what she had expected, and, as in those June card games, there was, from first to last, the sense of something terribly gone wrong.

"Perk up," said Berenice. "I'm planning a big surprise for you. I'm just sitting here planning. Don't you want to know what it is?"

Frances did not answer even by a glance. The wedding was like a dream outside her own power, or like a show unmanaged by her in which she was supposed to have no part. The living room was crowded with Winter Hill company, and the bride and her brother stood before the mantelpiece at the end of the room. And seeing them again together was more like singing feeling than a picture that her dizzied eyes could truly see. She watched them with her heart, but all the time she was only thinking: I have not told them and they don't know. And knowing this was heavy as a swallowed stone. And afterward, during the kissing of the bride, refreshments served in the dining room, the stir and party bustle—she hovered close to the two of them, but words would not come. They are not going to take me, she was thinking, and this was the one thought she could not bear.

When Mr. Williams brought their bags, she hastened after with her own suitcase. The rest was like some nightmare show in which a wild girl in the audience breaks onto the stage to take upon herself an unplanned part that was never written or meant to be. You are the we of me, her heart was saying, but she could only say aloud: "Take me!" And they pleaded and begged with her, but she was already in the car. At the last she clung to the steering wheel until her father and somebody else had hauled and dragged her from the car, and even then she could only cry in the dust of the empty road: "Take me! Take me!" But there was only the wedding company to hear, for the bride and her brother had driven away.

Berenice said: "School will begin now in only three more weeks. And you'll go into the A section of the seventh grade and meet a lot of nice new children and make another bosom friend like that Evelyn Owen you were so wild about."

The kind tone Frances could not stand. "I never meant to go with them!" she said. "It was all just a joke. They said they were going to invite me to a visit when they get settled, but I wouldn't go. Not for a million dollars."

"We know all about that," said Berenice. "Now listen to my surprise I've planned. Soon as you get settled in school and have a chance to make these friends, I think it would be a good idea to have a party. A lovely bridge party in the living room, with potato salad and those little olive sandwiches your Aunt Pet had for a club meeting you were so carried away about——the round-shaped kind with the tiny round hole in the middle and the olive showing. A lovely bridge party with delicious refreshments. How would you like that?"

The baby promises rasped her nerves. Her cheap heart hurt, and she pressed her crossed arms over it and rocked a little. "It was a framed game. The cards were stacked. It was a frame-up all around."

"We can have that bridge party going on in the living room. And out in the back yard we can have another party at the same time. A costume party with hot dogs. One party dainty and the other one rough. With prizes for the highest bridge score and the funniest costume. How does that strike you?"

Frances refused to look at Berenice or answer.

"You could call up the society editor of the *Evening Journal* and have the party written up in the paper. And that would make the fourth time your name has been published in the paper."

It would, but a thing like that no longer mattered to her. Once, when her bike ran into an automobile, the paper had called her Fankie Addams. *Fankie!* But now she did not care.

"Don't be so blue," said Berenice. "This is not doomsday."

"Frankie, don't cry," John Henry said. "We will go home and put up the tepee and have a good time."

She could not stop crying and the sobbing had a strangled sound. "Oh, hush up your mouth!"

"Listen to me. Tell me what you would like and I'll try
to do it if it's in my power."

"All I would like," said Frances, after a minute, "all I
wish in the world, is for no human being ever to speak to
me so long as I live."

And Berenice said, finally: "Well. Then bawl, then,
Misery."

They did not talk the rest of the way back to the town.
Her father slept with a handkerchief over his nose and
eyes, snoring a little. John Henry West lay in her father's
lap and slept also. The other passengers were drowsy quiet
and the bus rocked like a cradle and made a softly roaring sound. Outside the afternoon shimmered and now and
then there was a buzzard lazily balanced against the blazing pale sky. They passed red empty crossroads with deep
red gulches on either side, and rotten gray shacks set in the
lonesome cotton fields. Only the dark pine trees looked
cool—and the low blue hills when seen from miles away.
Frances watched from the window with a stiff sick face and
for four hours did not say a word. They were entering the
town, and a change came. The sky lowered and turned a
purple-gray against which the trees were a poison green.
There was a jellied stillness in the air and then the mutter
of the first thunder. A wind came through the treetops with
a sound like rushing water, forewarning storm.

"I told you so," said Berenice, and she was not speaking
of the wedding. "I could feel the misery in these joints.
After a good storm we will all feel much better."

The rain did not come, and there was only a feeling of
expectation in the air. The wind was hot. Frances smiled a
little at Berenice's words, but it was a scorning smile that
hurt.

"You think it's all over," she said, "but that only shows
how little you know."

They thought it was finished, but she would show them.
The wedding had not included her, but she would still go
into the world. Where she was going she did not know;

however, she was leaving town that night. If she could not go in the way she had planned, safe with her brother and the bride, she would go, anyway. Even if she had to commit every crime. For the first time since the night before she thought about the soldier—but only in a glancing way, for her mind was busy with hasty plans. There was a train that passed through the town at two o'clock, and she would take it; the train went north in a general way, probably to Chicago or New York. If the train went to Chicago, she would go on to Hollywood and write shows or get a job as a movie starlet—or, if worse came to worse, even act in comedies. If the train went to New York, she would dress like a boy and give a false name and a false age and join the Marines. Meanwhile, she had to wait until her father was asleep, and she could still hear him moving in the kitchen. She sat at the typewriter and wrote a letter.

Dear Father:
     This is a farewell letter until I write you from a different place. I told you I was going to leave town because it is inevitable. I cannot stand this existance any longer because my life has become a burden. I am taking the pistol because who can tell when it might come in handy and I will send back the money to you at the very first opportunaty. Tell Berenice not to worry. The whole thing is a irony of fate and it is inevitable. Later I will write. Please Papa do not try to capture me.
                                   Sincerely yours,
                                        Frances Addams

The green-and-white moths were nervous at the window screen and the night outside was queer. The hot wind had stopped and the air was so still that it seemed solid and there was a weight against you when you moved. The thunder grumbled low occasionally. Frances sat motionless before the typewriter, wearing the dotted Swiss dress, and the strapped suitcase was beside the door. After a while the light in the kitchen was turned off and her father called from the foot of the stairs: "Good night, Picklepriss. Good night, John Henry."

Frances waited a long time. John Henry was sleeping across the foot of the bed, still dressed and with his shoes on, and his mouth was open and one ear of his glasses frame had come loose. After waiting as long as she could stand it, she took the suitcase and tiptoed very quietly down the stairs. It was dark down there, dark in her father's room, dark through the house. She stood on the threshold of her father's room and he was snoring softly. The hardest time was the few minutes she stood there, listening.

The rest was easy. Her father was a widow-man, set in his ways, and at night he folded his pants over a straight chair and left his wallet, watch, and glasses on the right-hand side of the bureau. She moved very quietly in the darkness and laid hand on the wallet almost immediately. She was careful opening the bureau drawer, stopping to listen each time there was a scraping sound. The pistol felt heavy and cool in her hot hand. It was easy except for the loudness of beating heart and for an accident that happened just as she crept from the room. She stumbled over a wastepaper basket and the snoring stopped. Her father stirred, muttered. She held her breath—then finally, after a minute, the snoring went on again.

She put the letter on the table and tiptoed to the back porch. But there was one thing she had not counted on—John Henry began to call.

"Frankie!" The high child voice seemed to carry through all the rooms of the night house. "Where are you?"

"Hush," she whispered. "Go back to sleep."

She had left the light on in her room, and he stood in the stairway door and looked down into the dark kitchen. "What are you doing down there in the dark?"

"Hush!" she said again in a loud whisper. "I'll be there by the time you get to sleep."

She waited a few minutes after John Henry had gone, then groped to the back door, unlocked it, and stepped outside. But, though she was very quiet, he must have heard her. "Wait, Frankie!" he wailed. "I'm coming."

The child wailing had waked her father, and she knew it before she reached the corner of the house. The night was dark and heavy, and as she ran, she heard her father calling her. Behind the corner of the house she looked and saw the kitchen light go on; the bulb swing back and forth, making a swinging gold reflection on the arbor and the dark yard. He will read the letter now, she thought, and chase and try to capture me. But after she had run a few blocks, the suitcase bumping against her legs and sometimes nearly tripping her, she remembered that her father would have to put on pants and a shirt—for he would not chase her through the streets dressed only in pajama bottoms. She stopped for a second to look behind. No one was there. At the first street light she put down the suitcase and, taking the wallet from the front pocket of her dress, opened it with shaking hands. Inside there was three dollars and fifteen cents. She would have to hop a box car, or something.

All at once, alone there in the night-empty street, she realized she did not know how. It is easy to talk about hopping a freight train, but how did bums and people really do it? She was three blocks from the station and she walked toward it slowly. The station was closed and she went round it and stared at the platform, long and empty under the pale lights, with the Chiclet machines against the station wall and scraps of chewing-gum paper and candy wrappings on the platform. The train tracks gleamed silver and exact and some freight cars were off on a siding in the distance, but they were not hooked to any engine. The train would not come until two o'clock, and would she be able to hop a car, as she had read about, and get away? There was a red lantern a little way down the tracks, and against this colored light she saw a railroad man come walking slowly. She could not hang around like that until two o'clock—but as she left the station, one shoulder dragged down by the weight of the bag, she did not know where she should go.

The streets were lonesome and idle with Sunday night. The red-and-green neon lights in the signboards mixed with the street lights to make a pale hot haze above the town, but the sky was starless, black. A man in a tilted hat took out his cigarette and turned to stare at her as she passed by. She could not wander around the town like this, for by this time her father would be chasing her. In the alley behind Finny's Place she sat down on the suitcase, and only then she realized that the pistol was still in her left hand. She had been going around with the pistol held right in her hand, and she felt that she had lost her mind. She had said that she would shoot herself if the bride and her brother would not take her. She pointed the pistol at the side of her head and held it there a minute or two. If she squeezed down on the trigger she would be dead—and deadness was blackness, nothing but pure terrible blackness that went on and on and never ended until the end of all the world. When she lowered the pistol, she told herself that at the last minute she had changed her mind. The pistol she put in her suitcase.

The alley was black and smelled of garbage cans, and it was in this alley where Lon Baker had his throat slashed that spring afternoon so that his neck was like a bloody mouth that gibbered in the sun. It was here Lon Baker had been killed. And had she killed the soldier, when she brained his head with the water pitcher? She was scared in the dark alley and her mind felt splintered. If only there was someone with her! If only she could hunt down Honey Brown and they could go away together! But Honey had gone to Forks Falls and would not be back until tomorrow. Or if she could find the monkey and the monkey-man and join with them to run away! There was a scuttling noise, and she jerked with terror. A cat had leaped up on a garbage can, and in the darkness she could see its outline against the light at the end of the alley. She whispered: "Charles!" and then, "Charlina." But it was not her Persian cat, and when she stumbled toward the can it sprang away.

She could stand the black sour alley no longer and, carrying the suitcase toward the light at the end, she stood close to the sidewalk, but still inside the shadow of a wall. If there was only somebody to tell her what to do and where to go and how to get there! The fortune of Big Mama had turned out true—about the sort of trip and a departure and a return, and even the cotton bales, for the bus had passed a truck of them on the way back from Winter Hill. And there was the sum of money in her father's wallet, so that already she had lived up all the fortune Big Mama had foreseen. Should she go down to the house in Sugarville and say that she had used up the whole future, and what was she now to do?

Beyond the shadow of the alley the gloomy street was like a street that waited, with the winking neon Coca-Cola sign on the next corner, and a lady walking back and forth beneath a street light as though expecting someone. A car, a long closed car that maybe was a Packard, came slowly down the street, and the way it cruised close to the curb reminded her of a gangster's car, so that she shrank back closer to the wall. Then, on the opposite sidewalk, two people passed, and a feeling like a sudden flame sprang up inside her, and for less than a second it seemed that her brother and the bride had come for her and were now *there*. But the feeling blew out instantly and she was just watching a stranger couple passing down the street. There was a hollow in her chest, but at the bottom of this emptiness a heavy weight pressed down and bruised her stomach, so that she felt sick. She told herself she ought to get busy and pick up her feet and go away. But she still stood there, her eyes closed, and her head against the warm brick wall.

When she left the alley, it was a long time after midnight and she had reached the point where any sudden idea seemed a good idea. She had seized on first one notion and then another. To hitch-hike to Forks Falls and track down Honey, or to wire Evelyn Owen to meet her in Atlanta, or even to go back to the house and get John Henry, so that at least there would be somebody with her and she would not have to go into the world alone. But there was some objection to each of these ideas.

Then, all at once, from the tangle of turning impossibilities, she thought of the soldier; and this time the thought was not a glancing one—it lingered, stuck, and did not go away. She wondered if she ought to go to the Blue Moon and find if she had killed the soldier, before she left the town forever. The idea, once seized on, seemed to her good, and she started for Front Avenue. If she had not killed the soldier, then when she found him what could she say? How the next thought occurred to her she did not know, but suddenly it seemed she might as well ask the soldier to marry with her, and then the two of them could go away. Before he had gone crazy, he had been a little nice. And because it was a new and sudden idea, it also seemed reasonable. She remembered a part of the fortune she had forgotten, that she would marry a light-haired person with blue eyes, and the fact that the soldier had light red hair and blue eyes was like a proof that this was the right thing to do.

She hurried faster. The night before was like a time that had happened so long ago that the soldier was unraveled in her memory. But she recalled the silence in the hotel room; and all at once a fit in a front room, the silence, the nasty talk behind the garage—these separate recollections fell together in the darkness of her mind, as shafting searchlights meet in the night sky upon an aeroplane, so that in a flash there came in her an understanding. There was a feeling of cold surprise; she stopped a minute, then went on toward the Blue Moon. The stores were dark and closed, the pawnshop window locked with criss-crossed steel against night robbers, and the only lights were those from the open wooden stairs of buildings and the greenish splash of brightness from the Blue Moon. There was a sound of quarreling voices from an upper story, and the footsteps of two men, far down the street, walking away. She was no longer thinking of the soldier; the discovery of the moment before had scattered him from her mind. There was only knowing that she must find somebody, anybody, that she could join with to go away. For now she admitted she was too scared to go into the world alone.

She did not leave the town that night, for the Law caught her in the Blue Moon. Officer Wylie was there when she walked in, although she did not see him until she was settled at the window table with the suitcase on the floor beside her. The juke-box sounded a sleazy blues and the Portuguese owner stood with his eyes closed, playing up and down the wooden counter in time to the sad juke tune. There were only a few people in a corner booth and the blue light gave the place a look of being undersea. She did not see the Law until he was standing beside the table, and when she looked up at him, her startled heart quivered a little and then stopped still.

"You're Royal Addams's daughter," the Law said, and her head admitted with a nod. "I'll phone in to headquarters to say you're found. Just stay right here."

The Law went back to the telephone booth. He was calling the Black Maria to haul her off down to the jail, but she did not care. Very likely she had killed that soldier, and they had been following clues and hunting her all over town. Or the Law maybe had found out about the three-way knife she had stolen from the Sears and Roebuck Store. It was not plain just what she was captured for, and the crimes of the long spring and summer merged together as one guilt which she had lost the power to understand. It was as though the things that she had done, the sins committed, had all been done by someone else—a stranger a long time ago. She sat very still, her legs wrapped tight around each other, and her hands clasped in her lap. The Law was a long time at the telephone, and, staring straight ahead of her, she watched two people leave a booth and, leaning close against each other, start to dance. A soldier banged the screen door and walked through the café, and only the distant stranger in her recognized him; when he had climbed up the stairs, she only thought slowly and with no feeling that a curly red head such as that one was like cement. Then her mind went back to thoughts of jail and cold peas and cold cornbread and iron-barred cells. The Law came back from the telephone and sat down across from her and said:

"How did you happen to come in here?"

The Law was big in his blue policeman's suit and, once arrested, it was a bad policy to lie or trifle. He had a heavy face, with a squatty forehead and unmatched ears—one ear was larger than the other one, and had a torn look. When he questioned her, he did not look into her face, but at some point just above her head.

"What am I doing in here?" she repeated. For all at once she had forgotten, and she told the truth when she said finally, "I don't know."

The voice of the Law seemed to come from a distance like a question asked through a long corridor. "Where were you headed for?"

The world was now so far away that Frances could no longer think of it. She did not see the earth as in the old days, cracked and loose and turning a thousand miles an hour; the earth was enormous and still and flat. Between herself and all the places there was a space like an enormous canyon she could not hope to bridge or cross. The plans for the movies or the Marines were only child plans that would never work, and she was careful when she answered. She named the littlest, ugliest place she knew, for to run away there could not be considered so very wrong.

"Flowering Branch."

"Your father phoned headquarters you had left a letter that you were running away. We located him at the bus station and he'll be here in a minute to take you home."

It was her father who had sicked the Law on her, and she would not be carried to the jail. In a way she was sorry. It was better to be in a jail where you could bang the walls than in a jail you could not see. The world was too far away, and there was no way any more that she could be included. She was back to the fear of the summertime, the old feelings that the world was separate from herself—and the failed wedding had quickened the fear to terror. There had been a time, only yesterday, when she felt that every person that she saw was somehow connected with herself and there was between the two of them an instant recognition. Frances watched the Portuguese who still played a mock piano on the counter to the juke-box tune. He swayed as he played and his fingers skittered up and down the counter, so that a man at the far end protected his glass with his hand. When the tune was over, the Portuguese folded his arms upon his chest; Frances narrowed and tensed her eyes to will him to look at her. He had been the first person she had told the day before about the wedding, but as he gave an owner's look around the place, his glance passed by her in a casual way and there was in those eyes no feeling of connection. She turned to the others in the room, and it was the same with all of them and they were strangers. In the blue light she felt queer as a person drowning. At last she was staring at the Law and finally he looked into her eyes. He looked at her with eyes as china as a doll's, and in them there was only the reflection of her own lost face.

The screen door slammed and the Law said: "Here's your Daddy come to take you home."

Frances was never once to speak about the wedding. Weathers had turned and it was in another season. There were the changes and Frances was now thirteen. She was in the kitchen with Berenice on the day before they moved, the last afternoon that Berenice would be with them; for when it had been decided that she and her father would share with Aunt Pet and Uncle Ustace a house out in the new suburb of town, Berenice had given quit notice and said that she might as well marry T. T. It was the end of an afternoon in late November, and in the east the sky was the color of a winter geranium.

Frances had come back to the kitchen, for the other rooms were hollow since the van had taken the furniture away. There were only the two beds in the downstairs bedrooms and the kitchen furniture, and they were to be moved tomorrow. It was the first time in a long while that Frances had spent an afternoon back in the kitchen, alone with Berenice. It was not the same kitchen of the summer that now seemed so long ago. The pencil pictures had disappeared beneath a coat of calcimine, and new linoleum covered the splintery floor. Even the table had been moved, pushed back against the wall, since now there was nobody to take meals with Berenice.

The kitchen, done over and almost modern, had nothing that would bring to mind John Henry West. But nevertheless there were times when Frances felt his presence there, solemn and hovering and ghost-gray. And at those times there would come a hush—a hush quivered by voiceless words. A similar hush would come, also, when Honey was mentioned or brought to mind, for Honey was out on the road now with a sentence of eight years. Now the hush came that late November afternoon as Frances was making the sandwiches, cutting them into fancy shapes and taking great pains—for Mary Littlejohn was coming at five o'clock. Frances glanced at Berenice, who was sitting idle in a chair, wearing an old raveled sweater, her limp arms hanging at her sides. In her lap there was the thin little pinched fox fur that Ludie had given her many years ago. The fur was sticky and the sharp little face foxwise and sad. The fire from the red stove brushed the room with flickers of light and changing shadows.

"I am just mad about Michelangelo," she said.

Mary was coming at five o'clock to take dinner, spend the night, and ride in the van to the new house tomorrow. Mary collected pictures of great masters and pasted them in an art book. They read poets like Tennyson together; and Mary was going to be a great painter and Frances a great poet—or else the foremost authority on radar. Mr. Littlejohn had been connected with a tractor company and before the war the Littlejohns had lived abroad. When Frances was sixteen and Mary eighteen, they were going around the world together. Frances placed the sandwiches on a plate, along with eight chocolates and some salted nuts; this was to be a midnight feast, to be eaten in the bed at twelve o'clock.

"I told you we're going to travel around the world together."

"Mary Littlejohn," said Berenice, in a tinged voice. "Mary Littlejohn."

Berenice could not appreciate Michelangelo or poetry, let alone Mary Littlejohn. There had at first been words between them on the subject. Berenice had spoken of Mary as being lumpy and marshmallow-white, and Frances had defended fiercely. Mary had long braids that she could very nearly sit on, braids of a woven mixture of corn-yellow and brown, fastened at the ends with rubber bands and, on occasions, ribbons. She had brown eyes with yellow eyelashes, and her dimpled hands tapered at the fingers to little pink blobs of flesh, as Mary bit her nails. The Littlejohns were Catholics, and even on this point Berenice was all of a sudden narrowminded, saying that Roman Catholics worshiped Graven Images and wanted the Pope to rule the world. But for Frances this difference was a final touch of strangeness, silent terror, that completed the wonder of her love.

"There's no use our discussing a certain party. You could not possibly ever understand her. It's just not in you." She had said that once before to Berenice, and from the sudden faded stillness in her eye she knew that the words had hurt. And now she repeated them, angered because of the tinged way Berenice had said the name, but once the words were spoken she was sorry. "Anyhow, I consider it the greatest honor of my existence that Mary has picked me out to be her one most intimate friend. Me! Of all people!"

"Have I ever said anything against her?" said Berenice. "All I said was it makes me nervous to watch her just sitting there sucking them pigtails."

"Braids!"

A flock of strong-winged arrowed geese flew over the yard, and Frances went to the window. There had been frost that morning, silvering the brown grass and the roofs of neighbors' houses, and even the thinned leaves of the rusty arbor. When she turned back to the kitchen, the hush was in the room again. Berenice sat hunched with her elbow on her knee, and her forehead resting in her hand, staring with one mottled eye at the coal scuttle.

The changes had come about at the same time, during the middle of October. Frances had met Mary at a raffle two weeks before. It was the time when countless white and yellow butterflies danced among the last fall flowers; the time, too, of the Fair. First, it was Honey. Made crazy one night by a marihuana cigarette, by something called smoke or snow, he broke into the drugstore of the white man who had been selling them to him, desperate for more. He was locked in the jail, awaiting trial, and Berenice rushed back and forth, canvassing money, seeing a lawyer, and trying to get admission to the jail. She came in on the third day, worn out, and with the red curdled glare already in the eye. A headache, she said she had, and John Henry West put his head down on the table and said he had a headache, also. But nobody paid any mind to him, thinking he copied

Berenice. "Run along," she said, "for I don't have the patience to fool with you." Those were the last words spoken to him in the kitchen, and later Berenice recalled them as judgment on her from the Lord. John Henry had meningitis and after ten days he was dead. Until it was all over, Frances had never believed for a serious minute that he could die. It was the time of golden weather and Shasta daisies and the butterflies. The air was chilled, and day after day the sky was a clear green-blue, but filled with light, the color of a shallow wave.

Frances was never allowed to visit John Henry, but Berenice helped the trained nurse every day. She would come in toward dark, and the things that she said in her cracked voice seemed to make John Henry West unreal. "I don't see why he has to suffer so," Berenice would say: and the word *suffer* was one she could not associate with John Henry, a word she shrank from as before an unknown hollow darkness of the heart.

It was the time of the Fair and a big banner arched the main street and for six days and nights the Fair went on down at the fairground. Frances went twice, both times with Mary, and they rode on nearly everything, but did not enter the Freak Pavilion, as Mrs. Littlejohn said it was morbid to gaze at Freaks. Frances bought John Henry a walking stick and sent him the rug she had won at Lotto. But Berenice remarked that he was beyond all this, and the words were eerie and unreal. As the bright days followed one upon the other, the words of Berenice became so terrible that she would listen in a spell of horror, but a part of her could not believe. John Henry had been screaming for three days and his eyeballs were walled up in a corner stuck and blind. He lay there finally with his head drawn back in a buckled way, and he had lost the strength to scream. He died the Tuesday after the Fair was gone, a golden morning of the most butterflies, the clearest sky.

Meanwhile Berenice had got a lawyer and had seen Honey at the jail. "I don't know what I've done," she kept saying. "Honey in this fix and now John Henry." Still, there was some part of Frances that did not even yet believe. But on the day he was to be taken to the family graveyard in Opelika, the same place where they had buried Uncle Charles, she saw the coffin, and then she knew. He came to her once or twice in nightmare dreams, like an escaped child dummy from the window of a department store, the wax legs moving stiffly only at joints, and the wax face wizened and faintly painted, coming toward her until terror snatched her awake. But the dreams came only once or twice, and the daytime now was filled with radar, school, and Mary Littlejohn. She remembered John Henry more as he used to be, and it was seldom now that she felt his presence—solemn, hovering, and ghost-gray. Only occasionally at twilight time or when the special hush would come into the room.

"I was by the store about school and Papa had a letter from Jarvis. He is in Luxembourg," said Frances. "Luxembourg. Don't you think that's a lovely name?"

Berenice roused herself. "Well, Baby—it brings to my mind soapy water. But it's a kind of pretty name."

"There is a basement in the new house. And a laundry room." She added, after a minute, "We will most likely pass through Luxembourg when we go around the world together."

Frances turned back to the window. It was almost five o'clock and the geranium glow had faded from the sky. The last pale colors were crushed and cold on the horizon. Dark, when it came, would come on quickly, as it does in wintertime. "I am simply mad about——" But the sentence was left unfinished for the hush was shattered when, with an instant shock of happiness, she heard the ringing of the bell.

ABOUT THE AUTHOR

When she was only twenty-three, CARSON MCCULLERS'
first novel, *The Heart Is a Lonely Hunter*, became a
literary sensation. Mrs. McCullers later wrote *Reflections
in a Golden Eye*, *The Member of the Wedding*, *The
Ballad of the Sad Café* and *Clock Without Hands*. Ed-
ward Albee's dramatization of *The Ballad of the Sad Café*
appeared on Broadway. *The Member of the Wedding* was
a prize-winning Broadway play and a motion picture.

Mrs. McCullers steadily acquired an international
reputation, with French and English critics ranking her
close to Faulkner and Hemingway. *Time* placed her
"among the top dozen contemporary American writers."
She died in 1967.

PRAISE FOR

BETTING THE RAINBOW

"Readers will root for their happily-ever-after and will be satisfied in the end . . . Gratifying emotional moments."
—*Kirkus Reviews*

"Ms. Thomas charms the reader once again with her sweet, warm touch at contemporary romance . . . in a story full of intriguing, distinctive characters who are vibrant, realistic people. Readers will feel right at home."   —*Affaire de Coeur*

"Thomas knocks it out of the park again . . . [she] is a master at creating damaged yet appealing characters, and their expressions of love—as siblings, as friends, as partners—are intense and beautiful."   —*Publishers Weekly*

"Told with a soft, gentle lyricism that parallels the town name, Thomas' tale takes readers on a lovely trip to a place that they'll hold in their hearts."   —*RT Book Reviews*

CAN'T STOP BELIEVING

"Filled with bittersweet endings and new beginnings, this is a heartwarming and heart-wrenching visit to Harmony. Prepare to laugh and shed some tears."   —*RT Book Reviews*

"Harmony, Texas, may be the most unusual series in the ever-growing subgenre of small-town romance."
—*The Romance Dish*

"[Thomas's] often beautiful turn of phrase and eloquent writing impart truths we spend lifetimes gleaning for ourselves . . . The best of the series so far."   —*All About Romance*

continued . . .

CHANCE OF A LIFETIME

"Tender, realistic, and insightful . . . Will appeal to fans of Debbie Macomber and Sherryl Woods." —*Library Journal*

"I've never met a Jodi Thomas book that wasn't absolutely dog-eared from being read many times. They are all like warm, cozy friends that just beg to be taken back from the bookshelves and revisited . . . [A] wonderful contemporary tale infused with humor and mystery." —*Fresh Fiction*

"Beautiful prose and a thought-provoking plot . . . [A] heartwarming romance and intriguing mystery. Like old friends, readers will love the chance to catch up with characters from previous tales." —*RT Book Reviews*

JUST DOWN THE ROAD

"A welcome return packed with cameos from familiar characters." —*Publishers Weekly*

"This book is like once again visiting old friends while making new ones and will leave readers eager for the next visit. A pure joy to read." —*RT Book Review*

THE COMFORTS OF HOME

"Even for readers new to the series, the intricate relationships between these affable men and eccentric women are easy to follow and even easier to love. Thomas skillfully juggles the many subplots, and the relationship between Ronelle and Marty, which inspires both to trust again, is especially touching." —*Publishers Weekly*

"There's always something brewing in Harmony and each story just adds to the richness of depth of the characters and town. If you haven't had a chance to meet the fine folks of Harmony, Texas, what are you waiting for?"
—*Fallen Angel Reviews*

"If you're a fan of small-town settings, heartwarming tales, and out-of-the-ordinary characters, you don't want to miss this book." —*Petit Fours and Hot Tamales*

Somewhere Along the Way

"A delightful story with as much love and warmth as there is terror and fear . . . This is terrific reading from page one to the end. Jodi Thomas is a passionate writer who puts real feeling into her characters." —*Fresh Fiction*

"Thomas once again brings to life this fascinating little Texas town and its numerous characters. The reader is expertly drawn into their lives and left eager to know what happens next." —*RT Book Reviews*

Welcome to Harmony

"The characters are delightful, and a subplot about mysterious fires balances the sweet stories about being and becoming family." —*Publishers Weekly*

"A fast-moving, engaging tale that keeps you turning pages . . . Thomas's characters become as familiar as family or friends." —*Fresh Fiction*

continued . . .

"A heartwarming tale, with plenty of excitement, *Welcome to Harmony* is Jodi Thomas all the way—super characters, lots of riveting subplots, and the background of a realistic Texas town. Don't miss this terrific novel."

—*Romance Reviews Today*

ADDITIONAL PRAISE FOR THE
NOVELS OF JODI THOMAS

"Compelling and beautifully written, it is exactly the kind of heart-wrenching, emotional story one has come to expect from Jodi Thomas."

—Debbie Macomber, #1 *New York Times* bestselling author

"Jodi Thomas is a masterful storyteller. She grabs your attention on the first page, captures your heart, and then makes you sad when it is time to bid her wonderful characters farewell. You can count on Jodi Thomas to give you a satisfying and memorable read."

—Catherine Anderson, *New York Times* bestselling author

"Thomas sketches a slow, sweet surrender."

—*Publishers Weekly*

One True Heart

JODI THOMAS

BERKLEY BOOKS, NEW YORK

THE BERKLEY PUBLISHING GROUP
Published by the Penguin Group
Penguin Group (USA) LLC
375 Hudson Street, New York, New York 10014

USA • Canada • UK • Ireland • Australia • New Zealand • India • South Africa • China

penguin.com

A Penguin Random House Company

ONE TRUE HEART

A Berkley Book / published by arrangement with the author

For information, address: The Berkley Publishing Group,
a division of Penguin Group (USA) LLC,
375 Hudson Street, New York, New York 10014.

ISBN: 978-0-425-26841-4

PUBLISHING HISTORY
Berkley mass-market edition / April 2015

PRINTED IN THE UNITED STATES OF AMERICA

10 9 8 7 6 5 4 3 2 1

Cover art by Jim Griffin. Handlettering by Ron Zinn.
Cover design by George Long.
Interior text design by Kristin del Rosario.

Chapter 1

MILLANIE MCALLEN USED THE BACKS OF THE AIRLINE SEATS to hop her way from the tiny toilet to the exit as the flight attendant pulled out her crutches from the front storage.

"Sorry, Captain McAllen, I thought everyone was off." The girl apologized with a quick smile at Millanie.

"No problem. I needed a few minutes to change." Millanie's army jacket rested over her arm. Her name bar and ribbons sparkled in the plane's lighting. She traded the attendant her uniform for the crutches as she read the girl's name tag. "Trudi, would you mind folding this into my bag? When I walk off, or rather limp off, this plane and into Texas, I'm no longer in the army."

While the attendant did as requested, Millanie tried to straighten the wrinkled long-sleeve blouse and gathered prairie skirt she'd changed into. They weren't her style, far too lacy, but when she'd bought them at the airport in Dallas all she'd been thinking about was something easy to get on over the cast on her right leg.

"I could call for a chair." Trudi looked at her with trained sympathy in her eyes. "This time of night they're never busy."

"No, thanks. I can handle this." After four plane changes and an all-night layover at LaGuardia with a leg hurting like they'd left shrapnel in it, simply walking out of the last airport seemed a piece of cake.

"What time of night is it?" Millanie guessed she sounded a bit crazy, but she'd lost all track of time flying from half-way around the world.

"Almost eleven. The airport will be closing soon. We're the last flight, I think."

Looping her purse over one shoulder so it was out of the way and wrapping the bag strings around the long strap, the newly decommissioned Captain McAllen hobbled off the plane. She refused to look back and take one more glance of sympathy. She'd had enough to last a lifetime.

The air was different here in West Texas. Unlike any-where in the world. Thin and pure with the smell of the earth spiced in by the wind. She hadn't been back to Harmony for six years, but she swore she could smell cattle and oil cir-culating in the air-conditioned breeze even inside the terminal.

Part of the crowd who'd come to stand and wave flags and cheer for hometown warriors returning on her flight were now milling around, picking up streamers they'd thrown and rolling up flags. She'd heard soldiers talking when they'd waited at the USO in Dallas. One had been told about the welcoming group that would be waiting for them when they landed in Amarillo. All the men got excited to be going home to a place where they would be welcomed by a crowd of friends, family, and fellow veterans.

Millanie had limped her way down half a mile of crowded gates at DFW to find a clothing store. It sold the gaudiest Western clothes in Texas. Her choices had been jeans with rhinestone crosses on her butt or a gathered skirt that looked like it had been hanging around since the sixties. Her choice was made simply on which would go over her cast.

Looking down at her attire, she decided her great-great-grandmother probably wore the same kind of outfit when she climbed off the covered wagon almost a hundred and fifty years ago to homestead. Patrick and Annie McAllen hadn't been much more than kids when they'd helped start Harmony. Maybe that was why, no matter where she traveled, the little town would always be home. Her roots were here and maybe, somehow, she'd find a life here.

She took a deep breath and smiled. Two more hours and she'd be able to rest. She'd be in Harmony.

By the time she made it downstairs to baggage claim, everyone else on her flight was long gone, and she'd sweated so much her brown curly hair lay plastered as if it were a swim cap. Her army-issued duffel bag was circling like a homely drunk after last call.

I can do this. She set her mind. *Grab the bag. Drag it the thirty feet to the rent-a-car booth.* Somehow she'd manage to get her right leg in the car and drive with her left.

The thought crossed her mind that she was an idiot for not calling Major Katherine Cummings or one of her dozen cousins in Harmony to come get her. But Millanie, as always, had to prove she could handle everything on her own. She'd been that way since she was nineteen and lost both her parents within a year.

Besides, the major had married the local funeral director and had a baby since they'd seen each other, and Millanie had no idea what her married name was. They weren't really friends, just two soldiers who had a town in common. Millanie had listed Harmony as her hometown and Katherine had been going there when she retired.

And now I'm returning, Millanie thought. Something she figured she'd do after twenty or thirty years in the army, not after twelve. One stranger in a crowd outside an embassy one night had changed all her plans and ended her career. Nothing personal. She was just in the wrong place when he wanted to kill himself.

Correction, the wound ended not only her career, but every plan she had ever made. Now she had no direction, no life, and no future in a job she loved. She was simply drifting, and any direction, even Harmony, Texas, seemed a good place to go.

As she reached down, trying to balance on one leg while she grabbed for the duffel bag, the strap of her purse slid forward, causing her to miss the handle.

"Damn," she mumbled.

A laugh came from just behind her.

She straightened and turned slowly, shifting her weight to regain her balance. No matter the injury, she'd be ready to fight. Twelve years as a soldier didn't wash away overnight.

As she'd been trained to do, she sized up the man standing a few feet away. Tall, lean, in his midthirties with hair too long to be stylish and intelligent eyes behind his dark-framed glasses. A teacher or an accountant by the way he dressed, unarmed of course, and single she'd guess. Men who had a woman in their lives gave it away in more ways than wearing a ring.

She relaxed and faked a smile.

"Sorry." He waved his hands in front of him as if erasing his outburst. "I shouldn't have laughed, but for a moment you looked like you were playing some kind of strange game people waste their money on at the county fair. Reaching for the impossible."

"You hang out at a lot of county fairs?" she asked, thinking this guy didn't look like he ever left the library, or study, or lab, or wherever geeks like him hid out. She could almost picture a tiny hoarder's apartment with stacks of books serving as tables. He probably drove one of those compact cars that could almost serve as a paperweight when it wasn't puttering along.

"I hang around them all the time. Can't stay away from the great fried food." He lied, of course. "How about I grab your bag when it comes around again as my apology?"

She nodded her thank-you, guessing he wouldn't be able

to lift her bag. But she wasn't a captain in the army anymore; maybe she shouldn't be so critical. She must simply look like a woman, poorly dressed and stranded in an airport. Maybe she'd play the role all the way to the rent-a-car counter. Then she'd say thank you and he'd leave, thinking he'd done his good deed for the day.

The bag circled and, to her surprise, he picked it up.

Without lowering her one piece of luggage to the ground, he said, "Where you headed? I'll carry it for you."

She smiled, thinking this plan was too easy. "I'm going to a bed-and-breakfast in a little town called Harmony, but that's too far for you to carry my bag. How about just dropping it at the car counter over there?"

They both started toward the far end of the terminal just as the light above the last car booth blinked twice and went out.

"Great," Millanie muttered. "Now I'll have to find a cab and stay in Amarillo tonight."

The professor-type next to her spoke. "You could ride with me. I'm heading that direction and would be happy to give you a lift."

No was already on her lips, but when she looked at him she almost laughed. The man couldn't look less like a serial killer. Odds were he'd be a safe driver who never traveled more than five miles over the speed limit. Her mother's warning of not getting in cars with strangers surely didn't apply to this geek.

When she didn't answer, he must have felt the need to testify. "You're in no danger, miss. I have a cabin out near Twisted Creek. It's no trouble to drop you in Harmony on the way." He didn't seem to be trying to talk her into the ride, just stating facts.

"I wouldn't mind paying for half the gas," she offered.

"Oh, no. I'll be happy for the company. A little conversation will keep me awake. I make this flight to visit my mother in Chicago, and this last leg on the road home always seems endless when I'm driving alone."

Now she knew she was safe. He'd been to visit his mother.

How sweet. He'd have to live near Harmony if he knew about Twisted Creek, and everyone out there knew everyone else.

"I'll hike out to the far parking lot and get my car. You wait here by the side door. I'll be right back." He shoved her duffel bag by the side entrance and disappeared.

She blinked, then had to force her eyes to stay open. The endless traveling without sleep was catching up to her. The stillness of the empty terminal offered her nothing to focus on, nothing to help her stay awake.

She wasn't sure which way the professor-type had gone. Between the pain in her leg and the lack of sleep, she might have drifted off while still on her feet, suspended like a fashion nightmare of a scarecrow between two crutches.

Moving through the side door, she welcomed the cool air of the Panhandle-Plains night. Since she'd been injured, her life had gone completely to hell. The doctors patched her up, but she'd had no close family to call. She could handle this part of the recovery on her own. Her one brother lived in New York and would have just complained that she should have listened to him and not joined the army anyway if she'd bothered to call him. Or worse, want her to come to New York until the cast was off.

Millanie needed peace, not people. She needed time to find a direction, to find a life.

Breathing deep relaxing breaths, she stared up at the full moon. In a few hours she'd be back to where she'd spent the first ten years of her life. The day before she'd turned eleven, her dad got transferred to Dallas. The family moved to a bigger house, and her father made more money, but she'd never felt she belonged there. Dallas was just where she lived for a while; Harmony would always be home. Harmony was a place where all the world seemed balanced, even if it was mostly just memories in her mind.

Out of the darkness behind the terminal building, Millanie heard movement and tried to focus her tired mind on reality.

The noise came again, muffled laughter, hurried footsteps.

Custodians taking a smoke break? Teenagers painting the outside of the building? Huge rats? She didn't really care. All she wanted to do was get to the room she'd rented at the bed-and-breakfast and sleep for three days.

Then, out of the corner of her eye, she saw them. Three men advancing in the tall, dry grass. For a moment she was back on embassy guard duty. Listening. Standing ready. On alert.

Opening her eyes, and her ears, she took in her surroundings in the circles of light that she stood between. Amarillo, Texas. Not another country. Not a war.

Her vision adjusted. The three men were shadows now, crouched low, hiding behind the bushes made from pampas grass. They were keeping off the sidewalk, but she could hear their every move.

She knew the moment they spotted her. Halted footsteps. Lowered voices.

The one in front straightened and slowed his pace. The other two followed. Now, the men who'd been creeping closer appeared to be simply walking toward her. They were young, loose jointed probably due to drugs or too much alcohol.

"Hey, lady, that door still open?" the leader asked casually, as if he couldn't have easily guessed she'd just come out.

She nodded, her tired body feeling adrenaline begin to pump. They all three wore old ball caps and dirty, baggy jeans low on their hips. Druggies, early twenties, probably armed but untrained. Out of habit, her mind filed facts about each.

Only one came nearer and looked in the terminal. "No one's around," he whispered back to the others.

"Well, let's grab it and go." The second one moved closer, his whisper carrying easily on the wind.

Millanie kept her head down as if she were paying them no attention, but their planning drifted to her in the midnight air.

"We could grab this woman's purse," one mumbled. "It's probably got more cash in it than we'd get for that laptop Cherie left out on her counter for us."

Millanie fought the urge to glance back and see which one of the rent-a-car counters had a laptop sitting out. She'd bet it was the counter below where the last light had blinked twice.

The leader took off his hat and scratched his head as if to stimulate his thinking. Then he nodded and all three advanced toward her.

"You waiting for somebody?" the leader shouted. "We could help you to your car, lady."

She forced her body to relax as she shifted just enough that her purse slipped to the concrete at her feet. The bag followed. "I'm fine." She finally turned her full attention to the pack. "You boys don't want to do this."

"What?" the talky one said, still edging closer. "We're just offering to help a poor lady in distress. How about you let me carry that expensive-looking purse you just dropped? I don't mind taking it off your hands."

"Step away," Millanie said with cold calmness. "I don't want to hurt you."

All three laughed and showed their teeth like wild dogs.

"Step away," she repeated just as the leader jumped forward, bending to grab the bag at her feet.

The instinct to react, trained into her muscles by practice and combat, fired her movements.

She swung her crutch, hitting the leader in the knee and sending him down hard on the concrete. When the second one advanced from the other side, planning to grip one of her arms, she let the other crutch fall against the building as she delivered a chopping blow across his throat, sending him to the ground fighting to draw air.

The third man had crept forward but hesitated when one of his friends gasped and the other began to cry as he whined that the bitch had broken his knee.

Millanie lifted her crutch as if it were a rifle and shoved it hard into the third man's abdomen before he could react.

When he winced in pain she said, "Pick up your friends and get out of here. I'm too tired to turn you three in, but if I ever see any of you again, you'll be sorry."

Holding his middle, the coward of the group, and probably the smartest, helped his friends limp away. Within seconds they were no more than whispered swear words in the darkness.

Millanie leaned against the building and closed her eyes as the sound of a car pulling around to the side of the building reached her tired senses. She remained still as the vehicle stopped and the driver jumped out.

"I'm sorry I took so long," an educated, low voice said as her professor/accountant approached her. "Oh, you've dropped your crutch. You poor thing. Let me help you."

A strong arm circled her waist and helped her to a battered van. She made no protest as the tall man from Twisted Creek settled her into the passenger seat, carefully lifting her broken leg and locking her seat belt. His hands were gentle, a caretaker's hands, as he spread a blanket over her and propped her cast up with a huge stuffed toy unicorn.

Of all the questions she could have asked this stranger, the one thing she could think of after he loaded her duffel bag in the back and climbed into the driver's seat was, "You carry a unicorn in your van?"

"It's my little sister's. She still believes in them."

Millanie knew she was safe. No man who carries around his sister's toy could be a threat to her. "How old is your sister?" she asked as he pulled onto the highway.

"Twenty-four. She's a fortune-teller at the bookstore in Harmony. For your own safety I'd advise you to avoid her."

He continued, but she was too far gone into sleep to think how strange his words sounded.

Chapter 2

THE HIGHWAY BETWEEN AMARILLO AND
HARMONY

AS HE DROVE THROUGH THE NIGHT, DREW CUNNINGHAM
decided he loved summers in Texas. Almost midnight and still
not enough humidity in the air to allow a mosquito to spit.

He glanced over at Sleeping Beauty in the passenger seat.
The lady in distress with her broken leg and tired green eyes
hadn't said a word since she'd settled into his van. He could
have raped and murdered her a half dozen times by now, or
married her off to some guy in a commune so she could be
his eighteenth wife. She already had the clothes for that
career.

If he weren't such a nice guy, he could have robbed her,
stolen her hundred-pound duffel bag, and rolled her off in
a ditch somewhere. She was so sound asleep she probably
wouldn't wake up until day after tomorrow if it didn't rain,
and it never rained in Texas. Not this year.

And another thing, he mentally corrected himself. *I'm
not a nice guy.*

Nice guys finish last. Nice guys never get the girl. His sister had been drilling that into his head every time she'd seen him for six months. Only her lectures were a waste of time. Everyone out by the lake where he lived knew him, and they all knew he was a nice guy. So, little hope of changing his image at thirty-four.

He went back to thinking about all the terrible things that could have happened to Sleeping Beauty if he hadn't come along. By the time he saw the first lights of Harmony, Texas, he'd laid out a whole scenario of how the end of the world had hit while she slept, and come morning she'd wake up to a town full of zombies and have no idea who to trust.

Drew frowned. Now he'd have to keep her safe and teach her all the facts on how to live among the undead. It wouldn't be easy for her to run in the cast, and with those clothes she might as well be waving a "come get me" flag at the monsters.

Tossing his glasses on the dash, he studied her in the blinks of the passing streetlights. She was pretty, in the down-deep, no-makeup kind of way few women are pretty. Smooth skin, dark brown hair, lips that would probably keep him awake tonight.

He couldn't help but wonder why she'd come to Harmony, a crippled-up woman with no family to meet her. It wasn't like this little town had healing springs or a world-class health spa. Harmony was barely on the map. If the world did really come to an end, the people around here would probably miss the apocalypse.

Drew turned off Main Street into what everyone called the old part of town. Houses were big, and every one on the street built different from any other. Narrow streets made it easy for old elms to cross over and touch. A heroine would live on a street like this, or maybe an old lady who'd had every pet she'd ever cared about stuffed. In these historical few blocks all the legends and secrets of the town were probably hidden away in attic trunks.

Sleeping Beauty said she was headed to a bed-and-breakfast, and as far as he knew there was only one in town:

Winter's Inn. The old place was run by the crazy woman who also thought she was in charge of the local writers' club. The group had asked him to speak a few times.

Martha Q Patterson made Drew think of stories about serial killers who preyed on chubby little women who talked all the time. Rumor was she'd had seven husbands. Some said she killed off half by talking them to death.

He smiled. Martha Q had told him that he made her wish for "afternoon delights," which made him more frightened of her than he usually was of the fairer sex. He had the feeling she wasn't kidding about the delights part and she had a dozen rooms at her place where they could work out the details. Just driving down her street and remembering her made his imagination move to overdrive. What if she'd stuffed those seven husbands and they were sitting in her parlor right now?

He pulled into the Winter's Inn's drive just as the image of old Martha Q, wrapped in a sheet, hanging from her third-story window flashed in his mind. That sight would be a great opening to a thriller. Maybe the ghosts of her dead lovers had killed her. Only with her weight, she'd be like Outlaw Jack Ketchum in the Old West. He'd gotten so fat on Clayton, New Mexico's jail food while he waited for the hangman to arrive, the rope had snapped Jack's head right off when the floor went out from under him. One of the not-so-romantic Western stories.

Drew shook off his imagination and tried to stay in reality at least long enough to get Sleeping Beauty delivered.

The porch light at Winter's Inn was burning bright. Foot-high LED lights, made to look like daisies, lined both sides of the walk. Drew had the depressing impression he was delivering Hansel and Gretel to the cottage in the woods. Maybe he should run up and ask if there was room at the inn before waking the beauty beside him.

As he stepped out of his van, Martha Q opened the door and waved at him just like the witch in the fairy tale must have done to the siblings. She was dressed in a short summer robe with huge pink birds painted on it. With the belt tied around her waist the flamingos appeared to be choking.

Drew fought the urge to throw the van in reverse and burn rubber, but then what would he do with Beauty?

Having no choice, he cut the engine and circled the rusty old vehicle to open the passenger door. There she was, dreaming away. Her warm brown hair, her perfect complexion, her kissable mouth.

Without much thought, he leaned in and brushed her lips with his as he reached to unbuckle her seat belt.

She made a little sound in her sleep and he fought the urge to deepen the kiss. It had been so long since he'd kissed a woman.

"That you, Andrew Cunningham?" Martha Q yelled loud enough to awaken the block. "I didn't know you'd be bringing my guest. When she called from London, I decided she couldn't be from around here even if her name is McAllen." The round little lady had waddled halfway down the walk. "If she was kin to any McAllen, she'd be staying with them, I'd bet. Probably one of them genealogy types tracing her roots."

Martha Q didn't offer to help, but continued to talk.

Drew brushed Sleeping Beauty's cheek. "Wake up, Miss McAllen. We're here." He fought the urge to kiss her again. That first kiss had certainly brought him fully awake.

In the background he heard Martha Q saying that Hank Matheson told her if another person came here claiming kin he planned to take a power saw to a few branches of the family tree. McAllens and Mathesons reproduced like rabbits around these parts.

"Rise and shine, sleepyhead," Drew whispered near her ear. "You're at Winter's Inn."

Green eyes opened and stared at him. "Who are you?"

He couldn't believe she didn't seem the least frightened. "I'm just your driver, miss." He pointed at the backside of Martha Q as she leaned over, straightening one of the daisy night lights. "And that is the innkeeper at Winter's Inn."

Sleeping Beauty yawned. "Noisy one, isn't she?"

Drew couldn't hold back a grin. "She has to make that noise if there's a chance she might be backing up."

While Martha Q rambled on about how dark it was around her place, Drew helped his passenger out of his van. "Just hold on to me and I'll carry your crutches. I don't think the walk's wide enough to maneuver on crutches in the dark."

She looped her arm over his shoulder and he circled her waist. At six feet one he rarely saw a woman near his height, but she was within three inches. They progressed down the walkway, her cast taking out every other LED light.

"I'm Millanie McAllen," she said as she hopped along.

"Andrew Cunningham. My friends call me Drew."

"Thank you, Drew, for bringing me here. I owe you one."

He knew he was probably being forward, but the lady was plastered against his side. "You staying long, Millie?"

She looked up with those tired green eyes, and he knew she was a woman who never lied. "I've always been called Millanie."

"All right. You staying long, Millanie?"

"I don't know," she finally answered. "Getting here was my first plan of action. I'll think of my second when I've slept the clock around and eaten a few meals."

Millanie McAllen might think she knew exactly where on the planet she was, but Drew saw the truth in those beautiful eyes.

She was lost. Had no direction. He knew the look well. He'd been there once.

"Andrew!" Martha Q yelled. "Any chance you two are going to make it in to sign the register before dawn? I can't stand here waiting if she's not interested."

Sleeping Beauty looked directly at him when she answered Martha Q. "I'm interested."

Chapter 3

WINTER'S INN

FROM THE SHADOWS OF HUNDRED-YEAR-OLD ELM TREES
Beau Yates watched a man almost carrying a woman with
a broken leg into the bed-and-breakfast. For a moment he
thought of offering help, but if he did he'd have to talk to
Martha Q and maybe Mrs. Biggs. He loved the old ladies
dearly, but he didn't feel like seeing anyone tonight. He was
just passing through.

The air was still and all the sounds and smells of the old
downtown area seemed to circle around him, carrying memories. The aroma of popcorn from the movie theater, the
faint beat of the drummer playing above the band at Buffalo's, the hollow sound of his boots tapping against the
sidewalk.

There was a time, when he'd just been starting out in the
music business, that he'd walk these sleeping streets for
hours listening to the beat of the town. Only now, his world
seemed to be spinning in double time.

Beau thought of how it had first been when he'd played

his guitar all day, writing songs and hoping his neighbor would cook something so he could eat. He'd been so happy when he got his first gig at Buffalo's Bar. The money wasn't much, but they were professionals, even if part of their pay came in a plastic basket with fries.

Now, he packed in thousands and had more money in the bank than he could count, but it was the music that drove him, and he could still count his true friends on one hand.

Funny, the old woman yelling on the porch of the bed-and-breakfast was one of them. Martha Q might nag him to cut his hair and ask him every time she saw him why he hadn't found a girl, but she'd also been the one who'd loaned him a thousand dollars when his car broke down in Winslow. She'd thump him hard if she heard him say he thought of her as a grandmother, and then she'd walk right up to Harley at the bar and tell the old biker that he should clean up his place when a big star like Beau Yates played there.

He crossed her lawn and slid down six feet to the bottom of the dried-up creek bed. The shortcut took him into the back of the Blue Moon Diner, and another few yards got him to the bar's parking lot.

Beau didn't want to talk to anyone. He just wanted to slip into the place and listen for a while.

It was late, maybe a half hour before closing. Few baskets of food remained on the tables; folks ordered drinks at this hour. Cowboys were leading their ladies around the floor to a slow song. Foreplay, Beau thought. That was always Harley's idea. Have the band play slow-country-loving songs so the crowd would leave thinking of romance and not complain when he blinked the lights and announced it was closing time.

Beau stood in the corner and watched, feeling like he was home. Harley yelled last call. The band played three more songs and then, to slight applause, picked up their gear and headed out the back door.

He waited as Harley locked up, leaving the empty bottles on the table as he rarely did. As he circled the bar the room grew darker, and then the huge, tattooed owner walked up the stairs to his quarters. The low glow of lights near the stage and the exit signs gave off a smoky illumination.

Beau walked over to where Harley had hung Beau's guitar after he'd been inducted into the Grand Ole Opry last year. Without hesitating, he took it down and pulled a chair to the stage. Amid the smell of beer and sweat and cheap perfume lingering in the dusty air, Beau began to play.

The songs, his songs, flowed out of him as if pieces of his life danced through the air. His first date, his fear of thinking he might never make it in the business, his loneliness of never being able to hold on to a girl long enough to fall in love and, worse, of never having anyone, including his parents, hang on to him.

After an hour, he returned the guitar to its place and walked out the back door of the bar, making sure it locked behind him. He crossed to the creek bed and followed it out to the edge of town, where his tour bus waited to continue the drive to Nashville.

He needed the music. He was addicted to it, but it couldn't be all there was for him. He wanted more. A life not only in the lights. A love who didn't care what he did for a living. Beau had no idea how he'd find what he was looking for, but he knew where to start.

Harmony. Where he was born. Where he'd learned music in his father's church and how to play from his grandfather. Where he'd first stood on his own five years ago. Someday he'd stop the double-time world and step off and, when he did, he knew his boot would land on Texas soil.

Chapter 4

WHEELER FARM

JOHNNY WHEELER WAITED UNTIL WELL AFTER MIDNIGHT before turning every light off in his big old rambling farm-house. He walked out the back door with a shovel in one hand and a grain sack in the other. He planned to bury the memory of Scarlet tonight if it was the last thing he did.

The moon offered plenty of light as he walked the rim of the ravine on the north side of his place. When a car passed, he just stood still, knowing it unlikely anyone would notice him. Across the road was an old rest stop used for picnics in the summer. Johnny figured it was too late for dinner out and too early for teenage parkers.

Johnny had to find just the right spot for what he thought would be his one love. Scarlet was a choosy woman; any old hole wouldn't do. Once, she'd dragged him around the mall in Amarillo three times before she found just the right nightgown for their honeymoon to Hawaii. Then she'd made him drive back the next day and take it back because she said the color didn't look good in daylight. He'd tried to help her with the flawed logic, but she didn't appreciate it.

Scarlet was picky, plain and simple, and now he'd take his time figuring out where to dig.

Finally, a half mile away from his house, he found the circle of dirt about five feet across that was surrounded by rocks. Weeds as high as his knee grew up in the place where a plow had never cut. His boot caught on one of the rocks and he took a tumble into the weeds. Several other boulders decided to join the fight, bruising his face and bloodying his left hand, but Johnny persisted in the burying.

Apparently, the earth didn't want any part of Scarlet either, but this was one battle he planned to win.

Propping his worn Justin boot on one of the rocks, Johnny opened the sack. He'd packed everything Scarlet had left behind, except him. Two pair of panties he'd found under the bed. Lotions, creams, and serums she was always lathering on herself. A picture of her and her best friend, Max. He'd found the photo in a book on her side of the bed that had been lying there since they married.

At the last minute, as he walked out, Johnny tossed in the funny playlike birdcages she called decorations and a few of the garden gnomes she thought looked good by the back door. If he didn't have Scarlet to put up with, he didn't have to tolerate her junk.

Johnny stared at the picture of his wife and Max in the moonlight, barely making out two people smiling. Hell, he'd thought Max was gay until he'd come home early to find them hugging just like they were doing in the picture. Only somehow, the day he'd found them, they'd both forgotten their clothes.

He swore. That had been the first hint he'd noticed that Max wasn't gay. Johnny decided that at twenty-seven, he should have known better than to trust the smooth-talking best friend of his wife.

Johnny rifled through combs with some of her bleached blond hair still in them. A nightgown he'd bought her in

Hawaii that she never wore. One shoe. Birth control pills. Those she'd probably miss. Several letters tied up with a ribbon. She'd said they were from her mother in Seattle, but he'd opened one earlier and found her mom signed them, "Love, Frank."

Somewhere about the time he'd collected all she left behind, Johnny figured out that he had to be too dumb to breathe. When it came to women, most men, including him, were cross-eyed. They seemed to see two of everything. Two big blue eyes looking lovable. Two long legs heading toward heaven. Two breasts peeping up as if saying hello.

He decided if men really saw most women, there wouldn't be a next generation.

He closed the sack. Scarlet was dead to him, and tonight he'd bury her memory and never think of her again. He'd wasted three years trying to make her happy, and now it was about time to get on with his life.

In the moonlight he dug the hole three feet deep and plenty wide. Then he dropped in what remained of Scarlet and covered the junk with dirt. Just to make sure some coyote didn't dig her up, he used his shovel to play golf with the rocks nearby so the opening would be forever blocked from future digging. No one would ever find Scarlet's left-behinds.

As he walked back across his dry farmland, he calculated that at twenty-seven he had about fifty or sixty years to live with what a fool he'd been. She'd gone through his savings within six months after they married, then complained every day he worked that he wasn't spending any time with her. When he didn't work, she complained they didn't have any money. On and on it went. The house was too small. They needed a pool. She never had anything to wear. He wasn't understanding, or sympathetic or empathetic. Hell, he didn't even know what that meant, so he might as well add *dumb* to her list. She was always telling him how great Max was on the computer. Johnny hadn't even seen the need to buy one.

Johnny stopped walking and debated hitting himself in the head with the shovel. "It's over. Stop thinking about her!" he yelled to himself as he lifted the shovel near his temple just to prove he meant business if his mind didn't turn off the flood of memories that had been drowning him for a week.

Luckily, before he beat himself to death with the shovel, Johnny noticed all the lights were on at his place. For a second he thought she might have come back to collect the minerals in his blood, and then he spotted his brother's pickup parked out front.

Wendell Wheeler, Wen; for short, was the one person he knew who got his days and nights mixed up when he was a baby and never recovered. He'd driven everyone in the family crazy running around all night and sleeping all day until he finally started school. Then he slept there. Their dad made him move out to a small apartment in the barn when he was twelve. He made so much noise out there the cow quit giving milk, but their dad said it was a small price to pay for the rest of the family to get some sleep.

"Evening, John," Wendell yelled from the porch. "You out planting by the moon?"

"Nope," Johnny lied. "Just taking a walk, just me and my shovel."

Wendell offered him a cold beer. "Here, take one of my drinks. I just got them out of your fridge. You might want to think about shopping, brother, you're running low."

Johnny took the bottle and sat down on the top step of the porch. "What brings you out here? Shouldn't you be at work? Who's watching Harmony's shopping center?"

"I asked off when I heard Scarlet left you. I didn't know if you'd be celebrating or crying in your beer, but I wanted to be with you."

"She left me for Max Dewy."

"I thought he was gay." Wendell looked shocked.

"I don't think that rumor is true." Johnny found little comfort in knowing his brother was as dumb as he was. "Not from what I saw, but he's probably real happy right now and she'll keep him that way until the ten thousand she pulled out of our checking account runs out."

Both brothers gave up talking and just drank for a while. Finally, Johnny broke the silence. "Did you ever think that maybe we're doing something wrong in this life?" Johnny had always thought of himself as fairly good looking, and he'd had enough brains to finish two years of college before he started farming. Only luck never seemed to go his way. Not in love or business.

Wendell shook his head as he tossed his beer bottle into the flower bed, taking out the last garden gnome. "Maybe you, John, but I know I'm doing it all right. Staying single suits me just fine. Play the field."

Johnny didn't bother to tell Wendell that he probably didn't even know where the field was, and working as a mall guard wasn't exactly living an exciting life. "I just want to settle down with someone I can love and who can love me. I want to raise my crops and maybe someday a few kids. That's all. Is that too much to ask?"

Wendell thought as he stared at the moon. Finally he answered, "That's boring, John. No wonder every girl you ever had ran. I love you, brother, but watching okra grow is more exciting most days than talking to you. Nothing ever happens to you. You got about as much depth as spilled table salt."

Johnny hated the thought that his brother was right. He was boring. He always had been. Standing, he stomped his way across the porch. "Good night, Wen. I'll see you tomorrow."

"Wait. While you're drowning in your bad luck, think about me. You got the great build, the looks, Hell, you even got Momma's brown eyes. If you can't find a woman, what chance do I have?"

Johnny didn't feel very lucky. "Right, Wen, I pretty much emptied the good side of the gene pool before you came along. Too bad you got all the luck."

Wendell stood. "What you going to do tomorrow?"

Johnny glanced back and smiled. "Change."

Chapter 5

WINTER'S INN

THE STRANGE MAN WHO'D DRIVEN HER TO HARMONY stood behind her, his hands lightly bracing her waist as Millanie McAllen wrote her name in the guest book of an old inn that looked to have been one of the first homes in Harmony.

"Should I lay out towels for one or two?" Martha Q asked in her not-so-subtle way of seeing if Drew Cunningham planned to stay.

Millanie was exhausted and the warmth of Drew near her made her want to cuddle close to this man she'd just met, but she had no plans of sharing a bed with a man she didn't know.

She glanced over her shoulder and caught the shock on his face that the innkeeper would even ask if he planned to stay. He obviously was a very proper gentleman with his professor clothes and polished manner. Men like him would never have a one-night stand.

When she looked back at Martha Q, she saw the slightly

raised eyebrow as the corner of her lip twitched. The innkeeper was having a joke, knowing Drew wouldn't be staying. Knowing she was embarrassing him.

Millanie decided to surprise this woman who obviously thought she knew the shy, sweet man who'd taken the time to be a Good Samaritan. She leaned in, pressing against his side, and whispered loud enough for Martha Q to hear, "You're welcome to stay, but I know you have to get back to Twisted Creek tonight."

So he wouldn't say anything and ruin the innkeeper's shock, Millanie kissed him, quickly, a short, impersonal kiss. He took her full attack without retreat, which surprised her. Maybe he wasn't as shy as she'd thought. She was so tired her judgment might be slipping.

When she pulled away she'd expected him to be angry or flustered at her action, but he simply studied her and acted like he'd kissed her before. Her action hadn't surprised or shocked him. More accurately, she'd have to say, intrigued him.

Now it was Millanie's turn to be surprised.

"Well, I'll say good night," Martha Q managed as she moved away to allow them some privacy. "Your room is right behind you, dear. Breakfast is between eight and ten on Saturdays."

"Don't set me a place. I plan to sleep late." Millanie pulled away from Drew Cunningham as she took her crutches.

"I'll get your bag," he said, already halfway to the door.

She left the door to her room open and had made it to the bay window when he rushed back.

"Well, that's it. Delivered safe and sound, Miss McAllen. I hope you have a pleasant stay here in Harmony."

"Thank you," she managed. "You're very kind." She almost added, *and forgettable*. He was totally one of those men who didn't linger in a woman's mind. If she saw him a week or a year from now she'd have trouble remembering anything about him, except for the kiss maybe. That had been nice.

He took a step toward her. "About that kiss," he said, as if planning to apologize for something he'd done.

"Sorry about the kiss." She stopped him. "I shouldn't have done that. It's not like me. You do know the landlady was teasing you about the towels. I just wanted to fire back, but I may have laid it on a little thick."

He opened his mouth as if to apologize for her apology, and then he stopped and grinned. "You're right. Martha Q was probably shocked by such a display. Maybe we should talk about the damage you've done to my reputation."

She laughed. The geek was making fun of her and she found it sweet. Embarrassing him had been unkind, but his good-natured comeback let her know he'd forgiven her.

"That's why"—he took another step—"I'm giving the kiss back." His hand slid around her waist and pulled her against him so fast the crutches tumbled.

She grabbed his shoulders to make sure she didn't fall as his mouth captured hers. There was nothing shy or hesitant about the way this man kissed. He was taking no prisoners.

Maybe it was because she was tired or maybe she just wanted to feel something other than pain, but Millanie let the kiss wash over her. His fingers dug into her hair and fisted in her curls, turning her head slightly so he could deepen the kiss. His warm body felt so good pressed against her that all she wanted to do was drink him in.

The kiss turned tender, loving almost. A kiss between lovers who knew how each liked to be kissed.

Slowly, he pulled her deeper into the pure pleasure of feeling wanted to the point of losing control. No one except doctors and therapists had touched her in so long. It felt wonderful to have a real hug and know the man giving it was attracted to her.

No, not just attracted to her. This kiss was born of a need, almost as if this moment might be life and death for them both. She held on tight, wanting what he offered. Wanting to feel something more than duty or pain. This man was no one she'd ever get to know, but for a few heartbeats he filled her senses.

When he finally raised his head, his hands still caressed

the small of her back. "You're tired, Millie; you need some sleep." His words were those of a stranger, but his touch seemed familiar.

She nodded, too surprised to form thoughts. Drew was so far out of the realm of anyone she would ever be interested in, yet right now she didn't want to let him go.

He shifted and lowered her to the window seat. "Get some sleep. We'll continue this discussion later."

He was gone before she could ask what discussion.

She leaned forward and grabbed one crutch, hopped to the bathroom, stripped off her clothes, locked the door, and fell into bed.

Twelve hours later she woke, realizing she hadn't moved all night. It took all her effort to climb out of the warm covers, put on a sweatshirt and baggy shorts from her bag, and unlock the door.

The aroma of coffee greeted her.

She followed the smell to a kitchen three doors away and found a thin, white-haired woman making bread.

"Morning." The granny type smiled up at her. "I'm Mrs. Biggs, the cook here. I kept the coffee warming thinking you'd be wanting it when you woke."

Millanie collapsed in the nearest chair and took a cup. Before it was cool enough to drink, a plate of sandwiches and cookies sat before her.

Mrs. Biggs was polite but didn't fuss over her. Millanie liked that.

"Did you just get out of the army, dear?" Mrs. Biggs pointed at the shorts and shirt that both were stamped with the *ARMY* logo.

"Yes." Millanie took one of the sandwiches and stuffed it in her mouth. She wasn't ready for all the questions yet.

Mrs. Biggs seemed to understand. "With that leg, I'd be happy to deliver you a tray to your room every morning."

"Thanks." Millanie didn't want to think about how terrible she probably looked. She took a few cookies off the plate before Mrs. Biggs kicked her out. The clock had probably circled twice since she'd bothered to comb her hair.

"Room service is no trouble. You're our only guest. We'd love to pamper you. I'll bring breakfast at nine and serve tea anywhere you like at three. The porch might be a good spot this time of year. You'd rest easy in one of those wicker rockers. It has a stool that rocks right along with the chair."

"You're very kind." She downed her cup of coffee and two more cookies. "Do you know that man who delivered me here last night? Andrew Cunningham."

"Oh, yes, Dr. Andrew Cunningham. He's lectured at our church a few times. Very intelligent. I feel smarter just sitting in the audience."

Millanie didn't look up. If she had she might have been tempted to call the sweet woman a liar. No man who kissed like hell on wheels would be lecturing at a church. Mrs. Biggs hadn't seen Drew. Maybe she had him mixed up with someone else. He did have that nice-guy look about him; it had almost fooled her.

"Tall guy, thin, looks like a teacher or an accountant?"

"That's Andrew," Mrs. Biggs nodded. "I'm not likely to get him mixed up with those two hulks who came by yesterday to see if a McAllen had arrived."

Millanie pulled out of her own thoughts and paid attention. "Mrs. Biggs. No one knows I'm here." The sweet old lady must be losing her mind. "So no one would have called for me yesterday."

"Maybe I'm mistaken. I wish Martha Q had been here. She would have asked them questions. They wore dark suits as if it were their uniform. Dark glasses too. Both wide shouldered and frowns firm on their mouths."

"Did they ask for me by name?" Millanie tried again.

"No, dear, they asked for Captain McAllen. I told them we had a McAllen, but it wasn't the one they were looking for. Now, seeing those clothes, I may have made a mistake." Mrs. Biggs hurried out the kitchen door toward a phone ringing somewhere down the hall.

Millanie let her mind drift. In a town with so many McAllens there could be another captain besides her. She had no idea what the two men had wanted, but it probably wasn't her. She'd told no one where she was headed when she left the hospital in Germany. Her army days were over. Now all she had to do was finish recovering and find a life.

When she'd finished both the plate of sandwiches and all the cookies, Millanie limped back to her room and found extra towels, a box of trash bags, and duct tape. Everything she needed for a proper shower.

An hour later she felt almost human. Except for underwear, everything in her bag was either army issue or too small to fit over the cast. She made it out to the porch with her laptop and propped herself up in a huge old wicker chair. About the time Mrs. Biggs delivered afternoon tea to the porch, Millanie had ordered a half dozen outfits online, along with several books she'd always wanted to read, and chocolates for fun.

After enjoying the warm tea and blueberry scones, she lay back among the extra pillows Martha Q thought she might need and decided to take a nap. Now and then a car would pass or she'd hear the bells in the clock tower, but peace surrounded her. She'd finally made it home. Nothing in Harmony had changed since she'd been eleven. She'd visited now and then over the years for family weddings and once for a family reunion, but after her parents passed away, it had been too painful. Six years ago she'd returned for one day, her grandmother's funeral. She'd expected the sadness to still be there, but no sorrow remained. Only peace. Good memories. Home.

Maybe she'd stay here a while. Maybe she'd go to New York and visit her brother. Maybe she'd stay on Winter's Inn Bed-and-Breakfast's porch and just daydream the rest of the summer away.

But one man, one kiss, kept walking through her thoughts. She didn't know who or what he really was, but no man who kissed like that could be the shy professor type. He had to have a wild side, a reckless past, an alternate life he didn't let the people of Harmony know about.

She had to see him again and she wasn't sure if it was because the kiss had affected her or because she'd misjudged him so completely as harmless. For twelve years her job, her life, had depended on being able to size people up at first glance.

Millanie's memories blended with her dreams as she drifted. At thirty-two she'd never loved any man, at least not long enough or hard enough to give up the army. She'd had many men as friends, and a few had become casual lovers, but none made her think of settling down.

Andrew Cunningham wouldn't either. When she got to know him better, if she got to know him at all, she was sure he'd disappoint her. Or, worse, *she'd* disappoint him.

Evening shadows stretched across the porch when she finally awoke. The outline of a stocky man blinked into her peripheral vision and for a second she stiffened, preparing for trouble, and then she saw the uniform he wore.

Reality pulled her fully awake and she turned to the man leaning against the railing a few feet away. Short, thirty pounds overweight, and silver-gray hair. He was older, but she knew him immediately. "Sergeant Hughes." Shoving her hair away from her eyes, she stared at the induction officer who'd sworn her into the army twelve years ago.

"You remembered me." He smiled. "I'm touched, Millanie, or should I say Captain McAllen?"

"I'm out of the service now," she said, tapping her leg. "But I'll never forget you." She'd skipped her graduation from Texas Tech to talk to him. They'd spent hours planning what she'd like to do as a career. That evening Sergeant Hughes and his wife had taken her out to dinner to celebrate the degree she'd earned. It wasn't part of his job, he just didn't want her to be alone on such an important day. Graduating and joining the army. Stepping out of one life and into another.

"How's the boss?" Millanie remembered that was what he'd called his wife.

"Hard to live with as ever. Now she's a grandmother. I haven't seen an R-rated movie in years and I know all the words to the *Frozen* songs."

Millanie smiled, remembering how much she liked Hughes. "You just come by to check on me, Sarge?"

The smile slid off his face. "I wish it were that, kid, but I'm here with orders for you."

"I'm out of the army, remember. Odds are this leg will never heal to normal. At best, I'll limp. At worst, I'll always wear a brace. So, no more assignments. No more orders."

Hughes didn't offer her any sympathy. "The higher-ups are delaying those discharge papers for a while. There's something Uncle Sam wants you to do here, Captain."

For a blink she wondered if she might be still dreaming. What could she do for her country in Harmony? With one leg in a cast the only assignment she was ready for would be "speed bump". The height of her agenda lately seemed to be eating, sleeping, and kissing some guy she couldn't figure out.

Sergeant Hughes pulled up a ladder-back chair that crackled with his weight. He leaned in close. "I can't do much explaining. I think they thought you wouldn't talk to anyone but someone you knew, so they dug around and found me. The government wants you to do what you've been doing for twelve years, Captain. They want you to do it here."

"That makes no sense. Nothing ever happens in Harmony. There is no threat here." She considered the possibility that Hughes had cracked up in his old age. "I'm trained to spot the needle in the haystack. The one person out of hundreds who might be a threat to all."

"This time you won't be looking for someone who is about to cause trouble. This time they want you to look for someone trying to blend in and be invisible. A year ago the feds figured out that a man with ties to funding trouble all over the world just might be from, or hiding out in, the Panhandle of Texas. We've got men in Lubbock, Amarillo, and Plainview, but this guy is leaving little paper trail. He could be anywhere."

Millanie shook her head. "I can't help."

"You can, Captain. You'll take this assignment." He softened slightly. "It's what you're trained for, spotting people who don't belong. Plus you know folks here, or have family who know everyone for a hundred miles around. This guy may be faking it, but he doesn't think like most people do. He thinks of hurting and killing people as a political statement, not a crime. He lives by a different set of rules and he's been here long enough to think he's safe."

Millanie's mind began to work. "He'd be hiding out here, not from around here. He'd stick out unless he was very careful."

Hughes smiled. "Right, and my guess is he'd be rich or close to it. He'd have all the updated computer equipment. Maybe a private plane. Definitely a fast car. Correction, he'll have more than one."

"If he's smart, he'd be social too. Folks would be quick to point out a loner who moved to town." She could almost see him. "He'd be involved in the community. Maybe join a church or donate to a cause for charity. He might even date, or marry a local girl. Men who have years to embed go deep, and then when it gets too hot for them, they walk away from everything, including families they've started."

The sergeant laughed. "That's it, use that brain. Keep your eyes open. Get involved and when you spot him, watch his every move while we investigate him. Men who make up their history always have holes."

Millanie had no choice but to accept the assignment. "What else do you know about him, Sergeant?"

"Nothing except for a message intercepted from a pilot saying he had to make sure he had enough gas in a plane to make it to the Panhandle. He crashed over near Pampa with enough arms onboard to start a small war. The guy embedded here had been giving the orders, but the pilot was a ghost. No ID and burned too badly to check fingerprints."

"We'd better add a small airstrip to the list of things about the man we're looking for." She knew several of the big ranches had strips. Not that they needed them. In most places the land was so flat a plane could land just about anywhere.

Millanie mentally started a list of what she'd need. A car. A secure computer. A contact person she could trust. A weapon.

A half hour later when Hughes stood, she hugged him, knowing that she probably wouldn't see him again until someone found this threat among them. The next and only person she'd discuss her progress with would be her contact. Not even her family could know what she was doing.

"A contact will get in touch with you. He'll have the computer skills you'll need for tracking. I'll have the rest of what you need sent over."

She watched him walk away, already filing away possibilities of where to start in her brain.

Millanie stared out at the shady street in the heart of town. Sarge didn't know it, but he'd just given her a reason to stop feeling sorry for herself and wake up. She could do this mission. It was what she'd been trained for. If evil lived in this town, she'd find it.

Chapter 6

Drew Cunningham planned to drop by and check on Millanie McAllen at the bed-and-breakfast, but calamity came in small doses. He taught a class at the little college in Clifton Creek, an hour's drive from his home. One flat tire. Then Drew ate lunch on the drive home. One spilled drink. All afternoon he worked at his computer until he had to stop and fight a gang of wasps who'd decided his cabin would make a good home for them. Three stings. Toss in one bloody knee from trying to avoid stings.

But no matter what happened, the kiss he'd shared with Sleeping Beauty still lingered in his mind. He'd never kissed a woman like that in his life. All out and free. Like it meant something. Like he could learn to care. Most of the women he knew near his age were just friends. A slight kiss on the cheek, that's all. It played in with the image they had of him, he guessed. That old nice-guy thing again. So why had he stepped out of his usual role with a woman he hadn't said more than a few words to?

In his college days he'd always been too busy for more than an occasional one-night stand and, after college, his work as a teacher had consumed him until one day his world shattered. After one school shooting, his normal changed. He needed silence. He needed to be alone so he didn't have to worry that one day someone near him would be bloodied. Would be dead. It was hard to think of developing a relationship when his whole life was broken.

Drew had crawled into reclusiveness and never planned to come out. The world was too deadly a place to roam. He had learned that the hard way. Every night, even in his dreams, he always smelled blood and heard the screams. In daylight he could escape into his work, or he'd run until he was too tired to remember for a while. Slowly, he was able to think of other things and be content to live in his simple, safe life. For a while, until the nightmares returned.

Two years ago he'd finally stepped out and agreed to teach one class at a nearby college. The class was small. The door was always locked to outsiders.

At first teaching had been hard, painful almost, but slowly he relaxed and gained an ounce of the love he once had for it.

Only Monday morning, the lady he'd driven to Harmony Friday night was still there, walking through his thoughts. When he remembered her, he could push the horror back into the shadows, let it lie in the past for a while. She was different than any woman he'd known. Strong, confident one moment, then somehow broken the next. In her eyes, he saw the same fear that he lived with. Maybe what drew him to her was simply that she knew the same secret he did. The only difference was that he'd had years to hide his away so that no one saw it.

The world was not a safe place. But he could pretend, and maybe she'd learn to do the same in time.

When he'd held her, kissed her, he felt so alive. Just thinking about it made him smile. He hadn't been the only one losing control Friday night.

Control was something he never lost, and from the look

in those green eyes, she wasn't used to stepping off the safe path either.

Even today he couldn't seem to concentrate. He stared out his cabin window, watching the wind attempting to blow down the trees while he tried to figure out why he was so attracted to a woman he barely knew. She had no fashion sense and looked wounded in both body and soul. If she was as broken as he was, they couldn't be good for one another.

If he had a type, which he didn't, she would definitely not be it.

Flipping off his computer, he decided to walk.

The lake was down because of the drought, but the house he'd rented was in the woods, not near the water. He passed the cute country café and general store owned by the Morgans. The place looked like it belonged on the cover of a travel magazine and not nestled in the middle of a small lake community.

Luke Morgan had retired from a job with the ATF to take over as the first sheriff of Twisted Creek. All the folks at the lake had formed a town and hired him. Since they'd incorporated and begun improvements, the population had doubled. There was even talk of rebuilding the old lodge that burned years ago, and most of the new cabins looked like they belonged more on a fancy golf course than at a lake.

The cabin Drew rented was old, basically one room with a loft barely wide enough for a bed. He always laughed and said he never lost anything because he could see everything he owned from any spot in his house.

Luke Morgan had been his friend since college. Luke was a grad student during Drew's freshman year, but they'd always gotten along. After college, like most people, they lost touch.

When Drew had been wounded and shattered five years ago, Luke, without calling to ask if he was needed, had flown halfway across the country to stand by his side. The media had been everywhere, wanting to know about the young teacher who'd faced down a killer, wanting Drew to tell how he felt, what he'd thought when he'd heard gunfire on campus. Why he'd carried a lifeless student out of the building.

Drew had no family to go to. He couldn't think after the hospital released him with a pocket full of painkillers and two healing gunshot wounds.

He couldn't sleep or eat or think.

Luke had loaded him on a plane and they'd flown away from the life he'd known since college. At Twisted Creek Drew had mended, body and soul. Except for once a year when he flew back to Chicago. The same day, the same month. Drew flew back to stand before the graves of the two students he couldn't save. There in the silent graveyard he'd say he was sorry one more time. He should have acted faster. He should have seen the danger. He should have blocked more than two bullets.

Drew had made up the lie about going to visit his mother as he got to know people in Twisted Creek. He wasn't ready to tell anyone but Luke the truth about why he made the flight to Chicago. He just wanted to let his two students know that even if he couldn't talk about them, he'd never forget.

Then he'd catch the last plane back to Texas and his life. He didn't like to think he was hiding out; he was simply resting. Only Drew wasn't sure he'd ever grow stronger.

His half-sister Karaleen, who called herself Kare, had found him a few years ago, but none of the media had. Maybe after five years no one was looking for him. She bought into the fact that her brother was simply a professor working on a book in his free time. She knew nothing of the violence that had driven him to Texas. Now and then, she'd tell him his lifeline didn't match his life, but he explained it away by saying he wrote about exciting people, and their stories must have somehow flowed through his blood and become a part of him.

She might know little about him since they'd connected two years ago, but he hadn't known she existed until she showed up at his office door at the college.

She'd somehow found him, thanks to the Internet. He'd just stared at her when this wild child of twenty-two explained she'd just dropped out of her third college and needed a place to hide out until her parents got over the shock of her grades. Apparently, she'd known about him since birth and thought now was the time for them to meet.

Drew had no memories of his father except what Kare told him. Cunningham had left his first wife and Drew before Drew could walk. Then, years later, Cunningham married again and had one more child, Kare.

Maybe it was the fact that they had different mothers, maybe it was her growing up in California and him in New York, but they were as different as night and day. He loved watching her and wondering what it would have been like growing up knowing he had a little sister. She'd lived in the same farmhouse, fifty miles from any town, with two parents until she'd left and started college *hopping*, as she called it. He'd lived in a different apartment every year with his mother in Queens. Nature was nothing more than a subject in science. He never had a pet or saw grass that wasn't surrounded by concrete as a child.

Walking through the woods, heading back to his cabin, he thought about how hard he'd studied for a scholarship. Back then he'd known exactly what he wanted—out of the life he had. His mother died from a drug overdose the summer before he left for college. That fall he registered, taking two part-time jobs and a full load of classes. Everything he owned was packed in two boxes. He wasn't sure where he was going or what he'd become, but he knew he was never going back.

By his senior year he decided. He wanted to be a great teacher in a school like the ones he'd gone to. He wanted to inspire his students to climb out of the world of poverty, gangs, and crime. Until the shooting, it had been working.

After the shooting, he felt the same as he had when his mother died. He had to get away, and he could never go back to where he was the day before he heard gunfire.

Five years ago he'd stepped away from the life he'd built

and started all over. Like a chameleon, he'd changed everything. When he walked away from Chicago, he left no for-
warding address. His one friend, Luke, had helped him build
another life. No tough high schools. This time he'd make
his living researching and writing. Drew finished his doctorate online and finally became Professor Cunningham for
one small class.

Luke Morgan had proved a good friend. When Morgan
agreed to help Drew, he kept both his promise and Drew's
secret. It seemed natural for Drew to move close, and there
was an open cabin at the lake that he could rent. Paying cash
for everything. Staying off the grid, he claimed.

Drew moved into a ready-made life, and Luke's friends
became his friends. The job at the college was easy and
offered him plenty of time to write. Now there was peace,
his teaching, the writing he never seemed to finish, and his
half-sister. Yet he never forgot where he came from. Every
day when he walked the woods, he took in the silent beauty
of nature like a rare gift he'd never tire of seeing.

The late-afternoon sun touched the treetops as he circled
back to his cabin. He noticed the front door was wide open.
An odd hour for a break-in, he thought.

Drew didn't straighten, didn't show any sign of alarm.
He simply walked. The last break-in at his place had been
a masked raccoon.

When he stepped onto the porch, he saw wet footprints.
Small. Human. Drew shoved the door slowly open. "If you're
a robber you're dead meat."

A child squealed with laughter. "What would I steal?
Books? They're no good. Most don't even have pictures."

Drew puffed up as if ready to defend his cabin. "I'll take
no prisoners." He saw a flash swing up into the loft of his
cabin on a rope he'd tied to the ceiling for that very purpose.
"This is my castle and I'll defend it fully."

"You don't frighten me," the intruder shouted. "I got
Indian blood, white man. I'll have your liver for lunch."

Drew grabbed the boy as he swung again from the loft
railing to the top of the windowsill a few feet away. Laughing,

tickling, and swearing threats from *Treasure Island*, Drew tossed the boy and let him tumble onto the couch.

Jefferson Morgan bounced up and began to jump on the old couch. "I didn't break in. The door was unlocked, and all I stole was your graham crackers. You should buy Oreos. I like them more."

Drew walked to the wall that served as his kitchen. "Did you leave me any?"

"Two, but you won't need them. Mom says to come over and eat leftovers. We got meat loaf and lasagna plus a lot of no-name, no-good vegetables."

Leftovers at Allie Morgan's place were better than anything he could cook. "Come on, Jeff, I'll race you through the trees to your back door. If I win, you have to eat your no-name vegetables." He almost tripped over his briefcase and jacket as he rushed out ahead of the kid.

They were off toward the café, beating down paths the boy knew by heart. Jeff, despite his hatred of anything green to eat, was getting faster. Drew was breathing hard by the time they hit the back door of an addition built onto the original café and store.

"We tied," Drew announced. "You have to eat a carrot and some lettuce."

Jefferson Morgan frowned. "Don't give them names. Vegetables are just leaves and roots and seeds. They don't need names."

Drew laughed as he followed the boy to the small café.

Luke and Allie joined them for the late lunch they always had on Monday after Drew taught his class. The couple was within ten years of the same age, but there was something about Luke that made him seem older than his years and something about Allie, with her small frame and quick laugh, that would always make her seem more girl than woman. But together they worked. Her teasing him, him adoring her.

Drew sometimes thought that if life were a circus, Luke would be the lion and Allie the lion tamer. Since he'd shown up at their place, he'd always known them as a couple and he had a feeling neither would be whole without the other.

Her grandmother had died the year Allie and Luke's son, Jefferson, was born. They said even after Alzheimer's had taken her mind, she never forgot the boy's name. She'd sit on the porch of the general store and talk to the baby like they had a lifetime of things to say to each other, and he never cried when in her arms.

The little café on Twisted Creek had become so popular it was open all weekend. Monday the locals always ate what hadn't sold. On Saturdays and Sundays folks from town came out to eat and sat in the wooden chairs facing the lake to watch the sunset.

Drew liked Mondays the best, with locals dropping by to take potluck on a half-priced meal. The conversations were usually about fishing and weather, but Drew didn't care. He still craved normal.

After lunch, Jefferson asked Drew if he wanted to go fishing, but Drew had already made up his mind he'd be making the drive over to Harmony. "I've got to go to town and buy cookies and more books."

Thirty minutes later when he backed Luke Morgan's Jeep onto the main road, cookies and books were not on his mind. It was time to see if Sleeping Beauty was awake.

Maybe he'd drive by the inn. Maybe he'd stop.

Chapter 7

WHEELER FARM

JOHNNY WHEELER THOUGHT ABOUT HIS LIFE ALL MORNING and decided his brother was right. He was the most boring man in the world.

That afternoon, while he was fixing irrigation pipe, Scarlet's lawyer served him with divorce papers and by sundown he'd come up with a plan to make her sorry she left him. After discarding several devious plots he thought might do the job, but end up with him serving time, Johnny settled on the perfect answer.

He'd do a home improvement project on himself. When she got back to town she'd be so sorry she'd left him she'd drop Max and beg to come back. Of course, he wouldn't take her back; he would break her heart, just like she broke his.

He dropped by the senior citizens' center, where his grandfather lived from breakfast to supper. Then, just before dark Pops would walk the half block to the garden home he'd bought when he handed over the farm to Johnny. Funny thing was, after sixty years of working the farm, Pops retired and never asked a single question about how it was doing. Johnny asked his grandfather once if he'd like to drive out and see the land. The old man said he'd rather drop by the Dairy Queen. Evidently a hamburger meant more to him than the land he'd worked.

Johnny found Pops, but the eighty-year-old was playing poker for cheese balls and didn't want to visit. When Johnny ate a few of his winnings, Pops suggested he move on.

Walking over to the senior citizens' office, Johnny volunteered to help out with the dance lessons. There were always three or four times as many women as men, so he'd get lots of practice. He'd seen the parties they had and noticed some of the old girls could really dance. Lessons couldn't hurt, and they might help. Scarlet always complained about his two left feet.

Next, he drove a block over and joined the gym in town. He'd farmed since he was old enough to reach the gas pedal, but he guessed his muscles were probably in the wrong places.

When he circled Main, he decided to stop by the bookstore and read a few novels. That was bound to make him more interesting.

As usual, the bookstore was silent as a tomb. "Mr. Hatcher. It's John Wheeler," he yelled, not wanting to frighten anyone lost in the stacks.

No answer. The old man who ran the place often left for meals without locking up, which was fine with Johnny. He'd rather look for a good book than be followed around the store with Mr. Hatcher giving him a synopsis of every hardback published since '53. That must have been the year Hatcher stepped out of the children's section and into the rest of the bookstore.

As he wandered toward the back, his head bumped against a sign hanging from the ceiling. KARE CUNNINGHAM. PALM READINGS—HALF PRICE. TWO HANDS READ FOR THE PRICE OF ONE.

A green door with funny little charms glued to the wood

was hidden in between the shelves of *National Geographic*. It was open just enough to be inviting.

Johnny had no idea why he fell off the sensible wagon at that moment, but he tapped on the green door.

"Come in," a voice whispered.

He shoved with his foot, not sure he wanted to touch anything just in case he might catch crazy. "I . . ." That was all he said. His brain hadn't figured out the rest of the sentence.

"I know," a black-haired young woman with a purple scarf banding her wild curls answered. "You want a reading. I could take time out from my studies to do a reading. I've been waiting for you, John."

"You're good," he said, amazed she knew his name already. Then he remembered he'd yelled it out five minutes before when he'd walked in. "I think I do want a reading." He didn't believe in fortune-tellers, but the lady wasn't bad on the eyes in a space-case kind of way. She looked like someone who would dance in the midnight moonlight. Kind of like a blend of sixties hippie and Tinkerbell.

The room was small. The ceiling almost brushed the top of his head. Books lined the walls, but the area smelled of spices and incense. The woman was in her early twenties and, with her dark features, she looked like she'd be from somewhere far away but her voice was soft and almost southern.

"My name is Kare. You know, like empathy. Please sit down." She pointed to a chair on the other side of a short table barely wide enough to hold one book. "I'll read your past and your future."

"I know my past." Johnny folded his big frame into a flimsy chair. "How about we just go for my future?"

She took his rough hand in her soft one and began to move her fingers over his palm. "You're very strong in mind and body."

Johnny figured she was a fraud and said that to everyone. What kind of fool would argue with that diagnosis?

"You've loved deeply and passionately, but I fear true love hasn't found you yet."

Maybe she was for real, he decided. There was something

in her touch that made him think of foreplay. He had no idea
about the "loving deeply" part. Scarlet was the one love he'd
had. They'd married the weekend after they'd discovered
they both liked sangria. He'd thought they were waltzing
through life and it turned out she was line dancing.

"You have trouble trusting," the fairy named Kare said
in her midnight voice.

She got that right. He watched her finger circling over
his hand. Whatever she charged was worth it just to feel her
light touch. He sure hoped she couldn't read his mind
because his thoughts were definitely turning R-rated.

"You come from the land. You're a part of nature. A son
of pioneers."

He frowned, guessing that anyone who walked into this
bookstore would probably be the same. "Tell me something
I don't know."

Her big brown eyes looked up at him and her whispered
words brushed against his face.

"You are in great danger."

He swore he felt a chill as her eyes looked above him as
though a spirit of some kind were standing just behind him.
Fear flickered in her beautiful eyes as she whispered,
"You're about to be arrested."

Johnny grinned and leaned back in the little chair.
"You're going a little overboa—" He froze as his chair
bumped into something behind him.

Turning slowly, Johnny saw first the boots, then tan trousers, then a starched shirt with a star above the pocket.
"Afternoon, Deputy Gentry," Johnny tried to sound friendly,
but handcuffs were in the lawman's hand.

"Mr. Wheeler, I wonder if you wouldn't mind coming
with me over to the office."

Johnny stood still, staring at the handcuffs. "Are those
necessary?" Once, he'd let Scarlet handcuff him in bed and
it hadn't turned out well. He guessed this would have the
same ending without the fun.

"They are, John," Gentry said formally. "I'm arresting
you on suspicion of murder."

Johnny stood. This had to be some kind of bad joke. "What? Who am I supposed to have killed?"

Gentry clicked the first wrist. "Your wife."

Before he could lock the second wrist, the fortune-teller fainted and both men had to work together to carry her out of the tiny room and get her water. When she finally came to, Gentry continued with the arresting.

Chapter 8

MILLANIE HAD SPENT SUNDAY SLEEPING. SHE FELT LIKE HER mind needed to heal as much as her leg. She wasn't sure she was up to taking on an assignment, but Sergeant Hughes wouldn't take no for an answer, so after her breakfast on Monday, she stumbled out on the porch with her laptop and tried to get organized. Once her partner did show up, she planned to have a ton of work for him to do.

To her surprise, a little girl was sitting in one of the wicker chairs on the porch. She looked about ten and was winter pale even though wearing a summer dress.

"Hello." Millanie smiled down at the child. "Nice to find someone else on the porch this morning." She didn't miss the brace on the girl's thin leg. "Are you lost?"

The guest straightened, growing older as she faced Millanie without returning her smile. "I'm Saralynn Matheson, and though I'm small for my age, I'm twelve, so don't talk to me like I'm a kid, okay? My aunt told me to wait until you finished breakfast and came out. She said you're crippled up like me."

"I do have a broken leg and I would never treat someone who looks as intelligent as you like a child." Millanie was out of her comfort zone. "I'm just not used to talking to children of any age."

Saralynn leaned forward and relaxed as if silently accepting the apology. "I was born with my legs not working right, but my aunt says you got yours hurt while being a hero. She says you saved many lives by facing down a man with a bomb."

Millanie figured it would have taken far longer than three days for word to get around that she was back in town. "Who is your aunt, Saralynn?"

"Sheriff Alex Matheson, but she was a McAllen like you before she married my uncle. She says you two are second cousins."

Millanie took the other wicker chair on the porch. "That's right. I've only seen her once since we've been grown, but we are cousins."

Saralynn rocked in her chair. "I thought so. The two of you look kind of alike. You both got the McAllen height. My grandmother Matheson says all McAllens look like they've been stretched. Does your leg hurt?"

"A little. How about yours?"

"A little." Saralynn leaned forward and put her hand on the cast. "I know a secret that will help with the pain."

"I'd appreciate any advice." Millanie loved talking to this bright child.

"When it's bad and you've been pushing yourself, remember this story my uncle Hank told me. He said when he was little, several older boys were going to swim the lake. An old man with a boat agreed to follow them across. If one of the boys gave up and had to climb in the boat, the other boys would call him a baby. Hank said he couldn't swim all that well, but he didn't want to back down. About halfway across, every part of his body was hurting. He claimed his muscles turned to Jell-O. He went close to the boat knowing that he'd have to be the first one to give up, but the old man said one thing that saved him from being marked as a baby."

The child was a natural storyteller. She even waited for Millanie to ask, "What did he say?"

Saralynn hesitated, then added, "The old man said, 'Just float.' Uncle Hank did for a while, until he was strong enough to go on. He didn't win the race, but he didn't quit." She leaned back in the wicker chair, propped her foot up on the rocking footstool, and whispered, "How about we float for a while?"

Millanie tossed an old quilt over them both even though the air was warm. After a few minutes she whispered to the little sage, "Good idea."

When the sheriff walked up an hour later, Millanie felt rested. She stood, hugged her cousin, and said good-bye to Saralynn.

As the girl headed to the car, Alex lowered her voice and leaned in close to Millanie. "She's a real joy, isn't she?"

Millanie watched the child limp to the car while Alex continued, "She wanted to come over here after her piano lesson this morning to talk to you. I told her it would be a while before I could pick her up, but she said she had plenty to do."

"She did." Millanie waved at the girl. "She taught me to float."

They talked for a few more minutes, promised to have lunch soon, and exchanged e-mails. Each knew they could count on the other; they didn't need to say the words.

With the air still and the heat of the day still not weighing down on everything yet, Millanie decided to lean back in her chair and float some more. She woke once about teatime and ate everything Mrs. Biggs brought on a tray, then worked on her laptop a few hours before leaning back in the chair and floating again. All the days and nights she'd been in too much pain to sleep seemed to be catching up to her.

The shadows were long when she heard a Jeep pull into the drive. For a few minutes she didn't move, just watched Drew Cunningham walking toward her. He had his hands in his pockets, his head down, his strides long. A man thinking as he walked, unaware of his surroundings, she decided. A man so different from all the fighters and schemers she'd known.

He was almost to the steps before he looked up and saw her. He slowed. Hesitated. Looked unsure of what he was about to do. She almost laughed. Stepping on Martha Q's porch wasn't exactly charting new worlds.

"Evening, Millie," he finally said in his low, educated voice.

"Evening, Dr. Cunningham." She had no doubt that he'd learned more about her, just as she had about him in the three days since he'd brought her here. "You coming to check in, or check up on me?" The gossip was that he'd traveled and lectured for a few years all over the world before finally settling here to write a textbook. One of Martha Q's friends said he taught a class over in Clifton Creek, but no one knew or seemed to care what the class was about.

Millanie had looked him up online. He had a great credit rating, rented his place, and apparently owned no car in his name. If he weren't so harmless looking she would have put him on her list of people to watch, this man who left no footprints of where he'd been.

His intelligent gaze took in her loose cotton slacks and casual shirt. "You look like you should be on a yacht somewhere. Quite a change from the *Little House on the Prairie* look."

"These were the only pants long and wide enough to fit over my cast. That seems to be my one rule of fashion these days." She didn't miss the approval in his gaze. Maybe the outfit didn't look as bad as she thought it did. She hadn't been out of uniform long enough to feel comfortable in anything else. The hospital nurses had cut off one leg of her trousers so she could walk out of the hospital.

He climbed the first two steps. "In answer to your question, I'm here to take you out for a drink, if you'll join me."

"Martha Q called you?"

"Of course."

His bottom lip twitched at the corner and she knew he lied. The man was an open book.

She decided she wouldn't know him long enough to bother making him call her by her proper name. Shortening names seemed to be a habit in the South.

Leaning closer, he added, "Martha Q can't have the wounded hero of Harmony sitting on her porch all day and night; it's bad for business. I agreed to kidnap you."

Millanie filed away another fact. Drew Cunningham was a very poor liar.

She found that intriguing, but the hunger pains she couldn't seem to get rid of answered his question. "I'll go, if any kind of food comes with the drink. Just let me comb my hair and grab my purse."

"You won't need a purse. I'll buy, and your hair looks perfect. We're eating on the deck of Buffalo's Bar and Grill. You know the place? Even the cockroaches know how to two-step."

"No. I was underage when I left town."

"It's a joint where oilfield workers and cowhands stop by for a beer before they clean up. All food comes in a plastic basket with ketchup and jalapeños on the side. I've heard they've got a new cook and have expanded the menu to include sweet potato fries and hush puppies."

She grinned. "In that case, I'm ready. What do they have for dessert?"

He offered his hand and pulled her gently out of the rocker. When his arm went around her waist she felt the familiar nearness of him. That sense of being safe returned, even though reason told her, even with a cast, if trouble came she'd probably be the one to get them out of it.

"Fried apple pies. Trust me, you'll love them."

When he winked, she laughed.

She'd never been around anyone like him. He was kind, sweet almost, caring for sure. All the men she'd known in the army were hard and well trained and thought foreplay was simply asking, *Your place or mine?* The man before her didn't look like he knew how to fire a weapon and probably didn't even play tennis to stay in shape, so why did she feel safe near him?

He helped her into the Jeep with no top and all the windows down. It smelled slightly of fish and looked like it had always been left out in the weather. As he climbed in the other side, she asked, "Did you trade in the van?"

"Nope. I have several vehicles I borrow. Haven't found one I want to own yet. This stays mostly at the lake, but I thought the night was so nice you'd like the breeze."

The truth, she decided. It would have been easy for him to lie, but he'd admitted he didn't own a car. A fact she already knew and thought very strange.

"Oh, so this kidnapping was planned." She fought down another giggle. "You premeditated abducting me off Martha Q's porch?"

"Of course. I'm organized. My plan is to take you for a windy ride, stuff you with all the bad fried food we can order, and bring you back here so I can kiss your socks off. That's it, but I'm open to suggestions."

She wondered if he was kidding or if he'd thought of her as much as she'd thought of him. *Not my type*, she reminded herself, but the memory of their shared kiss wouldn't leave her mind. Maybe now, in recovery, in transition, this gentle man was exactly what she needed.

He was right about the drive. Even on a still day in Texas the wind blew. By the time they made the few blocks to the bar, her hair was a mess. She usually wore it shorter, but since the accident she hadn't given her hair or makeup much thought. Now the chocolate-brown strands covered her eyes if she didn't push them away.

When he came around to her side of the Jeep to help her out, he lightly touched her hair as if he couldn't help himself. "I like your curls. My sister's got curly black hair, but she wears her hair long."

"Your fortune-telling sister?"

He nodded. "You remember. Maybe you weren't as out of it as I thought. Yes, that's her. I have one sister that I know of and, to tell the truth, she's about all I can handle."

Millanie read what he didn't say. "When did you find out about her?"

He studied her as if surprised she'd read between the lines. "I learned of her existence a few years ago. Apparently, she found me on the Internet. We share the same father, but I'm ten years older than her. Our father left me before I had memories of him, which is probably for the best because he's always calling her just to bug her. She claims if there was an eight hundred number for Dial-A-Lecture it would be his home phone."

Millanie logged facts about him in her brain. Drew was so normal. Normal people always tell more than needed. People who have something to hide just deliver what they feel they have to. A few drinks and she'd know every detail of this boring man's life. She'd bet that when he had traveled the world he'd stayed at American hotels, eaten American food, and never ventured too far off the campus where he lectured.

Drew helped her to a chair on the deck before going in to order their food from a little takeout window on the side of the building. She liked sitting out on the porch watching people heading into the bar. Most were near her age, but she felt so much older. Something about being on her own early made her grow up fast.

When he brought back two beers, Drew sat across from her and stretched his long legs out on the chair next to her. Surprisingly, he didn't seem to want to talk, he just wanted to stare at her. She considered the possibility that he'd had very few dates.

There was absolutely nothing wrong with him, but women want a man with a touch of danger or an ounce of style. He was too easygoing, too laid-back. The only thing really interesting about the man was the way he kissed, and she couldn't see that as enough to hold a date together, much less a relationship.

After several minutes of silence, he said casually, "We could swap life stories, talk about our college days and what we hate about our jobs, but how about we skip that part of the conversation?"

Millanie was shocked. If this was some kind of line, she'd

misjudged the shy professor. "All right," she said. "What do we talk about? Politics, movies, the weather?"

He shrugged. "I've already talked about the weather today and I don't care what your politics are. I haven't seen a movie in a year, so that topic's out."

"So, what does that leave?"

"Well, later tonight I don't plan to talk to you at all. I think I've made that clear, but for now I'd like to know why you came back here to Harmony. I'm a good judge of people and you don't seem to belong here. Not your style, I'm guessing."

Millanie almost laughed at him. Folks who said they were good judges of people rarely were. So, either the professor was simply making conversation, or he tended to lie to himself.

The waitress delivered baskets of chicken fingers and sweet potato fries. A couple walked by and stopped to talk to Drew about how the fishing was down at the lake. One of her McAllen cousins rushed out of the bar and said she'd heard Millanie was back in town. They rehashed everything they could remember about being in the third grade together. Millanie had the feeling her cousin would have joined them for dinner if Drew had suggested it. Thank goodness, the professor was silent.

By the time the cousin finally went back inside, the deck had filled with people. Millanie forced herself not to study each one. This wasn't the army. These people didn't pose a threat. This was Harmony. She could relax. The man she'd be looking for wouldn't hang out here. He'd more likely be at the country club or at a fund-raiser.

Drew disappeared to get two more beers, and a slender woman in her early twenties with long black curly hair dashed over and plopped in his vacant chair. "You've got to help me," she whispered, like a spy from an old suspense movie.

"You're Drew's sister? Kare, right?" Millanie had no doubt. The girl looked like she still believed in unicorns.

"How'd you know?" Wide brown eyes stared at her in surprise.

Millanie played along. "I've got a bit of the gift myself, you know. I can sense things before they're said."

Kare bounced in the chair, making the twenty-strand necklace she wore jingle like tiny Christmas bells. "That's grand. We need to stick together. There are many who don't appreciate our talents. I grew up an only child of two people who didn't like company dropping by. Would you believe I thought everyone had gifts, except my dad, until I got to college and found out most people don't?"

"I understand." Millanie said what she knew the girl wanted to hear. She'd learned years ago that if you want the truth out of anyone, simply mirror what they are. Everyone automatically likes someone who understands them. "Now, how can I help?"

The little sister of Drew Cunningham leaned close. "Johnny Wheeler is about to swing for something he didn't do. I read his palm. He couldn't have killed anyone. It would have shown up on his hands. But everyone thinks he offed Scarlet, so he's going down the river for sure for murder one. I think the one thing slowing down his trial is the fact they haven't found her body, but in a few days when it starts to smell, Johnny will be officially charged."

Millanie tried to piece together facts within her rambling. Kare had definitely watched one too many prison movies. A dozen questions came to mind and she had no idea where to start. Finally, she settled on, "Who'd Johnny Wheeler kill again?"

"Well, they say he killed his wife, Scarlet, and maybe her lover, Max Dewy. Half the folks argue that one because most think Max is gay, so that cuts him out as her lover. But Johnny didn't kill them even if his own brother admitted he saw Johnny the night she disappeared. The brother said he'd looked like he'd been in a fight and was carrying a shovel with fresh dirt on it." Kare finally took a breath and added, "Two kids were parked out across from his place and swear they saw him bury something. It's hard to miss a big guy like Johnny Wheeler, even in the dark. They said what he tossed in the hole wasn't very big, but Scarlet was a little bitty thing. She was thirty and still getting carded."

"How can I help?" Millanie said again. She considered

that this might be some kind of bar game she didn't know about just to see how gullible the newcomer was.

Kare looked really worried when she begged, "Tell my brother he has to help me this time. This is real. A man could die and I'm the only one who believes he's innocent. Drew's got brains. He'll think of something."

"Get out of my chair." Drew's voice boomed from just behind Millanie. "I'm on the first date I've had in years and you're not invited to join us. Whatever this week's crisis is can wait, Kare."

She flashed her brown eyes at Millanie, begging one more time for help.

Millanie nodded and patted the girl's hand as if silently swearing to oblige.

Kare jumped up. She kissed her brother on the cheek and danced away as if they'd somehow solved her problem.

Drew sat down and offered Millanie one of the drinks. "I warned you to stay away from my sister."

"It wasn't easy to run with this leg." She saw the lift of his lip and knew he wasn't serious. "You always solve her problems, don't you?"

"It's my mission in life, it seems. Last week she was convinced there was a ring of catnappers running wild in the streets. A week before that she thought she met a man who didn't have a heart. I mean really didn't have one. She claimed she'd read about heart thieves in an old book. Last month I put a dozen holes in her wall because she swore she heard something trapped inside. Now you know why I don't have time for TV or movies."

"Or dates, apparently."

He shook his head. "Not dating was by choice." He grabbed a fry and pointed it toward her. "Now, answer my question. Why'd you come back to Harmony?"

Their meals were half eaten since he'd asked. He waited. She stalled by acting like she was starving.

Finally, when all her chicken was gone, she said, "I don't know why I came back. I lived here as a kid and I guess it's as close to being home as anywhere. My roots are here. My great-great-grandparents started this town." She couldn't tell him she'd returned here simply because she had nowhere else to go.

He ate a few bites without speaking, then said more to himself than to her, "That's not the answer, but it'll do for now." He pushed his food aside and added, "You want to go for a ride?"

Millanie tilted her head and studied him. "What about your sister's emergency?"

"I talked to a friend about it when she woke me up from my afternoon nap. The law doesn't think Wheeler killed his wife. In fact, she did a pretty good job of mentally beating him up before she left. If he hadn't said he buried her, the sheriff wouldn't have arrested him. But it's hard to ignore a confession and everyone's talking."

"Small towns." She'd never understood them. "I remember some of my mother's stories about growing up here, but we moved before I paid much attention."

"You got to love them. They have two jars on the bar for money. One to bet on how he killed her and the other to help pay for his defense." Drew put his arm around her to help her up, as casually as if he'd done it a hundred times. "Let's get out of here before my sister comes back."

The wind had died and the night was warm and rich with the aroma of summer. He drove her through the streets of Harmony. Neither talked much. She pointed out a few places she remembered. He gave no hint of where he grew up.

Finally, she asked, "You said you didn't date, so why me? Why now?"

"Maybe I haven't run across a woman who had what I wanted?"

She laughed. "What? Two lips?" She liked the low laugh he had when she caught him off guard.

"No, it's more than that. I don't know what, but you have something, lady. Something very rare. Maybe something only I see."

She thought of saying that whatever she had must be very rare because no one else had ever mentioned it. Maybe he was a romantic, looking for a magic that wasn't there. The stars weren't aligning for love. They were simply two people who were probably a little lonely, a little bored.

When they made it back to the bed-and-breakfast, Millanie wasn't sure what to do. He walked her to the porch, held her back steady as she climbed the steps, and opened the front door for her. A perfect gentleman.

"Want to come in for a glass of wine? I know where Martha Q hides the bottles."

"No, thanks," he answered politely. "I've a full day tomorrow."

She almost asked, *Doing what?* but she didn't know him well enough yet. Maybe she never would. She now had a mission in Harmony, and getting to know him would just be a distraction.

He opened the door to her room, then stepped back.

She walked through and turned to say good night. The words died in her throat when his hand gently brushed her arm.

"Put the crutches down, Millie. I'll hold you up." His hand slid along her waist. "We've finally gotten to the reason I came by tonight."

She thought of making a joke or acting surprised, but one look in his eyes told her the man was dead serious. Propping the crutches between the door facing and the window-sill, she waited.

His hands moved to the small of her back as he closed the few inches between them. He moved against her, his mouth brushing her ear as he whispered, "Now is the part where I kiss your socks off."

Millanie closed her eyes, realizing she'd been waiting for another kiss since the moment he'd left Friday night. But he seemed in no hurry as his face brushed against her hair, and then he slowly kissed his way down her throat. By the time he finally covered her lips with his, she was starving for the promised kiss.

This one wasn't sweet or tender but hungry with need. Something deep inside her responded and the kiss turned wild. It washed over her like a storm, leaving her shaken and starving for something she'd never felt. She couldn't pull away. She wouldn't let go. She wanted to be closer to him. She wanted more.

Then, as suddenly as the storm had started, he broke the kiss and straightened, their bodies still touching, their breaths mingling. If his hands hadn't been holding her, she felt like she might melt to the floor, boneless.

His eyes reflected her feelings. Shock. Passion. The edge of control. She watched as he silently fought to rule his emotions.

She knew the minute he won. His hands were still firm at her back, but they no longer caressed her.

"Do all men go mad when they kiss you?" The question snapped in the air like an accusation.

"No," she answered, surprised at his sharpness. The predictable professor was losing control and he didn't like it. If she hadn't been trying to untangle her own feelings, she might have found the situation funny. "You're the only one. Tell me, does it happen often, this going mad?"

"Never," he answered.

She reached for her crutches as he continued. "I'm not planning to get involved. This is . . . I'm not really . . ."

She got the message. "Look, Drew, I'm not in a place where I can start a relationship either. I don't plan to be in town that long. How about we just be friends?"

"We're not friends now," he corrected as his hands left her side.

"True." She shrugged. "Okay, how about we not be friends. If we just happen to run into each other again, we'll just kiss and part. Not friends or lovers, just kissing buddies."

He relaxed, then took a step backward as if in fear they might start a fire, again. "If that didn't sound so ridiculous, I'd agree to it."

"Me, too," she answered as she closed her door without saying good-bye.

Chapter 9

TUESDAY
HARMONY COUNTY JAIL

WHEN JOHNNY WHEELER WAS TOLD FOR THE TENTH TIME that he had a visitor, he almost refused to leave his cell. He'd been at the county jail for less than twenty-four hours and half the people in town had dropped by to talk to him.

Every lawman within a hundred miles drove over to test out his interrogation skills trying to crack the case. They were calling it a "crime of passion." Johnny spent an hour trying to tell them there had been no passion between him and Scarlet for six months but realized "a crime without passion" didn't sound much better.

Anyone related to him rushed in to cry and ask why. Apparently, he was the first Wheeler to show outlaw blood since his great-great-uncle rode with the James Gang. It seemed no one from his brother to his preacher thought he was innocent, and all said that even if Scarlet deserved to be punished for what she did, he wasn't the one who should have pulled the trigger, or slit her throat, or smothered her with a pillow. Wendell seemed to think he was playing cha-rades. Every time the guard turned away, he'd make some kind of killing motion and wiggle his eyebrows, expecting Johnny to nod when he guessed right.

Johnny had a feeling there were bets on at Buffalo's Bar about how he killed his wife. One of his aunts even dropped by to tell him the stories she'd heard about Scarlet while in the beauty shop. Max Dewy wasn't the first "friend" his wife had enjoyed. Dozens, apparently. Aunt May gave details as if somehow the news that he was not only dumb but blind would make Johnny feel better about murdering his wife.

"Mr. Wheeler," the young deputy said. "You all right?"

Johnny wanted to scream *No*, but he didn't think that would help much unless he planned to go with an insanity plea. "I'm fine."

"Did you hear me say you had a visitor?"

"I heard. Is it another relative?"

"No."

"A lawman?"

"No. I don't think so."

Johnny stood, trying to decide if he wanted to talk to anyone else. This was his last question. "It's not Tyler Wright from the funeral home?"

"No." The deputy smiled. "It's a pretty young woman with long black hair and a skirt that looks like it's made out of scarves. Real sweet, but she seemed a little scatterbrained."

"Oh." Johnny moved toward the open cell door. "Must be my lawyer."

He walked into the visitation room. Harmony's jail didn't have the glass windows and telephones like he'd always seen on TV. All they had was a long table. He'd been told to sit at one end and to make no attempt to touch the visitor. His Aunt May had paid no attention to the rule; she'd bolted for him and gotten in a good hug before they pulled her off. Then she had to be patted down twice because of spontane-ous hugging. She hadn't looked like she minded.

The opposite door opened and the fortune-teller slipped

in. The only way Kare Cunningham had helped him was that he now knew what *empathetic* meant. It meant he cared. Scarlet had been right about that one; he rarely cared about what she was talking about, and to her that must have translated to meaning that he didn't care about her.

The fortune-teller opened the door far enough to hurry through as if she feared one of the murderers imprisoned might accidentally slip out if she left extra room.

"Hello, John," she said in that low bedroom voice as she sat down at the other end of the table.

He had the strangest urge to stretch out his hands to her, but he didn't. "If you've come to tell me I'm in trouble, Kare, it's too late. Apparently my wife and her lover disappeared without closing out their hotel bill and everyone seems to think I'm to blame."

"Why you?" she said simply.

"It was my credit card they left on file. Problem was their shopping spree had already pushed the limit of the card. So now I not only have to pay the bill, but I'm going to jail for life for murder." His smile didn't feel right. "Seems a little unfair when I didn't get to have any of the fun."

"You had nothing to do with killing her. If she's dead, that is. I can't answer to that since I've never seen her lifeline." Kare fanned both hands in front of her face. "If she ever shows up, bring her by and I'll tell you how long she'll live. Well, not exactly. We don't deal in dates."

"I doubt we'll be going out together again," he said, wondering why this fairylike creature spoke in plural like she was sitting with a crowd at the other end of the table.

"You never know. Life takes its own turns and twists." Kare smiled as if she'd just remembered the thought for the day.

He looked directly at her. If it were another time or place he would have thought her pretty, but flirting with a space case while you're handcuffed didn't seem like it would be a relationship going anywhere. "You sure about that, lady? You seem to be the only one who doesn't think I belong here."

She shook her head, sending wild hair bouncing around her shoulders. "I know you didn't ask me to, but I read your past. No murders behind you. I would have seen it in your palms."

"Great, I've got one witness I can count on. The way my luck is running they'll probably hack off my hands and file them as evidence, but I'd appreciate it if you'd tell them."

"Oh, I wouldn't testify. It's against our code. Too many skeptics. Something we never do."

"Then why did you come?" He was in far too much trouble to even joke around about how their few minutes together had seemed like a beginning to something there right before the handcuffs clicked around his wrists and she fainted.

She looked straight at him with those big brown eyes and said simply, "You forgot to pay me."

Johnny stood and walked back to his cell, thinking he'd give up on women, and relatives, and all thought he'd had of improving himself. Maybe he could talk the county into putting him to sleep the way they do old dogs.

When he stepped in his cell, he noticed a package wrapped loosely in brown paper on his bunk. "What's this?" he asked the deputy.

The young deputy smiled. "A gift for you."

"You shouldn't have."

The deputy looked embarrassed. "It's a book. I had to open it. The girl you just talked to brought it to you."

Johnny pulled the paper aside and turned the well-worn book over in his hands. *Gulliver's Travels.* What a strange gift to give a man going nowhere.

Chapter 10

BEAU YATES FINISHED HIS INTERVIEW AT A RADIO STATION in Nashville before he finally answered an unknown caller on his private line.

"Yates here," he snapped, hoping it wasn't some nut who'd found his number. He'd had to change phone numbers half a dozen times last year. Fans wanting to talk, wannabe song-writers insisting he listen, one nut who said he wanted to kill Beau because he thought Beau was singing about his sister.

"Beau"—the caller sounded official, all business—"this is Addison Spencer at the Harmony County Hospital. Your agent gave me your number. I hate to call, but your father has had a heart attack."

He nodded, then realized the doc couldn't see him. "Hello, Doc," he got out before her last sentence caught up to his brain.

She continued, "He's stable, Beau, but it was close. I thought I should call and let you know."

Beau thought of saying that he'd lost his father years ago when his old man kicked him out, but he really didn't think the doc needed to hear about the past. For the first seventeen years of his life Beau had been his father's favorite sinner to preach to. The older Beau got, the more his father found wrong or evil about him. But the sin he couldn't seem to forgive was Beau's love for country music. No matter how much he preached, Beau wouldn't give it up.

Dr. Spencer had been talking, but all he heard was her last sentence. "Your father won't survive another one."

All the lectures Melvin Yates gave him during his teens now weighed Beau down like layer after layer of wool, smothering the life out of him. In truth, if he thought of his father at all, Beau thought of him in the past tense. Reverend Yates had been dead to him for years. Not one call. Not one letter. The first year Beau had made real money, he'd sent flowers with a note that said *Happy New Year*. The next day one of his friends said he'd seen the arrangement, pot and bow and card, out near the street next to the trash cans.

The silence on the other end of the phone finally brought Beau back to the present. "Thanks for calling and letting me know, Doc."

Addison hesitated, then added, "One of the nurses said that in the few minutes he woke in recovery, he asked for you, Beau."

Beau took a long breath, knowing what he had to do. "I'm on my way."

The last thing he wanted to do was go back home to see his father, but deep down, he knew he had to. A few years ago he'd still been angry enough that he might have wanted to tell the old man off, but now, that didn't matter. There was no love—or hate—left, it seemed. All he could hope for if he went home was closure.

Dr. Spencer rattled off details he didn't understand. Beau wasn't listening. Memories were circling like trash in a windy alley. Wasted, dusty memories he'd spent his life running away from. All that was left between him and his father was a good-bye.

Two hours later he was on a private plane headed toward Harmony. The sun had been setting when they headed west, and it seemed to last for an hour as they flew toward it. Beau had friends he could call or stay with, but he didn't want to talk to anyone yet. He'd go straight to the hospital, see his dad, ask his stepmother if she needed anything, and be back on the plane by noon tomorrow. He'd offer any help needed with the bills, but he wouldn't stand silent for another lecture. He'd had enough of those to last this lifetime and the next.

When the plane landed on a dirt strip, no one would be there to see a man in a black hat carrying only a guitar case climb off. Beau would step back into Harmony as silently as he'd stepped out.

A rental car was waiting when he got to the old hangar next to the strip. Keys under the right sun visor as he'd requested. Beau stashed his guitar in the trunk, climbed in, and started the car as the airplane taxied around to leave. The urge to jump out and run toward the plane was strong. He could be back in Nashville in a few hours. Back where he belonged.

Several guys in his band had offered to come along with him, but this was something Beau needed to do alone.

He drove slowly through the sleepy little town, seeing slices of his life hanging around like ghosts. The town had aged some, improved some, but he could still walk it blind and never miss a step.

There was no need to get a room. By the time he checked on his father and found something to eat, it would be midnight. He'd just find a quiet corner in the waiting room and sleep under his hat until morning. Then he'd talk to the doctor, thank her for letting him know, and return to his world. With luck, no one he knew here would see him and no fans would recognize him. Sometimes he felt like there were two versions of Beau Yates. The one he played for the public and the real one, shy and insecure as ever.

His dad was in the critical care unit, the maximum security of any hospital. Beau had to wait a half hour before they let him go in. He promised not to wake his father and said he'd stay just a few minutes.

When he entered the room, he stood in the shadows and stared at the man he'd once been so afraid of. His father was older, paler, not near as frightening. Bruises and dark marks spotted his hands. His hair was noticeably thinner. The hum of machines almost blocked out the sound of his slow breathing.

Beau counted the seconds between each breath as if his father might stop at any moment and be dead. Reverend Melvin Yates would never go like that, Beau decided. He'd go screaming from the pulpit or demanding God's attention to his prayers. He'd never just quietly stop breathing.

Beau waited five minutes, counting the spaces between breaths, but nothing happened. The nurse stepped inside to whisper that the reverend's wife had gone home early. When Beau asked, she admitted that no one else had signed in to visit.

Then the nurse added that his stepmother hadn't wanted to leave his father's side, but she looked so exhausted the doctor had insisted and promised to call the moment there was any change.

Beau wasn't surprised. Twenty years of living with his father would exhaust anyone. The thing he didn't understand was why she had never left the old man. She'd volunteered to live in the wasteland around his father where nothing grew, not even love. Beau had always felt he'd been drafted.

Walking over to the bedside, he thought of covering his father's hand with his, but couldn't. No memory of ever touching his father came to him. No hand holding when he'd been small. No pats on the back. No touching Beau when he was afraid or sad. Somehow, now didn't seem the time to start.

Beau walked out of the room and asked if there was a cafeteria. He wasn't hungry, but it seemed as good a reason as any to leave. If he stayed around any longer he'd start feeling sorry for himself.

The cafeteria was closed, but vending machines lined the back wall. He bought a cup of coffee and a bag of chips and found a corner where anyone coming in this late wouldn't even notice him.

The chair by the smoky window was air-conditioner cold,

almost damp, but he barely noticed. He sat down and stared out the window into the night. For a moment he saw nothing, maybe because he expected to see nothing, and then his eyes adjusted. A table outside on the patio had been shoved against the glass, looking like it mirrored his table. A shadow of a woman sat on the other side of the table. If the sheet of glass hadn't been between them they would have been eating across from one another.

The woman wasn't aware of him as she stirred her coffee. Her head jerked up slightly now and then. She raised a napkin to her nose. She was crying. He couldn't hear her. She was no more than a shadow crying, but he saw her sorrow.

After a while, she left. Beau was careful not to look up as she stepped inside and crossed the area, now a graveyard of scattered tables and chairs. She gave no hint that she saw him, but sorrow flowed around her shoulders like a long gray cape.

He turned back to the window, thinking he could almost still see her outline in the night. Maybe she hadn't been a mourner, but the ghost of a newly departed soul. Funny, he thought, how your mind dances with strange thoughts when you're waiting for death to drop by.

As he always did when he talked silently to himself, a song began to whisper through his mind. It was so soft at first he could barely hear it, and then slowly the words began to fit together. A sad melody of a hollow man wishing any feeling, even sorrow, could reach him and the woman he watched crying, not for herself but for him.

Beau pulled a napkin from the box and began putting words to the music whispering in his brain. When he walked back toward his father's room, he took a side door out to his car. Deep in the night when the hospital slept, Beau sat alone in the small critical care waiting room and played his songs. They echoed softly throughout the hallways, but no one came by to tell him to stop.

Maybe they all knew that the famous Beau Yates was among them and the shy private Beau Yates needed to grieve the only way he knew how . . . through his music.

Chapter 11

JOHNNY WHEELER WASN'T SURPRISED WHEN, ON THE THIRD day of his incarceration, the deputy woke him from his afternoon nap to tell him he had a visitor.

He grumbled, a habit he'd developed of late. His lawyer had been by twice yesterday trying to bail him out, but the food was good and Johnny wasn't ready to go home. Once he got back to the farm, there would be a hundred chores to do from dawn to dusk, and then he'd spend the night trying to figure out why he was so terrible at loving someone. At least here, he could relax and read the book the fairy lady brought him.

His brother, Wendell, claimed he'd accidentally turned in Johnny for murdering Scarlet and had agreed to do chores until Johnny got out. So there was no hurry.

Johnny looked up at the deputy. In a strange way, they'd become friends. Maybe when he got out, if he ever got out, he and the deputy could go have a beer. "If my court-appointed lawyer finds a way to get me out, I'll shoot him."

The deputy didn't look interested in the death threat. "It's not your lawyer, John; it's that girl with all the hair. I swear she smells like French toast."

Johnny stood. "Brown eyes?"

"I guess. I wasn't looking at her eyes when she floated in. If I didn't get to pat her down I'd wonder if she was real."

"Real pretty?" Johnny asked, thinking she also fit in the "real crazy" category. She was probably the last thing he needed in his life right now.

The deputy opened the cell and Johnny turned around to be handcuffed for the walk. He'd learned the routine.

"She's pretty, I guess." Deputy Rogers was far too married with five kids to have enough single cells left for looking at other women.

Apparently all he was allowed to do was smell.

Rogers patted Johnny on the back, indicating Johnny should move forward, as he continued, "Your brother was talking about her last night at the bar and said he wouldn't kick her out of bed."

Johnny swore. "My brother doesn't have a bed. He sleeps in a tree like all other buzzards. When I get out of here I'm going to have a few words to shove down his throat. My own kin telling the sheriff that I looked like I killed someone." Johnny swore again. "I swear if I ever do commit murder, it'll be a sibling."

The deputy held Johnny's arm tightly just above his elbow, as if he didn't quite trust the farmer. "John, how many brothers and sisters do you have?"

"One, and if you ask me, that is one too many. Wendell better start for the border now. If he's still around when I get out, he'll be talking out of his nose in no time because I'm going to shove all his teeth down his throat."

"John," the deputy whispered. "Stop making death threats. It's not the right thing to do while you're already locked up."

Johnny didn't have time to say more. The deputy almost threw him into the visitation room. Conversations with lawmen were often ended abruptly, Johnny had learned recently.

He stumbled a few steps and then raised his head. There

sat his little fairy, looking as dingy as ever. Walking to his side of the long table, Johnny sat down thinking she was even prettier than she had been a few days ago, if that were possible. Maybe they could have a jailhouse romance. He'd heard of women who go for men behind bars. Right about now, with an allegedly dead wife and a brother getting death threats from him, Johnny figured he must look pretty eligible in the prison lover market. Of course, if Scarlet really was dead, he'd be available.

"How are you, Kare?" he asked. It wasn't exactly a pickup line, but then if he picked her up, where would they go?

"I'm worried, John. No one is listening to me about your innocence. I've consulted with the cards and called a 'phone a spirit guide' hotline. I've even talked to my brother. It appears we are the only two people who think you're innocent."

"What about Scarlet and Max?"

The fairy lady jumped up so fast he thought she might be levitating for a moment.

"That's it," she said. "All I have to do is find Scarlet and Max, make them come home, and then you'll be cleared. I'm so happy I could kiss you."

Johnny didn't get his hopes up, but he had to ask, "Does this mean we're dating?"

He'd expected a laugh, or maybe a yes, but Kare looked at him with those big brown eyes tearing up. "Oh no," she cried. "Prison life is getting to you. The bars can sap your sanity. You've got to be strong, John. Don't worry, you've got me out here in the free world fighting for you."

He tried to smile, but knowing she was helping frightened him more than the murder charge. He stood. "I need to go back to my cell."

Now tears were running down her cheeks. "I understand. It's the one place you feel safe. Locked away from all the world. I've read about how not being free can imprison your mind as well as your body."

Johnny walked back to his cell thinking that after meeting Kare Cunningham, if he ever did get out of here and divorce Scarlet, he'd move to his farm and become a hermit.

Chapter 12

THURSDAY

THE NOON SUN WAS SLICING THROUGH THE BLINDS IN THE
waiting room when Beau Yates woke. He lifted his hat
slowly, taking his first peek at life circling around him. Several families, huddled in groups, were in the room or just
outside the door in the hallway. They were talking quietly
like strangers might as they waited for a train. Only the
loved one about to leave was beyond the double doors.

Apparently, Beau was as invisible as the silk plant in the
corner. No one noticed him. They simply moved around
him, sharing their grief with one another with hugs and pats.

Standing, he walked to an empty desk near the entrance
to the critical care unit. Any volunteer who might have sat
there in the past had been replaced by a single sheet of paper
with visiting times printed in bold letters.

Fifteen minutes until he could go in again and stare at
his father. Then, Beau promised himself he'd call for a plane
to come pick him up. By the time he ate lunch and drove

out to the airstrip, the plane would be waiting. It was time he got back to work.

He leaned against the wall, watching the others. Most looked sad. A few seemed more worried or afraid. All appeared tired, weary of waiting, anxious of what would come next. Something about hospital air sucked hope out of all who breathed it.

Beau wasn't even sure what he hoped for. If his father lived, they'd just go on ignoring each other. If he died, Beau would have to stay a few days and at least offer to help out. Maybe if he survived this heart attack, Beau wouldn't rush home next time.

When a nurse started letting people into the critical care unit, Beau's stepmother walked into the room. She looked smaller than he remembered. A little mouse of a woman void of any joy in life. She'd married his father when she was almost forty. Beau used to wonder how bad her single life must have been if she'd settled for his old man.

"Hello, Ruthie," he whispered when she was three feet from him.

She jumped, then met his gaze for a moment. "How'd you know, Beau? I didn't know you'd be here."

Her words told him that she hadn't asked that he'd be called. Which meant what he suspected: His father wouldn't be happy to see him.

"The doc called me. I flew in last night." He noticed that she was thinner than she'd been when he left years ago. "How you doing, Ruthie?"

He touched her shoulder, letting her know he cared. In truth, she'd always been kind in a quiet, shy way. Even after he was kicked out she left food for him in the fridge on Sunday mornings when he knew his father would be out. He used to sneak back in his room, get clean clothes, and take food packed away in plastic for him. The next week his clothes would be clean and pressed, waiting.

"I'm fine, Beau. Have you seen your father?"

"Not awake." Beau stuffed his guitar under the desk and followed her through the door. "You mind if I go in with you?"

She shook her head. "I don't mind. He doesn't talk about you like he used to. I don't think he's angry anymore. It's more like he thinks of you as dead."

"Oh, that's comforting," Beau answered, wondering if Ruthie was trying to cheer him up. He would bet she'd had to listen to hours of his father raging over a son who had gone bad.

They walked into the room where his father lay and moved to either side of the bed. Beau observed that Ruthie didn't touch her husband. They just stood watching him breathe until the nurse poked her head in and told them it was time to leave.

When they walked out, Beau asked the same question. "How are you doing, Ruthie?"

"I'm . . ." She started to lie, then hesitated and added, "The bank . . ."

He touched her arm. "I'll take care of it."

She nodded. "He can't know. He'd be mad if he thought I mentioned it to you."

Beau understood. "He won't." On impulse Beau leaned in and kissed her cheek. He'd never thought of her as his mother, not even a substitute one, but he did care about her.

Ten minutes later, he was standing in the bank before he bothered to notice his wrinkled clothes. The black tailored shirt, jeans, and boots no longer looked polished and pressed. He'd lost the leather tie that always held his dark hair back, and two days' worth of stubble darkened his jaw. He looked so bad the bank probably wouldn't take his money. In Nashville he was proud to be an outlaw, but here it might not be a good idea to look the part.

"May I help you, sir?" a suit, who could have played Scrooge in *A Christmas Carol* without bothering with makeup, asked in a cold, professional way. While he waited for Beau to answer he rocked onto his toes as if trying to appear taller, more important. There was a nervousness about him. A clock watcher, Beau guessed.

Beau decided to bluff his way through. "Yes, I'd like to see the president of the bank."

"He's not here, sir." The suit lifted his chin as if preparing to die rather than give out more information. "I'm one of the loan officers. I'm sure I can help you with any questions."

Beau stood his ground.

The suit broke first. "I can check with the vice president, if you'll wait here. She's new, but maybe she can be of some help."

Beau nodded and waited. A minute later the nervous guy came back and pointed in the direction of an open door. He didn't look interested in making introductions and Beau wondered if he'd even notified the vice president that she had a customer.

Beau took off his black hat, raked his fingers through hair far too long for Harmony style, and silently walked through the open door.

For a moment he watched the woman who sat behind the long desk. Though computers banked her on both sides, she concentrated on papers organized in neat piles before her. She was about his age but didn't resemble anyone he remembered from school. Blond hair, tucked up in a tight knot on top of her head. Dark blue suit, slightly too big. Maybe she was trying to look like a banker the same way he felt like he tried to look like a country-western singer.

He took another step, his worn boots echoing off her polished floor.

"How may I help you?" she said as she reluctantly lowered the paper she'd been reading.

Her gaze met his.

The air froze between them. Memories and feelings tumbled over him. The night he'd first seen her drive up in her red convertible. The weeks, years ago, when he'd tried to find the girl who now stood before him. She'd been his midnight ride across the moonlight. A wild, rich girl who'd picked up a struggling singer. Both in their teens. Both too young to understand what they'd felt.

He broke the trance first. "Hello, Trouble." She'd once said her daddy called her Trouble, and he'd thought the name fit.

In a fluid movement she was around the desk.

He opened his arms, but she stopped a foot out of his embrace. They'd been an "almost was" years ago. Now they were older. No more than strangers with a shared memory. He hadn't known then how she'd haunt his dreams, and looking into her sky-blue eyes he had the feeling she felt the same.

"Beau," she whispered. "I didn't think I'd ever see you again."

He wanted to hold her tight, but all he held was the memory of how she used to drop by to hear him play at Buffalo's Bar and how, now and then, she'd take him for a drive in her classic Mustang. When he began to climb, he saw her less and less. Until finally, she vanished like a midnight dream at dawn.

Lowering his arms, he studied the woman she'd become. "You look so good. I miss the ponytail and the red boots, but the lady you've turned into isn't half bad."

"You look terrible."

He laughed. "I know. I could explain by saying I spent the night at the hospital. My dad had a heart attack. Which is all true, but Trouble, darling, I don't look much different on any other day."

He knew he was playing at being Beau Yates, something he'd learned to do when in public. Say what the crowd expected to hear. Play the role of an outlaw. That was what the public wanted. As long as he played the rehearsed lines he didn't fall over words.

"I'm sorry about your father." Her words sounded rehearsed as well. Maybe they were both playing a part.

The girl he remembered had matured into a beautiful woman. Educated, successful, and totally out of his league. When he couldn't think of anything else to say, he noticed her straightening, pulling away mentally. Maybe she knew he was playing her, or maybe she was simply molding into her own shell.

Beau tried again, but all signs of what they'd meant to each other were gone. "Doc says my father is stable now. I wouldn't put it past him to be pretending to sleep so he doesn't have to talk to me." Beau backed a few inches away. "Looks like you're doing well."

She smiled. "I finished my MBA from UT last year."

"And became vice president of a bank," he added.

She grinned, and he saw the twinkle in her blue eyes that he'd always loved. "It helped that my daddy owns several branches. I'm just training here. But you, Beau, you're the shooting star."

He shook his head. "I'm still doing the same thing I was when you met me. I'm playing my music."

"Only now, millions listen."

They stood, a foot apart yet unable to close the distance. Too much had happened in their worlds. They were no longer two wild kids driving through the night dreaming of the life that could be.

"How can I help you, Beau?" she asked in her most professional voice.

"I need to pay off my father's house."

"Do you know how much he owes?"

"No. It doesn't matter." He pulled out a card that had no limit. "If he has any other loans here, I'll pay them too."

She understood. While he waited, staring at the nameplate on her desk, she took care of everything. ASHLEY L. POWERS, VICE PRESIDENT. The name didn't fit her.

When she walked back in, she handed his card back. "He owed thirty-two thousand on the house and had two signature loans out for eleven thousand total." She hesitated until he looked up, then added, "Everything is in your father's name. It looks like your mother can't even write checks on the account. That might be a problem if he's in the hospital."

Beau wasn't surprised. "Open her an account with ten thousand in it. She'll just need a debit card. I'll explain how it works. That should get her through until he gets out of the hospital. She's not my mother, but I wouldn't want her to do without." He almost added that his stepmother had probably always done without.

"I'll take care of it." She stepped to the door and passed his request along, then returned. While they waited, she sat on the desk in front of his chair, almost close enough to touch. "Are you staying awhile?"

"A few days." He made up his mind as he watched her, wishing he could see her once more in moonlight. "I'll see if I can get a room at Winter's Inn. It might be nice to look up a few old friends."

He wanted to ask her if she'd like to have dinner, or go for a drive, but the girl he'd dreamed about for so long, the woman who'd whispered through so many of his songs, wasn't here now. She'd vanished. Molded into someone else.

The guy in the suit stepped in her office and handed Beau his receipts. Beau didn't miss the forced politeness in his stance.

"Thanks," Beau managed.

"Of course, sir." The nervous man almost jumped out the door.

Beau smiled at Trouble, feeling sorry for her because she had to work with such a jerk. She lowered her gaze to the floor. Nothing left to do but leave, he realized.

They shook hands like strangers, neither knowing how to climb over the years that separated them. He wanted to hug his Trouble, but she'd disappeared.

He drove over to Martha Q's place and ate lunch with her and Mrs. Biggs. Martha Q was thrilled to go along with his plan to keep his visit a secret. She put him upstairs in her best room and charged him full price.

In the silence of his room, he wondered why he'd even stayed. He'd done what he came to do—see his father, take care of any money they needed—but still he couldn't leave. Not yet. Something wasn't finished here.

Maybe it never would be, but he had to stay a few days and find out.

Chapter 13

FRIDAY MORNING

DREW WAITED ALL WEEK BEFORE HE DECIDED TO DRIVE
back to Harmony. The woman he'd called Sleeping Beauty
had haunted his every thought. He couldn't figure out what
it was about her that pulled him so strongly. She was pretty,
but he'd gone out with pretty women before. She was intelligent, well, maybe. He hadn't really talked to her enough
to know.

The night they'd gone to dinner together and ended up
back at the bed-and-breakfast for a good-night kiss, he
thought of tossing her on the bed and taking their evening
to another level. Her broken leg, or rather the cast, reminded
him that might be a bad idea. Yet the way she'd melted
against him had kept his heart running double time for an
hour.

Besides, he wasn't some romantic hero. He was simply
a man trying to hold his life together. Women went for the
adventurous types. They wanted excitement. If the talk
around town was true, Millanie was a wounded hero. A

woman like that would find a man like him about as interesting as watching a snail.

So, he argued with himself, how could she feel so good in his arms?

It made no sense. Men and women were naturally attracted to the opposite sex, but not like this. He'd seen her twice and she'd become an addiction. He could stay in his cabin and read or take long walks, or try to write, but it didn't matter. He was addicted.

Logic told him he could shake this need. After all, it was just a kiss. It wasn't like they were lovers. Hell, if they ever were lovers it might be a big enough overdose to kill them both. Drew smiled to himself, thinking it would almost be worth the risk. He'd like to see if the sparks between them exploded when they made love. His logical mind didn't want to accept what his body kept telling him. He wanted her.

He had to be sensible. He didn't have a future to offer a woman, and he had a feeling Millanie wouldn't settle for less. He was at peace with his one-room cabin and simple life of teaching one class and working on a book he'd probably never finish. The class and occasional lectures were his idea of pushing the limits. This existence he'd built from the ashes of his life after the shooting was all he could handle. Too many people around bothered him. Noise bothered him.

His relationship with Kare, his little sister, was the only ordinary thing in his life. Somehow her being a half bubble off plumb made it okay for him to be not quite normal. She seemed wild and crazy, but she had a big heart and cared about people deeply. Slowly, she was pulling him into life again.

He liked to think she'd settle here and be part of his life forever. She'd probably marry one of the locals. He'd see her often. Drew could even see him playing the part of the best uncle in the world.

As he walked through the trees toward the café at Twisted Creek, he tried to remember what it had been like to want something or someone. Once, he'd wanted everything.

Teaching in a school few teachers would have picked was a challenge. He'd wanted to make a difference in the world. He wanted to grow every day. Drew poured his whole life into teaching during the day and working on his doctorate at night. At twenty-eight he'd almost graduated and his dreams were turning toward teaching future teachers. He could have picked any college in the country to move to, but he wanted to finish the year out and watch his high school seniors graduate. Three days before graduation a student smuggled a gun past security and opened fire in the first classroom he encountered. Drew's open room. Drew's class.

Branches began to slap against Drew's face and he realized he was running in the trees by his cabin.

He slowed, pushing the past away, forcing himself to come back to today, not five years ago. Not that day.

When he'd come here, it had been a rebirth. His friend Luke must have seen how close Drew was to breaking. For weeks he didn't see anyone except the locals at the lake. No phone, no TV, no Internet. He read and slept and healed. Dr. Andrew Cunningham turned twenty-nine working on old cars that weren't even his. Andrew, the professional, the educator was dead and Drew Cunningham slowly came to be.

Drew smiled when he cleared the trees and headed up a path to the café. The first night he'd seen this place he thought he'd finally made it to the end of the world. Now, it felt more like home. As he reached the half dozen cars he and Luke had overhauled the past few years, he picked the old van that looked like it belonged in the dump but drove like a race car. Least noticeable. Invisible.

Luke had told him a dozen times to pick any car he wanted and it was his, but Drew didn't want to own anything. Somehow the paperwork would tie him down, make him easier to find.

Only being invisible was another kind of death. Maybe it was time he stepped back into life. He'd stayed under the radar. He'd been careful. Stayed away from crowds. Never got his picture in the paper. Paid cash for everything. It may have been five years, but the last thing Drew wanted was a reporter showing up now. If the people knew what had happened to him, they'd look at him differently.

He had to continue to be careful. Open himself up to the world one breath . . . one kiss . . . at a time.

A big shadow moved across the back porch of the café.

Drew slowed his steps but forced his body not to tense.

"You heading into town, Drew?" Morgan's low voice sounded sleepy.

"Yeah," Drew answered, "I thought I'd drop by and check on the McAllen woman that I picked up at the airport last week. Who knows, she might be hungry again and I could talk her into another date."

He saw Morgan's wide smile. "Or, just in case she needs you to 'kiss her socks off' again."

Drew laughed. He'd shared every detail of his evening out with his friend while they were fishing a few nights ago. "I know I rated it the worst date ever except for the kiss, but I figure I'll give her another chance to seduce me."

Luke Morgan saluted him as if wishing him luck. "Ever figure she might be too much for you, Professor?"

"I'm pretty sure if I catch her when she's not exhausted or on painkillers that handling her will be more than my unused heart can take. Just bury me out here by the lake."

"Will do," Luke yelled as Drew climbed into the van and backed away.

Chapter 14

MILLANIE LEFT THE DOCTOR'S OFFICE WITH HER COUSIN Noah McAllen by her side. The minute her kin found out she was in town, they'd taken turns calling every morning to see if they could help. Noah just happened to be the unlucky one who phoned the day of her first doctor visit.

She smiled at the good-looking cowboy beside her. Noah was seven or eight years younger, but he'd made a killing riding bulls in his late teens and early twenties. Someone said that he now owned one of the finest ranches around.

"Sorry I'm taking up your time." Millanie stuffed her medical files in a satchel she carried from hospital to hospital. "I could have made it here by myself."

"No problem." He grinned. "I was glad to get out of the house. My wife's planning our wedding. You'll have to come. We'd love to have you there. It's tomorrow night. She's decorating the barn in fall colors and just leaving all the boxes of apples out for decoration. They'll be dancing after the ceremony."

Millanie was shocked. "You're getting married tomorrow?"

He shrugged. "It's no big deal. We get married every month. Or have since August thirtieth, last year. This one will make the twelfth time I've said *I do* and I'm hoping it's the last. We're running out of preachers to perform the ceremony. The one month we didn't get married was February and I missed it, to tell the truth."

"Why marry every month?"

"My Rea says she wants to make sure I remember I'm married." He grinned again. "I'm not likely to forget. We have a huge party, invite everyone in town, and then spend a few days honeymooning. I kind of like that part." He helped her into his truck and tossed her crutches in the back. "I figure I'm the most married man I know, and that's right where I want to be."

Noah might be years younger than her, but when he winked Millanie blushed.

"I'll be there tomorrow," she said, thinking it might be just the place to watch people. All week she'd watched and waited. The assistant she'd been promised had never shown up. Looking for a person pretending to belong in Harmony wasn't easy. She could use a local's help. After listening to Martha Q talk at breakfast every morning for a week, Millanie had already decided that half the folks in Harmony belonged in an asylum. Most of Martha Q's stories were wild love affairs or tales of the horrors after one divorced.

"You mind if I stop and see Rick Matheson?" Noah interrupted Millanie's filing of information. "He's a lawyer who is handling the adoption of my son. It won't take long, and then I'll drive you anywhere you want to go."

Martha Q had told her the story of Noah and Reagan's baby. He had been dropped off at Reagan's farm a little over a year ago by a friend of hers who didn't want the child. Word was when Noah came home and saw the baby, he called the boy his son. Everyone knew the baby shouldn't have been the young couple's problem, but no one dared bring it up to Noah or Reagan.

When Noah pulled into the mini strip mall housing a used bookstore and a laundry below, and several offices above, Millanie relaxed, knowing she'd have something to do while she waited. "I'll browse for a few books. You take as long as you like."

Noah helped her to the bookstore's door and tipped his hat as she entered. A moment later she heard his boots bounding up the metal stairs.

Millanie hobbled in and smiled at the old guy behind a desk almost covered with books. Early sixties, she'd guess, shirt stained with coffee probably, ink on his right hand. Fifty pounds overweight, thinning gray hair that curled around the back of his ears. Intelligent, single, probably high blood pressure and allergies, judging from his red nose and several wadded tissues near the cash register. "Morning," she said. "I'm—"

"I know who you are." He puffed up as if insulted she'd think he wouldn't know her on sight. "Martha Q told me she had a guest at the inn who was on crutches. I figured you'd be in here at some point looking for books. Would you like a cup of coffee or do you just want to wander through the stacks? You're welcome to look but if you read past the first chapter, I expect you to buy."

Millanie felt like she'd just been tossed a multiple-choice question and he'd forgotten to say, *A, B, or C.* "No coffee, thanks. I'll just wander for a while, I guess. My cousin is—"

"I know." He stopped her again. "Who could miss Noah McAllen standing in the doorway blocking most of the sun? I'll yell when he comes back to pick you up."

Millanie moved away from the man. Definitely lived alone, for he was used to talking to himself. Correction, he had a cat. Hair ten inches up on his trousers gave that fact away. She added *not interested in making money* to her list. Nothing about the place welcomed shoppers. Even the big round reading table was piled high in the center with discarded books and used paper cups.

As she maneuvered throughout the stacks, she noticed Kare Cunningham's sign above a tiny green door tucked away in one corner. Drew had said her *office* was in the bookstore. On impulse, Millanie tapped on the door.

"Come in," Kare's voice answered above the sound of shuffling.

Millanie had trouble getting into the room. She finally set her crutches inside and hopped over the threshold. The space was cluttered with books, a laptop, and stacks of paper. The office reminded Millanie of *I Dream of Jeannie*'s home in a bottle. Scarves and tiny wind chimes were hung in every corner.

Kare jumped up and ran to help, knocking the crutches over and almost tripping Millanie.

"I'm so glad you came," Kare whispered when she finally stopped bouncing around like a hiccuping butterfly. "I've been waiting for you to drop by for a visit. I knew the minute I saw you who you were."

"So"—Millanie fought to keep her face blank—"you've read the future and you knew I was going to drop by."

"No, not really," Kare said as she helped Millanie lower into the chair. "Remember, I invited you to come see me. If you hadn't come today, I'd decided I'd try dropping by the inn. Only that wouldn't be my first choice for us to have a private conversation. The walls of that place have ears and they are stuck on Martha Q's head."

Millanie was trying to figure out how to tell Kare she hadn't come in for a reading when Kare whispered, "I'm here to help you, Captain McAllen."

For a moment Millanie's mind seemed to freeze up like an old air conditioner on a hot day. Kare couldn't be the contact sent to help her. Not this pixie of a girl who read palms for a living.

Walnut-brown eyes stared up at her. Intelligent eyes hidden by long overmascaraed lashes. Kare's lips were caked with red lipstick and a fake mole dotted her left cheek.

"I'm your contact," the fairy creature whispered again. "I quit the bureau two years ago for family reasons, but I sometimes take research jobs for them. You know, part-time work helps pay the bills until my career takes off. They called me the night you landed. By the time you checked into the inn, I'd already started my research."

Millanie thought of screaming *No*, but with her luck, the bookstore owner would rush in. So she simply said the first thing that came to mind. "You're kidding."

The girl waved one hand with nails long enough to plow a garden row. "Nope, I'm at your service. I'm a great researcher and I have a high enough security rating to get you whatever information you need."

Millanie saw it then, a disguise so good she doubted another person had cracked it. The flashiest woman in town wasn't real and no one knew.

Not even her brother.

Chapter 15

MILLANIE LEFT THE BOOKSTORE WITH TWO BOOKS SHE'D bought after barely looking at them and a huge bag with a quilt stuffed inside. Mr. Hatcher commented that he'd been staring at the quilt for a year wondering who'd be fool enough to buy it off the palm reader. He'd also commented that the little lady must have not needed the money because she never lowered the price.

Millanie said simply that she loved orange and brown blended together. In truth she couldn't wait to get home and read all the reports Kare had printed off and folded into the bulk of the quilt. For someone Millanie thought was tiptoeing around sanity, Kare appeared to have done her homework.

"Where to?" Noah asked with a wide smile. A hint of the rodeo cowboy still lingered in the way he stood and how he wore his hat low over his eyes. "I'll be your taxi all day."

She read him easily. "It went well with the lawyer, didn't it?"

"It did. Looks like my son, Utah, will be legally ours within the month. He's a great kid. Says *Dada* and *up*. Loves it when I let him sit on my horse. Rea throws a fit, but I could ride before I could walk and I'm guessing he will too."

Millanie had to ask, "Is he going to be a bull rider?"

"Nope. He's going to raise horses like his old man. Rea says we're stopping the next generation of McAllens from eating arena dirt." Noah shrugged. "But my dad says we can start him on sheep in a few years. If he's not interested, I'm happy with that, but if he wants to ride I'll be there for him. It's in our blood."

Millanie didn't want to bring up the fact that little Utah was adopted so it might not be in *his* blood.

"Thanks for taking me to my doctor's appointment this morning, Noah. I'll try to make your wedding." She noticed an old van parked beside Noah's truck. Drew sat watching her as if he had nothing else in the world to do.

"You mind if I bring a date?" she added.

"Nope." Noah turned in Drew's direction and waved as he opened the truck door on the passenger side. "Morning, Professor. If you're picking up laundry they got a new drive-through window on the side."

"Thanks, Noah." Drew climbed out of his van. "The only thing I was hoping to pick up is that cousin of yours." He looked directly at Millanie. "Want to have lunch with me?"

Noah took one glance at her standing there and winked. Without a word, he handed her crutches to Drew.

Drew held the crutches in one hand as his free arm circled her waist and he helped her to his van.

The familiar warmth of him felt so good, but her logical mind wondered when Drew Cunningham worked. Shouldn't he be at Clifton College or home writing? Of course, he obviously didn't spend money on new clothes or cars. Maybe if he cut out all the extras in life, he could live working one day a week.

"Now you take good care of my cousin, Professor," Noah yelled. "She's got a broken leg."

"I know," Drew whispered so low only Millanie heard. "It's the only thing keeping her upright."

Millanie smiled, knowing he was just joking, but still it was flattering to think Drew was interested in her.

She was vaguely aware of Noah backing out in his truck as Drew's hands slid over her arm when he carefully put her in the seat and secured the seat belt. Before he straightened he turned toward her and kissed her lightly on the mouth as if it were something he did every time he buckled her in.

It never occurred to her to protest. Watching him was like observing a species she'd never seen in the wild. She'd grown up with a father in the military; she'd gone through school in ROTC. All she'd ever been around were men who were driven by a mission.

Drew didn't seem to be driven by anything. Near as she could tell he wasn't even walking in any particular direction through life. His clothes were out of style, his hair in need of a haircut. He didn't seem to fit in any category and she was an expert at tagging people.

Between trying to place Drew and his sister in the right type, Millanie felt like she was slipping. Kare hadn't been what she seemed, and Drew didn't fit into any category.

They drove through the narrow streets of Harmony and out toward the highway. In her head she had the conversation they weren't having. He'd ask how the doctor's visit went and she'd lie and say all was great. She'd talk about Noah and how happy her family was that he'd settled down. Then Drew would say something about how everyone in town talked about Noah's rodeo days. She'd invite him to the wedding and he'd say he'd be happy to go. Maybe they'd drift into conversation about the weather or fall coming on, and then they'd be silent and just enjoy the drive. Like they were doing right now.

Along the interstate Drew turned off at a truck stop restaurant. He didn't ask her if this place would do. He just cut the engine and climbed out of a vehicle that didn't seem to fit him at all. Vans were for people who had kids or men with heavy hobbies to carry around, not professors whose usual load was probably papers to grade.

By the time she got her door open he was at her side helping her.

As he balanced her so she could stand, their bodies brushed. Both froze. She felt the warmth of him and one look into his eyes told her he wanted her. Not the how-about-we-hook-up-sometime kind of feeling, but something she'd never experienced, like maybe finding one true love in a world where such a thing had been extinct for years.

She considered the possibility that they'd both caught some disease at the airport that night they'd met. That theory made as much sense as any. She'd always been level-headed, reasonable, and he didn't seem the passionate type. After all, he'd lived to his thirties without putting a ring on his finger. In fact, she could almost see him as a dear old professor in forty years wandering the campus.

Nothing about the man was exciting or mysterious. He wasn't even flirting. His speech, his manners, his caring all seemed real. As real as the need he seemed to have for her. It occurred to her that he didn't understand it any more than she did.

Millanie pulled her warring feelings into check. She was too old to be reacting like this. He wasn't the kind of man she would ever be attracted to. He was nice and maybe a little mad to be infatuated with a woman with whom he couldn't keep a conversation going.

As they walked into the dive, she asked, "Aren't you going to say anything to me, Professor?"

"Not much worth eating here except the burgers." He held open the door.

"Then why did we come?"

"It's the only place around where we won't run into people we know. I wanted to be alone with you." He took her crutches while she lowered herself into the chair.

"So we could talk?" She laughed at her own joke.

He sat down, opened his menu, and answered without looking up. "I thought I made it plain to you before, Millie, talking isn't what I have in mind." His leg accidentally brushed hers under the table. "I've got wild plans, girl."

Giggling, she bumped his leg. "No one's called me *girl* in years and I hate the name Millie. It's not real important that we talk, but at least try to get my name right, Andrew."

"I'm making no promises. You distract me. You're lucky I can manage simple sentences when I'm around you."

She wondered if the harmless professor had any idea how cute he was, even with his dark glasses on. If another man at another time had said such things, she might have been on guard, but not with Drew. A man who went to see his mother in Chicago, had a fortune-telling sister he worried about, and lectured at church couldn't be dangerous.

He smiled at the waitress and ordered two hamburgers.

The waitress was trying to flirt with him, but Drew didn't seem to notice. He simply went back to reading the menu as if it were fascinating.

Millanie added that she wanted hers with no onion or lettuce and to add cheese. The waitress wrote it down without ever taking her eyes off Drew.

When they were alone, Millanie bumped her good leg against his again. No reaction. "What's so interesting?"

He rested his leg against hers as he looked over the menu and smiled when she didn't move away. His contact was definitely no accident this time.

"This menu has seven grammatical mistakes," he whispered.

She blinked. Maybe the bad guys had sent Drew to confuse her. No, not even drug lords hired professors. Could it be possible that he thought spelling to be a topic worth discussing?

The waitress dropped off their drinks without glancing at Millanie. She asked Drew twice if he wanted a straw. He politely said no, twice.

When they were alone again, Millanie leaned forward and asked, "What did your sister do before she became a fortune-teller?" They needed to talk before daydreaming took completely over in her mind. The heat of his leg resting against hers seemed to be warming her entire body.

"Went to school, I guess, but I don't know how well she did. She told me once she had her own computer by the time she was five and since then she could learn anything she wanted to know online. It's the one thing we share in common. I do most of my research for my book on the Internet and she plays on the thing all day between palm-reading customers."

"She's making a living at palm reading?"

"Must be. I've asked her several times since she dropped into my life if she needed any money and she always says no."

Millanie thought of asking how he got his money. She doubted teaching one class left him with enough to loan his sister money. Only the feel of his leg against her kept distracting her.

They ate lunch without bothering to keep a conversation going, and then he paid the bill and helped her back to his van. Before he could buckle her belt, she completed the task. He didn't look disappointed or seem to even notice, but he didn't kiss her this time. She'd been trained to read people, but she couldn't read him.

Again, he didn't tell her where they were going, but as they passed through town and headed out on Lone Oak Road, she guessed. "My ancestors had a place out this direction. A few acres they got for being one of the founding families of Harmony."

"I know. I looked it up last night on the library's Web page about the town's history. Have you ever seen the place?"

"No. If my folks took me out there as a kid, I don't remember it. Once we moved, it was rare to come back. The family always wanted to come to Dallas to see us. Lots more to do, they said."

As the van turned off on a dirt road, she felt like memory deep in her cells recognized the place. The line of trees must have been planted over a hundred years ago to serve as a windbreak, but the rest of the land looked almost the same as it had when Patrick and Annie McAllen homesteaded.

"From the looks of it," Drew said in what almost sounded like his lecture voice, "the land has never been plowed. Your great-great-grandparents must have been ranchers. Which would make sense in this uneven terrain. One of the records listed him as a carpenter."

"It's beautiful in a raw, wild way."

"I think so too." He slowed. "I'm guessing this old house holds secrets waiting. There is definitely a true beauty here."

When she glanced at him, Drew was looking at her, not the landscape. She remained perfectly still as he reached over and caught one of her short curls.

The van stopped as his fingers moved into her hair. "I just need to touch you for a moment," he whispered as if apologizing.

She closed her eyes as he cupped her cheek in his hand. His thumb moved over her mouth. "I know this isn't the time or place, but when it's right I plan to know the feel of your skin completely."

Millanie let out a long breath as he straightened and began to drive. He'd finally said something interesting.

"You all right?" he asked as he picked up speed.

"I'm fine." She wanted to say she'd never felt so desired, but words didn't come.

"Nice place to homestead," he said casually, pointing to the pretty rolling countryside.

She nodded, even though he was watching the rough road and didn't see her. Finally, she moved her thoughts past his touch. "I remember my mother telling me that. She said after their fourth kid, they bought more land and built farther out. The homestead house was used as a weaning house when their children first married. Eventually it was just used for storage. I'll be surprised if it's still standing."

Drew turned first left, then right on a winding road that was little more than tire tracks. "From the looks of this road, they didn't really care if they had company."

Millanie laughed. "Legend was my great-great-grandfather had four sisters who lived in town. Maybe he planned the road this way."

As they circled a natural rise, the little house came into view. Sunlight sparkled across it as if showing off the old place. Windows had been boarded up on the north and west sides, but the house still stood.

Drew slowed the van. "Not long after I got here, I met an interesting man, Tyler Wright, the local funeral director. He's spent years collecting maps and was tickled to have some help in logging the history of this area. He brought me to this homestead house once. Said most of the McAllens have never come out here. The square of land is too small for any ranch operation these days. He claimed most of them don't even know who owns the original square of land now."

Millanie couldn't stop staring at the house with wild rosebushes still growing on one side and a walk that looked like it was built from river rocks. When Drew didn't say anything for a long time, she put the pieces together. "Why'd you bring me out here?"

He turned in the seat to face her, gently bumping his knee against her good leg. "I looked it up last night. There was only one name listed as owner on the tax rolls." He hesitated. "I don't know who has been paying the taxes on this place, but they're paid up. The one owner was Patrick F. McAllen III, your father. I found his obituary online. I'm guessing if you inherited from him, this is your land, Millanie."

The memories of those horrible days after her father's death came rolling back. Her mother had died in a crash six months before. She and her brother were called home from college when her father told them he had cancer. He'd said he'd taken care of everything for them. Philip got the stocks. She got the land. She'd thought he meant the few acres surrounding the house in Dallas. She'd sold it to pay for college, never dreaming there had been more.

Drew brushed tears off her cheek. "You didn't know about this place?"

She shook her head. All her years in the army she'd never known where to list as home. Not Dallas, no family there; not Harmony, it was too far in her past. Now she knew. This land had been waiting for her to come back.

"This is your home, Millie." Drew said the very thing she was thinking. "Your roots are here."

When she looked up to thank him, she saw the sadness in his eyes and knew Drew had no roots to go back to. He was a wanderer and maybe always would be. Maybe that was why he didn't own anything, not even a car.

He leaned in and kissed a tear away, and then his lips covered hers in a gentle mating.

"Thank you," she whispered when he pulled far enough away to look at her.

"You're welcome," he answered, then kissed her again. A quick, happy kiss before he suggested they go inside and have a look around.

It was impossible to walk the stone walk on crutches, so she maneuvered through the grass to the steps. The bottom one was broken, but by leaning on him she made it to the porch. Slowly, with Drew testing every board, they reached the front door, now weathered but still standing.

Drew found the key above the door frame and they walked into the dusty old house occupied by birds, spiders, and tumbleweeds that blew in from the open back door. While Drew fought to close the door, Millanie stood perfectly still, letting the house surround her, welcome her. Generations of McAllens had grown up here. Of all the places she'd traveled and lived over the years, she'd never felt a pull so strong to one place. It was almost as if the house were whispering *Welcome*.

They took less than five minutes to explore the downstairs. Half the space was taken up by one room with a door leading off to the kitchen and another to what might have been a bedroom or study. A very basic bathroom had been built onto the side of the house, probably when they put in indoor plumbing. The big room had wide windows on three sides and a huge fireplace in the center of the house.

"This place was well built," Drew pointed out. "Looks like the roof is still good. Not a water spot on the ceiling." He tried the faucet on the old steel sink. "Put in new plumbing and a few windows, this place might be livable."

She flipped a switch. Nothing happened. "And new electrical."

"Of course. I didn't even see lines running from the road to the house. I'm guessing it hasn't been lived in for fifty years or more. There's a cabin across the road that your cousin Alex said was probably built about the same time. The sheriff said she thinks it must have belonged to your great-great-granddad's brother."

"How is that possible that they're both still standing?" She could almost see the ghosts of McAllens running up the narrow stairs or laughing as they talked around the huge fireplace.

She circled, studying the house. It was protected on two sides by the bluff, and the tree line would cut wind from the west.

"Your ancestor must have given this some thought. He wanted this house to be around for a long time."

"For me," she whispered. "Maybe he wanted it to last until I came along and needed a place to call home."

"Maybe," Drew agreed. "You're starting to sound like my sister. Don't suggest this place is haunted or she'll be running out here." He took a few steps toward Millanie. "By the way, why'd you tell her you have 'the gift' also? You'll only encourage her."

Millanie smiled. "Maybe I do. Maybe I don't need palms to read you. You're a very easy man to read, Professor."

He stood close, widened his stance to balance both their weight, and leaned in. "So, Millie, read my mind." His hand slid around her waist and tugged her full against him.

She raised her arms and rested them on his shoulders as he kissed her tenderly.

When he moved to her neck, she whispered against his ear. "You're a man who enjoys learning, likes order, and I think somewhere you must have taken time to learn exactly how women like to be kissed."

He mumbled something against her throat as she continued, "Only, it's been a long while since you've touched a woman. There's a hunger in you that your logical mind can't push down and, apparently, I seem to be the object of that hunger."

He returned to her mouth, stopping all conversation for a while. His hands moved along her back, holding her as he caressed her. When he reached into the V of her collar and pulled her tunic off her shoulder, she was surprised by his boldness. He lowered his head and began tasting her skin from her throat to her bare shoulders.

For a moment she couldn't catch her breath. It had never been like this for her. There was a need in this man that went far deeper than just attraction, and she wasn't sure he understood it any more than she did. This nice man with his logical mind and kind ways was opening up a world she'd never stepped into. Passion.

Chapter 16

SATURDAY

EVERYONE STILL CALLED THE PLACE WHERE NOAH AND Reagan lived the Truman Farm, even though no one named Truman lived there anymore. Reagan managed a very successful apple orchard that shipped apples all over a three-state area. Noah got up and went to work every morning on his ranch farther down Lone Oak Road. It seemed right that they were together; everyone in town talked about them as a couple and had as long as Beau could remember.

As Beau Yates pulled his rented car behind the barn, he laughed to himself. Noah and Reagan were the most married couple in the county and they were doing it again tonight. Since he was still in town, he agreed to play a set with the band Noah had hired.

Beau asked the not-so-newlyweds to keep his part in the party secret, but he doubted that was possible. He'd been in town three days and no one had bothered him. He always visited his father at night, then played his guitar and wrote music between the midnight visit and the four o'clock one. After that, he went home and slept until noon. Beau didn't worry about being interrupted at the inn; he had Martha Q on guard.

Only every night he sat out on the porch and wished a red Mustang convertible would drive by. The girl he'd called Trouble was out there somewhere and she knew where to find him. But she never came. Maybe she hadn't spent as many nights thinking of him as he had of her.

The sun was spreading out on the horizon when Beau swung up on the Truman Orchard's porch. "Evening, Noah," he said.

Noah sat near the steps, his long legs blocking his son from breaking free.

Utah shifted from slat to slat trying to find the way to escape, but the porch railing held him prisoner. Chubby little bare feet danced as he moved along as if eventually he'd find a hole big enough to slip through.

Noah motioned to a chair. "How's your dad?"

Beau shook his head. "I don't know if he's totally out of it or just doesn't want to talk to me, but every night I'm visiting a snoring man. I keep saying I'll give it one more day, then I'm heading back to Nashville."

Noah shook his head. "Relationships with dads are hard. When I was growing up, half the time I thought my dad was mad at me and the other half he wasn't around. Turns out he only had me to get a grandson. Now, when my folks come over they walk right past me to Utah. I've become the invisible man. My father, who I always thought was a relatively intelligent man, talks baby talk to Utah and the kid talks right back in the same language."

Beau laughed. Everyone knew Noah's father had watched over him every time he rode bulls, even in high school. One night, when Noah had been hurt, his father had climbed over the fence and pulled his son out from under a thousand pounds of hide and horns.

Beau watched the one-year-old keep moving back and

forth for a while before he asked, "You know that young vice president at the bank? I think her name's Ashley Powers."

"Sure. She came in to straighten a few things out. I hear she's a real hard boss. Half the folks in the bank are worried they'll lose their jobs. Someone said she's not here to make friends."

Beau didn't like what he heard. He wanted the wild girl in the ponytail, not the banker. Maybe he'd be wise to just keep her in his dreams.

Still, as the night wore on, he caught himself looking for her in the crowd. He knew most of the people on sight, though few he called friends. They were just people he'd seen in school, or church, or Buffalo's Bar. Funny thing, he could never remember which place.

His best friend, Border Biggs, was fishing off the Galveston coast. He'd made enough money playing backup for Beau that he'd bought a boat, put the rest of the money in savings, and said he planned to live off the interest.

The wedding was all party, with Noah hesitating as if he might not say "I do" again and Reagan tossing her flowers to the eighty-year-old priest who married them. The wedding cake was a carousel of pies, all made by Reagan, with the sheriff serving.

After the wedding ceremony, Beau played one set, then packed up his guitar and headed to his car. He'd learned never to stay too long at any party, even a wedding. As the wannabe singers drank, they always felt the need to tell Beau how they could have been bigger than he'd ever be. Somewhere the conversation ended with them telling him he'd been lucky. From then on there was nothing left for him to do but walk away. So tonight he'd do just that before the conversation even started.

In the shadows behind the barn, he walked across uneven ground, wishing he'd thought to bring a flashlight. He was almost to his rented car when he saw a red Mustang parked under the barn light. There was no mistaking the classic or the blond girl with a ponytail.

He felt like he was stepping back in time.

Beau dropped his guitar in her backseat and moved to the driver's side. "Move over, Trouble, I'm driving." He fought to keep from stuttering. He'd done enough of that in his teens when around girls.

She smiled up at him and shifted to the passenger seat. In the shadows she looked the same as he remembered. They might both be well into their twenties, but tonight they'd be teenagers again.

They drove for a while, letting their hair blow in the wind. He remembered the back roads where they could go ninety and never see a patrol. Finally, they stopped in the middle of the road. The moon was billboard bright and a wisp of rain lingered in the air. "What does the *L* stand for?" he asked as he shifted to face her. Somehow *Ashley* didn't fit her.

"Lark," she answered.

"You're rich, Trouble. I guess I always figured that but I never thought that your daddy might own the bank."

"So are you," she shot back as if he'd just insulted her. "I've kept up with you. Three million in royalties last year."

Beau shook his head. "There's an old saying I heard somewhere that says *once poor, never rich*. I got money, but I'll never think rich. You were driving this car when we first met. I checked it out once. A car like this is worth about fifty thousand and I'm guessing you've got others in the garage just like it."

"What if I do? It doesn't mean anything. They're just cars."

Beau had no idea how to explain it to her. She wouldn't understand. Even now, when he could buy a restaurant, he couldn't go into one and order the most expensive thing on the menu. He never wasted money. It wasn't in his nature.

"Hell," he said aloud. "This is not what I want to talk about."

"Me either. I'm not even sure why I came tonight. At the bank I felt like you were thinking the same thing I was and I wanted to run backward, if only for one time, to that place in my life when everything was perfect for a few nights, a few moments."

He brushed her ponytail. "I'd like that." He pulled her close and kissed her. When he broke the kiss, he whispered, "You know, Trouble, half the songs I write are about you."

"I know. When I listen to your songs I swear sometimes I feel you're singing just to me."

The banker and the famous singer disappeared for a while, and they were just two kids again. Seventeen and racing the wind.

Chapter 17

❦

A LITTLE AFTER BREAKFAST RICK MATHESON, JOHNNY'S lawyer, showed up at the jail. Johnny guessed he'd finally be getting out. After a week of nothing but gray walls, even chores looked good. A man can only enjoy so much sitting around. He'd read all three books Kare, the fairy, had brought him. *Gulliver's Travels* wasn't bad and he made it through *Of Mice and Men* without too many thoughts of suicide, but *The Grapes of Wrath* almost did him in. Every time he fell asleep he dreamed of being on the road with everything he owned piled atop his car.

"Am I going home?" he asked Rick when he walked into the visitation room.

The young lawyer shook his head. "I'd about got you out, but this morning we collected another problem."

Scarlet always said Rick Matheson was one hunk of handsome man, but now with his face all twisted up with worry he looked like he was aging fast from his late twenties to seventy over one client.

Johnny straightened, determined not to add one more worry line on Matheson's face. "Well, whoever died or disappeared, I didn't do it this time. I've been locked up for a week."

Rick's smile didn't look very happy. "You know the sheriff searched your farm."

"I know. They can dig holes all over my land, but they won't find a body." Johnny didn't like the way Rick stared. "Not one I put there anyway." Hell, the way his luck was running half the town might have been planting not-so-dearly departed in his fields. It was the closest plowed ground to the city limits sign. Wendell was probably out there right now setting up a lemonade stand and selling maps.

Rick leaned forward. "They didn't find any bodies. Which I guess you'd say is the good news."

"What's the bad news?"

Rick stared directly at him. "They found drugs, John. Lots of drugs hidden in your barn."

For a second, Johnny thought of slamming his forehead against the metal table, but the way the cards were stacked against him lately, they'd charge him with destroying government property if he left a dent. Looking up at Rick, he asked, "I suppose you're going to tell me it's not as bad as it looks?"

"No, it's bad." Rick offered no comfort. "Is there anything else you need to tell me, John? I'm your lawyer. It would just be between us."

"Like what?"

"I don't know. I just don't want to be surprised again. I'm in the judge's office first thing this morning trying to get you out on bail and here comes half the sheriff's department hauling huge trash bags of pot into the courthouse. They were all looking like I was an idiot for standing there with my unsigned paper trying to get you out."

Johnny had never thought of himself as a selfish person, but he couldn't help but ask, "When did this become about you, Rick Matheson?" At the rate he was piling up crimes they'd hang him, and as he dropped, shoot him a few times for good measure. "I'm the one in jail and you're the one complaining."

Matheson laughed. "You're right. You're the one who is going to have to believe in reincarnation to serve out your time. I'll get paid one way or the other. In fact, if you keep piling up crimes I might buy a new car before this is over."

"Thanks for cheering me up." Johnny had always liked Rick Matheson. They'd played football in high school together, but Johnny had to wonder if the good-looking guy got his degree out of a cereal box. "So, what's the plan?"

Rick opened his satchel. "We tackle one charge at a time. I hired a private investigator. You'll be billed for him, by the way. And I've got a friend who works in missing persons in Chicago. Give me a list of everywhere you think Scarlet might have gone. If we can hunt her down, we'll have our first problem solved."

"So you think she's still alive?" Johnny couldn't believe she'd missed her beauty appointment last Friday. She never missed that. Last winter he'd had to dig her car out of the garage so she could get her hair colored. It took him two hours and she was so mad about being late she didn't even say thank you.

"Of course, I believe you, John, and I will until we find a body; then I'll come up with a different defense." Rick's smile didn't quite seem real. "I'm going to be with you, fighting for you all the way. If it doesn't go in your favor, I'll be there just behind the glass when they execute you."

"That's real comforting," Johnny lied, knowing that no one except the fairy thought he was innocent. He was piling up crimes and the only one in his corner was probably at breakfast with her imaginary friends.

They worked for an hour thinking of places Scarlet and Max might have gone or people they might have called. Over and over Rick asked where the drugs came from, and Johnny's answer was always the same. He had no idea.

Before he had time to go back to his cell and get even more depressed, his very own fairy showed up for a visit.

Deputy Rogers moved a chair into the room and sat down, but he acted like he was reading an old copy of *Reader's Digest*. Johnny figured now that he was in jail on more than one charge, he wasn't allowed to be alone with anyone but his lawyer. Hell, if things didn't improve soon he'd probably be a serial killer by the end of the week.

"He's here for your protection," Johnny whispered to Kare when she frowned at the deputy.

"I don't need protection," she said, jingling her necklace loaded with tin charms. "You're innocent. I know you are."

Johnny tried to take comfort in the fact that a woman who talked to dead people believed in him. "Maybe he's here for my protection."

His fairy grinned. "That's not a bad idea. I'm dangerous. Hang around me long, Johnny Wheeler, and I might just steal your heart."

Now he laughed. "Doesn't look like I'll be hanging around anywhere unless it's to haunt this place. Word is I could get the chair for killing two people with drugs involved."

"I don't think they do the chair anymore. Do they? If so, that would be just too cruel. Can you imagine having thousands of volts of electricity running through your body? I saw in a movie once that they wet the guy's head so most of the juice will plow into his brain."

"Stop trying to cheer me up, Kare. Do you think we could talk about something else?"

Kare nodded. "Sure. You're not going to be found guilty because you're innocent and I'll fight for you."

"You are the only one who believes that." He might have been depressed, but he looked into her big brown eyes about then and all he could think about was how nice it would be to hold her hand. He wouldn't mind if she did that thing of running her fingers over his palm. That had been real nice before they were interrupted by the arrest.

If he didn't count his aunts, it had been months since he'd touched a woman. They tended to hug on every occasion from weddings to funerals, or arrests in his case. Scarlet had moved to the extra bedroom last Christmas, saying she had PMS. Apparently it was terminal because she never moved back. At the time, he told himself it was temporary. If he gave her some space? If he worked harder? If he was more understanding of her needing friends and nights out with the girls or Max? Oh, correction, that part hadn't turned out to be such a good idea.

Charms jingling pulled him out of the memory of seeing Max, nude, hugging Scarlet, who seemed surprised that she was also nude. Max had just stood there, but Scarlet had jumped around yelling at Johnny because he wasn't supposed to be home yet.

His fairy jingled again. He could almost see her in school driving some teacher crazy by never sitting still. She was smart, though; she must have paid attention sometime. Today she brought him a book about a seagull who had goals. John doubted he'd have time to read that one even if it was short. Somehow he didn't think he'd be able to get into the plot.

He stared at Kare, wondering if all that curly hair was smothering her fairy brain.

"I don't just believe you're innocent, Johnny," Kare said in that voice that always sounded like a midnight whisper. "I know it. Did you ever meet someone and feel like you've known them all your life? Like you could tell them anything?"

"I was raised around here, Kare. Most of the people I see I have known all my life. Usually, if I do run into someone I don't know, the first thing I try to do is figure out who in town they're kin to."

She spread her hand out across the table as if she could reach the six feet to him. "I know you, Johnny. I know you're innocent. And I'm going to do all I can to help. I swear."

"What can you do, honey?" He was touched by her sympathy, but he didn't see how she could be any real help.

She smiled slowly and he thought his fairy was downright sexy. "I've been thinking about it and I think that your ex-wife and her lover are the ones who hid the drugs. They'll come back for the pot and I'll be waiting."

"No." Johnny panicked. "Don't put yourself in danger. No telling what they'd do if you caught them. I don't think Scarlet would get violent. She'd be afraid of breaking a nail, but Max? There's no telling what any man is capable of after he's spent two weeks alone with Scarlet. You can't risk confronting them. Promise me you'll forget this plan, Kare? I don't want you out there when they come back and find the drugs are missing."

She raised her hand high, shaking her arm like a first grader asking permission to go to the bathroom. A dozen bracelets clambered along to her elbow.

The deputy finally looked up from his reading and nodded once at her, as if giving permission for her to ask a question.

"You see, Deputy Rogers, I told you Johnny didn't do it. If he had killed them he wouldn't be so worried about me being hurt when they come back for the drugs. And they will come back. I can see it happening in the future."

Rogers looked up. "I'm not the jury, Miss Cunningham. I'm just here to listen and make sure you two aren't passing secrets."

Kare looked disappointed. Her first plan to save Johnny obviously didn't work. "I'll find a way."

Johnny stood and watched her leave. He didn't say a word as the deputy walked him back to his cell, which was starting to look like home. Cluttered and lonely.

"I don't think things can get much worse," Johnny said as Rogers removed his handcuffs.

Rogers pushed him into the cell and closed the door. "They might, John. Your wife just might come back and find out you're falling in love with someone else. Nothing makes a woman want a man back worse than another woman interested. It's strange, she may not want you but you can bet she doesn't want anyone else wanting you."

Johnny dropped on his bunk and shook his head. "You're wrong. Kare's not interested in me. She's just a zany person who lives on the fringes of reality. I've never done one wild or crazy thing in my life. I'm not the kind of man she'd need."

The deputy turned and said as he walked away, "Seems to me you're just the kind she'd need. If you were a free man, that is." He stopped and looked back. "By the way, that idea she had of watching over where the drugs were hidden wasn't that crazy. If we could keep the find quiet for a few days it might be worth staking out the place."

"You believe me?"

"No, but if that little lady wants to believe in you a hundred percent, I guess I could waste a few hours seeing if she's right. I'll talk to the sheriff about it. With school starting I wouldn't mind putting in some overtime."

"Thanks," Johnny managed. "When I get out of here, I'll owe you a beer."

"If you get out of here, I'll take you up on it."

Chapter 18

MILLANIE AGREED TO MEET KARE AT THE BLUE MOON Diner for a late lunch. The day was hot, but she decided to walk the block to Main Street. She could go out the back door of Martha Q's place and see the diner's big blue moon sign, but a dried-up creek bed blocked her path. On crutches, it was safer to go around.

Each day she felt stronger now, but she still tired easily. Kitten strength, a nurse at the rehab had called it. The feeling was new to her since the bombing. She'd always felt sorry for people not in top shape, but now she had become one. Millanie refused to think about what she might never do again. She'd consider only how she'd do one more thing, one more step each day.

Three people and a sheriff's deputy stopped to offer her a ride during the ten-minute walk, but Millanie wanted to prove that she wasn't helpless. The doctor hadn't given her much hope last week. The broken bone was healing, but there was damage to both the knee and ankle of her right leg. At best she'd be looking at a few more surgeries; at worst, she'd limp the rest of her life.

She'd always been so strong. She'd kept fit running and lifting weights. It was part of her job to always be mentally and physically alert and ready. Now, that job and her identity seemed to be vanishing. The undercover assignment she'd been given would probably be a waste of time. What were the chances that a powerful computer expert who could launder money all over the world would be hiding out in Harmony, or any small town? He'd go somewhere densely populated, where he could blend in among strangers.

As she slowly maneuvered the steps of the Blue Moon, she mentally raced through notes. An hour ago she'd called Sergeant Hughes and found out that Kare Cunningham really was the researcher assigned to her. The girl had a promising forensic accounting career with the government waiting for her when she graduated from college. But two years ago she'd tossed it all when she found her brother. She'd quit her job, pulled out her savings, and moved to Harmony. She still handled off-site assignments now and then, but Millanie would bet that Drew knew nothing about that side of his little sister's life.

As a man walked out of the diner, he held the door for her. Millanie looked in and saw Kare sitting at the back booth. Something a lecturer at the academy once said came to her mind: *About the time you think you've got people figured out, someone comes along who doesn't fit into any mold.*

Kare was one of those people. As Millanie neared, the girl was waving and bouncing in her seat like they were old friends reunited after years.

"Hi, Kare." Millanie lowered herself slowly into her side of the booth, letting her leg stick out into the aisle.

Kare straightened. "I'm so nervous. I've never done this undercover kind of thing. In the months I worked for the IRS I never saw the agents asking the questions. I just took the information and did the research. Now I feel like I should buy a trench coat and hat."

"Just act normal. If anyone sees us they'll just think we're friends having lunch." Millanie couldn't imagine ever having a fortune-teller for a friend, but who knew, it might be possible.

"Right. That should work. Everyone knows you're dating my brother, so it makes sense we'd be friends."

"I'm not dating your brother." Millanie shrugged. "In fact, he stood me up Saturday night. I'd invited him to go with me to a wedding." Millanie still hadn't figured out if she was glad he'd backed out or sad. In truth when she'd asked him, he hadn't really made a commitment one way or the other. She got the feeling a barn full of strangers wasn't really his thing, or maybe it was weddings he hated.

Kare leaned back. "Drew doesn't like crowds."

"Why?" The thought that the fortune-teller had just read her mind startled Millanie, but she had no intention of mentioning it.

"I don't know." Kare played with her napkin.

Millanie had no trouble reading Drew's little sister's body language. Kare was lying. Maybe to protect him, maybe because she didn't want to get involved, but Kare knew the why to Drew's reluctance to go to the wedding.

They ordered, giving both time to think. As soon as the waitress walked away, Millanie stepped into the reason for the meeting. "I read over your data. For what I assume was a fast job, you dug up a great deal of information. I feel like I know these people far better."

Kare nodded. "Information is easy to find if you know where to look. I thought the listing of every person who bought a house, applied for a driver's license in Harmony County, or signed up for a post office box might help."

"Can you get a list of people who opened bank accounts?"

"I can, but I can't legally get into the accounts."

Millanie nodded. "What about people who join churches or contribute large amounts of money to local causes?"

"The church records would be easy, and most charities are wide open in a town this size. I'll do what I can. Give me a few hints of what to look for."

Millanie leaned closer. "We're looking for someone who lives big, tries a little too hard to fit in. He's not from around here but acts like he is. He probably buys new cars and might have a plane and access to a landing field. I'm guessing he'll be someone who disappears on business often."

Kare smiled. "I could ask Derwood about the airstrips. He's an old local pilot. He'd know where all the strips are and probably who flies planes. He's one of my regulars. Comes in every week for a reading."

When the food was delivered, Millanie asked, "How'd you get into reading palms?" It didn't exactly fit with a degree in accounting.

Kare waited until she finished her first bite and dabbed her lips with the paper napkin. "A friend in college said I looked like a gypsy, so one night I dressed the part and read palms at a party. I was no good, so I studied up on it and the next party I impressed everyone. When I came here to keep an eye on my brother, it seemed like a fun thing to do to get to know people."

Millanie thought it strange that Kare came here to watch over Drew. He'd told a different story. Again she had the feeling that he didn't know his little sister as well as he thought he did. He'd said he didn't even know Kare existed until a few years ago. She'd found him after he took the teaching job at Clifton College.

One of them was hiding something, but which one?

Chapter 19

BEAU LOADED HIS ONE BAG AND HIS OLD GUITAR IN THE
trunk of the rented car. He told Martha Q and Mrs. Biggs
good-bye while hugging them both twice. He'd spent four
days in Harmony watching his father sleep. Beau had done
what he'd come to do. If his father had said one word to him
he would have been surprised. He wasn't sure if Melvin
Yates couldn't talk or wouldn't. At this point it didn't much
matter which. That longed-for father-son talk didn't look
like it would happen.

Walking away from Winter's Inn, Beau decided it would
probably be a long time before he came back. He'd driven
the moonlit roads with a girl named Trouble and neither of
them had talked of a future. They hadn't even bothered to
exchange cell phone numbers or e-mails.

The time they'd spent together had been more like a
dream than real, and he thought it best if they left it at that.

As he drove the streets of Harmony one last time before
he headed out to the airport, he was tempted to stop by the
bank, but he didn't want to see Ashley L. Powers. He'd rather
keep the dream named Trouble. Her father would probably

have him barred from the bank if he even knew she talked to him. Beau might be something in Nashville, but he was nothing but a preacher's wild kid in Harmony and always would be to most folks here.

Maybe someday he'd send her tickets to one of his shows. But even if Ashley came, she wouldn't be the one he was looking for. He wanted the girl who'd stopped his heart one night when she'd pulled his hand from her shoulder to her breast. He wanted the wild child who'd taken her father's classic car out for a joy ride. He wanted Trouble.

Beau drove onto the airstrip an hour early and visited with Derwood while he waited on his plane. The old pilot was full of stories, and Beau had the feeling if he hadn't been there the guy would have simply talked to himself. He had frightening tales of Vietnam and brave accounts of flying through storms. He was always the hero in the stories, saving folks from dying and reuniting loved ones home. He even told one story of how he saved the whole Matheson clan during a tornado. They were trapped in their basement and would have starved to death if he hadn't flown out there.

Derwood watched the county from the air, and his view was often surprising. He told of planes flying in low just before sunup and landing on an old dirt road. Beau was only half listening when the old guy added, "You know the place. Out there near where you and that little lady of yours used to park in a red convertible."

"What girl?" Beau asked, more to see what Derwood knew than to deny it.

"I don't know. I can't see faces from that high up."

"Well then, how did you know it was me?"

Derwood giggled. "I didn't until just now. We ain't got that many long-haired men around here. If I see you two out there again, I'll dip low and wave. If there's a bright moon, you'll see me."

"You do that, Mr. Derwood," Beau said, knowing that he'd never be back again. "If I don't wave back, call the cops because I'm being kidnapped."

Derwood didn't know Beau was joking. He nodded and

raised two fingers as if he were a Boy Scout swearing an oath.

Beau's phone rang and he jumped to answer it. Talking to Derwood made him feel like he needed to take a motion-sickness pill. The man went up and down in thoughts faster than a stunt pilot.

"Beau here," he said as he walked a few feet away.

"Beau, it's Dr. Spencer. Are you coming in this morning?"

"No, Doc, I'm on my way home. Plane should pick me up in a few minutes."

There was a long pause, and then she said, "I think you'd better come in. We're losing your father."

For a moment Beau wanted to say that he lost his father a long time ago, but he just nodded as if the doctor could see him. Finally, he said, "I'm on my way."

With a wave to Derwood, Beau climbed back in his car and dialed his agent. "Cancel the plane, George. I won't be heading back today," he said, without bothering with hello.

"The pilot just called in to say they had a problem with their inspection and hadn't left Nashville yet. I'll call him back and tell him not to bother. I'll also call the car company. Want to tell me how long you're staying?"

"No idea," Beau said in a business tone. He and George hadn't had time to become friends. "A few more days. But when I get back, I'll want to try out a few new songs with the band."

The agent's voice relaxed. "That's what I want to hear. I don't care where you are as long as you're writing."

Beau rolled his head from side to side, trying to relax. "I'll call you when I'm headed home and you can get the band ready to work. There's something about this place. It's almost like I hear melodies in the air."

"Whatever works."

Both hung up without saying good-bye.

Beau barely remembered driving to the hospital or parking the car. It was like a moment went by and he was standing alone in the hallway outside surgery. No one seemed to know anything except that his father was behind closed doors fighting for his life. For a man who'd talked of what a great day it would be when he'd walk through the Pearly Gates he seemed to be fighting hard not to reach his goal.

Finally, Dr. Spencer came out. She looked tired and sad. The news wouldn't be good, Beau thought.

"Where's your mother?" she asked.

"My stepmother," Beau corrected. "I have no idea. I thought Ruth might be in with my father."

The doctor shook her head. "I called her a few minutes before I dialed you. I left her a message to get back to me as soon as she could."

"Tell me what's going on. I'll explain it to her when she gets here." Beau didn't plan to wait for her to show up. Knowing his stepmother, she was probably cleaning house. That was all he ever remembered her doing. She cleaned and cooked and waited for his dad to come home. When he did, she'd fill Melvin's plate and he'd eat at his desk or in front of the TV.

"Do you have any other kin?" the doctor asked.

"No, none that would come. My father cut himself off from what family he had years ago."

She straightened. "Your father had another heart attack almost an hour ago. We rushed him to surgery, but we weren't able to save him. He passed away a few minutes after I called you. I'm so sorry, Beau."

Her words were caring, and something she'd probably repeated many times, but they were no comfort. There was a river of things he needed to say and even more he needed to hear his father say. Words he'd never hear.

"Thanks, Doc, I'll try to find my stepmother. If she comes here, ask her to wait, then call me, would you? I don't want her to be alone."

Dr. Spencer gave him a caring look. "I understand."

Beau turned and almost ran from the hospital. He drove toward his father's house, thinking that he'd get through this and never come back to Harmony again. In a few days this life he'd hated so much would be behind him, but first he wanted to be kind to Ruthie, who had seen far too little caring in her marriage. He'd always felt the woman married the preacher and had to live with the man.

The house was unlocked and everything looked exactly as it had when he'd left years ago. He walked through the rooms half expecting to see his father asleep in his recliner or working at his desk off the dining room. No one. Somehow in the days he'd been in the hospital the echoes of his father's booming voice had settled into an eerie silence.

Beau crossed the street to the little church his father had pastored for twenty years. The place was locked up tight.

He circled the market and drove downtown. Unless they'd traded cars, which was unlikely, his stepmother had vanished. She'd known her husband was dying, or at least that he was close to death. The doctor had tried to call her. If not home or at the church or on her way to the hospital, where could she be?

Finally, Beau stopped in front of the bank. He needed an ounce of balance right now and he could think of only one person who might provide it.

Very few people were in the bank. Two tellers were looking busy with their backs to the lobby. A young woman, with three little children holding on to her skirt, waited. Two of the kids were making sounds just to listen to them echo off the high walls.

Beau walked straight to the vice president's office. No one seemed near to try to stop him. Scrooge must be out to lunch. The loan officer gave him the creeps, but Beau couldn't put his finger on exactly what he hated about the jittery guy.

He pushed past the open door of Lark's office and closed it before turning around.

Ashley L. Powers stood slowly. Surprise and alarm reflected in her face. He was obviously someone who didn't belong in this orderly world of hers.

He didn't move but guessed she could see the worry in his eyes. The pain. The fear. She moved around her desk and came toward him.

Beau swore he wouldn't cry for a father who hadn't loved him. He promised himself he wouldn't fall apart, but when she reached him he grabbed her and held on tight. He didn't know if she'd heard about his father or if she just felt his pain, but she returned the hug.

For a long while she just held on. Slowly his nerves calmed, his heart slowed. He could do this. He could face whatever happened next. All he needed was her near for a few minutes. He wasn't sure who started talking but he knew he did most of it. They held each other until his world settled.

"I have to go make arrangements," he finally said.

"I'll pick you up tonight. We'll drive." She brushed a tear he hadn't seen fall from her cheek.

He smiled, remembering the old pilot who flew in moonlight and almost said, *Just you, me, and Crazy Derwood.*

"Tonight," he echoed as he pulled away and walked out of the bank without looking back.

An hour later he found his stepmother sitting in her backyard. He pulled up a rusty folding chair and just kept her company for a while.

Finally, she said in a voice she hadn't used in a while, "He's dead, isn't he?"

"Yes." Beau wished he could think of some words of comfort, but she didn't look like words would matter.

She appeared so tired, like a woman worn out in body and soul. "Will you make the funeral plans?"

"I will if you want me to."

"I do." She waited awhile before she began to organize. "He'll want his black suit and a white shirt. Any tie will do. You pick it out. The service can be tomorrow if Mr. Wright can work it in the schedule. The church secretary will call all the parishioners. I doubt many will come, it being a weekday."

Beau added, "I'll let the paper know anyway and order flowers."

She shrugged as if neither thing he suggested was important. "Buy him a plot in the new section of the cemetery.

They're not as expensive. He'll want no headstone, but a marker would be nice. Tell Mr. Wright that we won't need a family car; I'll just ride out with you. I've spent years listening to him complain about how folks waste money on burying."

"Should I buy two plots? One for you?" He hated asking, but he didn't want to make a mistake.

"No. As soon as I get my things together, I'll be moving back to Kansas. I don't need to stay around for anything and I wouldn't want to be buried here. When my time comes, I've got a plot by my parents' graves."

"This house is yours," Beau said. "I paid off the mortgage. If you want to, you can stay here for a while or sell the place. Either way, this house is yours."

She shook her head. "I don't want it. I don't want anything. He always said when he died he didn't plan on leaving anything to me or you. He said he'd leave it to the church. Only all he left was bills."

"I don't want the house either," Beau echoed. "How about I offer it to the church?"

"I think that would be the right thing to do." Ruthie finally faced him. "Beau, you were a better son than he had a right to ask for. The trouble between you and him was on his shoulders, not yours."

Beau stood and slowly folded down by her side. He held her gently as if she were thin glass and might shatter. "Thanks for being kind to me," he whispered.

Part of him expected her to cry, but she didn't. She just patted him on the shoulder a few times. "You go set up the funeral and I'll go pack. If it's all right with you I'd like to just have a graveside service."

Beau knew his father would have wanted the works. Open casket, church full of flowers, folks crying, a long line of cars slowly snaking to the cemetery. But his father wasn't here. "I think a graveside service would be nice," he said.

They walked back inside as the warm air cooled and clouds crowded across the sky. Something had changed inside as well. The house seemed cold, void of color, a place where no one lived. It was no longer a home; maybe it had never been.

Leaving her to pack, Beau drove over to the funeral home and made all the arrangements. As he knew Mr. Wright would, Tyler said he'd take care of everything.

It was afternoon when Beau left the cemetery. He drove back to Winter's Inn and asked if his room was still available. Martha Q had heard about his father's death, so she hugged him twice, and Mrs. Biggs set a basket of cookies in his room while he went out to collect his guitar and bag.

Beau closed the door. Finally, he was alone. He fell atop the bed and closed his eyes. He thought of all the things he should feel, but all he really felt at the moment was tired. One deep breath and he was sound asleep.

When he woke it was almost eight. After a shower and shave in the fancy, overdecorated bathroom, he grabbed his guitar and moved out on the porch to watch the night move in. As he always did, he began to play, letting the music drift in the air. Some sad songs came to him, but he played all the old favorites of his grandfather, who'd been his first teacher.

Long after dark, Trouble pulled into the drive and just sat in her car listening. He played a few of the songs that he'd written while thinking of her.

When he finally stopped, he set his guitar inside and joined her. She drove while he leaned back and let the wind and memories circle round him.

Chapter 20

MONDAY AFTERNOON

LOW ROLLING CLOUDS LOWERED THE TEMPERATURE SEVERAL
degrees as Millanie drifted half asleep on the porch. Martha
Q left with her friend, a very distinguished-looking man she
introduced as Mr. Carleon.

The two made an odd pair. He stood watching the owner
of the inn as if she were a great actress and he was simply
one of the stage props. The white-haired man smiled when
Martha Q said anything outrageous. He adored her and she
relished the attention.

Millanie had almost laughed aloud when Martha Q
claimed they were just friends because Mr. Carleon had
winked. She couldn't decide if the old couple were lovers, or
if they just got a kick out of letting the world think they were.

"Don't look for me home tonight," Martha Q yelled back
as Mr. Carleon helped her into his expensive black Lincoln.
"We're going over to one of casinos in Oklahoma and I
might get lucky."

They both looked like they were laughing as they drove away.

Millanie thought about being almost thirty-three and she hadn't settled anywhere or even made a friend she could laugh with. The McAllen homestead gave her the first sense of belonging anywhere, but one old house wouldn't be enough to hold her here. Maybe she'd always be a drifter, comfortable in any place but at home in none.

She heard the familiar sound of Drew's Jeep but she didn't open her eyes. He hadn't committed to the wedding last Saturday night and, in truth, she hadn't been sure she wanted to go, but still she felt like he'd somehow let her down. It would have been a good opportunity to ask a few people about folks who were new in town.

Drew's footsteps tapped lightly on the porch. "Evening, Sleeping Beauty," he whispered as he leaned down and kissed her lightly.

Millanie opened her eyes. "You stood me up Saturday."

He studied her. "I never said I'd go."

"Your sister told me you don't like crowds."

"Don't talk to my sister. It'll mess with your brain." He lowered into the chair beside her. "You mad at me?"

"No, I don't know you well enough to be mad at you. How about answering a few questions, Dr. Andrew Cunningham? If you're going to drop by and kiss me, I'd like to talk to you now and then."

He shrugged. "All right, Captain McAllen, but no name, rank, and serial number. I'm no good at the hard questions."

"So you know I was in the army?" She wasn't surprised.

"Word gets around; besides, a woman who packs in a duffel bag was a strong clue." He reached over and took her hand as if he'd done so a hundred times. "If it's all right with you, I don't want to hear how you were hurt. I would, however, like to know how the recovery is coming along when you know me well enough to discuss intimate details like what's under that cast."

The last thing she wanted to talk about was her injury,

past or present, and she wasn't sure he really wanted to know the damage under the plaster.

"Did you know your sister thinks we're dating?" Millanie had no idea where to start with this man. She had the impression if she asked too personal a question he'd bolt.

"Is that the first question?"

"Yes."

"All right, yes, Kare mentioned it to me and I didn't correct her. I'm not exactly sure when the *dating* tag gets slapped on, but I wouldn't mind. Going out with you sounds good. Staying home sounds even better."

"How do you feel about everyone knowing, Professor?"

He squeezed her hand. "I don't much care what people say or what they think of anything I do. It's been so long since I've had a date I'm not sure I know how to play the role. You'd think there would be a guidebook somewhere I could download."

"You're lying, Professor. Everyone I meet thinks highly of you. They all say how intelligent you are. What a nice guy you are. If you didn't care, you wouldn't talk to church groups and work on every community project from Clifton Creek to Harmony."

Millanie didn't miss the fact that she'd just described one trait of the man she was tracking. Add *new to the area* and she had two matches. "Next questions. What did you do all day?"

He laced his fingers in hers. "I taught my class this morning, then spent the day at my computer doing research. I'm working on a book or, more accurately, a series of stories."

She felt, in the tightening of his touch, that he didn't like this game they were playing, but she planned to continue. "You good at computers?"

"I told you before that my sister and I share a love for computers. Sometimes, at night, we link and play games. She's so smart. Beats me every time."

Millanie closed her eyes. Third trait the dangerous man she sought might have. Only Drew wasn't rich; he didn't spread money around. He must not fly a plane or he wouldn't have been at the airport. He didn't have a car. He had family here.

She was cracking up if she thought this gentle man could be an underworld mastermind involved in drug trafficking and money laundering.

"No more questions?" he announced.

"One," she said. "Tell me about your last date."

He relaxed. "It was Friday. We ate hamburgers—no, correction, cheeseburgers at the truck stop and then—"

"No, not our last date. The last date you had before you met me."

He was silent and she waited. If he lied he might not be the criminal she was looking for, but she decided she'd make it plain she didn't want to see him again. This was a tough time in her life and she didn't want to complicate it with someone with whom she had to pick lies out of the conversations.

He leaned back as if debating whether to tell her. Finally, he said, "My last date was late in August five years ago. This time of year when the air cools at night and the leaves seem darker green just before they turn. I don't remember the exact date but I know it was close to school starting. I took out a girl named Holly Lee O'Neal. I'd known her since college and always thought she was pretty as her name. We bought hot dogs from a street vendor and walked to a concert in the park. The night couldn't have been more perfect. We were good friends and she was leaving for Europe the next day to do graduate work. We were both excited about fall coming and where we were heading. We were close friends back then."

"Sleepover kind of friends?"

"Yes, when we were in college. Not that night," he answered. "I heard she ended up getting her master's degree in Celtic legends, but I'm not sure about that."

"And you never saw her again?"

"No. I never saw or dated her again. She married some guy from Lake Forest. Lives in a house that looks over the water, and last I checked, she had two kids."

Millanie knew she was getting far too personal, but she asked, "Did you love her?"

"No. I cared about her, still do, but I've never caught that illness called love. How about you?"

She smiled, knowing he was tired of talking about himself and wanted to turn the tables. It was only fair. "I'm thirty-two, Drew, and never had the illness either. I don't think I ever will. I've had a few sleepover friends but no one I couldn't walk away from."

He leaned forward. "Can we stop with the interrogation, Millanie? If we keep going you're bound to ask a question I don't want to answer, and I don't want to lie to you. I came by to see if you want to go to a fund-raiser in Bailee. All the chili and cornbread you can eat, and then there's a baseball game we have to watch between the Baptists and the Methodists."

"I'd need to change."

"Believe me, you're fine just the way you are. As far as I can tell there is no dress code."

"But the crutches. I don't know how I'd manage the stands at a game."

"I'll catch you if you fall. I promise." He stood and pulled her up. "If we're dating, we might as well go out."

"I thought you didn't like crowds."

He leaned in close. "This will be nothing but locals. No big crowds and it's outside." His cheek brushed hers and he whispered, "One more answer to a question you forgot to ask. I don't want to be a sleepover kind of friend with you. This attraction I have for you is different than that. What's between us won't be shoved away in a dark corner to be kept secret. If we're dating, then we do it in front of everyone. If you're not comfortable with that, you'd better tell me now."

His hand moved along her side, caressing. She felt his need to touch her and saw the fire smoldering in his eyes. He'd answered her questions; now it was time for her to answer his.

She took in the nearness of him, the way he almost brushed along the side of her breast as his fingers moved and how he stayed close enough that his words tickled her ear. He was right; whatever this was, it was not a casual one-night stand. The need to be near him went all the way to her soul.

For the first time ever she whispered, "We're dating."

His mouth closed over hers in a kiss that made her forget all about questions. Part of her wanted to demand the names and addresses of Holly Lee O'Neal and every girl he ever dated. She needed to send them all thank-you cards for teaching him exactly what a woman wants in a kiss.

On the drive over to Bailee, Millanie tried to get her mind and body to settle, but all she could think about was that no one had ever warmed her blood so completely. *It was just a kiss*, she kept saying to herself, but she knew it was much, much more.

What they were doing, what they'd done from the first night, was foreplay and they both knew it.

Maybe Drew Cunningham was starved if he hadn't had a date in five years, but there was something that rattled her to her toes about the man. He was nice looking, but with his shaggy hair and out-of-style clothes he was not a man women noticed in a crowd.

His hand rested on her left knee as he drove, singing softly to an old seventies song on the radio. The Jeep ran like it had a powerful engine encased in an old frame.

"How many cars do you have that you drive and don't own?" she asked when he slowed to turn off the highway onto a farm-to-market road.

"Do you always talk in questions?"

She realized he was right. "I do."

"I'll answer, but this is the last question of the night." He looked at her and stared until she nodded, and then he continued. "When I first went to college, I got a job sweeping up at a garage. I found it interesting to see how cars worked. Before long I'd figured it out. A mechanic's pay was higher than a janitor's. Most kids going to Yale don't even know how to change the oil. I made a killing."

"You went to Yale?"

He pulled off the road and stopped. "Last question, remember."

"You're right." She was surprised he didn't look angry, just determined.

"I like working on cars. A friend of mine and I like to fix them up so they could race, but don't tell his wife. She'd throw a fit if she knew we hit the back roads now and then to see just how fast we can go."

Millanie thought of a dozen questions, but she didn't ask. He was sharing and maybe if she gave it time she'd learn all she needed to know.

Only, her logical mind checked off two more things on her list that Drew had in common with her invisible bad guy. Fast cars and invisible in crowds. She told herself the friend he mentioned might also be a person of interest, but the man before her was fast becoming a suspect—or a possible lover.

Neither talked until they got to the baseball field. True to his promise, he held her close as they maneuvered over the uneven ground.

Several tents were set up beside the roped-off field he called a parking lot. For ten dollars they got a badge that said *Official Judge* and a quart jug of sweet iced tea. Drew sat her in the middle of the cooks and went from tent to tent picking up samples of chili. Some were great, others so hot she downed half her tea to put out the fire.

He circled back to the tents until they picked their favorite chili. She wasn't surprised he liked the mild and she went for the spicy.

Their conversation was easy. He introduced her to a few people from the college and one old couple he said lived out at Twisted Creek. When he finally brought her peach cobbler, he sat down beside her, letting his leg brush against hers. No matter where they were, he seemed to feel a need to be touching her and she didn't mind.

"You know, chili was invented on the cattle drives. They had trouble keeping meat fresh and the spices made the questionable beef, or whatever landed in the pot, taste better."

"Thanks, Professor." She liked the way he slipped into his role. He was a man of many layers. She was both attracted to him and worried about some side of him she hadn't yet seen.

"Anytime," he answered, as if she hadn't been being sarcastic.

As the sun set, the lights on a roped-off field came on. The dirt could only very roughly be called a ballpark. Tumbleweeds half the size of a man rolled back and forth in the changing winds. Big white chalk lines marked squares for bases, and two rows of boards stretched over barrels formed the stands on either side of home base. About the time Millanie hobbled over and found a safe place to sit out of the way of any traffic pattern, men leading donkeys took to the field.

They were playing baseball with huge bats and softballs, and every player had to be in the saddle. Unfortunately, the donkeys didn't get the point of the game. They refused to move or ran the wrong direction or on several occasions bucked their rider off. Once the batter's donkey got hit with the ball and ran the bases in reverse order. One Methodist couldn't get his animal to move and played left field while his own team batted. The Baptists offered to baptize him on the spot.

The general chaos was hilarious. Millanie almost toppled off her bench seat so many times Drew permanently kept his arm behind her as a brace. By the fourth inning both sides agreed to call the annual game a tie. The players were starting to look the worse for wear and the donkeys appeared bothered by the whole game.

Drew made no move to leave as they watched all the families pack up and go. When the field lights went out, the heavens seemed to open up with a show of stars. She looked up, remembering all the times she'd watched the night sky in other lands. Sometimes she'd stare at the moon and remind herself it was the same moon that shined in Harmony.

"This was fun," she whispered as she leaned into him.

He kissed her cheek and tightened his arms around her. "When I came here to live, this was one of the first public events I attended. It's crazy, playing a game that makes no sense with teams that don't care who wins, but somehow I felt like all was not as mixed-up in the world as I thought."

She realized he was right. The laughter had helped.

Ten minutes later, when the wind kicked up, he stood and helped her to her feet. Side by side, with him carrying one crutch while she leaned against his ribs, they moved back toward the car.

"Evening, Drew," a voice whispered in the darkness as they passed the tents.

She tensed, but Drew didn't. "Evening, Pastor. I thought everyone was gone."

"They are. My wife packed up the kids and the food and left. She forgot me. When she realizes it, she'll come back."

"We could give you a lift."

The shadow moved a little closer. "No, thanks. I see her car lights turning off the road heading this way. I'll walk with you two to the parking lot."

As his wife neared, the pastor added, "Thanks, Drew, for sponsoring this again this year."

"Don't mention it," Drew said. "It was nothing."

The shadow waved and climbed into an old station wagon loaded down with kids.

Millanie waved good-bye, though she doubted anyone in the car could see them. "You sponsored this?" she asked in a low voice.

"It wasn't that expensive. Flyers, and donkey rental. A farmer used to offer them free, but then he found out people would pay to make fools of themselves."

They were at the Jeep, but he didn't open the door. He leaned her against the fender and took both her crutches. While he loaded them in the back, she started to ask another question. Drew didn't add up. How does a man who only works one day a week afford to sponsor anything? All she got out was "How does—"

He swung around and pushed her against the car, leaning into her body. "No more questions," he whispered as his mouth found hers.

This was no friendly kiss. This was full-out need, and for a moment she just hung on and rocked with the wave of passion. If she'd been able to reason she would have said she could have easily stopped his advance. Even with her leg in a cast, he would be no match for her in a fight. But reason deserted her and pushing him away couldn't have been further from her mind.

His hands moved over her body, making it obvious that he needed to touch her. Once, he pulled away and let her slow her breathing. The air blew cool between them. As she calmed her rapid heart, he leaned against her once more, letting her body feel the lean warmth of him.

"I can't—" The rest of his thought was lost as he lowered his mouth once more and his hand slid under her blouse and spread out along her warm skin.

A few minutes later when he threaded his fingers into her hair and deepened the kiss, she wasn't sure if she'd been about to say that she couldn't keep doing this or that she couldn't stop. The need to have him touch her like this had been growing all night with every brush of his arm and every slight contact between them.

Raindrops seemed to sizzle off their skin for a few minutes before they both realized it was raining. He helped her to the passenger seat, covered her cast with an old jacket he pulled from the backseat, and ran around the Jeep putting up the top. When he finally made it inside, he shook like a shaggy dog and she laughed so hard she got the hiccups.

He combed his hair back with his fingers and smiled at her.

Millanie couldn't breathe. With his hair back, not half covering his eyes, Drew Cunningham just might be the handsomest man she'd ever seen. She'd never noticed that behind his glasses were crystal blue eyes. The small scar on his jaw left just the right imperfection.

He leaned over and buried his face in the hollow of her neck. "You look great covered in wet silk, Millie."

She glanced down, realizing her blouse was plastered against her like a second skin. Closing her eyes in horror, she didn't move as he kissed his way up her throat and opened her mouth to a slow, deep kiss.

Other than kissing her, he didn't touch her. Maybe he knew if he did they'd be taking the relationship to another level and both of them probably didn't want their first time together to be in an old Jeep that smelled even more like dead fish when it rained.

When he finally straightened, he kissed the tip of her nose and whispered, "I could so get used to this dating thing with you."

Millanie simply smiled. She was getting to know Drew in more ways than one.

All the way back to the inn they shivered because of the drafty ride and laughed at all the funny things that somehow had made the evening perfect.

A man was sitting on the front porch when they returned. Millanie introduced him to Drew as Beau. Martha Q hadn't said his last name. She'd simply tagged him as just a drifter passing by, but Drew took the time to talk to the inn's other guest.

Millanie had studied him earlier when he joined her on the porch for tea. Drifters don't take the most expensive room or drive rented cars. His hair was way too long, but well cut. His clothes were wrinkled but well made, and he played his guitar like a master.

Drew said hello to Beau as if he knew of him but didn't talk long, telling her the two men didn't know one another well.

Without waiting to be invited, Drew followed her into the kitchen, where Mrs. Biggs had left instant hot chocolate and brownies. Without discussing it, they sat down at the kitchen table. Neither seemed to want the night to end. After two cups of hot chocolate, they moved to the cluttered front room that Martha Q called the parlor and sat on either end of the couch while they listened to Beau playing his guitar out on the porch.

Drew talked about a book he was working on as his hand rested on her cast, which she'd stretched between them. He wanted to record the history of this northernmost part of the state before the stories of the first settlers vanished. She tried to pay attention, but the music drifted through her thoughts as she watched his fingers moving along the cast.

Funny how the man wouldn't talk about himself, but he loved telling her details of history. She couldn't stop smiling, knowing that he must be a very gifted teacher even if he only taught one class.

Sometime while they talked the rain stopped. She thought she heard Beau open the front door and set something inside the entry, but Millanie was far too interested in watching Drew's eyes as he told her about a legend he'd heard from several people in the area. A rancher sold his herd and took payment in gold. On his way home with two of his men as guards, he disappeared along with the two men and the gold. Some said the men killed him and ran for Mexico. Others claimed one guard killed the other, then the old man. Maybe an Apache band got all three.

When Millanie demanded to hear the end of the story, Drew laughed and said she didn't understand the concept of legends at all.

Martha Q and her Mr. Carleon came in while Millanie was pouting. Drew said good night and planted a kiss on her cheek.

"I'll see you soon, Millie," he whispered, then disappeared before she could ask him to name exactly when *soon* was.

Millanie lay awake most of the night remembering the way his hand had brushed along her cast as if he were touching her. She couldn't feel his fingers caressing her, but she could see them and reacted as if no cast separated them.

One of Beau's songs about catching first love in the

midnight wind kept drifting in her mind as sleep called. The idea of finding first love at her age was ridiculous. She was thirty-two. Long past dreaming of love. What she felt for Drew was simply attraction. Pure and simple.

Yet the song kept circling as she finally fell asleep.

Chapter 21

AFTER A SLEEPLESS NIGHT, JOHNNY WHEELER SAT IN HIS cell eating breakfast and worrying.

The food wasn't bad, but then he'd been eating his own cooking for six months. Apparently when Scarlet moved out of his bedroom she also left the kitchen. Some nights when he came in too late from work to drive into town, his choices were peanut butter and jelly on toast or on stale bread. Scarlet lived on diet food. One night he found her high-fiber-no-sugar bars and ate the whole box of compressed cereal sprinkled with seeds. The stuff tasted like it should be used in bird feeders.

Johnny's philosophy about food was simply two rules: If it didn't crawl off the plate fast, he ate it, and everything tasted better with ketchup on it. He'd seriously considered the possibility that some small country somewhere, one that hated Americans, made and shipped those tiny little packs of ketchup that every fast-food place used. He could almost see them stuffing three drops in every impossible-to-open pack as they giggled about all the trouble they were causing.

Only this morning he didn't have time to worry about that conspiracy theory; he had to worry about Kare. His fairy was going to get herself in big trouble and he couldn't do a thing to help.

Johnny wasn't sure how she became *his* own personal fairy. After over a week in jail with two charges that could keep him locked up for the next hundred years, he was starting to wonder what he'd done wrong. But not Kare; she was telling everyone he was innocent and should be let out immediately.

If he'd done something bad to cause karma to dump this trouble on him, he must have also done a few things right to have Kare believe in him.

He grinned, thinking about how she talked Deputy Rogers into staking out his farm. If Scarlet really was the one who'd stashed the drugs in his barn, which he doubted, she'd be real surprised to find two hundred pounds of deputy waiting for her.

Johnny couldn't imagine her handling anything as smelly as drugs, but Max might. There was a great deal about the man that he didn't know. Obviously wearing buckled-up sandals and silk shirts didn't mean he was gay. In truth, Johnny could never remember talking to the man for longer than two minutes. Max didn't talk the language of farming or ranching, and Johnny didn't know about anything else. The few times he'd been forced to say a few words, the silk-wearing, bootless guy had talked about wine and said things like *The smellier the cheese, the better it tastes.*

"Deputy Rogers," Johnny yelled, knowing that the deputy was sleeping at his desk ten feet farther down the hallway.

"Yes," Rogers answered, sounding groggy.

"You know anything about wine?"

If Rogers thought the question was a strange thing for a man facing death row to ask, he didn't comment. "I know you don't drink it with breakfast."

"Everybody knows that. What else you know?"

Rogers walked into sight. "I know that you should always look for the twist-off caps 'cause those corks are more trouble than they're worth to mess with."

Johnny nodded. "What do you think of a full-bodied Cabernet?"

Rogers shrugged. "I married a full-bodied Debra and I like her just fine."

Both men laughed as the deputy collected Johnny's tray.

Ten minutes later he was back telling Johnny that he had another visitor.

"They don't let me have visitors this early," Johnny argued as he tried to get his hair to stay down. He needed a cut badly, but he wasn't about to settle for a prison cut. He'd seen a few of those on TV. If the days kept passing behind bars he'd be braiding his mud-colored locks before long.

Rogers was all business. "They do when it's your wife."

Johnny felt like a bolt of electricity had jumped through his body and they'd forgotten to wet his head. He slowly turned around far enough to see the deputy. "My wife? The one everyone thinks I killed?"

Rogers shrugged. "I think the department's pretty much given up on that theory."

Johnny tossed the comb in the sink. "Well, look on the bright side. You finally found her body and I can bet she's talking."

The deputy unlocked the cell and didn't bother with the handcuffs. "Now don't get mad and hit her, Johnny, or you'll be in trouble. All it takes is a few bruises and the judge will give her everything when the divorce comes up."

"I'm not going to hit her," Johnny answered. "I'm going to ask her how she liked her vacation with Max. Then she can go right back to him because she's never coming home with me."

"She could get half your farm, John."

Johnny smiled. "To do that, she'd have to marry and then divorce my grandpa. The farm is still in his name. Or it was the last time I saw him playing poker. Who knows, the old man might have bet the farm up against a stack of cheese balls."

As usual the deputy didn't know what he was talking about and, worse, didn't seem to care.

Rogers opened the door and Johnny walked into the visitation area, well aware that something could come flying at him at any moment. His wife had a good pitching arm and she loved to toss things like their wedding picture, or food, bowl included, at him.

But Scarlet was sitting calmly on the table. Her favorite weapon, her purse, rested beside her. She looked pretty in a dress he'd never seen and heels so tall she would be almost his height if she stood. Only he figured she wouldn't stand, because if she did, she wouldn't be showing near as much leg, and Scarlet liked to show skin when she felt an argument coming on. It used to give her the advantage, but Johnny wasn't falling for it this time. She could be standing nude in a six-foot bottle of beer and he wouldn't be thirsty.

He might have yelled at her, but when she looked up she was crying those big alligator tears he could never take. In fact, that was why he proposed. They were dating and she cried when he brought her candy and not a ring for Valentine's Day. He felt so bad he got down on one knee.

That wasn't happening again, but he couldn't yell at her when tears were running down her cheeks. "What's the matter? You and Max run out of money?"

"Oh, Johnny, don't be mean. You know I needed a break. What's so wrong with taking a vacation? Max got a great deal online."

Since the vacation seemed to have been planned as they ran, putting their clothes on in flight, from the house to Max's car, Johnny wasn't as sympathetic as he might have been. He'd never forget how Max had made it to the car first and Scarlet had to bang on the passenger window several times before he unlocked her door.

"Go back to Max, Scarlet. It's where you belong. We're finished. We were over a long time ago. There's no need to fight. I'll see you in court." He'd said all he needed to say. Johnny turned to walk away.

She screamed so loud Rogers jumped up, but Johnny stood the length of the room away from her. The deputy looked annoyed, then he just shook his head and sat back down.

She calmed now that she had everyone's attention. "I can't go back to him, you idiot. They arrested Max while we were at the farm and it's all your fault."

Now both the deputy and Johnny stared at Scarlet.

"And how is that my fault?" For three years everything had always been his fault. But since he was in jail, he had a hard time believing it this time.

She pointed her finger like it was a weapon. "When we got to the farm, Max wanted to pull his car into the barn; it's a seventy-thousand-dollar Lexus, you know, so it needed to be out of the sun while I was looking for my things. During the time I was inside the house, he got to looking around the barn and found some bags. Naturally he thought they were my things you'd hidden in the barn, so he started stuffing them in the trunk fast, fearing that you might be coming back soon."

She was huffing like a boxer in the ninth round. "The sheriff showed up and arrested him for drug possession. You tricked us, didn't you? You put those drugs in there hoping we'd think they were clothes and take them by mistake, but it won't work. Max and I have never seen the drugs."

Johnny fought to keep from smiling. He looked over at Rogers and the deputy was grinning from ear to ear.

"Looks like you'll be buying me a beer, Johnny," he said.

"No, he won't," Scarlet screamed, and stomped her high heel. "He's not going anywhere. Johnny, it's your farm and you've got to tell them the drugs are yours. I tried to tell them but they wouldn't listen. Half the people I run into in this town tell me I'm dead. This is all your doing, Johnny Wheeler. Those bags were on your land and therefore the drugs are your problem."

Johnny shrugged. "Well, Scarlet, you were on my land

and you're not my problem. However, I will say I'm very glad you're alive."

She stormed toward him with such rage he wouldn't have been surprised to see flying monkeys circling her. Any love he had left for the woman died.

If Deputy Rogers hadn't stopped her Scarlet would have killed him right there in the visitation room of the Harmony County Jail.

Chapter 22

TUESDAY

BEAU DROVE HIS STEPMOTHER TO THE CEMETERY AND WAS surprised how few cars were there. Seven, eight counting the hearse. They waited until ten minutes after eleven before Beau finally nodded for Mr. Wright to start.

Beau walked Ruthie to one of the empty chairs in the first row and looked up to see his friends lining the back row. Ronny Logan, who used to feed him when he was seventeen and on his own. Mrs. Biggs and Martha Q had their tissues out ready to do their duty and cry. Even Harley from the bar was standing at the back of the tent. Noah and Reagan were there with little Utah asleep in Noah's arms. A few others stood around. Some he recognized as men from the church, but most were his friends or teachers he'd had in school. They'd come to be with him during this time.

Two men from the grounds staff of the cemetery filled in as pallbearers. They carried the casket to the stand over the open grave as Beau stood watching it all. The flowers looked nice over the wooden coffin. He had asked Mr.

Wright to find a preacher to say a few words. The young man didn't look twenty, but he read from the Bible and offered a prayer. He said he didn't know Melvin Yates but any preacher surely was on the fast train to heaven.

No one in the crowd said an amen to his thought.

When the preacher finished, Beau played a few songs. If one cell had still been alive in his father's body, Melvin would have pounded on the coffin for him to stop.

When Beau finished, he thanked everyone for coming and hugged them all except one woman standing several feet away in the morning shadows of an old elm. Tall, blond, and dressed in a black suit.

He glanced back toward her a few minutes later and she was gone.

Trouble. She'd come.

Finally, when everyone was gone, Beau stood beside Ruthie and watched the men from the funeral home lower his father into the ground. As the casket sank, Beau let go of all the anger he'd had. Who knew, maybe knowing how much his father hated his music was the one thing that kept him driving forward. Maybe in an odd way he owed his success to the old guy.

Ruthie didn't say a word on the drive back to the house. Beau offered to help any way he could, but she just said that her brother would be in tonight to drive her back to Kansas. The things she'd packed and set by the door wouldn't fill a trunk.

He hugged her good-bye, knowing he'd probably never see her again.

For a while he drove around. Several of his friends who'd moved away from Harmony had called, leaving messages about how sorry they were, but Beau didn't want to call them back. He wanted to be alone.

Finally, he stopped at Buffalo's Bar and did something he'd never done.

He ordered a drink, laid a hundred on the bar, and told Harley to keep them coming.

Chapter 23

TUESDAY

AT FOUR FIFTEEN IN THE AFTERNOON JOHNNY WHEELER walked out of the Harmony County Jail a free man. He'd gained six pounds on a body that needed the fat and felt like he'd aged eight years over the past eight days.

His lawyer, Rick Matheson, shook his hand on the steps and wished him a happy and peaceful life.

Johnny thanked Matheson, deciding if things had gone a different direction they might have been real friends. Rick had always been straight with him, even when days looked bad. "You were a good lawyer," he managed to say. For a man who rarely thought to compliment anyone, Johnny was trying to say the right thing. "I don't plan to ever be in trouble again, but if I am, I'll call you. If you ever need me, I'll be there for you. I owe you, Matheson, and I'm a man who likes to pay his debts."

Rick smiled, looking more like a college boy than a man three years into his career. "I'll do that, and you watch out for Scarlet. Last time I saw her she threatened to kill me.

There's no telling what she'd do to you. She also told me her boyfriend was worth big money and he'd have me disbarred for trying to blame the drugs on him."

"You worried?"

"No. If every guy who made threats toward me decided to pay me a visit there would be a line around the building." Rick patted Johnny on the shoulder. "Take care. I might need that favor sometime if Scarlet doesn't get you first."

"I plan to be careful. I'm thinking of getting a guard dog, and an electric fence, maybe a guard tower. Something tells me she's not finished blaming me for the trouble Max is in."

"The drugs were his. No telling how long he'd been storing shipments there." Rick tugged his tie loose. "My cousin told me they found hard drugs in his glove box. He's mixed up in some bad stuff. How long have you known him?"

Johnny shrugged. "I don't know. Scarlet met him when she was dating around. He was new in town and needed a date to fund-raisers and fancy stuff. Scarlet told me she just went along for the fun of it. Said there was nothing between them." Johnny barked a laugh. "Last time I saw them together she was right. There was nothing, including clothes."

Rick shook his head. "Sorry about your marriage, John. You deserve better."

Johnny didn't know about that. When he married Scarlet, he thought he was marrying up. She'd had a fancy condo in Austin that her parents had given her and told him she'd been a model in Dallas for a year. She used to complain that all he'd ever done in his life was play in the dirt. After they married and she found out the farm wasn't in his name she'd been so upset she'd gone shopping for a week.

Rick turned back toward the courthouse and Johnny walked over to the bookstore. He hoped his car was still parked in the back lot. He'd waded through a river of emotions in the past eight days. People he'd thought would always stand with him had disappeared. Family seemed more than willing to believe the worst about him.

On the up side, he'd made two new friends. Deputy Rogers had done his job with a kindness Johnny appreciated, and the little fairy never stopped believing in him. She'd dropped by the jail every day just to remind him he was innocent.

He decided to walk through the bookstore, not around it. If Kare was there, he planned to thank her and hug her tight.

Mr. Hatcher was sitting at the counter reading and didn't look up when Johnny walked by. The dark green door to Kare Cunningham's tiny space was open. She was curled up around her computer studying something on the screen.

Johnny tapped on her door and she jumped, then looked up and saw him. A smile covered her face.

"You're out!" she shouted as her computer bumped against a pillow on the floor and she jumped toward him.

Johnny felt like he'd caught her in flight, and every sense exploded: the tinny jingle of necklaces, the silk of a dozen scarves floating around her, the smell of spices, the softness of her wet cheek as she hugged him.

He pressed his hand into all that curly hair and smiled, really smiled for the first time in years. He didn't want to talk to her, he just wanted to hold her for a minute and let time move on without them noticing.

She pulled away first and, to his surprise, he took the loss of her against him like a blow.

"I came by," he hurried to say as she floated back to her corner. "I came to say thank you for visiting me and believing in me."

"Oh, you're welcome. The thought of someone locked away who is innocent upsets me." She giggled. "I guess it reminds me of my childhood."

They were obviously going back to being strangers. Johnny had thought they had a bond. "I read all the books you gave me."

She picked up her computer. "I know, you told me. I'm glad you liked them." She reminded him of someone who'd been interrupted and had to get back to work. She was polite, friendly, but he'd thought there had been more between them.

"I thought, if you have time, we could go out to eat and celebrate."

Kare looked up at him. "That is sweet, John, but I can't tonight. I'm very happy you're free. May peace follow you like a river forever flowing."

Johnny decided he should go back to jail, walk out again, and start completely over. He must have taken a wrong step somewhere and walked into somebody else's life. She'd cared so much about him? Now she didn't even add *Maybe another night* to her excuse for turning him down. He had no idea what peace flowing like a river meant. It sounded like she'd read the line sometime in a fortune cookie and had been waiting years to use it.

Stop. He almost slammed his palm into his forehead. She hadn't cared that much about him, she'd only cared that he was innocent and being charged. She was probably one of those people who worried about folks she didn't even know and global warming, or endangered frogs in the rain forest. Hell, he didn't even know where the rain forest was and he figured he'd have to be a vice president to understand global warming. How could he have thought they shared something special between them?

"Thanks again for all your help," he managed, and walked out of her funny little office. One of the charms pasted to the door fell off as he exited, but he didn't stop to pick it up. She might get mad and take back her *river of peace* blessing.

All the way back to the farm he tried to figure out what had happened. Had he just imagined those big brown eyes looking at him with bedroom thoughts? How many times had she stretched out her arms as if trying to reach him across the table? Maybe he was right about thinking once that Kare was only interested in men behind bars. Now that he was out, she didn't seem interested at all.

Women. He'd never understand them. The hermit idea was looking better and better. If he raised chickens and bought a milk cow he could probably survive without ever going into town again. He was a farmer. If he could grow cotton and wheat, he could grow his own food. His grandpa had. Maybe he'd drop by the senior citizens' center and ask Pops a few questions.

A half hour later when he walked into his empty house, he felt like screaming until his voice gave completely out.

He was going mad. He'd been married to Scarlet for three years and didn't miss her at all, but, darn, if he didn't miss his fairy. All the magic in the world had dried up and blown away like a tumbleweed and he was left with nothing but a handful of air. He felt like a man who'd been asleep all his life and someone accidentally woke him up in the middle of a dust storm.

Now there was no going back to sleep and he had no idea how to move forward.

Chapter 24

BEAU STUMBLED OUT OF THE BAR AFTER SEVEN WHEN MOST folks were coming in to eat dinner. He didn't want to be around people, yet he didn't want to be alone. He'd thrown up most of the alcohol he'd downed and decided he'd never bother with it again. The stuff tasted nasty going down and worse coming up.

Walking past his rented car and skirting the Blue Moon Diner, he headed down into the creek bed, Winter's Inn already in his sight. Maybe he'd sleep off the way he felt in the quiet little inn. Nothing else seemed to work.

It wasn't near dark yet, but the shadows crossed above him, making the old scar in the earth look like the entrance to a cave. He walked along the dried ground as it crackled beneath his boots. The town, six feet above, was all around him, but Beau felt totally alone. As he always did, he heard the beat of Harmony. At midnight when he walked it was a soft haunting melody but now the beat was alive, fast, hurried.

Music began to play in his head. A car's horn became a crashing cymbal. Wheels rolling across the uneven boards on a nearby bridge were the drums. Church bells chimed in and the rustle of the trees added bass.

Beau closed his eyes and circled around on the uneven ground, loving that the music he'd always heard brushed against his skin and settled in his soul.

For a moment he heard something rattling, sliding across the dried leaves along the sides of the creek. The noise didn't belong in his music. It wasn't part of the town.

Then the sound of a branch breaking registered a moment before something slammed into the back of Beau's head and he fell face first. Another blow landed against the side of his head as shattered lightning exploded in his brain.

The music stopped.

Chapter 25

Kare worked on her research, prowling the Internet looking for a detail that marked one of the thirty people Captain McAllen had on her list of possible suspects. The man hiding out would fit most of the profile she'd listed, but maybe not all. He'd be new to the area within the last five years. Independently wealthy or showing no obvious means of income. He'd try to fit in, maybe a little too hard. Computer knowledge. Disappears from time to time. No family in area. Might fly planes or have airstrip on his land. Fast cars. Large amount of cash. Maybe speak more than one language.

Millanie had also provided her with possible jobs he might have or say he had. Stockbroker, banker, accountant, something freelance like writer or painter. He might tell people he was a trust fund baby or had recently inherited money. Only whatever he claimed wouldn't be traceable.

Two facts kept knocking on her brain like pesky neighbors who wouldn't go away.

One, Millanie had put Kare's brother, Drew, on the list as a person of interest. He should be on the "good guy" list.

The captain was dating him; surely she'd figured out what kind of person he was by now.

Maybe Millanie was simply testing her. If so, should Kare tell the truth? Her brother's secrets were none of the captain's business until he wanted to tell Millanie himself.

Since the day she walked into his office at Clifton College, Kare had wanted to tell Drew that she knew about the shooting, but then she'd have to admit that she'd stalked his every move for years. Just knowing he was there was enough when she was a kid. By college she'd begun making up stories of how they'd meet and how he'd be happy to be her big brother. When the shooting happened, she changed all plans. Within days he'd disappeared from the public eye and she knew she'd have to, first, find him and, second, help him through what happened.

Only two years ago when she'd stepped into his office and met the shy, intelligent man who was her brother, she couldn't admit to knowing about the shooting. It would have changed things somehow. The joy of finding him would have been shadowed.

As much as he kidded her about it, Kare really could read people. And she knew for his peace of mind he needed to keep one slice of his life a secret. She thought of how upset he might be when he learned that she knew about his past, so Kare promised herself that when, or if, he ever told her, she'd act like she'd just found it out.

Two years ago when he'd asked how she found him, she said she was checking colleges that might take her and noticed his name. Then she'd told Drew how her father talked about the boy he left behind who was ten years older than her.

She couldn't admit she'd known about Chicago or the real reason she'd come to Harmony. He was everything she'd dreamed a big brother might be and that was enough.

Kare often saw a sadness in her brother's eyes and knew he was remembering. When he made his annual trip back to the graves, she didn't ask where he'd been. She just did what she always did. She tried to cheer him up. Only this year she hadn't had to work her magic on his dark moods. He'd brought Millanie home and she'd changed his world. The two didn't match at all. A captain and a professor, but for some reason, they worked.

Kare shivered as she locked her office and walked out the back door of the bookstore. There was so much Drew didn't know about her. Her secrets seemed piled far higher than his. She'd told him she found him two years ago when she was checking out colleges in Texas and noticed a man named Cunningham had signed on to teach at Clifton Creek, but that was a lie too. Her father used to joke about how he'd left one child and he'd leave her if she didn't at least try to act normal.

Growing up, Kare sometimes thought of the big brother she had somewhere and guessed maybe he was the lucky one not to have their father around. If dads were ranked on a scale from one to ten, her pop would have been a negative two.

When she was alone in her teens, she'd talk to Drew, dreaming that since he was ten years older he was looking for her. After a few years she figured out that he couldn't know about her. To find her, he had to know where his father was, and that wouldn't have been possible. Her dad used to say he and his second wife *lived off the grid*. Their farm was fifty miles from any town and the deed had been registered to Kare's mother because she'd inherited the land just before she married. He'd also mentioned a few times that neither of them wanted children and Kare had been an accident, making both children he'd fathered mistakes.

Kare finally found Drew on the Internet when she was twelve. One night after her father had been drinking and telling her how awkward and homely she was, he mentioned that he should have kept Andrew and thrown her away. Unknowingly, he'd given her the piece of the puzzle she needed.

Searching, she'd typed Andrew Cunningham's name into

her computer. *Honor graduate from Yale* came up, complete with a picture. From then on she followed him like a silent stalker.

Two years later he had his master's in education and Kare had hidden away a dozen articles he'd written for the *Yale Review*. One newspaper article about him said he planned to teach history in one of the roughest high schools in Chicago. Kare was so proud. Her big brother was going to be one of those rare people who changed the world.

From then on there were other articles in professional teaching journals and once in a while in a parenting magazine. Drew wrote about his teaching and the tricks he'd learned to engage students. He said his goal was to make history come alive.

Four years after she found him online, he was very much a part of her and he didn't even know she existed. While her mother thought she was working on her homeschool lessons, Kare continued to keep up with her brother. He was working on his Ph.D. and winning recognition as one of the best teachers in Illinois. He was going places. She was staying home starting online classes from a junior college at sixteen.

When she was nineteen and away at college for her junior year, she saw a one-line news bulletin saying that an Andrew Cunningham had been shot in a school shooting. A few days later she mentioned it when she went home for the weekend.

Her father looked up from his supper, only mildly interested.

"Do you think this Cunningham could be kin to us?" she'd asked, already knowing he was.

"Nope," her dad answered. "The kid I left had a druggie for a mom; he'd be more likely the shooter than the victim. Biggest mistake of my life, marrying that woman when she got pregnant. I stayed with her until after the baby was born, but she got back on drugs and expected me to take care of the kid after I worked all day. Well, I showed her. I knew if I ever checked on the kid she'd come after me for child support, so when I hooked up with your mom I made sure everything was in her name. The old girl will never find me and neither will the kid."

Kare had heard it all a hundred times. Growing up on a farm, being homeschooled because her folks wanted her to finish her lessons by noon so she could help out, she'd heard every story. When they finally let her leave home for her last two years of college, she'd spent the first semester just listening to the way all the other girls talked and all they had to say about subjects no one in her family had thought to ever bring up.

She'd made a few friends, but Kare didn't fit in. She was alien to their world. She had no idea how to dress or what movies had been popular during her life, or a hundred other things.

Her social life, even while living in the dorm, became the Internet mostly. Her best friend, the computer. It was no wonder her closest relative was a brother she'd never met and who didn't know about her.

Tonight Kare walked toward the dried-up creek behind the Blue Moon Diner, thinking how college had also saved her five years ago. A few days after Drew had been shot while teaching, Kare lost track of him. She switched her major and studied harder, finishing in the top of her class as a forensic accountant. When the offers for jobs came in, she went straight to the IRS. If she was going to find Andrew, there would be a place to start. It took her two years, but one day his social security number showed up at a small college in Texas.

She saved and worked until finally she was on her way to Texas with a story prepared, enough money to carry her awhile, and a brother she'd been waiting half her life to meet. Her parents had thought she'd come home to work the farm, but when she didn't, they weren't upset. It turned out they didn't like people and that included her.

Holding on to a branch, Kare stepped down into the dry creek that wiggled through downtown Harmony. Her thoughts were on the day she'd found Drew. She couldn't have dreamed of a better brother. He'd accepted her as family, and somehow by being herself, the people in town accepted her too.

Her apartment was a few blocks away from the bookstore, and crossing the creek cut her walk in half. Most nights she liked to walk the streets downtown, but tonight she wanted to see Captain Millanie McAllen and drop off a few details she'd found. Nothing that would solve the mystery but enough to cross a few more suspects off the list.

The light shining over the back door of Winter's Inn told her she was expected. She'd sent Millanie a text. The captain would be waiting by the door. It wasn't much past dark, so someone at the bed-and-breakfast might be up. If they were, the captain would probably invite her in like Kare was simply a friend stopping by to visit. Maybe they'd share some iced tea. Kare would like that.

Her foot bumped into something along the path, almost toppling her over.

Kare looked down, pushing on the object with the toe of her shoe. The back porch light offered just enough glow for her to see a body. Long, lean, and dressed in black.

She screamed and ran toward the house. When she scrambled up the incline on all fours, she heard her skirt ripping but she didn't slow.

Millanie was on the back porch by the time Kare reached the steps. "There's a body in the creek bed! A body!"

"Alive or dead?"

Kare panicked. "I didn't take time to look. Was I supposed to look? Oh no! I didn't look."

Millanie seemed as calm as Kare was frightened. The captain leaned inside and ordered, "Martha Q, call the sheriff and an ambulance. Mrs. Biggs, bring flashlights. There's someone hurt in the creek bed."

"I should have checked," Kare repeated. All her life she'd felt like every other person got a rule book and somehow she'd lost hers before she'd had time to read it. "What if he's dead? What if he's not?"

Millanie moved slowly down the steps on her crutches. "Calm down, Kare. I don't think I can get down there on one leg, so you'll have to go back to where he is. Whoever it is might very well be hurt and need our help. If he's dead, he won't hurt you so there is no need to be afraid of him."

Millanie shoved a flashlight in Kare's hand as Mrs. Biggs joined them carrying two more.

The captain's request came as a command. "We'll be right above you, Kare. Go down and see if he's still breathing. Mrs. Biggs will keep a light on the body and I'll keep one on you."

Kare wanted to scream that she only worked part-time for the IRS. Nothing like this had ever been in her job description, but looking at an old woman and an injured captain, she seemed to be the only one for the job. If Martha Q or these two tried to slide down into the creek bed, there would probably be a pileup of bodies before the sheriff could get here.

"All right," Kare said, and marched back in the direction she came. The incline wasn't as steep on this side. She turned sideways and, one foot at a time, clomped her way to the bottom. Then she turned the light on her toes and took one step at a time until the glow splashed on a hand.

"What do you see?" Millanie called out.

"Black shirt. Black hat. One hand."

Mrs. Biggs screamed and Kare realized she probably should have said that the hand was attached to a body.

"Details, Kare," Millanie ordered from above.

It took all her courage to touch the hand. "It's a man's left hand. Warm. No ring."

"He's not married and he's still alive. Around here that's good news." Martha Q had joined them and felt the need to put in her assumptions. "I should have never let those steps go to ruin. If I hadn't, I'd be down there now helping. If there is one thing I know it's how to handle a man."

"Facts," Millanie repeated to Kare as she ignored Martha Q.

Kare moved the light over the body until she saw blood on the back of his head. "He's hurt. Bleeding from an open wound." She moved closer. "I hear his breathing. Oh dear God, there is so much blood."

The body moved, his fingers brushing her ankle. Kare yelped, then bolted, scrambling back up the side of the creek bed. She appeared so suddenly both Martha Q and Mrs. Biggs screamed in unison.

An ambulance sounded nearby but couldn't compete with the ladies.

"Don't try to move him, it might—" Millanie started to say but Kare was already gone.

Millanie gulped and whispered to herself more than Kare, "Good job. They'll be here in a minute. In fact, thanks to you they probably heard the screaming above the siren."

Kare and the two old ladies huddled while the captain moved a few feet so that whoever pulled in the drive could see her waving a flashlight beam back and forth.

About the time Kare got her heart out of her throat, she heard movement in the tree branches and turned just as the body pulled himself up.

All three women screamed again and he took a step backward, almost toppling into the creek bed.

Martha Q recovered first and yelled, "Beau Yates, you frightened ten years off my life! What do you think you are doing skulking around like one of the walking dead?"

"Sorry, ma'am, you want me to fall into the creek again? I could probably manage that. I think I was mugged down there." He touched his head and brought red fingers back. "My head hurts something terrible."

Kare fought to keep from fainting. All she could do was stare at the bright red blood on the man, formerly known as *the body*. She faded into the shadows as people flooded Martha Q's yard. The sheriff, firemen, the EMTs, and several people who'd heard the screaming ran from Main Street to help.

In her whole sheltered life she'd never seen a person bleed so much. Everyone was talking at once, trying to help and asking questions. Apparently they all knew the man who'd been attacked.

No, he didn't know how many or who hit him in the head.

Yes, he could walk.

He had no idea what time it happened. He came to when something kicked him in the side.

Now the sheriff turned to Kare and started shooting questions.

No, she hadn't seen anyone else in the creek bed.

What did she do? She ran screaming.

She was crossing to visit with her friend, Captain Millanie McAllen.

She didn't know why she took the shortcut. It seemed like a good idea at the time. On second thought, it probably wasn't.

Kare was starting to feel confused. A deputy asked her the same questions as the EMTs loaded the bleeding man up and rushed him to the ambulance. Both old ladies raced to the house to get their purses, claiming they were family and would be riding along with him to the hospital. Firemen fanned out around the place where he'd been found. They all shined their lights in the circle while the sheriff looked for clues.

When no one was looking, Kare went to the porch. In the dark corner, she curled up in a ball and buried her head on her knees. She hadn't done the right thing. She should have helped him, not run. Her dad was right; she was worthless in a crisis. She was worthless period. Lowering her head, she cried silently, as she always had when her father yelled at her or someone at college made fun or her, or people didn't understand her. Her whole body shook, but she held tight to her knees. She'd weather this time like she'd survived all the others. In a few days it wouldn't seem so bad. In a month she'd laugh about how dumb she'd acted.

Millanie found Kare in her dark corner. She spoke softly, her voice calming, reassuring. "Can you help me inside, Kare? I can't hold the door and manage my crutches."

Kare shoved her tears off her cheeks with her palms and stood. "Of course." She could help. That she could do.

"If you'll come inside with me, I could use an assistant for making coffee. When Mrs. Biggs and Martha Q get back they'll probably need some."

Logic told Kare what the captain was doing. Calming her down. Keeping her busy. But still, it worked. Kare stopped thinking about how upset she was and started worrying about others. All the while she made coffee and sliced banana bread and dug through the refrigerator for jelly, Kare listened to Millanie's calm voice going over what needed to be done.

One thought was born amid the panic in Kare's mind. If Millanie could help calm her, a coward afraid of the sight of blood, what could the captain do for Drew, a real hero who'd lost his way?

Magic maybe?

Chapter 26

WITH THE LIBRARIAN, MRS. PARKER, HOLDING THE DOOR for Drew, he slipped past her with his stack of books and watched her lock up. "Sorry to be so late. Thanks for finding these for me. If it weren't for interlibrary loan, I'd be driving all over the state."

"No problem, Dr. Cunningham. You should know librarians live for challenges like the ones you always present."

She looked down; her shy manner made her beautiful in her own way.

"Dr. Cunningham, I know few mention this, but those of us who know about your work think it's wonderful. Generations will learn from your books about the history of this area. They'll know the strong kind of people it took to settle here."

"Thank you," he said, surprised at the compliment.

She said good night as a man stepped from a powerful black pickup. Her husband, Drew guessed from the way she stood on her toes and kissed his cheek. He took her bag and helped her into the truck, then gave a short wave to Drew as if thanking him for walking her out.

As Drew stashed the books in the back of the Jeep, he thought of Millanie and doubted they'd ever have that comfortable easy way with one another. Each was attracted to the other, that was obvious, but he couldn't see himself settling down, moving into a real house, living a normal life. Most days he thought this very simple life he'd managed to cobble together here in Texas was all he'd ever be able to handle.

An ambulance passed by him with full lights and sirens flashing. In Chicago he'd seen them daily, but not here.

An uneasiness settled over Drew. The flashing lights were headed directly toward the historical part of town.

He climbed into his Jeep and decided to follow. Winter's Inn and Kare's apartment were both in the area. Millanie and his sister were all right, he told himself. Of course, they were. Only, Kare had been hanging out with a guy who just got released from jail and Millanie looked like a walking target with her crutches. If there was one bad guy in town, he might have crossed their paths.

By the time Drew turned off Main, worry had trumped concern. The sheriff's car was parked out in front of Martha Q's inn and the ambulance had pulled into the drive.

He stopped the Jeep a few houses down and waited. Drew wasn't sure he could walk in on a crime scene. He'd lived without any violence in his life for five years.

One man walked to the ambulance flanked by what looked like the EMTs. Drew climbed out of his Jeep and moved toward them as the emergency medical team put the man on a stretcher. One wrapped his head while the other belted him in.

Drew recognized Beau Yates. A local kid whose talent had made him famous. Now he looked nothing like his picture in the local paper. The singer's shirt seemed covered in blood. Dark shiny blood made even more striking in the blinking lights of the ambulance.

Drew's heart stopped pounding. Not Kare. Not Millanie. Maybe it was just accident. One of the EMTs was talking to Beau, so it couldn't have been too bad.

Drew joined a small group of people watching as others circled around. One man said the guy named Beau had left Buffalo's drunk. Another said he probably fell. Everyone, except Drew, nodded as if they'd solved the puzzle in the dark without a single clue.

Martha Q waddled at top speed out the front door, yelling for them to hurry up and get Beau to the hospital. "The boy's going to bleed to death and you men are doing nothing but talking."

The two EMTs lifted the stretcher into the back, with Beau telling Martha Q that it wasn't as bad as it looked.

She climbed into the passenger seat still talking loud enough for everyone on the block to hear her. "Great use of my tax dollars. Pay two healthy men to stand around and talk to the victim. At this rate, if you men had two calls on the same night you'd be in big trouble, or rather the bleeding would. I think if I have a heart attack I'll cross the county line before I call 911."

The men didn't seem to be listening to Martha Q as they helped Mrs. Biggs into the back. Drew had the feeling this wasn't the first time the chubby Martha Q had dealt with trouble.

The ambulance and the sheriff's car left. The crowd dispersed.

Drew stood in the darkness, unsure what to do. If he went inside there might be a crime scene. No one said where Beau had fallen. Maybe someone had broken into the house? If he didn't go in, he'd never know if Millanie was all right.

Of course, she was all right, he told himself. But he'd thought he was all right five years ago, and he hadn't been. The wounds he'd suffered had healed, but Drew still wasn't all right. Even the sight of the ambulance made memories pile up in his mind.

He'd thought the first shots were firecrackers in the hall-way of the high school where he'd taught the year he turned twenty-nine. It was almost the end of the spring semester. Pranks were common. His class was packing up, getting ready to leave.

He hadn't locked his door.

Another shot in the hallway.

Before he could stop them, the students moved toward the exit, wanting to see where the noise came from.

They were all between Drew and the door when one boy, not old enough to be called a man, blocked the exit.

When the first shot thundered into his room Drew had turned toward a student hit in the arm, not the shooter.

Another shot. Screams. They all ran to the back. To where Drew stood.

Drew pushed his way through a sea of students as he rushed to the door and the boy who held a gun.

Another shot. Then another.

Drew kept moving even when he heard someone behind him hit the floor with the sickening thud of a dead body.

He was ten, eight, seven feet from the shooter when the boy saw him and turned the weapon toward the only teacher in the room. Drew didn't even know him. He'd seen the kid in the hall a few times, but now he didn't miss the hatred in the shooter's eyes.

One bullet hit Drew's shoulder like a slug from a boxer's fist. Another ran like fire along his side, but Drew kept charging.

Five feet. Four.

A shot went wild over his head. Another missed him but he heard someone scream behind him. His students were crying and screaming as alarms went off all over the building.

Drew was three feet away from the shooter when footsteps thundered down the hallway, drawing louder and closer. Drew knew who they were. Every teacher asks himself the same question. *If I hear gunfire, do I run away or toward it?* Like Drew, many had said they'd run toward it.

The shooter heard the storm coming behind him and was distracted for a moment.

That was all Drew needed. He hurled himself full force toward a kid who weighed fifty pounds less than he did. The gun fired as it left the boy's hand and hit the floor. Drew's bloody body slammed the shooter to the hard tiles.

For a moment, all was silent. Drew held the boy down flat. He looked into the kid's eyes, fearing that he might have hurt him, but all he saw was surprise, almost as if Drew had interrupted a game the boy had been playing.

The principal and two other teachers reached the room at the same time the police stormed the hallway. They surrounded the shooter and took him out, handling him carefully as if he were a broken boy and not a heartless killer.

Drew turned back to his class. He didn't realize how bloody he was until he saw his students' faces. "I'm all right." He tried to keep calm. "Who needs help?"

Some were too upset to help, but others moved. Drew didn't feel any pain. He lifted a girl who'd been shot in the stomach and carried her out to the waiting ambulance. She clung to him and cried. Just past the school doors she stopped crying. She died.

In the darkness of Winter's Inn's front yard Drew relived it all. For five years he'd fought the memory, but it came back as if it had only been a day ago. Somewhere between the school that day and the hospital, he'd shattered. His dreams of teaching, of making students love history, of showing them they could climb out of where they were if they used the ladder of education, all stopped.

Even as his wounds healed, he'd known he couldn't go back. Not to his career, or the school, or his life. For five years he'd found a place to hide, only now he knew his wounds were still open and bleeding on the inside.

Two deputies walked within ten feet of him without noticing Drew in the shadows.

One said, "Don't you think it was strange the fortune-teller found Beau Yates? Maybe she knew he was going to be there. Maybe she's got a real gift. If she hadn't, Beau might have bled to death in that creek."

"Lots of folks cross the creek. She just happened to trip over him. If she'd known he'd be there, don't you think she'd have been more careful?"

They climbed in the cruiser and Drew heard no more.

He looked around. If Kare had found the singer, where was she now?

Only one answer came to him as he stared at the old house. She was inside.

Pushing his fears away, Drew walked slowly to the porch and up the steps. He didn't bother to knock, he just walked in.

The rooms were mostly dark with only a foyer light on and one lamp burning low in the parlor. He stood, listening, every sense fully alive, ready to run. Ready to fight.

Millanie's voice drifted to him from the kitchen. Silently he followed, letting his breathing slow, forcing muscles in his entire body to relax. They were all right. He was all right.

As Drew turned the corner and saw the two of them, he froze, too filled with relief to move. Millanie was sitting at the table and Kare stood by the sink. They were talking.

"Evening, ladies," he said as casually as he could. "What happened here?"

Kare dropped her tea towel and ran toward him. "Oh, Drew, it was terrible. I found Beau hurt behind the house. Someone knocked him in the head."

He hugged her tightly as he thought a big brother should do, then pushed her mass of hair away from her face. "You're all right, Kare. It's over. I saw Beau leaving and he was talking as they got him ready to transport to the hospital."

She sniffled as if trying to decide whether to cry again. "I know, but I could have hurt him when I stumbled over him. I was so scared, all I thought to do was run. I should have seen if he was breathing. I should have helped him, but all I did was run."

"You went back down there," Millanie added. "You did the right thing. You did help. If you hadn't run to me, the ambulance wouldn't have gotten here so fast."

Drew looked over his sister's head to Millanie and silently thanked her as he whispered to Kare, "We all do the best we can. You helped."

Kare stayed in his arms a few more minutes, then pulled

away. "What did I ever do growing up without you? Sometimes nothing works better than a hug."

In her whimsical way, Kare pulled away smiling with tears still on her face. "Want some hot chocolate?" She glanced at Millanie and giggled before moving to the smorgasbord of sweets on the counter. "We know it's a hot night, but we decided in a crisis nothing works better than chocolate, so we're having hot chocolate with brownies topped with chocolate ice cream and Martha Q's secret stash of M&Ms we found. She told us to make ourselves at home, but home was never this loaded with sweets."

"Whatever you mix up will be great," he lied as he took the chair next to Millanie. "Evening, Millie, thanks for watching over my little sister." His hand brushed the back of her shoulders.

To his surprise, she leaned over and kissed his cheek.

"What's that for?" he whispered.

"For being a great big brother," she answered.

The urge to kiss her back was a hunger that had nothing to do with chocolate, but his sister was too close. Drew moved his hand under the table and slid his fingers along her warm skin, exposed thanks to her shorts.

He saw her eyes darken, but she didn't move away as his hand slowly moved up from her knee. When he reached the hem of her shorts, he knew he'd better calm down or he'd shock his sister.

Turning his attention to Kare, he asked, "What were you doing in the creek?"

She didn't face him as she answered, "Millanie invited me over to visit. She may be your girlfriend, but she's my friend."

Millanie nodded. "That's right. I'm afraid you'll have to share me, Drew."

His fingers tightened around the upper part of her leg, hopefully letting her know that he didn't plan to share her with anyone.

Kare set a mess of different kinds of chocolate before him and turned back to the counter. "Unless you want more,

I'd better put up this stuff before Martha Q comes back and thinks we've robbed her."

They all talked. The girls told him every detail of the night and Drew told them how proud he was of them.

A half hour later Mrs. Biggs called from the hospital and said that Beau had a dozen stitches and was spending the night, but it looked like he'd be all right. The sheriff had been by to see him and said she thought the attack was a simple robbery. Beau had flashed a few hundreds in the bar and someone must have seen him as easy prey.

When they moved to the parlor, Kare curled up in an overstuffed chair and fell asleep midsentence.

"Does she always do that?" Millanie asked.

"I don't know. We didn't grow up together. Different mothers, same father." Drew lifted a light cotton throw and spread it over his sister. "I wish I'd been around to look out for her."

"Of course. That explains it," Millanie said, as if she'd figured out a puzzle.

"Explains what?"

"Why the two of you are so different. I've watched you. There's an edge to you that people from small towns or farms don't have. You're easygoing, but you keep things close to the vest like people raised in big cities."

"New York," he admitted as he sat down on the other end of the couch. She lifted her cast on the middle cushion between them. "How'd you end up here?"

"More questions, Captain?" His words were direct, but his hand rested on the cast between them.

"Just one," she grinned. "Why do you move your hand over my cast? You do know I can't feel it."

"I know, but I can imagine. If you want to switch places you could leave your cast on the floor and stretch out your bare leg that I've already had the pleasure of touching. I liked the feel of your warm skin, especially the place half-way up from your knee on the inside of your long beautiful leg. It's softer there, less tanned."

She breathed deep before she whispered, "How do you

know it's less tanned? You couldn't see my skin under the table when you were feeling your way along my skin."

"I wouldn't mind checking it out. We could easily settle the matter."

Millanie glanced at Kare sleeping, then looked at him. "Would you mind stepping into the entryway, Dr. Cunningham?"

"Not at all," he answered very formally as he stood and offered her his hand.

She let him help her away from the chance of a sleeping sister hearing or seeing what they were doing.

Once outside the parlor, he leaned her against the door to her room and flipped off the foyer light. They were so close her body touched his every time she breathed, but he didn't kiss her. He brushed his jaw against her hair and let out a long sigh.

"Aren't you going to kiss me?" she whispered.

"More questions," he said as he balanced her with his hands on her shoulders and moved his leg between hers. The contrast of the hard cast and her soft flesh only one layer of khaki pants away from him almost drove him insane. She was slim, but not thin. There was an odd mix of strength and vulnerability about her that fascinated him. His whole body seemed to want to say *I've finally found you. My perfect fit.* Even though the few brain cells still working reminded him he barely knew this woman who felt so right pressed against him.

Once she relaxed, knowing she wasn't going to fall, he moved his hands down her sides, taking his time feeling her through the light summer shirt. With each stroke his fingertips brushed the side of her breasts. He liked the sudden softness beneath her clothes.

He smiled when she leaned her head against the wall and closed her eyes. Her mouth was open slightly, inviting him in, but he didn't want a kiss tonight. He wanted to memorize every curve of her body.

As his hands grew bolder, her breathing grew deeper. He stayed so close that she kept touching him with her slight movements. Her head moved back and forth as his hands slipped beneath the hem of her shirt and spread out over her flesh. Her entire body was so warm. When his long fingers slowly slid over her breasts, she arched with the sudden pleasure and he leaned into her, letting his body feel her fully.

He brushed her lips but pulled away before they kissed. He wanted her to need him as much as he needed her.

She moved against him. He kissed her lightly again and she cried out softly.

"No, Drew, no."

He kissed her throat. "Now what?"

"Don't stop," she said so low he barely heard. "Please, don't stop. Don't pull away from me."

He grinned as his lips trailed up her throat to her mouth. Finally, she'd said something that wasn't a question.

Drew kissed her then, long and slow. She fit so perfectly against him. He loved seeing her need for him in her eyes. He loved knowing that she wanted this between them as dearly as he did. Her arms rested lightly on his shoulders as he unbuttoned a few buttons of her blouse, then pressed his hand against the side of her breast so the mound almost broke free of any material. Along the untanned flesh he took his time tasting her as she begged him not to stop.

His hand continued to roam over her for a few seconds even after he heard someone moving onto the porch.

"We'll finish this later," he whispered as he pulled away and flipped on the foyer light.

By the time Martha Q unlocked the door and stepped inside, Drew was lowering Millanie to her seat on the couch.

Chapter 27

JOHNNY WHEELER HAD SWORN HE WOULDN'T GO TO TOWN for a while, but by dark he realized there was no food in the house. The lettuce and grapes he'd bought ten days ago had turned brown and the bread was green. Even hermits had to have food. It occurred to him that maybe he should grow something next season that he could eat. After all, he was a farmer. How hard could it be to plant a garden?

He might even use his barn for something other than a place to leave his tractor, and of course, his wife's boyfriend's drugs. Max must have thought Johnny a complete idiot for not noticing the drugs in the barn or Max in his bed with Scarlet.

When Johnny climbed in his pickup, he couldn't help wondering where Scarlet's car had disappeared to. When Max had been arrested with the drugs, surely Scarlet had been brought in to the sheriff's office.

At first he'd thought maybe the sheriff just drove off with Max and left her behind. If so, Scarlet would have had to come inside the house for the purse she'd left behind over a week ago.

He grinned and walked over to the dryer. Opening the door, he noticed her purse was exactly where he'd put it. She'd never think to look in the dryer. He wasn't even sure she knew the thing had a door.

If she took her car after Max's arrest, someone had to drive out and help her.

"Wendell," he said to himself, knowing his brother always came running whenever she needed help.

She wouldn't have to sleep with Wendell to get whatever she wanted; she could just pat him on the head. Before Wendell worked in mall patrol, he'd owned a key shop. He'd never considered the possibility that only a dozen people might need keys made every month. After three months of not making enough to pay the electricity on the place, he moved his tools to his garage and went looking for another job.

As Johnny drove into town, he tried to think of where Scarlet might be. Last year she'd sold her condo in Austin and said she was making some investments. She didn't want to talk about it and Johnny had thought, since it was her money, she could do whatever she wanted with it.

He'd never seen a dime, or a statement, or anything that hinted at what she'd done with the windfall.

Maybe she'd bought a place in Harmony? Maybe tonight she'd invited Wendell over to dinner at her secret place so she could talk him into confessing to a drug possession charge.

No, he thought, if she'd planned something so devious, she'd have to cook and Scarlet never did that. Plus, she wouldn't go out because she might be seen with Wendell. Even having a husband in jail couldn't damage her reputation as bad as stepping out with Wendell.

Johnny pulled into a grocery store. It was late. If he got fast food first, the store might be closed by the time he circled back. As he walked across the parking lot he heard sirens from the direction of the old town square. Sirens were rarely heard. He thought of yelling that he wasn't doing anything but buying groceries, but despite his recent record, maybe this time the cops were looking for someone else.

Johnny shoved the door to the store open, knowing it would probably take him an hour to pick up enough groceries to last a month. Once he got settled in on the farm, he didn't plan on coming back to town for a while.

Like maybe until Max's trial was over and Scarlet died of old age.

When Johnny checked out, he heard that there had been trouble down behind Winter's Inn. A man came in and said he heard a drunk had been mugged while walking in the creek bed. Word was he might have died if that woman who read palms at the bookstore hadn't found him.

Johnny told himself it was none of his business. The bookstore was long past closed and he had no idea where Kare Cunningham lived. He drove home and put up the groceries with his mind still turning over what must have happened. What if Kare got scared? He didn't like to think of her frightened. What if there was blood? She might not like that, and one thing was for sure: Even if she didn't know the guy Kare would worry about him, probably cry because he was hurt. With her soft heart there was no telling what she might do.

"Damn," Johnny said to the empty house. "I'm jealous of some drunk who got mugged."

He made a sandwich and grabbed a beer. If he had to he'd wake the bookstore owner up and demand to know where Kare lived.

Halfway to town it dawned on him that his plan would probably get him arrested. He'd developed a fear of handcuffs lately. He couldn't just drive around asking where some woman he barely knew lived.

He had to come up with Plan B. Only problem was when you start out with such a terrible Plan A, Plan B's not easy. Finally, he decided he'd drive around and think. Gas was cheaper than a psychiatrist.

An hour later Johnny was standing in Winter's Inn's backyard staring at where Kare had found a body. He had no idea why the mugged guy had crossed at this spot. All he cared about was why Kare had been there. If she crossed she was either taking a shortcut, which meant she lived near, or visiting someone, which meant she had a friend in one of these old houses. Or a client?

He looked through the cottonwoods and saw the bright Blue Moon Diner sign. If she'd left the back of the bookstore and walked in this direction, she might still be near.

Staring at the big old houses, he guessed he could knock on every door, but at some point people might not see him as friendly, what with his new jail tan, hair too long, and a week's worth of beard. Hell, they'd probably all swear they'd seen him on a wanted poster.

Some of the houses had little apartments in back. Maybe she lived in one? He stared at the bed-and-breakfast. If she crossed here, this could be the place she might have been headed.

Johnny had heard of Martha Q Patterson. The crazy old lady was just the type to have her palms read by moonlight. It was as good a place as any to start.

Glancing at the three-story house, Johnny got a feeling. His first as far as he could remember. He felt like Kare was in there. The little fairy must be rubbing off on him.

Walking up to the door, he wondered if he was breaking any laws by just knocking. Surely not. After all, Winter's Inn was a business. People must come and go all the time.

He knocked.

A chubby little lady with chocolate on her chin answered the door. "May I help you?" She wiggled her eyebrows at him. "I'm afraid we don't take guests this late."

She must have looked down at his boots and worn jeans and figured he couldn't afford a place like this anyway.

"I'm not looking for a room, Mrs. Patterson. I'm looking for Kare Cunningham. I understand she had some trouble tonight and I'd just like to offer my help if she needs anything. We're friends." The last part wasn't exactly a lie.

"We both seem to know who I am, young man, but I don't know who you are. No one comes into my house without a name."

"Johnny Wheeler, ma'am. I have a farm out north of town."

Martha Q laughed. "Of course you are. I can see the Wheeler look about you. Tall and broad shoulders. I knew your father, boy."

He hadn't thought of himself as a boy in years, but he wasn't surprised she knew his father. Word was she knew half the men in town very well. Johnny took a chance with a story he'd heard once. "My dad said he saw you dance on the table at Buffalo's Bar one night. He said you were the most beautiful woman he'd ever seen."

She giggled. "I don't remember him being there that night, but he's right, I was beautiful. Three men proposed to me before midnight that evening." Opening the door wider, she added, "Come on in, Johnny. We're all here."

He didn't want to see anyone but Kare, but when a man's invited into the dragon's lair, sometimes he's got to go.

Martha Q walked him down to the kitchen and offered him a seat. Another old lady was there serving up ice cream, and a distinguished man a few years older than Johnny stood to shake his hand. The woman next to the brainy type didn't seem as friendly. In fact, she looked like she was sizing him up. He wouldn't have been surprised if she'd asked him to open his mouth so she could count his teeth.

"I just wanted to stop by and check on Kare." Johnny stumbled over his words. "I'm a friend of hers."

The intelligent-looking man frowned at him. "I'm her brother and I assure you she's fine. She's asleep right now. It's been a rough night for her."

"I heard. I'm so sorry." Johnny didn't want to see any of these people; he only wanted to know Kare was fine.

"Have you known her long?" the woman with a cast on her leg asked.

"No," he answered.

"New in town?" she shot back.

He shook his head. "I was born here. Mrs. Patterson knew my father." Johnny doubted that would be a recommendation, but he'd try it anyway.

The woman in the cast seemed to relax and so did Kare's

brother. Johnny might be a complete lunatic for all they knew, but at least he was homegrown.

"Well, folks, I'm sorry to have bothered you. I'll say good night." He started to back out of the room.

"Stay for ice cream, Johnny." Martha Q snaked her arm around his. "I want to hear how your dad and granddad are doing. They were both big good-looking men like you without an ounce of fat on them."

He let her lead him over to a chair, not mentioning that she'd forgotten to ask about any of the women in his family. "My dad died about six years ago. Heart attack. After that my grandfather lost interest in the farm and I took it over. It's not that big an operation. I only hire out help during the harvest."

"I think I heard about your dad's passing a few years back. I'm sorry. He was a good man. Liked to drink and gamble a little, but he always went home to your mother."

She'd just told Johnny what he'd wondered about. His father hadn't been one of the men she'd gone out with. He met her stare and another feeling hit him. Martha Q knew exactly what she was telling him with her statement.

"Yes, ma'am. He loved my mother. When he died Mom moved to Granbury, down near Dallas, to be with her two sisters. They're all widowed now and spend most of their time quilting. They've gone to shows as far away as Arizona and won a wall full of ribbons. My mom's an expert with the Lone Star pattern. I got them a long-arm machine for Christmas so the quilting part doesn't take long."

Johnny wasn't surprised Martha Q looked bored. He'd bored himself. Wendell was right, he needed to develop an interest in something, otherwise people would start sleeping every time he opened his mouth.

Kare's brother, Drew, tried to help him out by saying, "That's interesting. I've always thought of quilting as a truly American art form."

No one in the kitchen believed his lie.

The other old lady, who identified herself as Mrs. Biggs,

handed him a brownie and a glass of milk. Johnny downed it as fast as possible and said he had to be going.

To his surprise Martha Q insisted on walking him to the door.

When they reached the foyer, she pointed to the parlor. One lamp put off a low glow in the corner.

He saw his little fairy curled up in a huge chair. She was sound asleep. Before he lost his nerve, Johnny asked, "Would it be all right if I just sat in here for a while and watched over her? I was worried."

Martha Q seemed to understand. She nodded and wad-dled back to the kitchen.

Johnny sat down on the couch across from Kare. Her wild hair was spread out behind her like a huge midnight pillow. He wasn't sure how or when it happened, but Kare mattered to him. Knowing that she was here and safe settled his heart.

Leaning back, he felt his body totally relax. Something about her was so special. If she would just let him be her friend, that would be enough. Once in a while someone comes along and you just know that person would be a blessing to be around.

He drifted off with his eyes half open just to make sure she was safe. The others were in the kitchen talking and laughing, but he was right where he wanted to be.

When Kare moved, he remained still, not wanting to surprise her or, worse, frighten her in the shadows. She'd had enough fright tonight.

"Johnny?" she whispered.

"Yes," he answered. "Now, don't get mad. I'm just here watching over you."

"Good," she answered, and went back to sleep.

A half hour later, the people in the kitchen moved to the foyer and were saying good night. She woke again and the first thing she did was look at him, not the others.

Martha Q told Kare she was welcome to stay the night, and all agreed she shouldn't go home this late.

Johnny stood. "I better be going. You're right, it's getting late."

No one considered including him in the sleepover. "Good night," he said, and moved to the porch.

Kare followed him out and gave him a quick hug. "Thanks for watching over me," she said before running back into the house.

Johnny walked to his pickup and got his third *feeling* in one night. He had a feeling he'd be seeing a great deal of his fairy in the future. Watching over her had been more fun than he'd ever had.

Chapter 28

❧

BEAU YATES WOKE FROM A SOUND SLEEP A LITTLE AFTER
midnight. He had an IV in his hand and bandages covering
the back of his head. For a while he lay very still and tried
to remember what had happened. He recalled every detail
of his father's funeral yesterday. The preacher had said his
old man must have been on a fast train to heaven, but somehow Beau doubted that. Then he'd played songs, not caring
that his father wouldn't have liked it.

As he hugged everyone good-bye, he'd seen Trouble several yards away. She'd come to the funeral, not because she
knew his father, but to make sure he was all right. She had
on a suit that should have been worn by a woman twice her
age and her pretty blond hair was tied up in that knot he
hated. But still, it meant a great deal that she'd come.

He'd turned back, planning to walk over to her when all
the mourners were gone, but she'd disappeared.

After the funeral he'd talked to Ruth awhile, promising
help if she ever needed it. His stepmother just seemed to
want to go back home. Beau sensed that nothing in the boxes

she packed had anything of her marriage or her time in Harmony.

He'd driven around and finally ended up at Buffalo's Bar. In many ways Beau felt like he'd grown up in that bar. He'd learned to play for a crowd there. He'd seen the best in people and the worst. Only after the funeral all he wanted to do was drink until his mind numbed.

Now, hours later in the hospital, he could still taste the whiskey he'd downed and then thrown up. He wasn't sure if the effects of the alcohol were splitting his brain in two or if it was the tree branch that someone had swung at his head a few times like they were swinging for a home run.

As his eyes focused, he saw a slender woman in the corner with her hair in a ponytail.

"Hello, Trouble," he said, sounding like a frog.

She pushed away from the wall and moved closer. Without asking, she poured him a glass of water.

He drank it down, then held it out for another.

"I went by Winter's Inn tonight but the cops were there."

Beau loved her low southern voice. Southern women often have that sweet sound of Mother Earth and midnight passion in their voices. Beau closed his eyes wondering if he could play music that sounded like that.

She slid her hand lightly over the blanket covering his leg. "I heard you were hurt. How are you feeling now, Beau?"

He finished the second glass and waited for her to fill it again. "Terrible, Trouble. You sure you didn't run over me with that red Mustang tonight?"

"Nope. I'd rather have you in the seat next to me. If you could get out of that bed, we could race the moon again. Just two kids living a dream."

Her hand covered his and the warmth of her fingers spread over his body. She was dressed in a plain cotton shirt and jeans. If he hadn't known better he'd guess her at sixteen. He felt like he'd lived a hundred lifetimes in the years he'd been gone but she hadn't changed. She was still his fantasy of the beginning of summer love, first love.

"Come on, Beau, ride with me one last time. You could be seventeen again."

He shook his head and then regretted it. The drugs they'd given him made him fight sleep, but he knew what he had to do. "No, Trouble, we've got to grow up sometime."

Beau couldn't believe he was stepping out of a fantasy he'd had for years. She'd always been there in the back of his mind, racing the moon, wild in the night.

She took his hand and held it tight. "I don't want to," she whispered. "I like who I was, who I am with you." Lowering her head, she kissed his hand. "I'm afraid you wouldn't like the woman your Trouble has become."

Beau saw her then for the first time. He'd always seen the girl; he'd never really looked at the woman. Even when he'd met her in the bank, the woman had only been a mask his Trouble was wearing.

"Give me a chance, Lark." He used her middle name, knowing that it fit her far better now than Trouble or Ashley. "Give me one chance to see you. The real you. I have a feeling I'd like the woman who grew from Trouble very much."

She was just as beautiful as he remembered, but now he saw that she was playing a role. The mask she wore tonight was that of the girl he remembered, not the other way around. The red boots. The ponytail. Probably even the clothes were all part of pretending she was in another time, another place.

"My grandfather used to call me Lark." She laced her fingers with Beau's. "He always said it was a name I'd grow into someday."

"It does fit you." Beau watched her. "Would you take the ribbon from your hair?"

She let go of his hand and pulled her hair free. Long blond strands caressed her shoulders just as he thought they would. Lovely. Sexy.

He liked what he saw. "Tell me about you, Lark. I'll always see a little of Trouble in you, but I want to go deeper tonight."

She sat on the end of his bed and they talked. She told him about her schooling and how she hated banking but her father thought she should go into the family business. She told him of summer studies in Europe and how until she was twenty she rode her horse almost every day after school. He thought he saw the shy girl she must have been with everyone but him. He figured out how the girl turned into a woman who thought she always had to be in control.

"Racing the moon with you was the only wild thing I ever did. A guy like you wouldn't have given me a second look if you'd seen me in school."

"A guy like me?"

Touching the side of his face, she whispered, "Didn't you know that every girl, every woman, who saw you wanted you back then? They still do. Only you don't see past the music. I've watched you, Beau. You play for yourself, not the crowd. It doesn't matter to you if it's a drunken bar crowd or a concert in a stadium. You're playing from your heart and we're all voyeurs listening in as you pour out your soul."

"You're wrong, Lark, I would have seen you in high school, if I'd have been there. I missed most of my last two years. I was lucky to graduate. After high school I picked up classes online between gigs, but you'll find I have some real gaps in my studies."

He cupped the side of her face when he noticed she didn't look like she believed him. "You're wrong. I would have seen you. I think I've always seen you. I saw you then, Trouble, and I see you now."

She nodded as one tear drifted along her cheek.

As the night rolled on, he told her of life on the road and his fight to make something of himself. He described how failure was not an option with him because he had no fallback plan. He always knew he was going to make it in the music business because he wanted it with every ounce of his being.

When he'd signed his first big deal earlier this year someone asked him if he ever thought he'd make it so far so fast. His answer had been simply, *yes*. Making it big had been all he'd thought about from the beginning. Not for the fame or the money, but more because it was meant to be.

She swore her life was the opposite. She wasn't meant to be a banker, but somehow she'd stepped on the train heading in that direction and nothing she could do would stop it. Her parents insisted on her majoring in business.

They laughed about growing up in different towns thirty miles apart. How so many things were the same. They talked of their fathers and realized how both, in their way, had made Beau and her what they were today.

Finally, deep in the night they told each other how much the times they'd raced into the night had meant to them. For both, those nights they'd driven the back roads with the top down were their only taste of real freedom. He said he'd never looked at another woman without comparing her to Trouble, and she admitted she never could get serious with another guy because Beau had a piece of her heart.

A nurse came in about four A.M. and told Beau he needed to sleep. She obviously didn't know who he was. For him the night had always been his time to be alive.

Lark stood to go as the nurse shot medicine into Beau's IV, but he wouldn't turn her hand loose. When the nurse left, he whispered, "I don't want to lose you again. You may think what we had was more dream than real, but sometimes I swear you're the only real thing in my life."

"Which of me do you not want to lose?" she said, and waited for the answer as if it were the most important question she'd asked in her life.

"You, Lark. I don't want to lose you. I'll always have Trouble in my memory, but I'd like to think I'd have a chance with you in my future."

"We'll see," she said as she leaned in and kissed him good night.

He'd been too drugged by the medicine flowing through his IV to truly feel the kiss. She gently pushed him back on the pillows as she turned the kiss to a feather-light touch against his lips.

He drifted off thinking he didn't want this one kiss to end.

Chapter 29

WEDNESDAY

MILLANIE INSISTED ON GOING TO THE DOCTOR THE MORNING after Beau had been hurt. The happenings of the night before demanded it.

First she wanted to check on the singer, and second, she wanted to ask Dr. Spencer a few questions. Patience had never been a trait Millanie cultivated. In her organized way she realized she couldn't make decisions without facts, and she'd waited long enough for the truth.

After making it down a long hallway to Beau's room, she found him sound asleep. She'd read on the Internet that folks called him an outlaw in country music, but in a hospital gown and asleep he didn't look like much of an outlaw. There was something about the man, so talented, and probably so rich, yet he had a bit of the lost boy inside him. He was the kind of man every woman near his age took the time to flirt with, and as far as she could see every man he knew called him friend. Well, every man but one. The one who'd almost knocked his brains out.

The doctor had finished her rounds and was waiting in her office by the time Millanie managed to maneuver the hallways on crutches.

Dr. Addison Spencer was much loved and respected in Harmony. Many said she could have had a million-dollar practice in any big city, but she loved Tinch Turner and Harmony.

Millanie felt comfortable around the all-business Addison. She'd had enough medical people who wanted to baby her. Millanie got right to the point. "I need to know about my leg so I can make plans."

She didn't say that the plans were whether to fall in love for the first time. That wasn't important to the conversation. All she needed to know was how bad the crippling would be.

Addison stood and walked around her desk. "I've read your records and sent the X-rays to two experts. The wounds were bad enough to give you a medical discharge from the army, so we're not dealing with something that will heal without a great deal of patience and effort. The army did not think you'd be able to continue your duties, but that doesn't mean you can't live a full and normal life."

"I understand. But how bad will my leg be when all the work is done? I can handle anything if I have a hint of what's coming. I don't want to just hear the good news. I need to know it all."

To Millanie's surprise, the doctor said, "Let's take off the cast and see."

An hour later, after new X-rays and several tests, Millanie sat on the exam table and waited for the doctor to finish poking. Her right leg looked pale and slightly thinner than her left. Two large scars jetted across her ankle and her knee. A dozen other small wounds had healed into star-shaped scars.

"The knee seems to be healing fine. Much better than expected." Dr. Spencer wasn't sugarcoating the news. "The ankle will probably need at least one more surgery before you can put weight on it. We can leave the cast off, but you'll have to wear a brace until after you've had at least one surgery on that ankle." Addison met her gaze. "That means a brace all the time, night and day. Anytime there is the slightest chance you'd put weight on the ankle. One time coming down on that bone with your weight might cause more damage."

Millanie nodded. She could deal with anything as long as she knew the facts. She stared at the ugly scar running six inches across her knee. "I'll wear the brace. Day and night."

"If you use a crutch to balance you can take a shower without it." Addison touched the red scar as if she could brush it away. "You'll be able to use a cane with the brace, but you must be very careful of falling. I'd suggest a walker, but I have a feeling you wouldn't go for that. I don't think you'll have trouble balancing with the cane."

Millanie nodded.

"I've got a relative who is a great plastic surgeon. He'd come if I ask him. Maybe we could take this scar down to a thick pencil line when we do the surgery."

"Let's give it a try." Millanie could easily deal with a line. Maybe she wouldn't wear as many dresses, but she'd always preferred pants anyway.

"You're willing to stay in Harmony that long?" The doctor seemed surprised.

"I am." Millanie made up her mind. "I'm thinking of remodeling an old house."

Addison smiled. "This town has a way of taking in strays. It took me in and it looks like it's hooked you too, Captain. You know, if you stay here we'll be almost related. My husband's mother was a McAllen."

Millanie laughed. "Everyone around is either related to me directly or married into the family. But in your case, I'm glad to know we're almost kin."

"That has its advantages. You'll see." The doctor picked up her pen and began to write. "We'll start by setting you up with some physical therapy three days a week. On the other days you'll need to walk some. Not till it's painful, but as you get used to the brace you'll forget you have it on."

"I doubt it."

Addison stood. "While you get dressed, I'll call Martha Q to come get you. Will you be staying at the bed-and-breakfast during the recovery?"

"No, just until I get the old McAllen place in livable condition. I'm moving back there. It turns out I've owned the place since I was nineteen and didn't even know it." As always, Millanie made up her mind in a blink.

When Martha Q's line was busy, the doctor called Alex McAllen Matheson, the sheriff, to come pick up Millanie. She called back in minutes saying she had a problem at the station and was sending her husband, Hank Matheson, to drive Millanie back to the inn.

Millanie laughed. Apparently if your name was McAllen in this town, you never needed a taxi.

Five minutes later when Hank picked her up at the emergency room doors, he had two of her McAllen cousins in the backseat of his truck. They both wanted to see the homestead, so before she could say she was tired or didn't have time, Hank was driving toward the old house on the first piece of land the McAllens owned.

"It's only a few miles from town," Hank yelled back to the young McAllens. "You guys could run out there and back for exercise."

Both men in the backseat groaned. One made a comment that Mathesons were still trying to kill McAllens, so Millanie better be careful.

The cousins were in training to be volunteer firemen and practiced their fireman carry on Millanie all the way to the porch. She'd never felt young, even in her early twenties, but the visit to her new home was an adventure. Before they finished roaming through the place, everyone including Hank was rattling off what had to be done.

Millanie took notes. Every time she said, "How do I find someone to do that?" one of the men named a relative that would either offer to do it free or *give her a good rate*.

When she said she'd like to restore it as close as it was to the original design, Hank suggested they call around and try to dig up as many pictures as they could with McAllens standing in front of the old house.

Before Millanie knew it, the afternoon was gone and Hank was driving her home.

"I'll call a few McAllens and tell everyone who has pictures to show up at my ranch for supper tomorrow night. My mother and aunts always cook on Fridays and this time it's Mexican food. My aunts make the best green chili enchiladas in the state.

"You'll probably decide to move as soon as you see how many relatives you have," Hank added. "I'm a Matheson and I've got plenty kin, but my wife has relatives living around here she hasn't had time to meet.

"When the three families first came, Patrick McAllen was the youngest of the three men. The other two had a start on him as far as kids went, but he caught up and passed them all. Legend was that his wife could pop out a baby between loads of laundry."

"It's overwhelming," she said. "After my grandmother died, I never thought of having family here."

Hank grinned. "They were here, waiting. I've heard more than one mention you and comment on how proud they all are of you. You were in their thoughts and prayers, Captain, whether you knew it or not."

"Would you mind if I brought a friend to the dinner? He's fascinated with the history of this area."

"Sure." Hank pulled up in the inn's driveway. "Bring Dr. Cunningham along. We all know you're seeing him."

She frowned, at first a bit angry that everyone seemed to know her business, but it occurred to her that Friday night might be the perfect time to do a little research. These were just the people to ask about a stranger in their midst.

Once back in her room she called Kare and asked her to pass on a message to her brother. Tell him she was tired and going to bed early just in case he'd planned to drop by. She also asked if he'd take her out to the Matheson ranch Friday night for supper.

Kare said, "Sure, but don't you just want his number?"

Millanie said no. Somehow she thought Drew should give her the number.

When she ended the call, Millanie hadn't set her phone down before it rang.

Drew's voice sounded out of breath. "Hello, Millie," he said. "I just walked into the bookstore and Kare said you called."

She repeated the message and he agreed to pick her up at six Friday night. He didn't ask any questions, just said he would be there and, with a quick *good night*, hung up.

She stared at the phone a moment, thinking that for a man who couldn't keep his hands off her last night, he sure didn't seem like he wanted to talk to her tonight.

Maybe it was for the best. Her recovery would take months, maybe longer. She couldn't ask him to hang around and just be friends until she found out if she wanted to be involved. Maybe she should slow things down.

On impulse she picked her phone back up and hit redial.

"Bookstore." The gravelly voice of Mr. Hatcher was unmistakable.

Millanie hit end, hating herself for checking Drew's story. Why would he lie?

Chapter 30

EVERYONE WAS SURPRISED WHEN BEAU DIDN'T COMPLAIN about having to stay in the hospital for a few days of further testing. They didn't know that while he slept most of the day away, he sat up talking all night to Lark.

She'd stand in the corner of his room, watching as the nurse did her final check and tucked Beau in, then she'd appear like a favorite dream and curl up on the bed with him. To their surprise they never ran out of things to talk about.

The second night she'd brought hamburgers and Cokes from Buffalo's Bar and Grill. When she told the bar owner, Harley, they were for Beau he wouldn't let her pay.

"The guy looks rough, like an old biker left in the rain, but he said you were a son to him."

Beau laughed. "Yeah, right. The first few years we played he locked us in that cage he calls a stage and half the time he forgot to feed us. If we'd been at the pound there would have been citations written for animal cruelty. By the time

I turned twenty, the crowds were getting so big I didn't want out of the cage."

Lark passed him a hamburger. "Just imagine what he would have done if he hadn't liked you so much."

"You're right. The first night we only knew four songs. We'd play the same four fast and slow, with words and without. The crowd was so drunk that night Harley was the only one who noticed. He told us not to come back without knowing at least one more song. I had to skip two days of school to teach another one to Border."

They laughed so hard they bumped heads, making Lark burst into tears thinking she'd hurt Beau.

Just before dawn, she opened the hospital's window blinds and they watched Harmony sleeping. One subject led into another and, by the time she left the third morning, he felt like he'd talked to her more than he'd ever talked to all the other girls he'd known put together.

She'd bought him real pajamas so he could get out of bed without being embarrassed by the open-backed gown. She smuggled in R-rated movies for them to watch, and popcorn, and his guitar.

The last night he played all the songs he'd written while thinking of her and she cried, this time because she swore his words brushed across her heart.

He was falling in love with Lark, only when he touched her, she pulled away. Maybe she thought that the hospital wasn't the right place or maybe she wasn't interested in him that way. He couldn't tell. The few times he'd been attracted to a girl it had been a one-night romance and he didn't want that with Lark.

She hadn't commented on what would happen after he left the hospital. He'd hinted that they could still have their midnight talks at the inn. She could even stay for breakfast. Only she never gave him an answer and he was afraid to push it.

"I'm getting out tomorrow," he finally said as he walked her to the door of his room. "Promise I'll see you tomorrow night. I could ask Mrs. Biggs to fix us dinner and we could have a quiet evening, or we could go out someplace. There's a little café over in Bailee where no one would know us."

She kissed his cheek and shook her head. "I've got bank examiners coming. I may not be able to get away. I'll call you."

The door closed behind her before he thought to tell her his phone number. She'd disappeared out of his life once before, and he promised himself that he'd never let that happen again.

Chapter 31

✦❧

FRIDAY

MILLANIE LET KARE IN THE BACK DOOR AT WINTER'S INN at seven thirty on Friday morning. They had work to do on the investigation, but Millanie had simply told the innkeeper that she'd invited her friend for breakfast. If Martha Q thought it strange that an injured army captain and a fortune-teller might be friends, she didn't mention it.

As they talked of nothing while waiting for Martha Q and Mrs. Biggs to disappear, Millanie asked about Drew. The memory of the way he'd held her almost a week ago still warmed her blood. The polite professor wasn't so shy when they were alone. If they'd had a few more minutes in the dark foyer together, Martha Q would have walked into a very hot scene.

Kare didn't seem to notice she didn't have Millanie's full attention. The small, young beauty said she hadn't seen her brother since Tuesday night when she'd found Beau. He'd called a few times but he'd sounded busy. "He's working on a book and when he's deep in his research I sometimes don't hear from him for days. I tell him he's lost in the past. If he'd had my mother, who dragged me to every historical site in California, he probably would have gotten over history years ago."

Kare continued talking as she ate her French toast. "Actually I kind of enjoyed those trips. Dad never came; for him it was always about watching sports and hunting, and the less time he spent with *the women* the happier he was. Mom drove me everywhere she thought I should go as part of my lessons. She was usually buried in one of her novels while I looked around, taking in the history of each place. Then when we got home she'd make me write an essay about what I learned."

Kare swallowed another bite and continued. "My mom didn't like people. Wouldn't even eat in a restaurant unless she had to. Most of the time I got the feeling I was included in the 'people.' Dinner when Dad was home was mostly sitting at the table listening to him talk. Dinner when he was gone was me eating while Mom read."

Millanie built a picture of the fortune-teller/assistant as Kare talked. A lonely picture. "She must have missed you when you went away to college."

A mass of curls bounced as Kare shook her head. "The week I left for a real college, I'd just turned nineteen and was going to spend a night without her for the first time in my life. With no friends around our place, sleepovers weren't an issue at my house. I asked my mom if she wanted to take me to the dorm. Her answer was simply, 'Surely you can read a map, Kare.'

"My bank account had twice the money I needed for living expenses those two years. I don't know if it was because she didn't want to worry about me or she and Dad were afraid I might come back if I ran out of funds. Even though Drew sometimes disappears on a hunt for some lost place in history, he still keeps up with me a hundred times better than my parents do."

He disappears for days, Millanie thought as she and Kare moved to the porch, where they could talk about the investigation. The two comfortable chairs were waiting for them. Thanks to Kare's help they were slowly crossing off name after name on the list of suspects. Several counties had checked in the past week saying the master criminal wasn't in their area, leaving Millanie less and less sure that she'd guessed right when she'd told the sergeant that no underworld criminal would be hiding in Harmony.

"You know, we may not have who we're looking for on the list," Millanie admitted. "I thought it would be easier than this, but our list may be cold. The chances are slim that he's even near Harmony and, if he is, he's an expert at hiding. He knows how to play this game."

"I agree. That's why I went back through all the info I've collected to make sure I didn't miss one person. The one we're looking for." Kare helped herself to one of the gingersnaps Mrs. Biggs had started leaving in a covered jar between their chairs.

Millanie smiled, thinking the next big mystery would probably be how such a small woman could eat so much.

Kare handed her a new file and whispered, "Remember, you've got a secret weapon. Me. I'm an expert at finding. I found Drew and that wasn't easy."

"Didn't you know his mother's name?" Millanie assumed it would have been easy to locate a brother.

"No. She died when Drew was eighteen. When I was a kid I dug through every piece of paper my father had and couldn't find any names or addresses."

Kare was buried in a file and didn't look up as she talked.

Millanie fought to keep her face blank but she wasn't winning the war. Drew, the first man she'd ever thought she could maybe get serious about, had lied. Almost the first thing he'd said when they'd met at the airport had been that he had been traveling to visit his mother.

Drew Cunningham didn't have a mother. He hadn't had one for almost half his life.

"How did she die?" Part of Millanie wanted Kare to be wrong.

"She overdosed on prescription drugs. Drew Cunningham was listed as her only kin." Kare shrugged. "I didn't catch it when I first searched. I'd always thought of Drew as Andrew."

How many red flags had to pop up before Millanie considered the possibility that he could be the man the government was looking for? Drawing her emotions in, she decided not to include Kare in her theory. The girl obviously loved her brother, maybe enough to lie for him.

Millanie stared at Kare and saw the dark circles under her eyes. Maybe the mugging three days before had bothered her deeply, or maybe she was working too hard, or maybe she was fighting to make sure Drew stayed off the list. "What's your gut feeling, Kare? Do you have any idea where we should look next?"

Kare shook her head. "I don't know about the list. I'll keep searching. One will eventually stand out." She hesitated, then lowered the files to her knees. "I should tell you I detected someone trying to break into my online files last night. Maybe it's just a hacker. I've developed extra walls to protect any government files I work on off-site." She took a slow breath. "But deep down I think maybe it's someone who noticed I've been searching for information about him. If he's good, he might spot me poking around. The man we're looking for may have found us first."

"So we may be close to the bad guy?" Millanie's pulse raced. The idea that she might actually find someone who was a real threat to the world was exciting. Once they had him, Kare's job was done and Millanie would take over. Thanks to the brace and the cane, she could watch the guy's every move. Every cell in her body longed to get back in the game and do some good. This might be a different kind of war, but it was war just the same.

"I don't know if we've found the man the government is looking for, but one of these men on the list is not happy about me tailing him online. I have no proof, but I think he's watching me, too. I mean really watching me." She let out a long breath as if a load had lifted off her chest by telling someone. "Yesterday as a precaution, I drove to the bookstore instead of walking. When I headed home, my tire was flat. I caught a ride with Mr. Hatcher but when I got home there were marks on my apartment lock. Like someone had tried to pick the lock."

"Do you think they got in?"

Kare shook her head. "I don't think so. Even if they did, I keep nothing there. I always leave my work computer in my little office where no one would find it. I use different passwords and codes on my laptop at home even if I look up something. Someone would have to be very good to locate me or even know I'm the person searching for them. But then, if this guy launders money, he's very good."

Millanie didn't want to alarm her. "Maybe the flat was just a flat. Maybe some kid was playing around trying to open your apartment door. The scratches could have been there for days or weeks. You were just more aware because of the mugging this week."

"True."

"Don't worry about it."

"You're right. Drew's the one person I know smart enough to break a fake code." She covered her mouth with her hand, obviously realizing what she'd said. "Only he would never do it, of course. He's not the one."

"I agree, but you never gave me his information. He was on my original list."

Kare tried to smile. "His background was too boring. My brother's not that interesting."

Millanie could hear the lie, but she didn't push.

"Keep me informed if you notice anything else, Kare. I don't want you in danger, understand."

"Got it. Don't worry, I'm afraid of my shadow. If anything else happens I'll come running to you."

"All right. That's settled. Now, let's go over every file again. I have two more names to add. A computer teacher who moved here three years ago and a loan officer at the bank."

Kare jumped into the search. "I've already checked out the teacher. He might have the skills, but his record is completely clean. Also, he worked his way through college, married young, and has three kids. If he's our guy, he's not spending any money. Last time I checked he pays the minimum on his credit card every month. I doubt if his wife lets him disappear from time to time. I wouldn't if I had three preschoolers."

Millanie nodded but still didn't cross him off the list. She thought she'd arrange to at least meet the guy first.

"As for the loan officer, he was transferred from another bank to handle the mess at Harmony's local bank. He has computer skills and was moved up to loan officer a few months ago. Far as I can tell he's made no friends, joined no club, or donated to anything. I might have scratched him off the list, but he does have a pilot's license and can speak Spanish, but then so can half the people in Texas. When I checked he'd used several sick days and all his vacation that he'd accumulated since he's been in town. One of the girls from the bank says no one likes him. Not the profile, but money laundering wouldn't be that hard for a bank officer."

"Being nice is not one of our essential criteria. Maybe our guy got tired of trying to fit in and is letting his true nature show."

Kare nodded. "Maybe."

Millanie had to ask, "How do you know the girl from the bank? She might be a good contact if we have to follow his movements."

Kare smiled. "I've been reading up on past-life regression. The fortune-teller before me at the bookstore collected books on it. The girl at the bank and I are working on her past lives. We discovered last week that she'd been killed in a concentration camp in Germany last life, and the one before that she was murdered in Scotland in 1870. It appears she's had many lives but always died off before she's thirty. Since she turned twenty-nine we've agreed to do double sessions."

Millanie tried to act like she understood. "Kind of a good news, bad news thing, I guess. Good news is she comes back. Bad news she dies off by thirty. I'm not sure I'd like to know how I died."

"That's what I told her, but she keeps wanting to search. I've noticed everyone who goes back always finds out they were a king or famous. No one's story is that they lived life after life in the lower class."

Martha Q interrupted them with a tray loaded down with a coffeepot and three cups.

They both shifted into a relaxed girlfriend-chat mood as Kare slid the files into her knitting bag and pulled out a ball of yarn.

"Thanks," Millanie said, inviting Martha Q to join them with a wave of her hand. "It is a little chilly out here. The coffee will be welcome."

Martha Q grinned. "I thought it might. The news says a cold front is coming in tonight. Might get rain." She made herself at home on the swing. "I hope you don't mind me joining you ladies while you visit. The vacuum cleaner noise is driving me crazy inside. I hate the sound of work."

"Not at all," Millanie lied. "We were just talking about people who believe in past lives. What's your opinion?"

Martha Q shook her head. "Never thought much about it. If people are supposed to learn from one life into the next, it seems to me after all these thousands or so years there's a great many people who weren't paying attention. Some must be dumb as rocks just rolling from one life into the next without picking up a single lesson."

She continued on, mentioning several people who were probably animals or insects before, if the life they had now was an improvement over the last.

Millanie did her best to act like she was listening, but her mind was turning over the people on the list. One investment broker whom no one seemed to have heard of before four years ago. Max Dewy, now in jail, who always drove new cars but had no visible means of income. The computer teacher. The loan officer at the bank. Drew Cunningham.

None fit the whole profile, but each had a few traits she was looking for.

While Martha Q went inside to get coffee cake to go with the coffee, Millanie asked Kare to run her off maps of all the suspects' work and home locations, then used her cell phone to call the sergeant and make sure she'd have a car and a weapon by tomorrow morning. It was finally time for her to start her part of the assignment.

"I'll keep searching," Kare whispered before Martha Q made it back. "How about you come to me for the next meeting? When I close my door Mr. Hatcher can't hear us talking."

"Fair enough," Millanie answered as Martha Q bumped through the door and hurried onto the porch.

"What did I miss?" she giggled. "I love visiting."

Millanie managed to look like she was embarrassed. "I'm afraid you caught us. I've just talked Kare into giving me a reading tomorrow. We're going to see if I lived any past lives. I've always had a desire to know."

"You'll not catch me trying that. What if I found out I was a man in my last life? One of the men in my writing group at the library said he dreamed once he was a general. All I ever dream is that I have to get up and go to the bathroom. Then I wake up and sure enough my dream comes true."

Kare laughed, but Millanie just smiled. She never thoroughly knew if Martha Q was telling the truth or playing to the crowd. The lady had lived and loved during her lifetime. Somewhere she'd learned that being funny was far more interesting than being wise. She'd told Millanie yesterday that there was an empty plot next to every one of her dead husbands, and when she died only one would be happy and the others would just have to sleep alone.

Kare stayed for lunch and then said she wanted to go over to county records. She promised to check in with Millanie when she got home that night and let her know if there was anything strange happening.

Millanie considered that *strange* in Kare's world was probably a larger category than in others' lives, so she added, "If you see anyone hanging around or even get a feeling that everything is not just right, send me a text where you are and I'll be on my way."

As Kare said good-bye she thanked Millanie for the meals and for caring but assured her she'd be fine. "I'm just overreacting. That's all," she admitted, then was gone.

After lunch Martha Q drove Millanie to her therapy. During the hour she worked out, Martha Q stayed in the lobby talking to everyone who walked in. As they left, Millanie thanked her for acting as driver but said she'd have her own car in a few hours.

Martha Q said, "Thank goodness. I don't know if I've got enough life left to listen to all those aches and pains again. The folks in the mental therapy waiting rooms are a lot better off. They may think they're crazy, but at least they're not dying."

Millanie didn't ask why Martha Q happened to be hanging out in a mental therapy waiting room. She wasn't sure she wanted to know.

After talking to the old lady and working a leg she hadn't used in over a month, Millanie decided to sleep the rest of the afternoon away.

She barely woke in time to dress for dinner. Martha Q interrupted her twice. Once to tell her a car and a bag had been dropped off for her and the second time to inform her it was almost six, as if Millanie didn't have clocks in her room.

Exactly at six o'clock, Drew picked her up for dinner and they drove to the Matheson ranch. He was nice and polite, but he seemed to have something on his mind. The kiss hello was on her cheek, and all the way out to the ranch he talked about the history of the area and mentioned nothing personal. Her gut told her Drew Cunningham didn't belong on her list, but she had to fill in the facts about him before she'd scratch off his name.

They spent the evening visiting with a dozen of her cousins and looking over old photos of the house she'd inherited.

One of her cousins admitted he'd leased out a slice of her land for grazing years ago when her father was alive. They'd agreed that he'd make his payment to a bank account in Harmony, then pay any bills on the place. The cousin had stopped needing the lease, but there was still money left in the account for her. He said it wasn't much, but it would pay to fix up the house.

Drew seemed far more involved in the old pictures and stories than she was. If a stranger had walked in he would have thought that Drew, not Millanie, was the long-lost relative. Drew was good at fitting in.

On the return to town she planned to start with why he'd lied about his dead mother. If he wouldn't, or couldn't, explain why he'd lied, maybe she needed to keep her distance. He might not be the bad guy she was looking for, but he wouldn't be someone she'd want to know.

Only one of her older cousins asked if they'd take her home, ruining Millanie's plan. The old widow didn't want to stay as long as her son did and it wouldn't be more than a few blocks out of their way. Her son needed to talk horses with Hank and she said she'd miss her show if she didn't get home.

So Drew drove home talking mostly to the old dear and leaving Millanie frustrated.

He circled the block and headed to the inn when they were finally alone in the car. They seemed no more than two strangers. She knew this wasn't the time or the place for a talk.

Drew walked her to the porch, his hand on her back to steady her. No longer a caress, simply an impersonal touch. She knew he sensed her coldness, but now wasn't the time to face the invisible wall between them.

He might have stayed awhile if she'd asked, but two newly arrived couples were visiting on Martha Q's porch. Drew had no choice but to thank her for the interesting evening. When he leaned in to kiss her cheek, she pulled back. The poor lighting didn't allow her to see his reaction. She didn't want to. She knew he was hurt.

Maybe she'd misread him, but he seemed in a hurry to be gone. He hurried to the van and didn't turn to wave as he pulled away.

She'd been cold all evening, but she had to protect herself. She had a job to do and right now she needed someone around who was honest.

Chapter 32

WHEELER FARM

JOHNNY STOOD ON HIS BACK PORCH WATCHING THE SUN set over his land. Heavy clouds were coming in from the northwest, but he didn't care. A good rain would cool temperatures into fall. He loved this time of day when it wasn't quite night, but the day had slowed. All week he'd been alone and he'd enjoyed the silence. Funny how a few nights in jail could make him forget how quiet it was in the country. As soon as the sun set, there wouldn't be anything but stars to keep him company.

Folks might think it strange or lonely out here, but he was at home. The farm had been in the family for four generations. It and all the equipment were paid for. Even if he had a bad year, he'd survive. Even with Scarlet and her boyfriend emptying their accounts, the farm's books were solid. Johnny had spent the day plowing and planning for next year. What he'd grow. When he'd plant. How many men he'd hire. Without a wife to distract him, he planned to work weekends and clear one more section by spring.

"I'm probably the poster child for boring," he said to the yard dog, who ignored him completely. All day he'd work doing the same things over and over, watching his progress in rows moving across the earth. Sometimes he'd think of all the people he was feeding by growing winter wheat, but mostly he just thought of what had to be done one step, one acre at a time.

Soon it would be winter. He'd work on his books, read up on what was new in equipment and seed, fix everything that broke all spring and summer that he never got around to during growing season. He'd rest too, like the land, so he'd be ready to go again when it came time to plow. Farmers didn't think much about living by the day, or even the week. They lived by the season. Work in the spring and summer happened from sunup to sundown. Scarlet could never understand that.

He hadn't missed her one bit. Wendell called once to say how sorry he was again about telling the sheriff that it looked like Johnny had just come in from burying his wife.

Johnny was thinking about forgiving his brother. After all, he had been the one holding the shovel and he might have said something like he'd just buried Scarlet.

But he reconsidered when he realized he and Wendell had just one thing in common: beer. Wendell hated the farm and had moved to town as soon as he got his first job. Wendell didn't want to get married and have kids. He thought he was living the wild bachelor life and planned to stay that way.

Maybe he'd put off forgiving Wendell a little longer and enjoy the peace for a while.

He was thinking of the money he'd save on beer alone when the house phone rang. Johnny almost didn't answer it. He didn't want to hear Wendell apologize again. There was nothing sadder than a mall guard crying.

On the fourth ring Johnny broke down and reached inside for the wall phone that had been hanging in the same spot all his life.

"Hello," he answered, already dreading hearing his brother's voice.

"John," a soft voice whispered.

"Kare." His heart stopped while he waited for her to say more.

"I'm at the county clerk's office just off Main. I was looking over some records and forgot about the time. When I packed up, I discovered everyone else must have gone home already and forgotten about me in the back."

"Are you locked in?" He hated the thought of having to call Wendell for help, but he would if Kare was trapped inside a government building. It'd probably be against the law, but he'd break her out.

"No. I can get out and the door will lock behind me." She sounded like she might cry. "But when I looked out there's a man standing in the parking lot and he's looking straight at my car. I think he's waiting for me."

"Do you know him?" Maybe some guy was just waiting to see if she was having trouble.

"No," she whispered, as if someone might hear her. "I think he's been following me."

Johnny didn't know what to do. He wanted to tell her she was just imagining trouble, but she might still be frightened from finding Beau Yates mugged. Or worse! What if she'd been the one the mugger had been waiting for in the creek bed and Beau just happened to come along?

"I'll be right there. Don't leave the building until you see me pull up."

He didn't bother to say good-bye. He just dropped the phone and ran for his truck. The night was growing darker by the minute and he didn't want her in danger one second longer. He hit ninety before he turned onto the main road and headed for the lights of Harmony. If he got picked up on radar the patrol car could follow him in.

Five minutes later he pulled into the side parking lot of the county courthouse. Rain was popping on the warm pavement and making the two lot lights shimmer like dying stars. An old Ford with peace signs on the bumper sat in the back of the lot. He had no doubt he'd found Kare. Between her car and the door was a man dressed in black with a hood over his head. He stood in the rain as if he hadn't noticed he was getting wet. His slick jacket reflected Johnny's lights but he didn't look up. He seemed faceless in the rain.

When Johnny circled and his truck lights flashed across him again, the stranger turned and disappeared around the corner of the building. He was built thick and his movements were uneven, like a man not used to running or someone out of shape. One hand remained tucked away in his jogging shirt pocket as he ran.

Johnny was tempted to chase the guy, but his first worry was Kare.

When he jumped from his truck and headed toward the steps, she flew out the door. She'd been watching for him. As he had once before, he caught the small woman in mid-flight and held her tight. He could feel her trembling.

"It's all right, Kare," he whispered. "I've got you." For a moment he stood, his feet wide apart, his body strong as an oak. He ignored the rain. He just held her.

Slowly, he carried her to his truck and lifted her across the driver's seat to the other side, then climbed in and locked the doors.

"Where to?" he asked as she curled around his arm. She was dripping wet and shivering.

"Not home. I think he may have been there earlier."

"Ok. How about your brother's place?"

"He's not there." She rubbed her tears on his sleeve. "He went out with Millanie and I don't know where they are."

"Martha Q is probably home. I'm sure she'd let you stay there until they get back. Or I could drive you over to the police station. We could report this guy."

"You saw him, too?" she asked.

"I saw him, too. Didn't look like anyone I know, but he could have been. I didn't see his face. Wish I had. I wouldn't mind having a short conversation with him. Maybe the sheriff should know he's hanging around?"

"What could I say? 'I saw a man I think has been following me. He may have tried to break into my apartment. He may have let the air out of my tire. He may have been watching me, waiting for me.' They won't believe me, and if they did, what could they do?"

Johnny saw her point. He threw his truck in gear and turned on the heater. He was wet but not cold. Kare, on the other hand, was still shivering. "You're coming with me. I'll watch over you. I think you're right. You are in trouble."

She didn't let go of his arm as he drove slowly home. He couldn't help but wonder why she was so afraid of the world. She wanted everything to be right and fair. Everything to be just and balanced. It was like she hadn't figured out yet that nothing makes sense. Maybe she always reads those strange books in her tiny office trying to figure it out?

"John," she finally whispered, "can I stay over at your house tonight? I don't want to go home."

"Of course." He started to make a joke that she sounded like she was eight years old, but he wasn't sure his frightened little fairy wasn't part little girl right now.

When he got home, he gave her his best flannel shirt to change into and warmed her a cup of milk. Looking around, he saw the rooms of his house through her eyes. Too much furniture. Too much stuff sitting on every table and stacked up in every corner. Plants that weren't real. Plaster teddy bears, art he didn't understand. She'd probably think he ran a used furniture store and this was where he stored the overflow.

On impulse, he picked up Scarlet's overstuffed flowery chair and hauled it to the sunroom at the back of the house. When he returned he brought trash bags. He was filling his third one when Kare stepped out of the bathroom looking adorable. Her pretty legs showing. Her wild hair curly and so damp it sparkled.

"What are you doing, John?"

"Making some room."

She laughed. "I don't take up much room."

"That's true, but all this junk does. I've decided to clear out everything that I don't use."

She smiled. "I do that sometimes. When I came here I decided I wouldn't take anything that couldn't fit in my car. Want some help?"

"Sure, stuff every pillow on the couch in this bag. I can't even see the leather."

Five minutes later all the gunk his wife had called decorations was gone and the room looked bare, but livable. "Now I can breathe," he said as he handed her the one remaining pillow and blanket. "Make yourself at home."

As she snuggled onto the couch, he brought her a cup of warm milk and a cereal bowl full of tiny graham cracker animals. "You know, I saw a program about Ireland once where they showed an ancient fairy tree growing in the middle of an old cemetery. Folks would stop by its low-hanging branches and tie ribbons and bright sparkly trinkets to the tree on the chance that they might attract a fairy.

"I think they'd look a lot like you, darlin', if they came to that tree. Small, dainty, and beautiful."

She smiled. "You're kidding me."

"No, I'm serious. Don't you know how pretty you are?"

She shook her head. "My father used to say I was as homely as a mangy chick. He was always trying to get Mom to cut my hair, but she wouldn't. I used to wonder why she never listened to his orders and then, finally, when I was about ten I figured it out."

"And what did you discover?" Johnny decided he could watch her all night. The way she talked, the way she moved was different than anyone he'd ever known.

"I figured out that my mom was the boss. You see, my dad thought he always had to have his way. He didn't want anything in his name because he feared his past would haunt him. It only took one fight with Mom and he realized his mistake. She owned everything. After that one argument, he still yelled from time to time and picked on me as much as he could get away with, but he never crossed the line again."

"You don't like him much, do you?"

"I haven't seen my parents for three years. Mom calls now and then but we never talk about Dad." She seemed relaxed as she curled up on his couch. "How about you? Did you like your dad?"

"I loved him." The simple answer surprised Johnny. He'd never really thought about how he'd given and received love so easily as a child. "He used to take me with him when he worked, and then we'd take an hour off and go fishing in the middle of the day like we were playing hooky. He'd always say, 'Don't tell Mom,' but I knew he was kidding because she'd packed the worms in a mason jar in the cooler. In the summers he worked hard and Mom would let me go with him in the mornings. In the winters we'd play games and travel around for days just looking for an adventure. He loved camping out in all the canyons around here."

"He died?" Kare covered his hand with hers.

"He died. I've always thought if I had kids I'd raise them like he did. They might not be rich, but they'd know they were loved."

"You should have kids, John."

He shrugged. "That plan's been derailed a bit." He pulled down a quilt from a pole on the wall. "You take my bed and I'll sleep here on the couch. If a car turns off the main road the yard dog will bark. I'll be on the porch with a shotgun before anyone can get near the house. You're safe here."

"What's the yard dog's name?" she asked.

"I don't know." He'd never thought to call him anything but *yard dog*.

Kare smiled. "I'll ask him tomorrow."

She stood on tiptoes and kissed Johnny's cheek. "Thanks. When I couldn't think of who to call or what to do, I thought of you."

"How'd you know my number?"

"I googled you." She pulled out her phone. "You don't have a cell, do you, John?"

"Never thought I needed one," he answered, realizing she must think him terribly backward. "I got a computer, though, but with the storm coming in I doubt it'll be much help."

"I told Millanie I'd text her. She said she'd have her phone off during dinner but she'd get my message." She tapped a dozen times on her phone, then turned it off. "I guess since you don't have a cell you don't have a charger. If the text went through, she'll know I'm safe. I can turn it off to save the battery."

She began rummaging through her bag like a squirrel looking for his last nut. Out came a hairbrush, a laptop, two notebooks, and half a dozen pens.

"Looking for supper?" he asked.

"No." She stopped suddenly and gathered everything around her like they were government secrets. "I was looking for my charger."

"No luck?"

"No luck."

He shrugged and offered his hand. "Then how about we go to dinner?"

"We're going out again? I can't." She looked down at the flannel shirt like she was Cinderella and the fairy godmother forgot to show up.

"You're in luck. I bought a month's worth of groceries. I can at least open a can or thaw you something."

"Can I cook?" She bounced up. "I love to experiment. You know, mix things up. Maybe make something that's never been invented."

He watched her rummage through his kitchen with the same panicked zest with which she'd tackled her purse. "Cook anything you like. I'll eat it." He walked toward the bedroom. "I'll change the sheets while you have fun."

He could tell the thunder made her nervous. Maybe cooking would take her mind off the storm.

An hour later, he wasn't so sure, but he sat down and took a deep breath. "Smells good," he managed even though he didn't recognize a thing on the plate, but she was so cute sitting across from him waiting for him to try everything he figured he could eat mud and smile.

To his surprise it was all good, except maybe for the corn and spinach taco with her secret mustard sauce, but he downed it anyway.

"You're a great cook," he said as he ate two of her little fruit desserts that tasted like fried pudding pies.

"I've always thought so." She looked amazed that he would agree with her assessment of her talent. "Who knows, someday I might give up fortune-telling and open a café. I could call it Kare's Kitchen."

He knew without asking that she was having a great time, and she hadn't looked bored once. While they did the dishes she talked about growing up on a chicken farm. They had lots of eggs so she'd pretty much learned to make every kind of egg dish in the world.

When they settled in to watch the late weather report, she paced in front of the windows. Her nerves were on edge and he didn't know if it was the storm or the fright she'd had tonight.

"How old are you, Kare?"

She faced him. "Twenty-four. I'll be twenty-five next month. How old are you?"

"Twenty-seven. Sometimes it seems like I should be older 'cause I've been farming all my life." He studied her. "I'm not a very interesting person. I mostly just farm. I'm honest despite my recent record. I'd like to be your friend. Partly, I'm guessing, because if you called me tonight you don't have many friends and partly because I just like being around you. You're the most fascinating person I've ever met."

"What kind of friend?" She moved closer and tilted her head as she stared at him.

"Good friends. The kind that if you needed me you'd know I'd be there and wouldn't complain or expect anything in return."

"Would you do things for me even if I didn't tell you why I needed them done?"

"I would, as long as it's not illegal. I really don't want to go back to jail." He figured she might ask something crazy, but if it wasn't illegal he might try it just to make her happy.

"But I'd come visit you and bring you books if you went back to jail."

He shook his head. "No. I'd have to draw the line at that, or hurting people that didn't need hurting." He'd always been big for his age and he was tall and strong now, but he'd never been the fighting kind.

She turned and went back to the window, and he couldn't stop wondering what kind of things she'd want a friend to do. Maybe he'd offered more than he could deliver. Finally, she walked back to where he sat in front of the news running on the TV.

"I'm not the airhead people think I am." She said the words calmly as if she'd practiced. "I have a college degree. I can read and write in three languages besides English, but haven't practiced much in speaking them. I finished high school at sixteen and made high enough scores on my entrance tests to get me into any college in the country. I'm not a child, John, so don't ever treat me like one."

"What do you want me to do, Kare?" He really hoped he didn't have to give his résumé to be her friend. He'd only made it two years in college and most days he probably didn't speak any language, including English, well.

"I want you to see me as an adult before I ask."

With her looking like a kid in his big flannel shirt, it wouldn't be easy, but he nodded. "All I see is a beautiful woman standing in front of me."

She closed her eyes as if her favor might be too big to ask, and then she said, "I want you to hold me until I go to sleep."

Before he could wrap his head around why she was asking, she crawled up in his lap and rested her cheek on his chest.

He circled his arms around her and held her against him. His college-educated high scorer who spoke four languages was afraid to go to sleep and, for some crazy reason, she trusted him.

He rocked her slowly as he hummed a hymn his mother used to hum when he was little and sick. Maybe the soft, low hum put her to sleep or maybe it was the vibration of his chest, but within ten minutes he felt her body relax.

For a while he just rocked this woman/child while he moved his hand over her hair. She thought he'd saved her tonight, but John knew deep down that she'd saved him the minute he'd stepped into her office.

Finally, he lifted her up and carried her to his bed. When he tucked her in he couldn't resist kissing her on the cheek. She had no idea how pretty she was or how funny, or even how loving.

When he walked back through the kitchen, he noticed the yard dog she'd thought should be invited to dinner. "Come on out on the porch, boy," Johnny said. "You've got a job to do tonight and so do I." He patted the dog's head. "Come morning the little lady plans to have a talk with you about your name."

He let the dog out, locked the doors, which he never did, and then turned his big rocking recliner to face the front of the house. For a long while he sat thinking and listening.

He was watching over his fairy tonight and he could think of nothing he'd rather be doing.

Deep in the night he thought he heard a phone ringing, but he didn't move. Right now the only person he was worried about was sleeping one room away.

Chapter 33

A LITTLE AFTER DAWN JOHNNY WHEELER STOOD PERFECTLY still on the front porch. His shotgun leaned just inside the door. He watched a Jeep he didn't recognize pull onto his land.

It was moving slow with the top down. A quarter mile away he recognized Kare's brother and Millanie McAllen. Johnny didn't move, he just waited for them to come to him.

Drew got out of the Jeep first, his long body moving fast, unaware that the farmer might see him as a threat. Nothing about the professor looked like he came to fight. If anything he looked worried.

Millanie, even on a cane, carried herself as if she were thinking about taking Johnny out with a few quick blows. Johnny had no doubt she could do the job. When he and Kare talked last night during dinner, she'd called Millanie Captain. He could see a bit of a military bearing about her and guessed that she'd been hurt in the line of duty.

"Morning, Professor." Johnny nodded once but didn't smile. Right about now he was wishing he'd put out a No TRESPASSING sign.

"Morning." Drew Cunningham reached the porch but didn't climb the stairs. "We're looking for Kare. She left a message on Millanie's phone saying she was safe with a friend and we thought you might—"

"She's safe." Johnny crossed his arms. "I went into town last night when she called."

Millanie slowly climbed the stairs. "I need to talk to her, John. You have any objection if I go inside?"

"She's asleep," Johnny realized he was saying almost exactly what they'd said to him earlier in the week. Maybe he should make an effort to be friendlier to her than she'd been to him at Martha Q's place. "Come on in. I've got coffee on." He wasn't used to company, but he could manage a few cups of coffee.

They sat around his kitchen table and listened as he told them everything he could remember about Kare's call and what he'd seen when he drove up in the parking lot.

"Was the guy alone?" the captain asked. "Did you see his car?"

"Yes, as far as I could tell he was alone and on foot."

"Can you describe him?"

"It was raining and he stood out of the parking lot light. I did notice he wore dark sweats—no, more like a jogging suit. Water was beading on it. Black or navy maybe and he kept his hand in the front pouch pocket. When he ran, he reminded me of someone out of shape, not used to running."

"Left or right?" she shot back.

"Left or right what?"

"Which hand was in the pocket?"

He thought a minute. "Right. Why is that important?"

The woman Kare called the captain looked surprised he'd had to ask. "From what you just told me, I'd say our man is over thirty and works a job, if he works, that doesn't require physical activity. Oh, also there is a good chance he's right-handed and was armed."

Johnny had never considered himself a very good judge of people, but even he could tell the brother was truly worried, and Millanie looked guilty for some reason. "I should have followed him," Johnny whispered to himself.

"No!" both snapped at him.

Drew took the lead. "You did right, John. Kare's safety was first priority. Millanie may be overthinking this."

No one including Drew believed his suggestion and Johnny felt like he'd just stepped into a spy novel.

About then, Kare walked out of his bedroom wearing nothing but his shirt. Her legs might not be long and tanned, but they were nicely shaped, he noticed, unable to pry his eyes off them.

"Morning," she said as she pushed her hair out of her face. The mass of curls seemed to have grown overnight. "What are you guys doing here?"

Johnny smiled at her. She didn't look the least embarrassed. Knowing his Kare, she had no idea what her brother was probably thinking about now.

The captain took charge. "We were worried. It seems you were right in thinking that someone was following you. We went by your apartment last night after I noticed the message. One of your windows was knocked out. The landlady said it was probably the storm, but I'm not so sure."

Drew moved in one fluid motion from the chair to stand in front of Kare. "You knew someone was stalking you and you didn't tell me." He glanced at Johnny with anger building. "You told *this guy* and you didn't tell me."

Surprisingly Millanie took Kare's side and made the point that Drew wasn't the easiest person to get hold of when he was writing.

Kare looked like she might cry as they shot questions in rapid fire at her. She'd done what she needed to do to take care of herself, but they were both acting like they should have been advised.

Johnny, who hadn't talked to anyone for almost a week, felt like he was in a tornado of words. Finally, he said the only thing that came to mind. "Anyone want breakfast? I'm having trouble keeping up on an empty stomach."

The room settled and everyone put the questions and the

worries aside. Kare knew the kitchen well enough to assign
duties and they all followed her orders. Twenty minutes later
over omelets, toast, and microwaved bacon, they ate and
moved into calm conversation.

Millanie explained that Kare was helping her do some
research on the town, and Drew apologized for being so lost
in his writing that he forgot to charge his phone. Johnny had
read enough mysteries to guess that there was more between
the two women and their little research project than they
were telling. He suspected that they hadn't been friends long
enough to be close, so the work was keeping them together.
Either way, he didn't care. He wasn't in the habit of poking
into other people's business or of discussing his own.

While Johnny and the professor did the dishes, the
women vanished into the bedroom. A moment later, Kare
ran out and grabbed her big bag with her computer in it.

Drew looked worried. "What do you think they're doing
in there?"

Johnny shrugged. "Planning world takeover. Oh, wait,
they already got that. So, that only leaves online shopping."

Kare's brother looked at him like he thought Johnny was
dumber than the leftover toast, and then suddenly, he
laughed. "Very funny, John."

"Thanks, I'm working on a stand-up routine."

Drew put his hand on Johnny's shoulder. "I can see why
Kare likes you and would come to you if she thought she
was in trouble. I got one piece of advice for you. Stay away
from my sister."

"Why?" Johnny wasn't sure he wanted to know, but it
seemed a good question to ask.

"I don't know. It just seemed like what a big brother
should say and you're the first man I've felt the need to say
it to."

"What did I do?" Johnny tried to act offended, but innocence doesn't come easy to a man newly out of jail.

"You didn't do anything." Drew laughed. "It was my
sister. She walked out of your bedroom wearing your shirt."

"We got caught in the rain. I slept on—"

"Stop. I don't want to hear the details. That smile she gives you whenever she looks your way tells me all I need to know."

Johnny nodded as if he understood. This being a friend was harder than he'd thought it would be, especially when it came with a big brother and a captain. He decided to change the subject. "How's things going with you and Millanie?"

Drew stared at the closed bedroom door where the women had disappeared. "Not so good. I thought we were fine, but something happened and she won't talk about it. We went to dinner last night and talked with some of her relatives, but on the way back home if the air between us had gotten any colder I'd have frostbite."

"Great," Johnny said low and angry. "If a man like you can't figure women out, I don't have a chance in hell."

Drew smiled. "Don't kid yourself, John. You had a woman sleeping in your bed last night and I went home without a good-night kiss."

"There's more to that story."

"I don't want to hear it, remember."

They both laughed, and then Johnny said, "I guess it's too early for a beer."

"Beers make less mess than another pot of coffee would."

Johnny opened the refrigerator. "You got a point, Professor."

Chapter 34

WINTER'S INN

SOMEHOW EVERYONE KNEW THAT BEAU YATES WAS BACK in town, thanks to the mugging. He'd often thought Harmony didn't need a paper. News spread like an airborne virus.

By the time he left the hospital and settled into Winter's Inn, girls were camped out on Martha Q's lawn, wanting an autograph. Every time he stepped out on the porch they screamed, frightening all the squirrels in the neighborhood.

Beau moved around the house like a caged lion. He didn't mention it to anyone, but every time the inn's phone rang he jumped. The women of the inn all offered him books to read or tried to feed him. Martha Q even talked for an hour about the soap opera she watched, hoping that he'd be interested enough to watch it with her. Millanie said she'd play poker with him, but he knew she'd beat him. Everyone beat him at poker. When he played, if he played, he always considered it a donation to the pot and not a game he'd have any chance at winning.

Lark didn't call Friday or Saturday. Beau finally got tired of making up excuses for her. It didn't matter if she had extra work or her family needed her or she had to leave town. She was a grown woman. She could have called if she'd wanted to.

The "why" ate at his gut and, by Sunday night, he'd turned to his music. A sad song flowed from his fingers with words about trying to see the future through a muddy telescope. Trying to find your way without a map. Trying to fall in love alone.

Martha Q took the country music fanatics' advances on Monday as if it were a storming of the palace gates. Thank goodness, a warm rain started about noon, driving the fans away.

As soon as the downpour stopped, Beau felt like walking. Everyone in the house warned him to stay on the main roads. Millanie, with a cane, even offered to go with him as bodyguard. Mrs. Biggs didn't say much, but he saw the worry in her eyes. They all seemed to think the mugger was just beyond the door waiting for Beau the rabbit to come out.

"I'll be fine," he stated as he passed all three waiting at the door. "I'll only go a few blocks." He pulled the hood over his bandaged head. "No one will even know it's me."

"You'll call if it starts raining again. I'll come pick you up," Martha Q ordered.

"I promise. Trust me, if I can walk the streets of Nashville at midnight, I can walk the streets of Harmony in the afternoon." He thought of showing the few scars he had from accidentally getting in the middle of bar fights, but Martha Q might want to show him hers and Beau had a feeling he'd have to live another ten years to equal the number of nights Martha Q had probably spent in bars.

Mrs. Biggs pointed out in her shy way that he hadn't been mugged in Nashville and another bang on the head might not do him any good.

"I'll stay on the main streets. I'll watch out," he said for the third time. "Nothing is going to happen to me."

Beau slipped out the front door before one of the ladies thought of a way to guilt him into staying.

For a while he walked down the old brick streets enjoying the sound of the rain dripping off leaves and the wind in the trees. As always the music came to him and all else shifted into the background. Since those magic summers with his grandfather listening to music flow out from the little tin-roofed cabin, Beau always felt like nature played harmony to every melody in his head. The words to songs came from his life, his feelings, his dreams.

As he walked, a hunger began to grow in him that had nothing to do with food.

Lark was always in his thoughts. He needed to see her. She'd stood him up four nights in a row. They'd been so close in the hospital. If she'd felt a tenth of what he'd felt those nights at the hospital, she would fight her way back to him.

Maybe she hadn't promised she'd come, but he'd thought it was understood. He thought they were starting something between them. They read each other's minds. They wanted the same thing. To be with each other. To be best friends. To someday soon be lovers.

Or at least he thought that was what they both wanted.

The hours they'd spent in the hospital were the most real time he could remember having. Even with the pain medication, he'd memorized all she'd said and how her fingers had felt laced in his. She'd kissed him as he fell asleep each night so that he drifted off with the taste of her on his lips. When they'd talked she'd rested her hand on his leg as if a part of him were already hers, just as a part of her, maybe the wild part, belonged to him and always would.

It occurred to him that no girl had turned him down since he'd left Harmony. In fact, he'd never chased one, or used a line, or done anything but be available. They'd just always been there to talk to if he had time, to flirt with if bored or to step into the shadows with if he needed a distraction. It was always just physical, nothing more. Nothing lasting. Nothing with meaning.

He didn't want that with Lark. He wanted more than sex. He'd never made love to a woman. He'd never said the words.

He wanted that with her. The thought of whispering just how much she meant to him while they were making love made him smile.

Beau turned toward the bank. Long ago, on a midnight road, they'd backed away from passion. Both had dreams they didn't want to derail. But now they were adults. They could handle whatever came their way.

Ten minutes later he walked into the bank just before closing. The guard at the door reminded Beau he only had a few minutes, but Beau just kept walking. The lobby was crowded with people taking care of business. He didn't care. He wasn't planning on standing in line.

The tall loan officer who'd frowned at him when he'd asked to see the president now sat alone at his desk looking tired and worried. Beau wondered if the bank exam Lark had mentioned on their last night in the hospital had anything to do with Mr. Not-So-Friendly.

Trouble's door was open. Without pausing, he walked through and saw her working at her desk. She looked so alone there. So unhappy.

When he closed the door and threw the lock, she glanced up.

"I'll just be a minute," she said with a quick smile, and turned back to the computer screen. "I have to get these sent before closing."

Beau moved slowly across the room, letting the beauty of the woman he'd always thought of as a girl sink into his mind.

She finally stood, closing up her computer. "I'm glad you dropped by. I was hoping—"

He reached for her and pulled her to him. "I didn't drop by, Lark. I came to do this."

His mouth closed over hers as his hand tugged the tie from her hair. He'd missed her more than he wanted to admit, and he didn't plan on wasting any more time talking.

She pushed away for a moment as if planning to remind him that this wasn't the place for them to be together.

This time he had no intention of slowing down. He advanced again.

He tightened his hold around her and deepened the kiss. He felt like he'd waited years to kiss her completely, and she tasted every bit as good as he remembered.

When he finally broke the kiss, she was breathless. "I couldn't wait any longer." His hand moved over the silk of her blouse until he gripped her breast. Trouble was a fantasy, but Lark was real in his arms and he wanted her more than he'd ever wanted a woman. "It's time we became more than friends, honey."

"Don't call me *honey.*" She stared at him, part angry and part need. She could have stepped from his loose hold but she didn't. The advance might have taken her off guard, but she'd recover.

He touched her forehead with his lips. "Whatever you say."

Her breath quickened as he took his time kissing his way across her face, then moved his hand down between her breasts. Before she could protest, his mouth closed over hers and the kiss turned wild. He fisted his hand in her hair and held on tight, turning her so that he could go deeper into her mouth. This was the ocean of feelings he felt like he'd been waiting all his life to fall into.

With one arm around her waist, he lifted her and carried her to the corner of her office so that no one passing the windows could see them. Pushing his body completely against her, he held her still as he kissed her hard, letting all his need for her show through. She didn't protest, or fight, but she stopped kissing him back.

Bracing the wall on either side of her, Beau lifted away an inch so he could watch her. Her cheeks were red. Her breathing fast. He knew without asking that she was not a woman who'd ever been handled so. If she'd had any lovers they'd been gentle, polite. She wasn't the kind to be picked up in a bar or who'd have sex in a dark hallway between sets. Yet in her office at the bank he'd treated her exactly like he thought she was.

He might know about passion, but he knew nothing about

loving. He saw anger and maybe fear in her eyes for the first time.

They were from different worlds and he'd been too rough. He moved his hands to her waist and held her gently. Then he kissed her softly. "I'm sorry, Lark, I didn't mean to frighten you. I just need to hold you for a moment."

She finally caught her breath. "No one's ever—"

"I'm sorry," he whispered, realizing his experience with women was so limited he didn't know how to treat her.

"Move away," she whispered. "You're pinning me in, Beau."

He stepped back, his hands in the air. "I don't know how to do this, Lark. Most romances I've had ended at last call." He looked at her, realizing she was so much more than he deserved. He wouldn't blame her if she slapped him hard and yelled for the guard to drag him out of her office.

"I want to be friends. I'd like to be lovers." He couldn't lie. "I want to do this right with you. We can go as slow as you like." He closed his eyes, fearing he was lying as he said, "What happened just now will never happen again."

Even as he said the words, he wanted her. She'd been the first girl he'd ever dreamed of. The one he'd left behind. The one who didn't seem interested in having sex just because he showed up to play the game.

She straightened her blouse, pulled her hair back into a bun, and faced him. "The bank is closing, Beau. You have to leave."

Her words could have been said to a stranger, but he saw the hurt in her eyes. Hurt and fear. He couldn't believe he'd just walked into her office and practically attacked her. "Can we talk, Lark?"

"Not now. Later. If my father had walked in I'm sure he would have had a heart attack. I think you should leave."

He took a step toward her and she put up a hand. "No. I can't talk now. I have to think. I'll call you."

"Can't or won't?" Anger mixed in his words. He'd gone too fast. The bank wasn't the right place, he got that. "I said I was sorry."

He fought the urge to reach for her when she walked past him and unlocked the door. All he'd wanted to do was see her, and he might have screwed the whole thing up.

"I'm not angry. I'll call later." Her eyes said she was lying.

"All right. I won't touch you again until you're ready. Not like that. Not any way, if that's how you want it."

She opened the door. "I'll call. I think I just need some time to think, Beau."

He crossed his arms. "Lark. We'll play it your way. Call when you're ready to talk." He grabbed a pen from her desk and wrote his number across her calendar.

"I thought we settled on friends?" She remained half a room away.

"We didn't settle on anything." Somehow he'd missed that conversation. Maybe he hadn't tried to kiss her at the hospital, but he was doped up. How could she have thought he wanted to be just friends? "How about dinner tonight or tomorrow night? We'll talk. Name the time and place and I'll be there."

"All right." She studied him.

Maybe she'd finally calmed down enough to realize he wasn't attacking her. Wherever she named, he'd go even if it meant running into fans. At least they liked him, which was more than he could say for Lark right now.

"I have dinner at my parents' house tonight," she said simply. "I choose there. I'll pick you up at six thirty and we'll drive over to Clifton Creek."

He didn't want to meet her parents. That sounded like torture. What could they talk about, how much he wanted to sleep with their daughter?

Finally, he decided if she wanted him to walk through fire, he'd give it a try. An hour to scrape off his rough edges seemed near impossible.

"I'll be waiting," he said as he walked out of her office without looking back.

Chapter 35

MILLANIE DECIDED TO SIT OUT BACK OF THE WINTER'S INN and catch the warmth of September. Fall already whispered in the leaves and for once she needed nature to calm her weary soul. The doctor's news hadn't been promising during her morning visit, or not overly hopeful. *It will take time* was beginning to sound like swear words to Millanie. The possibility of her not fully recovering was slowly seeping into her mind.

She unstrapped her thick padded brace and pulled her baggy pant leg up so her injured leg could get some sun. "It will heal," she whispered. "It will heal."

She hated the way her right leg looked, still slightly twisted, swollen at the ankle, battered and bruised. In a way it didn't seem part of her body. The pain was real, waking her up at night, making moving more than a few steps tiring, but this crippled limb wasn't her. She couldn't allow it to be. If she did, it would define her.

"Evening, Captain," Beau Yates said as he walked toward her. "Nice day."

After visiting with him for a week Millanie was becoming both a friend and a fan. She knew everyone in the inn stopped to listen when he played. She guessed that when he finally moved on, even the ghosts in the old place would mourn his leaving. "Evening, Beau. You look nice." She moved a sheet that Mrs. Biggs always left on the chair over her right leg so he wouldn't see the scars.

He stood tall and turned around with pride. "I bought new boots, a new hat, and this jacket."

She studied the western cut of his jeans and jacket. "What? No rhinestones on the cuffs. You playing somewhere tonight?"

"No. I got dressed up to go to dinner. I got a date, or at least I think it's a date."

"She must be very special."

He rocked in his new boots on the damp grass, not noticing he was muddying them up. "She is, but she may be mad at me. I swear, I can't tell. Maybe she's hurt. I can take mad, but not hurt."

"When you saw her last, what did she say?"

"She told me she had to think about there being an 'us,' then she said she'd call me, then she looked at me like I was smothering her." He pulled off his hat and dug his fingers through his long hair. "She's mad at me, but she invited me to supper with her folks. Which sounds like a bad idea, but I'm going anyway."

Millanie never had been into solving other people's problems. "Maybe you hurt her and she's planning the worst torture ever, meeting her parents."

He looked like he believed her diagnosis. "That's what I'm afraid of. Got any advice?"

Millanie almost felt sorry for the handsome singer. "Take your guitar, Beau. It'll block blows. Try to avoid another hit in the head."

"Thanks," he answered as both turned toward the rustle of leaves near the creek bed.

On instinct, Millanie reached for her cane.

A moment later a mass of black hair came into view and she relaxed. Kare pulled her way out of the leaves while colorful scarves flew around her.

"Hello," she said calmly as she picked brush off of her skirt.

Both Millanie and Beau started sentences with "You shouldn't" before they realized it was too late for advice. The fortune-teller was already across the creek bed.

Kare just shrugged. "I know, I shouldn't cross the creek, but it's *so* much faster and it's daylight. I wanted to drop by and see you"—she pointed toward Millanie as she rattled on—"before I head home. John is over at my place fixing the window and putting extra locks on everything. When he came by to measure, he said I needed furniture so he went home to collect a few chairs he plans to lend me. He said something about how furniture seems to run free-range around his place."

"Who's John?" Beau asked. "I've seen you a few times since the mugging. You got another brother, or maybe a boyfriend? With those beautiful eyes I'm guessing the men around here fall fast and hard for you, Kare."

"Stop teasing me, Beau. Just because I saved your life doesn't mean you can pry into my life." Kare giggled. "Besides, he's just a friend."

Beau offered her a chair and pulled up one of his own. He leaned in as if asking something very important. "Would one of you women mind explaining *a friend* to me? I thought I spoke the language, but obviously I don't. When a girl says *we're friends*, does that mean I can kiss her? I mean really kiss her on the mouth?"

"Of course," Kare answered, as if considering herself the expert.

Millanie just watched, finding the conversation interesting, but pointless.

"That's what I thought." Beau relaxed back in his chair.

Kare added, "But no passion. A kiss on the lips is fine, but no open mouth. No fire."

"Why bother if there's no passion?" Beau complained. "Maybe I'm not as dumb as I thought if women think a guy wants to kiss without heat involved. If a guy likes, I mean really likes a girl, he'll want passion involved. In fact, even if he doesn't care much for her, he'll probably vote for fire to be included anyway."

"Really? Even if he's not madly in love with her?" Kare's big eyes seemed to grow even larger. "That's not how it is in books."

"You were raised on a farm, Kare, surely you know romance isn't always involved." Beau sounded as if he knew from personal experience.

"Maybe you two should have had this conversation at fifteen." Millanie broke the silence as she wondered how these two ever made it into their twenties.

"I was too busy trying to make it as a singer," Beau confessed, as if it were all his fault. "Now I'm too dumb even to try to play the games."

"I was stuck on a farm with no one to talk to." Kare lifted her bag. "Go away, Beau, I want to visit with Millanie."

"Fine by me," he said. "I get the feeling it's the blind leading the blind out here." He looked at Millanie and pointed his finger. "You probably got the answers, Captain, but you're not telling."

A little blue BMW pulled up in the drive. Beau didn't bother to say good-bye. He just picked up his guitar and walked away while the women laughed.

"Let's get to work," Millanie said as the BMW backed away. "I have a possible person of interest."

"So do I, and we can work out here in peace." Kare looked up. "Rain is forecast later, but we'll be done before then. How about we start at the top of those left on the list? I got info that more money is being smuggled out of the country. People who hate America are using our own currency to buy weapons to kill us. It makes me angry."

"Me, too," Millanie answered, loving that they were getting closer. "Let's put what we know about the man you saw in the parking lot in the mix and see who matches. It's a long shot, but it might help."

They still had their heads together an hour later when Millanie looked up and saw Drew walking toward her. She knew it was him, but the picture seemed to be out of focus.

Kare jumped up, folding her papers away as fast as she could. "Drew," she squealed. "You look great. Where's my brother?"

He kissed her cheek. "Can't a guy get a haircut?"

"Sure, and new clothes and boots. I've never seen you wear boots."

Millanie just stared. Gone was the stuffy professor with his hair in need of cutting and his clothes ten years out of style. She wasn't sure she liked this man. She wouldn't have let this guy pick her up that night at the airport. He looked too polished, too handsome, too confident.

A chameleon, she thought. Just like a man who wanted to be invisible in a crowd.

"I thought since I've been in Texas five years it's about time I bought boots. Maybe I'll settle down." He looked at Millanie. "If I can get a certain woman to talk to me again."

Kare turned to first Millanie, then her brother. When neither said a word, she started packing up her bag. "I've got to go. I promised to feed John if he fixed my window."

"Call me later, Kare," Drew insisted when she was half-way down the drive.

"Sure," Kare answered, "but you'll probably be busy."

"I hope so," he said, too low for his sister to hear. Looking at Millanie, he added, "Am I still welcome here?"

"Of course." She remembered the ride home from the Matheson ranch Friday night. They'd both been at the meeting of McAllens. They'd looked at the pictures and he'd asked a dozen questions as if he were truly interested. He'd said a few things as they got in the car to leave, and then she couldn't talk to him. He'd lied to her, and that one lie colored all he'd ever said or would say to her.

"You're out of your cast and the new brace, I'm

guessing." He looked at the outline of her leg beneath the thin sheet.

Millanie glanced down, fearing the cover might have slipped, but it was still in place. "The doctor doesn't want me to put any weight on it without the brace, so I'll have to strap my foot in the brace to go inside."

She didn't move. She had no intention of putting it on with him watching. It was almost dark; maybe she'd go in then.

"I thought you might want to go out to dinner." He moved closer.

"No, thank you. I have some work to do here."

"I could help if it's about the homestead. I brought a few books that have pictures of houses your ancestors built in town. They aren't just like the old place, but I can see similarities. Would you like to see?"

"No thanks. Not tonight." She told herself he wasn't the terrorist she was looking for. He couldn't be. If the bad guy stalking Kare was the man they were looking for, it wouldn't be Drew. She'd have known her own brother, even in the rain. Plus, Drew was with her at the Mathesons' having dinner. He couldn't have been in two places at once.

Only he had lied.

He knelt beside her chair. "What happened with us, Millie? I thought we had something. You wanted what happened between us as much as I did the other night. Then Friday you changed. Are you ill or in pain?"

Millanie almost smiled, thinking Drew looked as confused about women as Beau had an hour earlier. Only Drew was ten years older and she thought far wiser. She couldn't tell him the truth. What if he was the man half the state had been searching for? He didn't fit all the profile, but he was close and smart. Maybe smart enough to fool his sister.

Closing her eyes, Millanie silently wondered if Kare couldn't be in on his plan. No. Impossible. She'd been through background checks.

Only, she had never done a profile on Drew even after Millanie asked her. When Millanie had asked about it, Kare's answer hadn't made much sense.

She stared at him in the dying light. If she was right and he was involved, this man she thought was kind could be responsible for hundreds of deaths, maybe more. If she was wrong, she'd just hurt an innocent man and maybe killed any chance of ever truly falling for someone.

"Answer me, Millie. You owe me that." His words seemed to circle in the sudden gust of wind.

"I can't," she said honestly. The knowledge that this just might be what it would be like the rest of her life frightened Millanie almost as much as the possibility that Drew could be a bad guy. She could see herself second-guessing everyone she met, never trusting fully, never running with her feelings.

The screen door popped open against the back of the inn and Martha Q shouted, "You two better get inside! Storm's blowing in."

Neither she nor Drew moved. Anger and hurt sparked between them like faraway lightning. She knew he wanted an answer. If he was innocent, he deserved an answer, but he'd told one lie. One lie might be the tip of an iceberg. One lie was all it took to break her trust.

"You need to snap out of it and run for the house!" Martha Q yelled again.

Millanie needed to put on her brace. She couldn't walk, much less run, without it, and she wouldn't move the sheet away with him watching. No one should have to look at her leg. If Drew truly was attracted to her, he wouldn't be when he saw the scars and swelling. She'd rather get wet than let him see her.

"Go on in," she ordered. "I'll be there in a minute."

A bolt of lightning popped, blinking the evening sky to white light for a moment.

"Come on." Drew reached for her hand as thunder rolled across the twilight like thousands of buffalo must have once stampeded across this very land.

"I can't!" she yelled as she glanced at the brace beside her chair and back at him. "Go on without me. I'll make it." If the rain hit, the grass would be wet. She'd barely managed the walk out. How could she make it back without putting on the brace?

In the next blink of lightning she saw his face and knew he understood. He leaned down close to her face. "Put your arm around my neck and hold on." It was an order, not a request, as huge droplets began to hit like tiny bombs.

She grabbed her brace in one hand and circled his neck with her arm. He straightened, lifting her off the chair as he stood. Then he was moving, not running, but taking swift long strides toward the porch.

Martha Q stepped out as rain began to pelt the house. She held the door with one hand while her other hand formed a tiny umbrella above her hair.

Drew didn't stop once inside, but rushed down the hallway and into Millanie's room. Martha Q followed a few steps behind, cussing mad that her hair had gotten wet.

Millanie held tight, fearing that he'd bump her leg against something. She didn't know if she fought panic because she was wet and cold or frustrated that she couldn't take care of herself. At that moment she hated her life, her leg, her crippled body, and Drew. She buried her head against his shoulder and tried to find the courage she'd always had. The order she'd lived with for years was slipping away.

Gently, he lowered her onto the bed and pulled the wet sheet off her shivering body. He grabbed a quilt and covered her up to her chin, then yelled that he needed coffee.

Mrs. Biggs must have followed them down the hallway with a cup in her hand.

Drew tossed his jacket onto a chair and knelt on one knee by Millanie's shoulder.

She was shaking so hard she couldn't talk. It wasn't the cold or the rain. Millanie, for the first time in her life, felt truly frightened.

He circled her shoulders and raised her up enough so she could swallow. "Are you all right, Millanie? Do we need to call a doctor?"

Downing one hot gulp, she answered, "No. I'm just cold."

He held her for a few more moments, and then Mrs. Biggs appeared with a stack of towels. "She's all right," he said to the old cook. "I'll take care of her."

Mrs. Biggs nodded. "I'll warm some soup after I check on Martha Q. She hates getting her hair wet worse than a cat." The cook closed the door as she left.

"I'm fine," Millanie said, hoping he'd leave. Drew didn't look so polished standing there with his new clothes dripping and his hair wet.

"Sure you are," he snapped, obviously not believing her.

Without asking, he tugged the blanket away and began patting down her hair, her face, her shoulders. "I'll get you as dry as I can first, then I'll pile the blankets on until you stop shivering."

Millanie closed her eyes, thinking the night could not possibly get worse. The man she thought might be a criminal had just saved her. It would have taken five minutes to get her brace on and slowly walk to the house. She didn't care about being wet, but she wasn't sure she could have made it on the damp grass and up the old wooden steps. If she'd fallen, even with the brace, she might have done some serious damage. One more break, one more injury to a leg finally starting to heal might leave her crippled for life.

She felt the towel slide down her leg. Her right leg.

"No," she cried.

"Am I hurting you?" he asked, worry thick in his voice.

"No. Don't look at my leg." Millanie closed her eyes so tight tears dripped from the corners.

"It looks bad, Millie, real bad." His tone softened. "You must have gone through hell." His warm fingers replaced the towel as he lightly brushed the scar across her knee. "It needs to heal, so tell me if I'm hurting you. I don't want to do anything that might cause you more pain."

He tugged her baggy trousers down and dried first her right leg, then her left before moving the blanket to her waist. Then, just as gently, he tugged off her top and patted her skin. The thin bra she wore hid nothing from view, but he didn't comment.

She was shaking hard even after he finally pulled the blanket to her chin.

She waited for him to finish and leave, but he didn't.

When she finally began to calm, she felt him push away the covers from her right leg. He lifted her swollen ankle and gently slid one of the socks the hospital gave her over her toes and all the way to her knee. Then he picked up the brace and turned it a few ways until he figured out how the contraption fit and began strapping it to her leg. Each touch was warm and gentle, and practiced, she thought. He'd done this before.

When he finished, he covered her with a second blanket and stepped a few feet away to the bench tucked into the bay window.

Millanie watched, too embarrassed to speak as he removed his boots with no skill, then pulled off his dripping shirt. When he turned around to hang the shirt on the bedpost, she was shocked at what she saw. A deep scar ran along his shoulder and another on his side. They were not the kind of scars people get from surgery. They were wounds, battle scars.

He turned around, his hair now wild. The styling that had made him look so polished was completely gone. Except for the scars his body was slim, but well-shaped like a runner's body. The scar at his side barely showed from the front, but the mark of a wound was clear on his shoulder. A bullet wound, she thought.

"I'm crawling under the covers with you, Millie." His voice was finally calm. "Nothing is going to happen except that I'm going to warm you up, so don't waste time complaining. When you're warm and rational, you can go back to ignoring me."

Without another word he slid in beside her and pulled her against him. The warmth of his flesh felt so good against hers.

The lights flickered a few times and went out, but neither of them said a word. One arm held her against him while the other moved atop the covers as if pushing the warmth gently closer.

Someone tapped on the door and asked if they needed any candles.

Drew said simply, "We're fine." In the total darkness, he brushed his fingers through her wet hair. "Relax, Millie. This old house has withstood a hundred storms worse than tonight; it'll make it through this one. I'm guessing your great-great-grandfather built Winter's Inn and he built it to stand."

He kissed her forehead as his warmth seeped into her.

Millanie closed her eyes and let the world with all its questions and problems slip away.

When the lights came on an hour later, Drew silently stood and flipped them off, then came back to bed.

Millanie was awake enough to be aware of him pulling her against him as he covered her shoulder with the blanket.

Chapter 36

BEAU MANAGED TO GET THROUGH THE MEAL WITH BOTH
Lark's parents staring at him. He was polite, feeling more
like an alien visiting another planet than a boyfriend. One
fact came through loud and clear, almost like a drumbeat
in the background. Lark was loved.

They weren't what he expected. In truth, he didn't know
what he expected. Servants maybe. A huge house where he'd
need a map to find the bathroom. But the Powers family
lived a fairly normal life. Their ranch-style home was big
and looked nice, but it didn't seem to be designed by some
fancy decorator. There were pictures of Lark and her two
sisters everywhere. The other two daughters were married,
and both had families. Mrs. Powers's favorite topic was her
grandchildren.

Mr. Powers asked questions about the music business,
intelligent questions. Beau had the feeling that maybe Mr.
Powers had spent his one hour's notice before the dinner
researching.

After they finished eating, everyone picked up their plates
and took them to the kitchen. To his surprise, they all helped

with the dishes. Lark's mother was in charge of putting up leftovers, even kidding his father that she'd be sure to save the peas for his lunch. Mr. Powers, a man who owned three banks, loaded the dishwasher. Lark cleaned off the table, handing things to both her father and mother.

Beau stood and watched until Lark finally shoved her dad out of the kitchen. "Show Beau the horses. He loves horses."

"Go on, Garth," Mrs. Powers ordered. "We'll make coffee and bring dessert out on the patio. It's too nice a night to be inside."

Garth nodded at his wife as if taking orders from her was no big deal and pointed toward the back door. Beau followed.

Halfway to the barn, Garth slowed. "So, you love horses, do you, Beau?"

"Don't know a thing about them," Beau answered honestly. "Don't let the hat fool you."

Garth laughed. "It didn't."

"Lark loves them, though, so I guess she wanted me to see them," Beau admitted. "One night in the hospital she told me all about her favorite pony when she was little."

"She sat with you in the hospital?" Lark's father asked.

"She did."

"You ill, Beau?"

"No, just dumb. I got mugged." He didn't want to tell Garth Powers all the details, so he asked as they neared the barn, "Which one is Spider King? She said she loved to ride him."

"That she does. All my girls grew up riding, but she was addicted to it. Whenever she has a problem or is worried about something, she saddles up and rides. She knows every inch of this place better than I do, and I grew up on this land."

They walked past the horse barn, with Garth pointing out a few horses, and Beau nodded as if he thought they were all grand. Beau didn't know enough to ask questions. He figured saying nothing was safer than making a fool of himself.

Mr. Powers must have gotten the hint. "How about I show you some horsepower you might be interested in?" He touched a code bar on the side of the next building and a huge garage door opened. Ten cars, all with plenty of space around them, were lined up in a spotless storage unit. Timeless classic cars, expensive cars.

"Nice," Beau said, seeing each one had been restored to perfection.

"It's my one hobby," Garth admitted. "I restore them myself. After all day at the bank nothing makes me happier than getting grease on my hands."

One by one they walked down the center row. These vehicles belonged in museums. Beau was almost afraid to touch a few. Each had been polished to shine like glass.

In the last space sat the red Mustang Beau knew so well. "Write-me-a-ticket red," he whispered to himself, thinking of the first night Lark smiled and said, *Want to go for a ride?*

Garth laughed. "I've heard a few call it that color before. Something about this car makes you want to drive fast. It was the first car I restored and it's still my favorite. My girls were all little and some nights it was nice to come out to the silence of this place for a while."

They were quiet for a few minutes while Garth ran his hand over the fender of the Mustang in almost a caress.

Beau had no idea what to say. Somehow he didn't think it was the time to mention that most of his sexiest memories were made in this car.

"You know, she likes you, Beau. She's dated some, but you're the first she's brought home to our family dinner," Garth said, almost more to himself than Beau.

He knew who Mr. Powers was talking about, but he wasn't sure Lark hadn't changed her mind about liking him. Maybe she'd invited him here just to prove how different they were. Family dinners and doing the dishes together had never happened while he was growing up.

Beau squared his shoulders and said as honestly as he could, "She's a part of me, my past, my present, and maybe my future if we ever get around to talking about it. Right now, I think we're just working on being friends."

Garth nodded. "She's my youngest, my smartest, but since she was a girl she's run from any feelings. Sometimes on her fast horse, and now and then in my favorite car. It's like she can't clear her mind if she's not racing. If she has feelings growing for you, son, you can bet she'll run."

Beau couldn't talk about how he felt with Lark's father. "How do you feel about her taking your car?"

Garth faced Beau as he leaned against the Mustang. "I love this car, Beau, but I love her more. If she wrecked it, my one and only question would be 'Are you all right?'"

Beau wished he could understand. Love, for him, was just a word used in songs. The man before him had power and wealth, but he valued family most. Beau had the feeling if he lost his money he'd still have it all.

They locked up the garage and walked back past the barn. Beau tried to help the conversation along but was out of his range. He'd spent most of his adult life talking to drunks. Lark's folks were nice, polite, and welcoming not because he was famous, but because he was their daughter's friend.

Over dessert they talked about music, obviously wanting to include him in the conversation. Her parents even got into a playful argument over which of the songs from the seventies had been their favorite. He swore "Sunshine on My Shoulders" was it, and she told him she was sure it had to be "Southern Nights."

Beau had brought the Gibson to play for Lark tonight when they were alone, but there might not be a later. She hadn't said four words to him since they'd arrived. So while they talked he went to collect his guitar from her car.

When he returned, he sat on the edge of the patio wall, opened his case, and said simply, "Let's end this argument."

He played the old John Denver song first. Slow and low like Denver would have played it on a small stage in a smoky bar. Then he played "Southern Nights." About halfway through Garth took his wife's hand.

When Beau finished, there was no doubt which song had been their favorite, their song.

He set his guitar back in the case and, for a moment, everyone was quiet. Then Garth stood and touched Beau's shoulder. "That was a real nice gift you gave us, son. You've a rare talent. I'll bet your parents are proud."

Beau just offered his practiced smile and said, "Yes, sir."

Then he was saying good-bye and walking back to Lark's little BMW. He reached for her hand but she turned away as if she hadn't seen him. The entire evening they'd always just missed touching.

As she opened her car door, she said, "You didn't have to play, you know. They didn't expect you to. I didn't bring you here to entertain."

"I know." He thought of telling her he hadn't minded. After all, it was what he did, but he didn't know how to talk to her anymore. Somehow the few minutes in her office had changed things between them. He thought about saying he was sorry again but doubted she'd believe him this time any more than she had before.

She'd made her point tonight. She wasn't one of his fans hanging around hoping he'd notice them. She wasn't a woman he could just grab and kiss. He'd learned that fact the hard way.

They drove the night watching the lightning dance across the sky. Neither knew how to start a conversation. Both seemed lost in their own thoughts. He longed for those old days in the Mustang when not talking had felt good between them.

The lights of Harmony spread across the horizon, making the little town look big in the night.

"Stop the car," Beau said as thunder rolled.

She kept driving. "I'm not in the mood to talk tonight, Beau. I don't want to park somewhere and watch the stars."

"Neither am I, and it's too cloudy to see any stars. Stop the car. I'm getting out."

She braked and pulled to the side of the road without

turning off her lights. "You're still five miles from town," she said as he climbed out.

"I don't care." He'd never been angry in his life, not like this, not mixed up with heartbreak.

"I'm not mad at you, Beau. I just need time. I didn't think you thought of me that way."

"What way?" he said as he held the door against the wind. "Like you're a woman and I'm a man? We can't be kids forever, Lark." For a moment, deep down he wanted Trouble back, but she was lost in a proper suit and blond hair tied up.

She lowered her head to the steering wheel and, if possible, he felt even worse than before. They might as well have been raised on different planets. She'd probably had a hundred dates that ended with a sweet kiss. She'd gone to prom and all the dances and held hands at the movies. He'd had none of that and what was the real kicker . . . he didn't want it.

He wanted passion, raw and real, and he wanted it with her.

He had no idea what the hell she wanted, but it obviously wasn't him. Which left them at good-bye. Both hurt. Both broken.

He slammed the car door so hard the BMW rocked. *Walk away*, he almost shouted. *Walk away before you do any more damage.*

The sound of a plane rattled over the sky as he headed toward town. Lark still sat in her car, probably watching him in the long beams of her headlights.

The plane flew low. Beau couldn't see the pilot, but he waved anyway just in case it was Derwood. The plane's wing tipped, then banked and headed off into the night.

Finally, Lark turned her car around and retraced her path. Beau just walked toward the lights of town. It was so dark he couldn't see his feet, but the tapping of his boots on the asphalt kept him going on the right path. If he got too far off, the gravel on the shoulder warned him.

The wind was cold from the west as a storm herded low

clouds toward town. Each time the lightning flashed, the night seemed darker when the light faded. As always, his surroundings came alive with the rhythm of the night. Leaves, crisp now with fall, rattled in the trees. There was movement in the fields. The swish of tall buffalo grass and the pop of a plastic bag caught on a fence. The thunder played bass and the wind strings.

Only Beau didn't want to hear the music tonight. He just wanted to walk and be miserable. A few trucks and cars passed by, but he stepped off the shoulder as they neared, making it plain he wasn't looking for a ride.

He needed to be alone. Apparently he didn't belong in polite society. He'd fallen for a nice girl and treated her like a tramp. He belonged out here with the storm and the coyotes and snakes. Shoving his hands in his pockets, he kept walking, not caring where he was going.

Finally, a car coming from town passed him, then circled back.

When the sheriff's cruiser pulled up, Beau thought of running, but where would he go? Whoever sat in the car could just watch him run until he gave out or fell over, then drive across the open field and pick him up.

"Beau Yates?" Phil Gentry called. "That you out here in the middle of nowhere taking a walk?"

"Yeah, it's me. Did Derwood turn me in?"

"Of course he did. Said the storm will hit long before you are near cover so I'd better come out and get you. We all got to watch over Harmony's rising star. How about you climb in and I'll give you a lift back to Martha Q's place?"

"Why?" Beau kept walking and Gentry followed in the car.

"How much money you got in your pocket?" the deputy asked.

"I don't know, a couple hundred. Maybe four or five."

Gentry swore. "Beau, you're a walking crime scene. Get in the car before I arrest you."

Beau might have argued, but the bandage on his head reminded him that Gentry was probably right. This time, if he ended up in the hospital, Lark wouldn't bother to come see him.

As rain began to fall, he gave up on his walk to nowhere and climbed in the deputy's car. "Don't you have anything better to do, Deputy Gentry?"

"Nope. It's Tuesday already. Nothing ever happens on Tuesday."

Chapter 37

JOHNNY DROVE KARE TO TOWN TUESDAY AFTER THEY HAD lunch. He didn't like the idea of her going back to her apartment, but just because she was his fairy didn't mean he could keep her. Talking to her was like breathing pure oxygen. She opened up his senses, his understanding, his world. If just being around her was making him smarter, he couldn't help but wonder if it wasn't somehow having the opposite effect on her. Maybe having him near was dumbing her down.

"I'm going to miss you, Kare," he admitted as he fought the urge to reach over and touch her. "I don't know when I've enjoyed a weekend more, even if it was a problem that brought you to me." He'd liked when they talked and when they were quiet. He probably should have brought her back Monday, but they never ran out of things to talk about and one day would never have been enough.

"I had fun, too. It's great to cook in a real kitchen. My apartment is so small I don't even have a drawer in my kitchen. If I did, the landlord would probably charge me for it." She sat with her legs crossed and folded beneath her as she rode in his truck. "I'm glad we built the chicken coop. Now you can get up every morning and collect fresh eggs."

"Promise you'll come back out and show me a few things about chickens when they arrive."

Kare laughed. "How could you have lived on a farm all your life and never had chickens?"

"Maybe when Mom left she took the chickens with her. I don't remember." The farm was pretty much an all-boys' club until he married Scarlet. He remembered asking her once if she wanted a garden, or chickens or even a cow. She said, "Why? The store is five miles away."

Kare pulled out a pen and notebook from her huge bag.

"What are you doing?" he asked after a few minutes.

"Making a list of all I'll have to teach you about how to be a farmer. It's more than just growing a cash crop every year." She pointed her pen. "Like, I'll bet you don't even know what song you have to sing every night to get chickens to sleep."

"You're right, I have no idea." Johnny acted as if he were giving it serious consideration while she giggled, obviously knowing he was teasing her. "It might take a while." He winked at her just like his grandpa had. "I'm a slow learner, so you'll be visiting lots." He liked the sound of that idea. "I thought you hated farming."

Kare's big eyes teared up. "I never hated the farm. I hated the loneliness of never being near anyone my age, and I hated never being able to go to a movie or a library or see a parade or go trick-or-treating or buy a snow cone, but I never hated the farm."

Leaning her head back, she added, "I love snow cones. I hang out at the stand so much every summer they think I'm an addict." She daydreamed for a while, then said, "I love watching plants grow and feeding animals and collecting eggs. I miss my home sometimes but I've never gone back, not since college."

"Why not?"

"My folks never really invited me. Mom had me by accident and did her duty to raise me. She did a good job and
loved me. She read me stories every night until I started
reading. Took me on educational trips. Bought my clothes,
taught me to cook. But once I left, she never invited me
back."

"I wish someone had taught me to cook. When my
grandpa moved to town he handed me a can opener and said,
'Good luck.'"

"No, he didn't." She hit him on the shoulder, knowing
she was being teased.

Johnny played the victim. "I'll probably starve now after
having real meals for three days. I won't be able to go back
to my ration of two cans of dog food a day." He'd told her
that once he'd been so tired when he fixed supper that he
opened dog food instead of beef stew. He was halfway
through the can before his taste buds woke up enough to
complain.

She rubbed away the punch she'd given him as if she'd
hurt him. "I'll come back, John. Plus you've got enough
leftovers to last the week."

He didn't have the nerve to tell her that it wasn't the food
he'd miss, it was her company. He didn't have the right to
say anything. A smart woman like her could never fall for
a regular farmer like him. So he'd better change the subject
before he made a fool of himself or they both started crying.
"You sure you want to visit my grandpa? Just because I go
every Tuesday doesn't mean you have to. I could take you
by your place first."

"I don't mind at all. I drop by the senior citizens' center
almost every week. Mr. Wheeler is one of my best customers."

Johnny thought of asking what she was charging his
grandpa for, but he'd learned Kare used her own vocabulary
and didn't always mean what he thought she said. He decided
to wait until they visited before asking too many questions.

As he watched her play with her scarves he thought about
how strange she'd seemed the first time he'd stumbled upon
her office. Now he thought other women looked plain

without all the colors floating around them. When he first met her, he decided there was something very simple about Kare Cunningham, more child than woman, but the longer he knew her he realized she had an intelligence, a complexity far beyond normal people.

Of course, his gauge had been Wendell and Scarlet. Both low bars to measure by. Conversations with Kare pushed him, made him pay attention, made him step in instead of zoning out of life. She quoted philosophers and statesmen. She worried about things happening in the world and what they should do about it like the two of them might make a difference. Every living thing mattered to her. When she'd walked up his front steps she'd noticed a caterpillar crawling across the top step. She'd helped him down and onto the grass.

A few minutes later, when they walked in the senior citizens' center, Pops rushed over to Kare, totally ignoring Johnny.

"We've been waiting for you, little darling," he said like she was a celebrity. "The coffee fund is almost dry and I need to know if I should play poker this week."

"Only if the stakes are eatable." Kare kissed his wrinkled cheek.

Johnny stood just inside the door as his eighty-year-old grandpa stole his girl. He didn't know whether to be angry or impressed. She was hugging on him and laughing at his dumb jokes and he was winking so much at her Johnny thought his grandpa might have developed a twitch since he saw him last.

A group of men in one corner all stood to welcome her. Some hugged her. One old man danced around with her as if someone had struck up the band.

Kare held up one finger asking them to wait a minute as she rushed over to the quilters to say hello and then the painting corner where everyone was supposed to paint the same picture but no two looked alike.

Johnny felt like he'd taken the prom queen to the dance. No one said hello to him. He was the invisible man until one of the activities coordinators, with a name tag that said Jeter Peters, motioned him over. Jeter was rubber-band thin.

His favorite time in school must have been craft time and he never got over it. In any other job he would have been the office pest, constantly organizing celebrations, surprises, and fund-raisers while he gossiped. But here, he was loved.

"Thanks for bringing Kare in, Johnny," Jeter said as if Johnny were nothing more than the delivery service. "We've all been worried about her. Mrs. Clark's son is a dispatcher for the sheriff's office and he told her someone was stalking Kare. After the questions Kare asked us last week we feared she might be in trouble. I was about to organize a Kare Watch to run round the clock."

"What questions?" Johnny thought of telling Jeter they didn't need a Kare watch, he already had that covered, but he wanted to know the questions Kare had been asking first.

"You know, like did we know someone who had a private plane or could we think of any newly arrived people in Harmony who didn't seem to have a job or attachments. Someone acting fishy, like a 'most wanted' type with no friends or family. I told her about Max Dewy being a pilot, and how he always smiled showing too many teeth, but I guess he'd don't fit as a loner now because he's attached to your wife."

Johnny wasn't surprised even the senior citizens knew about Scarlet and Max. Apparently, he'd been the last to hear. He didn't know, or care, that Max was a pilot, but if he ever got close to the man again Max might have a few less teeth.

"Which reminds me"—Jeter patted Johnny's shoulder as if they were buddies—"your wife dropped by the other day and asked the strangest question."

"What?"

"She wanted to know how your grandpa was doing and if there was any chance that he'd be dying in the next few months. She said she didn't want to upset him by hurrying the divorce if he was ill on account of how much it would hurt the old guy if you and she split up."

"Very considerate of her," Johnny said. The Wheeler farm was worth well over a million, but it was family land.

If she waited and divorced after he inherited, she could claim half of his half.

"I know." Jeter nodded. "I've never seen her visit or stop by for lunch with Mr. Wheeler, but she must really care about him."

He glanced over at Kare. She was at a table alone with one lady and it looked like Kare was reading her palm. She looked like a multicolored angel with all her scarves that were so light they looked like a breeze might rip them.

"You don't mind the fortune-teller doing readings?"

Jeter shook his head. "She makes them pay a three-dollar donation to the coffee fund as payment. You'd think as short as their lifelines must be it'd make them sad, but it doesn't. They all love her to come."

Johnny waved good-bye to Jeter and walked over near enough to Kare to listen.

"You've had a great love, Delta, and a blessed life, haven't you?" his little fortune-teller said to a lady with white hair.

"I have. I knew you'd see that in these old worn-out hands. I had Ollie for almost sixty years with me. We were blessed with eight grandchildren. Now that's a bushel full." White hair almost touched Kare's black as Delta added, "Do you see a peaceful passing for me, child?"

Kare smiled. "I do."

"I thought so." Relief relaxed the worried lines across a face that had seen eighty-four years. "I've always known he's waiting for me, so I'll go when the time comes. I thought he fought so hard because he didn't want to leave me. Finally, I promised him I wouldn't be long and he went on ahead."

Johnny moved over to the coffeepot before he started crying like a baby. When he made it back, Kare was holding hands with an old friend of Johnny's grandpa named Mr. Railsback. The old guy had farmed a mile down from them until a few years ago. He still lived on the farm, but he leased out his land.

"You're a very brave man," Kare said as she touched the old soldier's palm.

"I just did what had to be done. No more. It was war, you know. We all had to be brave men back then."

Kare patted his arm where a faded tattoo poked out beneath his sleeve. "I know, but that bravery has served you well over the years, Mr. Railsback. It got you through the hard times."

"I was in the Marines," he started, then added, "I remember the time . . ."

Johnny noticed Kare didn't say another word. Mr. Railsback talked the rest of her reading, then kissed her cheek for being brilliant and paid his three dollars.

The next man looked younger than the others at first glance. He still had a full head of sandy-colored hair with white at the temples.

"Hello, Mr. Gray. You here with questions?"

He shook his head. "Nope. Just thought I'd visit. Always good to see a new face."

"But don't you want to know how long you'll live or if you'll win the lottery?"

"Nope." He shifted in his chair. "I figure it don't matter how long you live, but how well you lived it. Maybe help a few people out, smile when you don't have to, and take time now and then to just enjoy the ride."

"You should be telling the fortunes, not me, Mr. Gray."

"No thanks, but I would like you to call me Brian or Brian Scott. That's what my folks sometimes called me."

"All right, Brian." She offered her hand. "I think I'd be honored to be your friend."

Johnny noticed the man's hands were stained but Kare didn't shy away. A working man's hands didn't frighten her.

"You see it, son?" his grandpa whispered so close to Johnny's ear that he jumped.

"What?" Johnny turned to the grandpa he'd loved all his life.

The older Wheeler smiled. "The kindness in Kare. Ain't one person in a hundred has that big a heart. She's fragile; she'll need protecting from time to time, I'm guessing. I'm thinking it'll take a man strong as an ox for that job."

"Not me. We're just friends. We're not seeing each other. I just stepped in to help when she needed it." Johnny wondered if he was lying to his grandfather or himself. Not that it mattered. He was still lying.

The old man frowned. "I don't need to read your palm to see what's happening. You start courting that girl proper or I'm leaving the farm to Wendell."

"Don't threaten me," Johnny stiffened. Whenever his grandfather wanted to control him, he always said the same thing. They both knew Wendell didn't want the farm. Inheriting it would be a curse for him. "You know you wouldn't do that to my brother."

Pops laughed. "You're right." He nodded toward Kare. "Marry that girl or I'll marry her myself. I think she's already fond of me and I got enough years left to have a few more kids if the ones I got don't start listening to me."

Johnny swore. With his luck, Kare would feel sorry for the old man and marry him. Then he'd be in love with his new grandma.

The world seemed a crazy place.

Chapter 38

DREW COULDN'T LET GO OF MILLANIE AS THEY CUDDLED safe and warm with the storm raging outside. All night he held her as close as he dared. It had been so many years since he'd slept with a woman. The feel of her against him, the smell of her skin mixed with rain, the softness of her hair tickling his chin. This one woman, wounded and stubborn, had brought him back into life. For the first time he cared too much to walk away.

Once she was asleep he'd banked her right leg on either side with pillows so he wouldn't accidentally brush her wounds. The sight of the twisted leg hadn't shocked him. He'd seen many injuries during his recovery, but hers broke his heart. The pain she had to have suffered. The effort it must still take to stand on the leg even with the brace. His brave Millie was fighting her way back as well to being whole. Only he feared part of the path had crumbled.

He wasn't sure why he'd removed his shirt last night. Maybe because he'd seen her scars and knew that his wouldn't matter. Or maybe it was time he stopped hiding and stepped out from behind the mask he'd been wearing.

He'd seen something tonight that made him reflect. He wasn't just his scars anymore than she was simply a broken leg, but the wounds were a part of them, a part of who they'd been, who they still were.

His strong, always-in-control Millie had cried when she knew he'd seen her leg. The weeks of surgeries and pain and endless discomfort she'd endured now tore at him as she relaxed in his arms, but he wasn't repelled. She'd been a soldier. He'd read the reports a few days after he'd met her. He'd gone over every detail he could find in every newspaper. She'd been listed as one of the casualties at first, and then she'd been critical for weeks. The last mention of her had said she was in therapy in a hospital in Germany.

As dawn filtered into her room, he couldn't help but kiss her bare shoulder. He had no idea why she was mad at him, but he didn't plan on walking away from her. Before they'd gone to dinner at the Matheson place, she'd wanted him as badly as he wanted her. They weren't wild kids. They both knew what would have happened if Martha Q hadn't picked that exact time to come home. Clothes would have littered the foyer and passion would have consumed them both.

He slid his hand along her bare waist, loving the feel of her skin. She felt so right.

She rolled on her back and whispered, "Go away. I'm sleeping."

"Not likely," he answered as he kissed the side of her throat.

"I don't want to be your friend."

"Great," he answered. "I don't want to be yours either, but that doesn't mean I don't want you." His hand moved over her stomach and began to slowly climb up her body.

She moaned, still half asleep, and stretched, arching her back into his touch.

His hand passed over her small breast covered with lace, then pressed harder as he moved downward, shoving her panties low.

She arched again like a cat being petted. "Go away," she whispered.

"I'm not going anywhere, Millie, so you might as well get ready for a good-morning kiss." His hand slid between her legs and she let out a little cry of surprise.

He covered her lips with his and caught the next moan before he kissed her deeply and passionately. Without slowing, he slid his hand back up to the middle of her bra and broke the clasp. His slender fingers seemed as hungry for the feel of her as her mouth was for his kiss, but he didn't lean into her. He wanted to feel every part of her first. She needed to know just how desirable she was.

When he finally broke the kiss, he moved to her ear and whispered, "I just wanted to say good morning, Millie." One hand still roamed over her while the other cupped the back of her head as he kissed his way down her neck.

"Beau was right," she whispered. "There never should be kissing without passion."

His head moved lower as his morning stubble tickled the valley between her breasts.

"You're not even listening," she whispered. When he didn't answer but moved down to kiss his way across her abdomen, she tried again. "I don't care if you hear a word I'm saying as long as you don't stop."

After he kissed each peak, he finally raised his head. "That bra got in the way. Don't wear one next time."

Millanie's smile was wicked with laughter. "What makes you think there will be a next time?"

He looked up at her, feeling half drunk on the tenderness in her eyes. "There'll be a next time, Millie, and a next and a next. I don't care if you ever speak to me again, I'll find you and you'll welcome me because you want me as dearly as I want you."

"You're pretty sure of yourself, Professor."

"It's only logical." He leaned above her and gently kissed her. Slowly, like a river of pleasure flowing over them, the kiss deepened. He silently proved his point.

Finally, he lowered his head next to hers, his words choppy and low. "I haven't held a woman in five years. I've been waiting for one who felt just right. Like it or not, you're a perfect match." He kissed her lightly, loving the fullness of her lips against his.

When her hand rested on his scarred shoulder, he didn't end the kiss but mentally he began pulling away. He knew he wouldn't make love to her today. Last night she'd broken and he'd been there to help. This morning she was too fragile. All she needed to know was that she was desired and that he'd be waiting when she was strong enough to finish what they'd started this morning.

He raised his head and kissed her on the nose. "I'm starving. You think Martha Q would feed me?"

Millanie grinned. "There's a good chance. I've seen her feed strays before."

Drew rolled from the bed and grabbed his wrinkled shirt. "You get dressed and I'll go tell her we're famished." He walked to the door, wanting to offer help but knowing she'd be upset if he did. Turning, he smiled at her still curled in the covers. "I don't know why you're mad at me, Millie, but I should admit that sleeping with you was the best night of my life. So, whatever I did or said or was, I'll start with, *I'm sorry, I'm innocent, I'll change*, and see if that works."

He stepped through the door before she answered.

Thirty minutes later Millanie walked into the breakfast room, her hair in perfect order and a touch of makeup brushed on her cheeks. She wore new linen pants and a blouse the same shade of green as her eyes. She held her head high, and only a slight leaning on her cane gave away any hint that she wasn't perfectly well.

Drew stood and pulled out her chair. "Good morning, Miss McAllen, I hope you slept well?"

"Martha Q let you stay," she guessed.

"Of course. After I asked her to keep my overnight visit a secret and offered to pay, she was all for it." Drew took his seat across from Millanie. All the food was on the table, so no one ventured in to say good morning to them. Drew had no doubt their absence was by design.

He held dishes out for her, noticing that her lips were slightly swollen from his kisses.

She didn't say a word as she filled her plate, but he guessed they were both thinking about last night.

"Back to not talking to me again?" Drew didn't really care. They seemed to be getting along fine this morning without carrying on much of a conversation. He could still smell her skin, all warm and rain washed.

"Want to tell me why you're angry?" How could she be mad? He couldn't remember a thing he'd done. The last time they'd been alone they'd enjoyed each other almost as much as they had twenty minutes ago. "How about saying something," he tried again. "Ask me a question. Yell at me. Complain about the weather, anything."

"When were you shot?" Millanie lowered her fork.

"I didn't figure you'd let that pass, but I thought you might at least eat breakfast first." He knew his voice had turned cold, but he'd hoped for more time.

She was back to being the captain. "You going to tell me?"

"No," he answered. "It was a long time ago. When I moved here I decided not to tell anyone. You're the only one who has even seen the scars. I meant it when I said there has been no woman for five years."

"A professor with multiple wounds—"

He stood suddenly and moved to the window. "I don't want to talk about it, Millie. Not now, maybe not ever."

"All right," she said, as if she were dropping the subject. "Let's talk about something else. How's your mother doing?"

He stared out at the gray day, thinking that this was the reason he never got close to people, never dated, never became too good a friend. At some point they'd want him to fill in the holes in his life and he couldn't talk about them.

Without a word, he walked out of the dining room. A few moments later he closed the front door behind him silently as if he'd never been there at all.

The best thing that had ever happened to him. The one person in years he'd wanted in his life. The budding of what could have been a deep relationship, maybe even love, had just ended. All that remained was to mourn in silence. Not all the scars were on his body; one was now on his heart.

Climbing into the old van, he headed back to his little cabin on Twisted Creek where he could hide away and pretend to live.

Chapter 39

❦

MILLANIE DOZED AFTER BREAKFAST IN THE PARLOR, BUT each time she almost nodded off one thought came to mind. *You're the first woman I've been with in five years*, Drew had said. Could that be possible? Drew had mentioned he was thirty-four. No man stayed celibate between twenty-nine and thirty-four.

He'd been so happy at dawn, kissing her, touching her. His hands were like magic to her body, making her feel things she hadn't felt since the bombing. For the first time since she'd met him, Drew seemed at peace with himself and his surroundings. She'd almost thought he was going to make love to her, but he'd stopped. Maybe he realized that if he hadn't pulled away, she would have. No man would want to make love to a woman in a brace.

Or would he? Would she?

Millanie groaned, thinking she was sounding like a teenager. Of course he wouldn't have continued. Or, she would have stopped them both before it had gone further. It was that simple. The kissing and the touching were nice, though. If he hadn't left, they could have continued more of that.

Only, he didn't just leave. She pushed him away. She'd treated him like a suspect needing interrogation. He had a right to his secrets. Maybe he didn't want to talk about his wounds any more than she did. Every brain cell she had told her he couldn't be the bad guy. He was too kind, too considerate, too loving.

The memory of how his twisted flesh had felt when she brushed her fingers over the scar on his shoulder came back so strong she could almost feel him now. The scar hadn't frightened her. It certainly hadn't turned her off. It simply brought up questions.

Questions Drew didn't want to answer.

Pulling up her laptop, she began to search. She didn't have to depend on Kare to do all the research; Millanie could do it herself. With Martha Q gone for her day of hair coloring and toe polishing, and Beau, as he did most mornings, sleeping away the day, Millanie felt like she had the place to herself. She could work in peace.

Not surprisingly, there were dozens of Andrew Cunninghams across the country. She narrowed her search to Texas and found him within minutes. Dr. Andrew Cunningham, professor of folklore and history, Clifton College. Several papers he'd written were mentioned. He'd been at a dozen community meetings listed as the speaker. Three awards for research in the past few years. No pictures. No address or phone number. No website or any social media that she could find. Kare had said he loved playing on the computer but he kept a very low profile.

An hour into the search she realized that until five years ago the man was a ghost. By early afternoon she'd widened the net and moved out of Texas. She tried California first, Kare's origin, then remembered Drew said he'd had his last date in New York five summers ago. She found his college. A Yale graduate with honors. Again several papers. Awards. But no pictures. Even before he hid out in Texas, Drew didn't like the camera.

The net she tossed was wide, catching hundreds of sites with other Andrews. It dawned on her that if he had been shot, it would have been in the paper. She began with the major cities. Dallas, Houston, Austin, San Antonio, New York, Washington, Boston, Chicago. Hundreds of shootings five years ago. She reasoned he wouldn't have been a cop. Not the personality. No training.

At Chicago's entry, the screen lit up. No Andrew, but a Drew Cunningham wounded in a school shooting.

Now there were pictures of a school in a rough neighborhood. A photo with students exiting, their hands in the air, their eyes to the ground as police cars surrounded the building.

The third picture that popped up stopped her heart. A tall, lean man. Bleeding. Carrying a girl of about fifteen or sixteen. He was cuddling her close to his chest as if he could shelter her from all the horror around. His hair was shorter, he wore jeans and a short-sleeve shirt soaked with blood, and he was even leaner than now, but she knew him the minute she saw the picture. Teacher now, teacher then, it fit.

She could imagine him five years ago. A shy, intelligent man trying to make a difference in the world. All the horror he'd seen and suffered. No wonder he ran away. As she followed the links she saw one headline that read, *First Anniversary of School Shooting*. The shot was long, showing the graves beside the pictures of the two students killed. A lone figure, thin and tall, was unaware of the camera as he knelt, brushing one hand over the grave. The grass was green. It looked like late August, when flowers and trees are heaviest just before fall.

The date matched the day she'd flown back home. Drew had been at the airport that night. He hadn't gone to see his mother. Millanie would bet her career that he'd gone, just as he had that first anniversary, to stand by the two kids' graves.

Lost in her thoughts, Millanie didn't move the first few times her phone rang.

When she lifted her cell, Kare's name came up.

"Hello, Kare, I need to talk to you as soon as possible." Millanie had to tell his sister that Drew was off the list. Then, she had to find a way to tell him she was sorry.

A man's voice, pure Texas twang, spoke slowly through the phone. "Captain McAllen, this is Johnny Wheeler. I'm talking on Kare's phone."

"I know that, Johnny." She smiled. The farmer obviously didn't use a cell.

"You do?" he said, then rushed on. "Is Kare with you?"

"No. I haven't seen her today. Is something wrong?"

Johnny didn't waste words. "She's missing. Her car is parked out behind the bookstore, but Mr. Hatcher said she hadn't been in. He said she always speaks to him on her way in and out of her office."

"Maybe she left her car there and walked home." Millanie could hear the panic in his pause. Johnny Wheeler was worried.

"No," he said. "She might have left her car home and walked in, but not the other way around. She drove her car to the bookstore this morning."

"Are you sure?"

Dead silence for a moment, and then he confessed, "Yeah, I'm sure. I watched her drive away. I wanted to take her into work, but she said she had something she had to tell you so she planned to drop by the bookstore, leave her car in case it was raining when she got finished, and then head across over to the inn. She told me that after she talked to you, she was planning to spend the rest of the morning online. She said she'd be safe at the bookstore, hidden away from the world." He paused. "She kept saying she'd be safe, like there was some reason she might not be."

"Where did you find her phone?" Millanie closed her eyes, praying that he'd say she left it in her apartment.

"I found it in the mud by her car. If it hadn't been pink I might not have noticed it. We were supposed to have lunch, and then I planned to head home. I finished building her a birdhouse this morning that she can see out her bedroom window."

He stopped and redirected. "That don't matter. Anyway, when she didn't show at the diner, I walked over to the bookstore. At first I thought she must have got busy doing what she calls research, but her office lights hadn't even been turned on. I checked the library and the county clerk's office after I talked to Mr. Hatcher.

"About one she didn't answer her phone when Mr. Hatcher called her and I called in reinforcements."

"The sheriff?" Millanie asked, knowing the police wouldn't normally help this soon with a missing person, but with the stalker and the broken window they might reconsider.

"No," Johnny answered. "I called the senior citizens' center. They were just finishing lunch and setting up for bingo, but when Jeter heard she was missing, he got them all organized, fanning out from the bookstore. I've got half a dozen cars with at least two in each. One driving slowly and the other on lookout. Those on walkers took the town square and the federal buildings; those that are steady on their feet are walking block by block. Mr. Gray and a few of his friends with canes are walking the creek bed looking for clues and haven't reported in yet, so I'm guessing the news isn't good. She's vanished."

Millanie tried to calm him down. "Johnny, you know she might have met up with her best friend and they went shopping." It didn't seem likely, but it would be a possibility.

"No. Jeter said those who can't walk have called every business in town. No one has seen her. Kare's not a woman people overlook." He hesitated. "Captain, I'm Kare's best friend, I think. She called me when she was afraid, and I've got a feeling she's afraid now. This time I've got her phone, so she may not be able to call anyone."

"Johnny, hang up. Find Drew's number in her phone. Write it down. Call me back and give it to me."

"All right," he said slowly. "I'll give it a try."

Millanie fought panic as the seconds ticked by. A whole minute passed before her phone rang.

She saw Kare's number, but she said, "Johnny?"

"I figured it out. These little things are neat."

"The number, Johnny."

"Oh, right." He gave her Drew's number, then promised to keep the phone close and report any change. Millanie said she'd be in touch with the sheriff and relay any messages. They didn't have to say more; they were both locked into one goal. Find Kare.

Millanie wasn't sure she even said good-bye. If Drew had a cell his sister might be the only one who had his number. Surely he'd answer her call.

Millanie dialed the number Johnny had given her.

Drew picked up on the second ring. "Whoever this is, I'm working. Leave a number and I'll call you back when I get hungry and stop for—"

"Drew?" Millanie's mouth went dry. "Don't hang up."

"I don't want to talk to you, Millanie," he snapped. "I've had enough questions."

"Wait! It's not about me. Kare is missing."

A long pause followed, and then in a low voice he asked, "Where are you?"

"I'm at the inn. But I'll be at the bookstore before you can get to town. She missed a lunch with Johnny and no one has seen her all morning."

"Give me ten minutes to get on the road. Then call back. I want details."

Millanie could hear the fear in his voice. "You'll have them."

Neither of them bothered to say good-bye. She dropped her phone in her pocket and picked up her laptop, her rental car keys, and the service weapon Sarge had brought her a few days ago. As fast as she could limp, she made it to the car and drove the few blocks with her left foot.

By the time she checked in with Johnny and the sheriff's office, Drew would have had time to be halfway to Harmony. She redialed his number.

"You took your time calling back," he yelled, sounding like he was in a wind tunnel. She knew without asking that he was driving the old Jeep over the speed limit.

"I know. I wanted updates before I called. Kare left her

apartment in her car before nine. After noon, when she didn't join him for lunch, Johnny Wheeler found her car behind the bookstore and no one has seen her. A dozen or more people are looking. They've combed the downtown area. Any place she could have walked to has been searched. She seems to have vanished."

"I'll be there in ten," he said, sounding worried. "Thanks for letting me know. I shouldn't have yelled at you, Millie. I guess I panicked."

"I know, I shouldn't have demanded answers. I wasn't being fair. We even now?"

"Even. When this is over, and we know Kare is safe, I'll answer your questions. I promise."

For the first time in years, the answers didn't matter to her. Drew did.

Chapter 40

JOHNNY FELT LIKE HE WAS GOING OUT OF HIS MIND. A FEW hours ago they'd been laughing about the colorful birdhouse he'd planted by her window. Kare had suggested they put little doors on each opening so the birds could have some privacy. He'd smiled all morning while he worked, thinking about Kare not wanting to watch the birds have sex.

She mattered to him, he knew that, but he didn't understand how much until she disappeared. He felt like he'd been growing inside every day since he met her. Since he'd left college to take over the farm six years ago, he'd been circling as if sleepwalking. Even marrying Scarlet was simply what he thought he should do. It was time. Life moved on like the seasons.

Only his little fairy woke him up. If she left, Kare would take half of a heart he didn't know he had. To make matters worse, his grandpa and several other senior citizens were parked around the reading table in Hatcher's bookstore staring at Johnny like it was all his fault.

"I told you to take care of that girl," his grandpa muttered every time Johnny circled. But Johnny didn't stop. He was too busy pacing and blaming himself. If the codger posse voted to hang him, Johnny had already decided he'd carry the rope.

Walking up and down the paperback aisle, Johnny tried to think of anywhere else he could look. The first person who came to mind who might have hurt Kare was Max Dewy. As far as Johnny knew, Kare didn't even know Max, but Max was a sleazeball. If styling and spraying his hair every day as well as sleeping with Scarlet didn't make him a criminal, Johnny didn't know what did.

Only, Max was out as a suspect. Max Dewy had been over at the courthouse bailing out about the time Johnny started worrying. One of the white-hairs said that the judge set his bail high thinking he'd never make it, but apparently Max had the money hidden away.

It must have been well hidden or Scarlet would have grabbed it. Last he heard she was still going around telling everyone who would listen that Max had been framed.

"Forget Max," Johnny said aloud, but no one seemed to notice. The bookstore was packed. Everyone in town loved Kare, including him. He thought of her as his little fairy, but apparently so did a dozen others. Two of the quilters were crying and the old Marine was claiming he'd rip anyone apart with his bare hands if he hurt Kare.

Johnny bumped into an abandoned walker and almost stumbled into the sweet old lady who cooked at Martha Q's place. Mrs. Biggs just smiled her sad smile and said nothing, but she'd brought cookies to the worry party.

Johnny continued pacing. If it wasn't Max, then who? Johnny knew most of the folks around. Something Kare said the other night when he asked her what she was doing on her computer bothered him. She'd said she was looking for a bad needle in a haystack. She'd even told him about asking the group at the senior citizens' center if they knew anyone who fit a profile.

The profile was simple: a guy relatively new to Harmony. Someone who flew, or had access to planes. Someone trying hard to fit in. Someone with no means of support but flashing money around. He'd know computers. He'd be intelligent. Probably speak several languages. Maybe join churches or charity boards to blend in. Had no family in the area.

Johnny mentioned that Max was the only one who fit that he knew of, but Max didn't have money. At least not lately. When Scarlet was dating Johnny she still went to charity balls and the like with Max. Also, Max had a job, if drug dealer could be called a job. It didn't pay much after his supplies were locked up.

One thing bothered Johnny. In the three years Johnny had seen Max around, nothing about him said "drug dealer." He had a big townhouse over on the south side of Harmony that Scarlet had helped him redecorate twice. He always bragged about buying his clothes in Neiman Marcus. He'd disappear for weeks and show up with whole new wardrobes. He was always using foreign words, too. Only for all Johnny knew they were pig Latin and not some other language.

Now, Johnny wondered what his ex-wife and Max were doing over at his townhouse all those months when she'd say she was going over to watch a movie with her best friend. She was probably drinking wine naked.

Suddenly, he realized, he didn't care. The marriage was over. It had been for a long time. He just hadn't buried the body.

Johnny looked up, making sure Wendell wasn't around. His brother would turn him in for killing Scarlet again. He'd heard she'd talked Wendell into unlocking the townhouse door for her. After all, she had to live somewhere, and a five-hundred-thousand-dollar townhouse would have to do.

When Kare's brother showed up, Johnny figured he could add one more to the list who blamed him for her disappearance, but Drew walked over and stood beside him. He asked questions and looked worried. They were about the same height, but where Johnny was thick with muscles, Drew was slim. Right now the worry on their faces was the same.

He poured Drew a cup of coffee, and it hadn't had time to cool off enough to drink when the men walking the creek bed came in through the back. Everyone gathered around and waited, hoping for news.

Nothing. They found nothing. Johnny had heard a few guess earlier that they bet she'd crossed the creek and the same guy who mugged Beau Yates probably got her. Only the men found no sign.

Johnny turned away as anger and fear built inside him. He'd run out of places to look and hope. Not even his fairy would just fly away.

"Show me where you found her phone," Drew instructed. "It's as good a place as any to start trying to trace her steps."

Johnny nodded. It was something to do, even if it wouldn't help.

They moved outside. The day was cloudy, as if the whole world were depressed.

"When I walked up I noticed her car door wasn't closed completely." Johnny had already been over every fact with the sheriff. "There was no sign of her big bag she carries her laptop in."

Drew studied the ground.

"We couldn't find any tracks thanks to the cracked black-top out here." Johnny gave the report. "If she walked to the bookstore or the alley, she wouldn't leave prints." Johnny followed as Drew studied the ground he'd already been over ten times. "The sheriff said if she'd crossed the creek heading toward the inn we might have picked up footprints, but Kare runs over to see the captain sometimes two or three times a day."

"Why?" Drew asked, more to himself than Johnny.

But Johnny answered anyway. "I think they're friends. They're working on some kind of puzzle together. I've heard Kare mention it a few times."

Drew raised his eyebrow and turned as Millanie limped over the broken back steps. "What kind of puzzle?"

Johnny started to answer, then realized the question wasn't directed toward him.

The captain straightened as if thinking about giving only her name, rank, and serial number. Then she looked at them both and seemed to reconsider. "Kare is helping me research people new to Harmony. We're looking for a man who may be living around here and handling illegal activity on a global scale. He may be laundering money or sending it overseas to fund criminal activity."

Both men frowned, Johnny because he didn't understand and the professor because he probably did.

Johnny threw out his one guess. The only man he hated in Harmony. "Max Dewy is probably your man. I wouldn't put any crime past the man."

"He's on the list," she answered honestly. "The criminal we're looking for may have found out about our investigation and is stalking Kare. If she uncovered something, he could have gotten to her before she could pass the information along to me."

Johnny had no problem moving to the next step. "He may have found her, you're saying. He could have kidnapped her. He's probably trying to frighten anything she might know out of her right now. Maybe he's torturing her." This was the worst-case scenario yet.

"When she called, she said she had news." The captain put her hand on Johnny's arm as if to calm him. "Maybe all he wanted was her computer. If he knows she's found him, that means she had some proof and that proof would be in her computer."

"If this man has her computer, he'll never get in." Drew's words were calm. "We've played a game before of trying to break into each other's systems. She cracked mine in five minutes, but I couldn't break hers. Knowing her, Kare will have more than one password and several walls protecting her find."

Johnny looked from Drew to the captain. "What does that mean?"

Millanie spoke first. "It means that Kare is still alive. If this guy is as bad as I think he is, he might kill Kare, but not before he knows what she found. Her life won't matter to him, but her information will."

Johnny felt like his head was exploding. "He's torturing

her! We have to tear this town apart. We have to find her."
Johnny stormed across the back lot, no longer able to stand
in one place. He had to think. The thought of someone hurting Kare was more than he could stand.

At the corner of the building where an old metal vent
from the cleaners used to release exhaust, a scrap of material
seemed to be waving at him. Walking a few steps, he stared
at the scrap, then grabbed it.

Kare was helping him out. Her scarf had wiggly gold
lines in it, just like this tiny piece of silk.

Drew must have seen him pull the bit of fabric down, for
he was at Johnny's side in a blink. "It's part of one of Kare's
scarves."

Johnny nodded.

Drew turned back to Millanie. "Stay here. We'll be back."

She moved toward them. "Not on your life," she announced.
"I'm going with you."

Within twenty feet along the back alley, they found
another scrap, then another. The wind had blown trash and
old newspapers into corners, but she'd managed to hook the
light silk on broken bricks and twigs.

No one spoke. They just moved, sometimes running,
sometimes backtracking. Johnny knew they probably should
go back and tell the sheriff, but if Kare was in trouble seconds might make all the difference.

The last scrap they found was wedged between the back
door of the theater and its frame.

Drew tried to turn the handle. "This place has been
closed for a month. Someone said the old guy who ran it had
a heart attack." He pushed and pulled, but the door didn't
budge.

Frustrated, Johnny backed away and ran full-out for the
door, slamming his shoulder into it and buckling the metal
enough to pop the lock. He stepped back a moment to
recover, and Drew disappeared inside.

Though the last to step inside, Johnny knew Kare was
inside. He could feel her near.

For a few minutes they moved in silence. Then Millanie whispered, "Spread out."

The low glow of the exit signs was the only light in the place. Johnny felt his way along the back wall, careful not to move his big feet too fast or he might bump into Kare. If someone had taken her and hurt her, Johnny would find the guy if it took him the rest of his life.

"I've got her," Drew shouted from somewhere in the blackness. "I've got her," he laughed. "She's alive but tied up."

Johnny turned as Drew stepped into the red light. He was cuddling his sister in his arms. Her colorful scarves now seemed like black waves floating below her, but she was wiggling. She was alive.

Within seconds they were out into the alley and untying her. As soon as the gag came off, Kare started talking. "He's coming back. He took my computer, but he knew someone would see him if he went any farther with me. We have to get out of here. He's coming back tonight."

"Who?" Millanie asked as she worked on the knots binding Kare's hands.

"I don't know. I've seen him somewhere, but I can't place him. I know I've never touched him because when I did, pure evil sent a shock through my senses. Maybe he works around here, somewhere in the background. You know, like one of those people you see but don't see."

Drew looked up. "Hundreds work around the square. There's shops, the courthouse, the sheriff's office, the fire house, the diner, Buffalo's bar. You could have seen him anywhere. We need to get you somewhere safe fast, Kare, and then we'll worry about him."

Johnny stood. "Stay here. I'll get my truck and come pick you up. Kare can identify this guy. There's no telling what he'll do next. You're right. We have to get her away."

He broke into an all-out run. Without stopping at the bookstore, he swung around the corner of the cleaners and jumped in his truck parked by the diner. Now he had a plan, and this time he wasn't going to fail Kare.

Drew had just pulled the last rope off Kare's legs when Johnny drove into the alley. He pulled his big truck to within three feet of them, careful to block Kare from anyone who might step into the alley.

Her brother helped Kare into the backseat of the pickup while Johnny lifted Millanie into the passenger seat. With all passengers' heads down, Johnny raced out of town.

"Where to?" he asked, already heading toward his farm.

"Not your place. Everyone knows you're looking for her," Millanie said calmly. "The guy who took her could be hanging out in the bookstore right now. If he's one of those invisible people we almost know, you can bet he's taking notes."

"I agree." Johnny fought down anger. The farm was the only safe place he knew, but this time it might not be safe for Kare.

"We can't go back to the bed-and-breakfast. If he's been following Kare he'll look there right after he looks at her apartment." Millanie rose up as they headed down Lone Oak Road. "I'll tell you where to turn off. I know just the place."

As she gave Johnny directions, Drew asked Kare questions.

Kare said that she'd just stepped out of her car when someone shoved what felt like a gun against her side and grabbed her bag. At first she thought it was just a robbery, but then he said, "Is this your research?" She knew then she was dealing with the man she'd been looking for.

Curling into a ball, Kare looked tiny in the rearview mirror as she added in a whisper, "He said he'd come back after dark and untie me as long as he got what he wanted off my computer, but I knew he was lying. When he came back, if he came back, it would be to kill me. I could feel it when I touched him. The guy didn't have a soul. I've heard about people like that, but I've never met one."

Johnny saw Drew hug her to him as if his little sister were freezing.

"Turn off here," Millanie said to Johnny. She pointed to a few dirt lines that looked more like a trail than a road.

"There's nothing down this path," he argued.

"Yes, there is. My house."

Johnny didn't say a word. He just drove as Drew and his sister talked. Both seemed calm. At peace now that they were together. Johnny couldn't help but feel like each other was all they had.

After they made a few turns on a road that hadn't been used since Model T days, an old house came into view. Millanie spoke softly as Johnny slowed the truck. "We have to be careful. This guy might be involved with enough people that even if we told only a few where we are, he'd hear about it."

They all agreed.

As Johnny cut the engine, he said, "I'm telling my grandpa I found Kare and I'm running away with her to China."

"What?" everyone said at once.

Johnny shrugged. "When I was a kid he used to tell me that if I ever found the perfect girl to run away and marry her even if I had to go all the way to China. Pops will know I have her and she's safe. He'll call off the search."

"This guy might go to your place, Drew," Millanie said as she shifted in her seat.

"Before he gets near my unlocked door, my friend Luke will spot him. I'll give him a call and let him know what's going on, but I won't say a word about where we're at. I agree, the fewer people who know the better."

No one made a move to open the truck doors. They were somehow cocooned inside. Together and finally speaking honestly. No more secrets.

Johnny leaned his arm over his seat, wishing he could touch Kare.

"What did you find, Kare?" Millanie asked, no longer worrying that Drew might hear.

"Something John said got me thinking, so I began putting the pieces back together one more time and this time they fit." Kare leaned forward and put her hand on Johnny's shoulder.

"Something I said?" Johnny turned to her, wishing she were close enough for him to hold her. He settled for laying his big hand over her small one. "I doubt I'd be much help."

"Yes, you were. Don't you remember when we were talking about the characteristics of the guy I was looking for, you said that he sounded like a two-headed snake. Well, when I was working late last night I figured it out. Millanie wasn't looking for one man, she was looking for two."

"But these guys are always alone," Millanie said to no one. "That's part of their MO. They blend in."

"I found two very different men, that if I put them together, they match every point on your profile. Maybe one leads and the other is in the background, but they're both needed to make the operation work. Only one got in too deep in playing the wealthy guy in town."

"Do you know their names?" Drew asked.

"Just Max Dewy. He got greedy with the drugs, and once he was arrested his background story began to fall apart."

Johnny hit the steering wheel so hard the truck rocked. "I knew it. I swear I'm getting downright psychic."

"And the other?" Drew said, showing no interest in Johnny's newly discovered gift.

"He moved here four or five months ago and took another man's name and job. I traced him as far as Dallas and it looks like he's still working with his contacts there to send money. He's in Harmony, though, I can almost hear his footsteps, but he's using another identity."

Drew's sharp mind was following his sister's clues. "Maybe he was sent to check up on Max. From what Johnny says, the guy wasn't doing a very good job of blending in with the crowd."

Kare nodded her agreement. "I'm not positive, but I think he was the man in the parking lot and the man who kidnapped me. I never saw his face, but they were both medium build and the man in the parking lot looked nervous. So did the guy who tied me up. He kept going back over the knots again and again as if he feared he might not have gotten them right."

"There could be a third man," Drew guessed.

"No," Millanie answered. "It's too tight an operation. Having someone working for them would only open up a hole in the system." She leaned back as if suddenly tired. "I see now why so many arrows pointed to Max. He had another man handling things even when he went to jail. For some reason, he must have run out of money and started branching out into other illegal activity like drug smuggling. Maybe he spent too much of the company's money and was desperate. It was probably between robbing a bank or dealing drugs."

"With both pilots, bringing the drugs in would be easy." Kare leaned forward closer to Johnny as she spoke to Millanie.

"Getting them distributed might be a little harder," Millanie added. "These guys might have started their careers running drugs, but they'd moved up and this would be foreign territory to them."

Johnny nodded. "And of course storage was a problem until they noticed my barn. It would have been so easy. Just watch me go into town or work the back section and they'd have all day to move the drugs into my barn. Scarlet was so wrapped up with Max, she probably didn't even notice."

Drew followed his line of thinking. "When Scarlet left, Max had no reason to come around. He couldn't get to his supply. He no longer had Scarlet to tip him off to when you'd be gone."

Johnny laughed. "He must have thought Wendell was guarding the place while I was in jail, or maybe Max and Scarlet really were out of town." Johnny didn't much care. "If Max is half of a team, that means he knows who the other man is, the one who kidnapped Kare. All we have to do is get to Max and beat a name out of him."

Drew didn't argue, but the captain objected. "We keep Kare safe and let the sheriff worry about Max and his partner. I'll call her on her cell and give her all the details we know."

Millanie finally opened the passenger door to the truck.

"We're surrounded by McAllen and Matheson land. When I call Alex with facts, I'll have her smuggle us some supplies. Until she gets this mysterious partner of Max in jail, none of us are safe."

"I'll need to talk to the sheriff also. My backup files are stored in my office. She'll never find them if I don't tell her where they are." Kare let Johnny help her down from the truck, and she didn't seem to mind when he held her tight for just a moment longer than needed.

They moved to the porch of the old homestead that belonged to the first McAllens to settle the land. Building supplies and tools had been delivered and now took up half the porch. Johnny rigged up a bench for Millanie to sit on. The afternoon was cool and cloudy with the hint of rain still in the air, a lazy kind of day that calmed them all.

Millanie talked with Drew while Kare and Johnny explored around the house. He could hear the captain telling the professor how she'd already hired men to put in the plumbing and electricity so that as soon as she was able she could move in.

Kare took Johnny's hand as they walked out the back door, where a ramp had already been installed. He fought the urge to pull her close and hug her against him again. He wasn't a man who knew the right words to say. He'd thought great sex with Scarlet meant love. They'd both said they loved one another on their wedding night, and he never remembered either of them saying it again. There was always some disagreement. She was unhappy about something or complaining or in her time of the month. Looking back, he realized he'd spent most of his marriage avoiding Scarlet. No wonder she'd turned to Max.

"Walk with me, John." Kare tugged him toward the shade of tall cottonwoods planted a hundred years ago.

"You seem all right." He tried to match her steps. "I would have thought you'd be half out of your mind with panic."

She shook her head, scarves and black curls flying. "I knew you'd come. I see it in your eyes, John. I feel it when

I touch you. You care about me. Our lives are linked. They have been from the moment you walked into my office and asked for a reading even though I knew you didn't believe in lifelines."

"But you believed in me. You always did and I'm not leaving your side until this is over, Kare. I don't think my heart could stand not knowing you were safe again." He knew the words weren't right, but they were all he could think of to say.

She winked. "I had a feeling that's what you'd say."

Kare linked her arm with his and they walked toward the sun. He knew, even if he never kissed her or slept with her, he'd love her the rest of his life.

And he had a feeling Kare knew it too.

Chapter 41

BEAU LEANED BACK IN THE WICKER CHAIR ON MARTHA Q's porch and propped his boots on the railing. A song about losing love before he could get a hold on it drifted in his mind. Reason told him he should have gone back to Nashville today, but he'd stayed. Location didn't matter. Wherever he was, he'd be thinking about Lark and what he could have done or said different.

He decided he couldn't leave until he got his Gibson back, but he'd had all day to drive over to the bank a few blocks away and pull it out of the backseat of Lark's BMW. But he hadn't. He could have driven back to her parents' house earlier in the evening. She might be there. He could have picked it up and rushed away, saying he had a plane to catch. But he didn't. It was after midnight and he hadn't moved farther than the porch. He'd made a fool of himself last night. Hell, when he'd grabbed her in her office, things started going downhill and he had no way to stop the slide.

Finally, he came to one simple conclusion. She deserved better than him. He lived in the night's smoky air and she lived in sunshine. Those few nights talking in the hospital had been the only *normal* he'd ever had. Tomorrow he'd go back to Nashville and the world he knew. The world he understood. Only it would be a world without Lark.

He could buy another guitar. The Gibson wasn't worth seeing Lark crying again. He'd hurt her so bad. First by practically attacking her when he tried to show how much she meant to him and then by making a fool of himself five miles outside town. If her father saw her crying he was probably heading over to beat Beau to a pulp.

Beau didn't care. He wouldn't even fight back. He'd take the blows.

Lark said she needed time, but guessing from the way she looked last night when he saw her crying in the car, he had about twenty years to wait.

Closing his eyes, he let the music circle in his head. He'd written more here than he'd written in months. This place had always been magic to him. This was where he'd been the happiest, living with the Biggs brothers and eating off paper plates. This was where he'd also had his heart broken by a girl who said her name was Trouble. All the days in between visits to Harmony were in-between days. This was where he lived, and a part of him always would. No matter what happened in Nashville, when he fell asleep every night he'd go home to Harmony.

The sound of a car turning onto the brick road in front of the inn drew him out of his thoughts.

A powder-blue BMW pulled silently into the drive.

Beau didn't move. Part of him feared if he did, the dream he was having might end. He watched through half-closed eyes as Lark stepped out of the car. She pulled his Gibson, along with a bag, from her passenger seat and walked slowly toward the porch. With her hair tied back and wearing jeans, she almost looked sixteen again.

He knew the second she spotted him on the porch. She froze for a blink as if she might turn and run, and then she straightened her shoulders and marched toward him like an executioner knowing he had to pull the switch.

He lowered his boots off the railing as she stepped on the porch. "Evening, Trouble," he said in a low voice. Somehow the nickname fit her tonight.

She set the small leather bag down by the steps as she handed him his guitar. "I figured you'd be up, so I drove over."

He stood slowly, not wanting to do anything to frighten her. He'd done enough of that lately. "You had enough time to think things over?"

"Yes," she said, folding her arms, making it plain that he might not like what she was about to say.

Beau leaned back against the railing, folding his arms to keep from reaching for her. "I don't guess saying I'm sorry for last night would help. You haven't forgiven me for the first mistake I made. I was a fool for thinking I wanted to walk to town last night with a storm coming in. If Deputy Gentry hadn't picked me up I'd probably still be out there. I've made a mess of what we might have had."

"I agree," she said too fast.

He could barely see her face in the low glow of the parlor lamp shining through the window. She didn't look like she was about to cry, so he guessed that was an improvement, but he wasn't sure her agreeing with him was a positive thing.

"Thank you for sitting up with me at the hospital, and I enjoyed meeting your parents." He knew he should stop while he was ahead, but he wanted to at least try to part as friends. "You mean a great deal to me, Lark, and I'd do anything if we could go back to being friends." He saw her bringing the guitar as a start, but she might see it as an ending.

Lark reached down and lifted the leather bag. "Put your arm on the railing."

"What?"

"Put your forearm on the railing. I want to have a little talk with you, but I don't want to worry about you grabbing me again."

"All right." He thought of swearing he wouldn't touch her, but maybe she needed proof. "I won't move from this spot."

"I plan to make sure." She pulled a few short leather straps from the bag and buckled his arm to the railing. "Now the other one," she whispered.

She was so close he could smell her, that wonderful fresh fragrance he'd always loved. She would always remind him of summertime and midnight drives. If he could just pull her close, maybe one kiss could change her mind. He'd let her know how he felt.

No, that was what got him in trouble to start with. He rested his other arm from elbow to hand on the railing and she strapped him to the wood.

"Now. You've got me just where you want me, Lark. I can't move so you can have your say. I guess my promise wasn't good enough." Whatever she told him, no matter how much she yelled or screamed, he'd give her the chance to tell him off. She deserved it.

Lark stepped a few feet away and smiled. "My father said you're like a wild horse, Beau, that's never been broke. You don't know how to act or even know how to love a woman. He says some men like you never learn."

Beau started to get a little worried about what else she might have in the bag. He'd heard of people who used whips and he wanted no part of that, but he didn't seem to have much choice in the matter right now. The way his luck was running she probably had a Taser gun. He twisted his hand, but his fingers couldn't reach the buckles holding his arms in place.

This was not a good idea and he'd stepped right into it.

Maybe he didn't know Lark at all. Maybe she was about to torture him. She thought she'd get back at every guy in the world who'd done a woman wrong. "Untie me," he said calmly. "We'll talk. I won't come near you."

"Not a chance."

Her smile was sexy as hell but her eyes looked a bit wicked in the dim light.

He heard the front door open. Martha Q waddled out in her fluffy Halloween-orange robe and slippers. His heart slowed. Finally, the cavalry to the rescue. The old lady would put a stop to whatever Lark had planned.

"Oh," Martha Q said. "Sorry, I thought there might be some of those crazy fans hanging around trying to peek in the windows. Evening, Lark."

"Evening, Mrs. Patterson." Lark, looking completely innocent, smiled at Martha Q. "I hope to see you at the bank Friday for the ladies' annual luncheon."

"Of course. Wouldn't miss it." Martha Q wiggled her eyebrows at Beau as she started backing into the house. "Good night."

"Wait!" Beau yelled. "Can't you see I'm tied up? Help me out. Untie me, Martha Q. There's no telling what this woman is planning to do to me."

Martha Q grinned so big her lips disappeared. "Been there, done that," she chimed as she crossed back into the house. "Have fun, kids, and Beau, try not to wake the other guests with your screams."

Beau swore. The whole world had gone crazy tonight. Correction, half the world. His buddy Border Biggs was right; women held all the cards and men didn't even know the rules to the game.

"Untie me," he ordered. "This isn't funny, Trouble."

"Or what?" She faced him, her hands on her hips.

"Or I'll have you arrested for kidnapping."

She laughed. "I didn't kidnap you, Beau, you're on the front porch right where I found you. You let me strap your arms down. No one would believe I held you down and tied you up against your will."

She had a point. Only an idiot would get in this mess. He tried to relax. "All right. I'm here. I'm listening. Say what you came to say. Let's get this over with."

She walked the few feet to stand in front of him. "Women don't like to be handled, or shoved into corners, or even kissed when they're not ready. They like to be touched gently." She moved her fingers along his shoulder and lightly over his throat.

Beau didn't move. He didn't even breathe.

She leaned closer and began unbuttoning his shirt, touching his chest as she moved slowly down. Her touch was a velvet agony, warming his skin.

"Stop this, Trouble," he said without anger. "What do you think you're doing, torturing me?" Her touch felt so good, but he hated not being able to return the feeling.

Her hand raked across his chest and he realized that was exactly what she was doing. Pure torment. She pulled his shirt open and kissed where his heart pounded. Her mouth moved over him, slowly kissing, tasting, even biting lightly. Again and again she almost kissed him, and then she'd pull away and start torturing again. She delved her fingers into his hair as she turned his head so she could trail kisses down his throat. Her body leaned into him. He'd never been so turned on. He'd never wanted a woman more. But not any woman, he wanted Lark.

Beau had no idea if he was in heaven or hell, but he wasn't leaving.

"Untie me," he whispered. "I want to touch you, too."

"No." She laughed. "I'm not finished." She tugged his shirttail, freeing it from his trousers so she could circle around and rake her fingernails lightly along his back. Just when he wanted to beg her to stop, she'd press against him until he could feel her soft breasts on his chest. Then all he could think of was begging her to continue.

"Loving is a dance, Beau." She whispered the words so low against his ear he felt them more than heard them. "You have the music in your head. All you need to do is learn the steps."

He was going mad with need, but her fingers kept brushing over him and her lips kept almost kissing him. His senses were overloading. The cool of the night and the warmth of her touch. The feel of her breath against his throat, the warmth of her hands sliding over his hot skin.

Her slim leg pushed between his and Beau's knees almost buckled.

He closed his eyes and rocked with her tender advance. "Tell me what you want, Trouble. Tell me why you're doing this."

She moved her body against his.

"Tell me," he whispered as he strained against the leather, wanting to press closer as she pulled a breath away.

"This is us, Beau. Me and you. We're not rushing what's between us. I won't let you. If we're going to be together, we're going to go slow. We're going to enjoy every step. This isn't one of your one-night romances. It never has been. I plan on driving you crazy for the rest of your life."

"If you'll untie me, I'll take you all the way, right now."

She pressed against his body, showing him how perfectly they'd fit together. "I know," she whispered. "That's why I'm leaving you here just like this." Her fingers ran down his chest to his belt buckle. "If you're interested in a real relationship, meet me at dawn at the diner. No public displays, Beau. No dark corners. No rush through passion." She finally kissed his mouth. One mind-blowing kiss before she pulled away. "But, in private, we'll write our own rules. We'll race the night until we're too exhausted to move."

One more long, hot, kiss. One last smile as she straightened.

"No," he shouted as she rushed down the steps. "Don't leave me like this. Come back."

She didn't turn around. She simply climbed into her car and drove away.

He thought about yelling until someone came. He thought about how good she'd felt against him. She'd driven him so insane he couldn't wait to try her plan.

About four in the morning he even decided that Lark's torture was better than full-out sex with any other woman.

For a while he concluded she hated him and had thought of the worst thing she could do to him short of killing him. Then he remembered she was feeding him breakfast. If she'd been showing him the preview of their loving, he wasn't sure his heart could take the real thing.

About six the paperboy tossed a paper on the porch, acting like he didn't notice Beau sleeping standing up against the railing.

A half hour later Martha Q came out and untied him.

"Don't say a word," he grumbled.

"I won't. I didn't see a thing. 'Course, if I had seen something it would have been a far more interesting scene than anything on late TV. Next time I'll leave the porch light on."

"There is not going to be a next time, and what part of 'Don't say a word' did you not understand, Martha Q?"

"Shut up or I'll tie you back up and leave you to the fans. Did you learn your lesson, Beau?"

"What lesson?" All he knew for sure was that the rest of his dreams till they put him in his coffin would be about Lark touching him.

Martha Q looked flustered. "That she may love you, but you got to be the man she needs you to be."

Rubbing his arms, he managed to say, "Oh, that lesson," as if he'd thought of it.

Martha Q shook her head. "I can see she may have to repeat herself to get you to understand. I swear, if they can make mosquito spray for tiny insects with their tiny brains, the same can should work on men."

Beau didn't have time to argue with Martha Q. "I need a pot of coffee and a shower if I'm going to meet Lark before dawn. I've got a feeling she's one woman I'll never keep waiting."

As he rushed away he caught a glimpse of Martha Q tucking the leather straps in her jogging pants pocket.

Chapter 42

❦

BEAU WALKED INTO THE BLUE MOON DINER AS DAWN sliced through the windows and lit the place up in golden hues. A few of the tables were occupied by people who looked like they'd been awake all night, but most were the early risers of the world. A group Beau had never trusted.

Lark, dressed in her banking best, sat at the center table where sunshine washed over her. She was so beautiful. All prim and proper. No one in the place would suspect she'd been a cute little dominatrix-in-training last night. He loved the different views of her and had a feeling there were many more to discover.

Beau was aware that everyone in the place watched him walk toward her table. When he sat down, the volume dropped by half. This wasn't going to be what he hoped for, a private conversation.

"Morning, Miss Powers," he said as he slid in across from Lark. "Thank you for meeting with me so early."

"You're welcome, Mr. Yates." Her smile was no longer than a blink.

Most of the heads who'd been watching turned back to

their breakfast. The few still staring could no longer hear as conversations around the room picked up. They might have been interested in the gossip of Beau Yates and one of the Powers girls meeting, but if it was business, it was none of theirs.

Beau opened the menu that hadn't changed in years and turned over the coffee cup already on the table. At least this was his territory. He was comfortable here; she looked like she wasn't.

The waitress, twice his age, winked at him when she poured his coffee, then giggled when Beau winked back.

Lark looked like she was trying to pout, but her eyes were dancing with laughter. "You're one good-looking man, Beau Yates. When you clean up and put on that black hat you can stop a woman's heart. I'm surprised women don't just run up and kiss you."

He shrugged. "It's the hat."

"That's what my father said," she agreed.

With the menu in front of him to hide his blush, Beau asked casually, "With the storm last night, I hope you slept well, Miss Powers."

"There was no storm last night. And I didn't sleep at all, thanks to you."

"Really, I could have sworn there was quite a storm blowing through." Beau looked up at her. He had no trouble reading her thoughts. The memory of the way she'd touched him came back so strong he swore he could feel her fingernails on his skin even now.

"Your father was right about calling you Trouble, Lark. I have a feeling I'm going to have a great many sleepless nights while we're together."

She played with her utensils as if considering them as weapons. "Are we together, Beau? I haven't heard the rumor."

He went back to reading the menu, his voice so low no one but Lark could have heard it. "We're together, Trouble, but don't get confused. This is not my surrender breakfast. This is simply a peace negotiation, and I think we've talked enough about your father for today, so leave him out of this discussion."

"All right. If this is a negotiation, what do you want?"

"I want you to stop being afraid of me." He began what he'd thought about saying all night. "You had no reason to be afraid when we were seventeen and you don't now. And, in answer to your comment about you not thinking we had *that* kind of thing going, as far as I'm concerned we always have and we do right now."

He studied her, wishing he could understand her. "In light of recent events, maybe I'm the one who should be afraid of you. Not that I'm complaining, but I think it was you who attacked me last night."

The waitress interrupted the negotiations. She took their order and walked away while Beau studied his very own Trouble. "What do you want, Lark?"

He half expected her to say that she wanted him to move a few tables down, but she didn't. She straightened. Her world was columns and numbers; she understood this kind of talk. She was in her element.

"I'd like you to come to dinner with my folks every time you are in town for a few days. I want you to hold me like you used to when we went driving. I'd like to fall in love with you slowly, Beau, one kiss at a time. I'm not looking for a hurricane; I'd prefer a gentle rain."

He shook his head. "I can't do that, Trouble. I'd like going to dinner with your folks now and then, and holding you sounds great, but I can't fall in love with you slowly. Nothing in my life has ever come easy, and I don't figure love will."

She looked like she might cry. "You can't or won't?"

He knew the third thing she'd asked for was a deal-breaker. She'd walk away if he didn't give her the kind of love she wanted and needed. "I can't fall in love with you slowly, honey. I'm already in love with you. I think I always have been. I may have to learn how to show you, but I've already taken the fall. How could you think otherwise? Half the songs I write are about you."

To his surprise tears rolled down her beautiful face. He knew he was pushing the line she'd drawn, but he reached across the table and took her hand. "I've never had a real girlfriend and I've never had a love. You may have to knock some sense into me now and then, but I promise I'll try. We may live in two different worlds, but I swear, my heart only beats when you're near."

She smiled and nodded. "Me too," she said, pulling her hand back. "I've been thinking that you have a wild side, Beau, and maybe, if we scheduled it and I knew it was coming, I wouldn't mind it so much."

He thought of telling her that scheduling a wild side didn't make sense, but he loved that she was trying to meet him halfway. He just wanted to love her and he didn't much care about the time or the place.

Beau couldn't stand being on stage any longer. The need to touch her was too great. "Are you hungry?"

"No," she answered.

He dropped a twenty on the table and stood. This time when he offered his hand she took it, and they walked out with everyone in the place staring.

Without a word he climbed into her car and drove back to the bed-and-breakfast. They ordered coffee and ran upstairs to the second-story study. There, with the curtains drawn, they sat on a small couch in the half light. She'd pulled off her shoes and dress jacket. He opened his arms and let her come to him.

He just held her for a long while, and then they talked in whispers. As time passed silently he touched her gently, rationing light kisses now and then.

About nine Mrs. Biggs brought up fresh coffee and apple-cinnamon bread. Even as they ate, they touched each other. He decided he could get used to this easy kind of loving.

Beau was learning her slowly. What she liked. How she wanted to be touched. As they cuddled, a song about gentle rain came to his mind. Someday, when loving came easy for them, he'd sing it to her. They'd start with these gentle touches and, who knows, they might end with them in sixty or seventy years, but in between there would be fire and wild nights to remember, to keep them warm.

At ten, her cell phone rang for the fourth time and she finally picked it up. After a short conversation, she dropped the phone into her purse and stood. "I have to get to the bank. Major things are happening there today. It seems one of our loan officers didn't report to work and his files are not in order."

"You'll meet me for lunch?" he asked.

"At one," she answered as they split the last bit of the bread. "I'll meet you at the diner. Same table."

"I'll be there," he said, then kissed her one quick time before following her down the stairs.

They didn't talk as he drove her to the bank, but when he stopped at the side door, she leaned over and kissed his cheek. "Thanks for this morning, Beau. It was nice."

"It can get a lot better than nice."

Her laughter was nervous, but her eyes darkened slightly with excitement. No fear. He was winning her over.

Three hours later Beau was almost late to lunch because he'd been writing. He rushed to the diner and ordered a couple of Cokes while he waited. After she'd left, he'd thought about how easy it would be to make Harmony his base. He could fly back and forth a few days a month, maybe even stay awhile when he wasn't touring. Maybe she could come to him on weekends?

At ten after one, she hurried in. "I'm sorry I'm late, but I got the problem at the bank solved and told everyone I was taking the rest of the afternoon off." She gulped down a breath. "The staff was all shocked, but no one said a word."

"You think they'll call your daddy?"

"No, but if he finds out, he'll call. I haven't missed an hour of work since I started. I've got weeks of vacation piled up."

Beau grinned. "I got a few ideas of how you might want to spend it."

They ordered hamburgers and talked while they waited. He couldn't stop staring at her. He was in a relationship. He had someone who would notice if he didn't show up. Someone worried about him, someone cared.

"You hungry?" he finally asked when she finished telling him about this guy at the bank who'd been embezzling.

"No," she answered. "Want to go back to the bed-and-breakfast? Maybe we could take a nap."

He stood so quickly his chair tumbled over. "Let's go. A nap sounds great." He dropped two twenties on the table and took her hand. "This is getting to be a habit."

For the second time everyone in the diner watched them leave.

No one was around a few minutes later when they climbed the stairs to his room. Beau locked the door while she pulled off her jacket and shoes. Then, as if she were perched on the edge of a cliff, she stood next to the bed staring at it.

Beau tossed his hat and tugged off his boots as he watched her. When she hadn't moved by the time he stood at her side, he took her hand. "We can go back to the study if you'd feel more comfortable."

"No. I want to be with just you."

He picked up his guitar and sat at the foot of the bed. "How about I sing you to sleep?"

As he played with the strings, she carefully lowered herself among the pillows and stretched her feet until they brushed against his leg. He sang his songs low, loving that she closed her eyes and breathed them in like air.

After a while, her foot relaxed against his thigh and her breathing slowed in time to the music. He sang one last song, then lowered his guitar and spread out beside her. His arm rested lightly across her waist, where he could feel her breathing as he went to sleep next to her.

He'd give her time to fall in love, but he'd never give her up. She'd always hold his heart.

Chapter 43

MILLANIE WOKE TO THE SOUNDS OF BIRDS. FOR A MOMENT she didn't know where she was. If the idea wasn't impossible, she might consider that she'd been wrapped on both sides in a huge taco shell.

Slowly, she opened her eyes a bit more. An old mattress ran up the sides of the bed of Johnny's pickup. She was cuddled amid blankets in the middle with her leg in a sling tied down on either side of the truck by bungee cords.

Slowly, the memory came back. The sheriff's husband had driven out to the old homestead after dark and delivered mattresses from the fire station along with camping equipment. Somehow, while she and Kare put together sandwiches, the men decided Millanie couldn't just sleep on the floor of the old house. She might hurt her leg and with the swelling, they needed to figure out how to elevate it.

Looking down at what the men came up with, Millanie rolled her eyes. They'd rigged up a bed and a sling in the pickup, making her feel very much like a cheap float in a small-town Halloween parade. She was so tired by the time Drew lifted her up she hadn't protested. In fact, she was asleep before Kare finished covering her up.

Now, in the early light she smiled at the plan. The bed was safe and warm, and her leg was quite comfortable raised in the sling. Of course, if the bad guys found them, she'd be the last one killed because they'd think that she was already being tortured.

"Morning, Millie," a familiar voice whispered.

She twisted her head enough to see the trousers of her professor. "Morning." He must have spent the night sitting in the front of the pickup watching over her. "Move down here so I can see you. I'm kind of tied into one place."

He carefully moved down, barely fitting in the space next to her.

"You must be freezing." She flipped one of her blankets over him.

"No, after the adrenaline rush yesterday, I think we were all exhausted. I was too tired to be cold."

He kissed her lightly on the mouth. "The few times I woke up all I had to do was think of you sleeping a few feet away and I warmed right up." He combed his long fingers through her hair. "You're so beautiful in the dawn light."

She brushed his sand-colored stubble. "Did you mean it when you said you haven't been with a woman in five years?"

"Yes, but I'm not interested in sex if you just feel sorry for me." He grinned. "Well, not too interested. If you're offering, I'm not turning you down."

"I'm not offering." She paused just long enough to keep him guessing. "At least not more than once or twice."

"You're in luck. I'm available both times or right now if you're in the mood."

She giggled. "We're not doing it in the back of a pickup with my leg in a sling and your sister probably watching from the upstairs window. I had something far more romantic and comfortable in mind."

"All right, Millie, but I'm telling you I think I may have reached the limit of my shelf life. I could go bad at any moment."

"I'll take my chances."

He fell backward, bumping his head on the side of the pickup. The old rusty truck made a dull gong sound. She laughed until she cried.

Before they could settle back into being adults, Johnny called from the porch. "You two want some coffee? I figured out how to boil a pot in the fireplace. It smells about ready."

Millanie raised her head and saw the big farmer, bare-footed and bare-chested, rummaging through the boxes of supplies Hank Matheson had delivered.

"I found the flashlights"—Johnny stood, showing them off as the sun sparkled across the porch—"and the bug spray."

"Any food to go with the coffee?" she yelled back.

"Health food bars and Baby Ruths. I'll sacrifice myself and eat the bad-for-you candy bars and you guys can have the healthy food." He hunted a little more and yelled, "Oh, I found some apples. Like we don't have enough on the tree fifty yards away."

Drew rose beside her and opened his mouth to say something, but before his words were out, Kare stepped out on the porch wearing nothing but Johnny's shirt. Her wild curly hair was bouncing to her waist.

Millanie almost laughed at the anger in Kare's big brother's face, but before he could say anything, Millanie jabbed him in the chest and yelled toward the others, "Drew loves apples."

He frowned at her, but his anger had disappeared. "I don't," he whispered.

She rested her hand on his heart and asked, "Help me out of this pickup bed. Before you make your sister mad by treating her like a kid."

"I would never—" He stopped. "You're right. She's twenty-four."

"Remember that, Drew."

He nodded, still frowning.

By the time Drew got Millanie down from the truck, Kare had changed into her own clothes but Drew's mood hadn't brightened. While he moved to his sister, Millanie slowed, taking in the beauty of her place. Her place, she repeated, with a million-dollar sunrise and a sky that doubled its beauty. Here she could heal. She could rest. She could put the pieces of her life together. She'd finally found home base.

In reality she might be limping toward the house, but in her mind she was twirling around with her hands outstretched.

"You all right, Millie?" Drew asked as he waited to help her up the porch steps.

"I'm wonderful." As his hand circled her waist, she leaned close and kissed him.

When she pulled away, Drew smiled and whispered, "Yes, you are," before Johnny and Kare invaded, bringing apples and laughter of their own.

After they ate, Kare helped Millanie to the new half-finished bathroom. When she'd called in different cousins to do the needed work, she'd insisted the bathroom and plumbing be a first priority. Electricity might take a few weeks to get, but as soon as she had water and the windows fixed, she wanted to spend her nights out here. From the looks of it, building supplies were stored in every room. The credit card she'd left at the lumberyard must be wearing out.

Though the tiny bathroom window was covered by a towel, they heard the two men talking on the porch as Millanie tried to wash her face.

"I thought I told you to stay away from my sister." Drew's voice didn't sound friendly, but at least he wasn't yelling.

Johnny's low tone came through the window loud and clear. "I'm afraid I can't do that, Professor. I'm crazy about her."

Millanie moved to the side of the window where she could see through the curtain, and Kare did the same.

"So you're not leaving?" Drew complained. "You're the

one with a truck. No one's looking for you. We'll be all right here. You probably need to go farm. Aren't farmers supposed to work from sunup to sundown? Looks like you're already running late."

Johnny fisted his big hands. "I'm not leaving Kare, Professor. Not now, not ever, if I have anything to say about it. But feel free to go back to your books and research. Nobody's looking for you either. I wouldn't mind taking you back to your Jeep."

"Well, you don't need to do that, Johnny. She's my sister, I'll look after her, and by the way, Kare's got better sense than to get involved with you no matter how crazy you claim you are about her."

Millanie choked down a laugh. She couldn't tell if Drew was serious or just playing around. She'd never heard the man say a bad word to anyone. It was almost as if they were putting on a show, but for who?

The answer to her question stood one foot away.

Kare leaned her head out the window and yelled, "Stop that right now, Andrew Cunningham." She giggled as if realizing she sounded just like a mother. "For once I don't need a big brother, I just need a brother. I'm crazy about Johnny too, you know, so quit pestering my new boyfriend. I've seen the future and I'm going to marry him Christmas Eve."

Both women watched from the window as the two men faced each other.

Drew took off the glasses he'd just cleaned and put on. "Are you telling me I'm going to have to put up with a farmer for a brother-in-law?" His question was for Kare, but he never stopped staring at Johnny as he said the words.

"You think you got it bad," Johnny answered back. "I've got to put up with a professor. We've never had one of them in the family. I don't know how the relatives will take it."

Kare squealed again.

Both men laughed and turned to the window as Millanie tugged the towel down. Kare had hidden her face with her hands, obviously fearing the worst. Now her big brown eyes peeked out between her fingers as she leaned her head out.

Johnny stomped across the porch and looked up at her. "You can't know we're getting married Christmas, Kare. I haven't even asked you yet. But after last night—"

"What happened last night?" Drew played his part.

Both Kare and Johnny said "Nothing" so fast it had to be a lie.

Millanie didn't say a word as she watched the men move to the big living area. Suddenly, they were both laughing. She and Kare joined them a few minutes later.

The men resumed frowning at each other as soon as Kare appeared. She patted on each as if she now bore the great burden of patching things up between the two men.

"Let's have some coffee." Millanie tried to break the silence as Kare poured.

Drew took a drink and coughed. "This coffee tastes terrible. It's full of grounds."

Johnny took a drink and shrugged. "Just drink it with your teeth closed. That'll catch most of the grounds. There's not a Starbucks around the corner out in the country, Professor."

Millanie elected to have water for breakfast. Coffee that didn't even slosh in the paper cup seemed a little strong. Funny, they were all tired and dirty and probably dying for a good meal, but she felt almost like they were a family.

Johnny suggested that since everyone was stuck here until the bad guys were caught, they might as well work on the place. Kare got all excited about drawing up plans. They all went to work.

Millanie was amazed at how good Drew was with his hands. She'd guessed that he wouldn't know how to hammer a nail, but he not only worked but thought of more efficient ways to do things. Every time she stood, one of the three walked by and told her to sit like she was the family dog. Finally, the captain showed her well-developed temper and ordered them all to stop.

From then on they flooded her with chores she could do sitting down. Johnny even rigged her up a table between two folding chairs Hank had brought.

Millie gave in and did her work from a stool with her leg propped up on a paint can.

Two hours later, Hank delivered real coffee and breakfast burritos. While they ate he gave the news. Everyone in town thought Johnny and Kare had run off, except Scarlet, who claimed the quickie divorce she'd decided to get online wouldn't be final until Wednesday. She wanted the sheriff to arrest him for bigamy. Apparently, she didn't want Johnny, but she didn't want anyone else to have him either.

Hank explained in great detail how Max had just proposed to Scarlet a few minutes before the sheriff took him in for questioning. He'd shoved a huge diamond ring on her finger about the time Alex clicked the handcuffs.

Millanie tried to think positive. "If he gives up the other guy's name, we could be back at Martha Q's for lunch." She couldn't imagine a man like Max Dewy confessing to any crimes, but he might point the finger at someone else.

Hank shook his head. "I don't think it will be that easy. Whoever kidnapped Kare is probably already out of the state. We found your laptop broken against the back door of the bookstore this morning. If he got into your files and found what he was looking for, he's running. If he couldn't get in, he must have given up but he's probably still running. If he can fly a plane, there's no way to stop him."

Drew had been pacing. He stopped and faced them all. "The answer for now is we all stay here. At least until we know something."

"I need to get in and collect my backup drive," Kare cried. "Alex said she couldn't find it in my office."

"It's too dangerous," both Drew and Johnny said at the same time, then nodded at each other.

Millanie didn't comment. She tended to agree with Kare. The danger might be worth the risk. If her files got into the wrong hands, it would do a great deal of damage.

Hank added a strong argument. "If Alex couldn't find your secret place, Kare, and you told her where to look, the man in league with Max Dewy won't have a chance. Mr. Hatcher is within sight of your door all day and Alex is having any deputy leaving the office drive by the bookstore. Your files are far safer in your office than they would be out here."

Kare nodded, but Millanie doubted she believed him. Highly trained researchers tend to protect their files with their lives. She'd once seen a programmer from one of the embassies tape a flash drive to his chest so he'd have all his files on him if a hurricane took out the island he'd been stationed on.

"Let's get back to work." Kare faked a smile. "If we can't go back to town, we might as well fix up the place."

Hank helped unload the supplies Millanie had called in when they'd started work this morning. They had no electricity, but Hank brought a generator for the power tools and wood for framing out rough beds for the mattresses.

"We'll have two beds finished by supper." Drew frowned at Johnny. "You two are sleeping in separate beds in separate rooms until Christmas Eve."

Johnny looked innocent. "Of course, Professor, and I'll be checking on you and Millanie several times during the night to make sure you don't need something out there all alone."

Drew frowned, mumbled an oath in Latin, and moved away.

Johnny turned to Millanie. "Is he ever in a good mood?"

"I never saw him in a bad mood until you came along." She tried her best to look serious. "It might help if you stopped patting on Kare every time she walks by."

"I don't. She's the one patting on me," he answered. "And I'm not telling her to stop no matter how much steam comes out of her brother's ears."

Millanie spent the next hour watching, and Johnny was right. Kare was doing all the patting and the farmer didn't seem to mind a bit. The little woman loved helping. Once the men passed carrying several long boards inside. Kare hung on to the middle of the stack, her feet walking on air. When Johnny put glass in the upstairs windows, she followed, painting flowers along the bottom of each pane. Her easy laughter and excitement made the workflow easy, and Millanie was amazed how fast the work went.

Midafternoon everyone voted to take a break. While Kare showed Millanie some of the work they'd done inside, she whispered, "I'm going after my files tonight. Are you with me or against me?"

Millanie knew it would do no good to argue, but she might be able to keep Kare out of trouble if she went along. "I'm with you. You get the pickup keys and drive. I'll ride shotgun."

Kare laughed. "Aye-aye, Captain. We'll leave about midnight. I've been thinking I could come out and tell Drew there is a big bug in my room. When he goes in the house, we pull out. I've got a key to the bookstore. We can be in and out of my office in three minutes."

"Sounds like a plan." Millanie weighed the danger. No one would be expecting them. With the sheriff's offices so close, a deputy could probably be there within minutes. Max Dewy's partner was probably out of the country by now. She had a Glock for backup and knew how to use it. Her bad leg wouldn't matter. She'd stay in the car in sight of the back door while Kare ran in and out. What could go wrong?

What could go wrong?

Chapter 44

NIGHT SPREAD ACROSS OPEN COUNTRY SLOWLY. DREW watched the sun disappear, thinking how he was tired and sore and worried but, all in all, it had been the best day of his life. He needed to be home. After three years of writing, a publishing house finally was giving serious consideration to his idea for a series of middle-grade novels about early Texas pioneers. They'd loved the first three stories he'd sent them and wanted at least three more as fast as possible.

But, for the first time in years, people and their problems and needs and desires were getting in the way. Even though he worried about Kare, he loved the feeling that he was finally stepping back into life. Messy as it was with doubts and fears, it felt so good.

Millanie stepped on the porch. "Getting cabin fever?"

He smiled at her. "I live in a cabin, remember? What I'm wondering is how you manage to look so good after sleeping in a pickup last night and working all day."

"Your glasses must be dirty." She tugged them off him and cleaned them with her shirttail, something she'd seen him do a dozen times. "I need a change of clothes, a hot shower, and something to eat besides health bars and tacos."

Johnny must have turned on one of the battery-powered lamps Hank brought out because a soft yellow light flooded the porch, making the new boards glow golden. Millanie lowered herself slowly onto the box that had become her bench.

Drew didn't have to ask if her leg hurt; he knew it did. They'd all tried to baby her, but the strong captain wouldn't allow it.

"I can't believe Hank only brought out tacos for supper. Couldn't he have added a few salads to the order the farmer turned in?" Millanie complained. "Johnny ate a dozen and we'll still have enough left for breakfast."

Millanie leaned back against the house. "I miss Martha Q. Well, not her so much as her food and the bed at the inn and the soft pillows. The first thing I plan to do when I get back is stand in the shower for an hour."

"Hank said he'd come out as soon as he has news. Who knows, we could be back at the inn before bedtime. Johnny and I talked about relocating, but if we did, we'd be exposed if only for a short time. The good thing is here no one can come up or down that road without us knowing it. We're safe here and despite the menu, I can think of no other place I'd rather be than with you right now."

He knelt in front of her. "I like being here knowing you and Kare are safe, but it's hard not touching you."

She laughed. "I was thinking the same thing. Besides the obvious reason we can't make love, it seems we have a chaperone."

"I'm a little old for a chaperone." He ran his hand along the brace over her leg. "You'll heal, Millie, and while you do I'd like to be right beside you. The scars don't frighten me."

"What if I limp? What if I'm never steady on this leg?"

"How about we make a pact to be totally honest with each other from now on?"

She nodded.

"I mean about everything, Millie."

"I promise." She smiled as if she'd just granted him a wish.

"Then I'm telling you true. If you limp, I'll walk closer. Just promise me you'll give us a shot." He thought of all he'd like to say to her, but now wasn't the right time. "Honestly, Millie, I had to work hard all day to keep from touching you." He leaned close, almost brushing her ear. "I kept remembering the feel of your breast in my hand and the lovely way you arch your back when your body is hungry and warm with need."

Johnny walked around the house with his flashlight, shattering their one private moment. "Well, it's dark," the big guy said. "I don't know about you two, but I'm going to bed." He shined the light in Drew's eyes. "That's what farmers do. We go to bed when it gets dark. Besides, tonight without much electricity we don't have any choice. Kare and I will take the upstairs. Millanie, you've got the big bed downstairs, and, Professor, looks like you got the cot in the kitchen."

"No way." Drew stood. "I'm sleeping upstairs. Kare will take the kitchen bed. You two aren't sleeping on the same floor until Christmas Eve as far as I'm concerned."

"But we're engaged." Johnny grumbled, then stomped across the porch. "I should have found a little fairy fortune-teller who didn't have a big brother. I'll go up and tell her the bad news."

When they heard him storming the stairs, Millanie laughed. "Being a little hard on the guy, aren't you?"

"I just don't want him taking advantage of my sister. She may be twenty-four but she doesn't have a lot of experience in this world."

"They just want to be together. Which is pretty much what we want. By torturing him, you're also pulling us apart."

Drew had to touch her. In the shadows he could barely see her. "Is that what you want, Millie, for us to be together? It seems like you spend most of your time pushing me away." He moved his hands over her shoulders. "What do you want, my brave Millie?"

"I want us to be honest and open with each other. So I'll only tell the truth. I want you in my life, but I should warn you, trust and love won't come easy for me."

Before Drew could promise to try, a huge rattling shook the house as breaking boards sounded above them.

He stood, thinking something must have hit the house. Maybe part of the roof had fallen in. Maybe Johnny had tumbled down the stairs. Drew wanted to run in, but he couldn't leave Millie. Offering his arm, he supported her as she pulled to her feet and they moved inside together.

"Are you all right, Kare?" Drew called up the stairs.

He was halfway up when he heard his sister's laughter and stopped climbing.

"I'm fine, Drew. I'll be down in a minute."

"What happened?" he demanded, fearing she might be hurt.

Johnny swore and said in a voice that echoed off the walls of the little house, "One of the beds broke, Professor, and I'm sure it was the one you hammered together."

Kare was still giggling as she floated down the stairs. "Looks like you men are going to have to flip for who sleeps on the floor. I'm glad I've got my bed in the kitchen."

Johnny came down frowning. His boots were off and his hair a mess. One side of his shirt was tucked out of his jeans. "Lucky we tested the beds, Professor. One of us could have been hurt falling out of a tumbling bed in the dark."

Drew backed down the stairs. "Johnny, I told you to stay away from my sister."

"And I told you I can't do that." He rubbed his head. "I might consider getting sturdier furniture once we're married, though. I didn't know she likes to jump on the bed. She said it was fun, but I don't agree."

"I've always jumped on the bed," Kare yelled from the kitchen. "It's like you're flying for a moment."

Drew almost felt sorry for the farmer. He slapped him on the shoulder before heading upstairs. "Good luck. She probably jumps off couches, too."

Johnny shrugged. "I have to admit it was fun until I hit the ceiling and came down on a bed that crumbled."

"You hit my ceiling?" Millie stepped into the fight.

Johnny shook bits of the ceiling out of his hair. "It didn't do much damage and I'm thinking that would be a good spot for a ceiling fan anyway."

Millie rolled her eyes, and Drew laughed, deciding he was going to love having the farmer in the family. A few minutes later with everyone settled in their own beds, they all did the Waltons thing of saying good night to everyone. It probably wasn't ten o'clock, but they were too tired to stay up.

Chapter 45

"I HEAR JOHNNY SNORING," KARE WHISPERED AS MILLANIE tried to put on her brace by the light of a flashlight.

"I'm ready." Millanie shoved her Glock in her bag and slung it across her body. "You've got the keys?"

"Johnny left his in the pickup and I've got the bookstore keys in my pocket." She helped Millanie stand and handed her the cane. Slowly, and silently, they moved toward the truck.

"I figure five minutes to the bookstore once we hit the main road. I can be in and out of the store with my backup files in hand within two, maybe three minutes. Then back here. The boys won't even know we're gone and I'll be able to sleep knowing the files are safe."

Millanie guessed Kare kept talking because she was nervous, so she didn't tell her to be quiet. In truth, with the lack of sleep and the hard work, she'd be surprised if the men noticed if lightning hit the house.

Kare started the truck. In the silence the engine sounded like a roar.

"Go," Millanie ordered. If Drew or Johnny woke she

wanted to be half a mile down the road before they could dress and get downstairs. The last thing she needed on this mission was two more people to worry about.

Kare kept talking as she drove. "This is so exciting. I feel like I'm on one of those TV shows with a fast car chase. I've never done anything this wild. Once I ran away from home when I was about seven. I got halfway to the main road before I ran out of food and water. Then I had to walk all the way back to the farmhouse exhausted, hungry, and dying of thirst. I found my parents eating supper when I stepped in the back door. They hadn't even noticed I'd been gone, much less missed me."

"Dim your lights when you head into town." Millanie wanted this to go smoothly. "When you pull behind the bookstore, turn off your lights completely. I'll hand you a flashlight, but don't turn it on unless you have to."

"I won't need it," Kare whispered, as if spies might be hiding close enough to hear them. "Mr. Hatcher put new bulbs in the back light. I just hope he remembered to turn it on."

"Take the flashlight just in case."

"Roger, over and out," Kare said as she slowed. "This is more fun than jumping on the bed. Don't worry, Captain, I've seen my wedding so I know nothing is going to happen to us. Or me anyway. Sorry," she squealed. "Never mind. Forget what I said."

"Great." Millanie wished she believed. This seemed like a good time to start.

Kare turned off the pickup lights, pulled to a stop, and slid from the truck, a flashlight in one hand and the bookstore key in the other.

Mr. Hatcher hadn't left the back light on, but there was enough moon for Kare to easily see the door.

Millanie rolled down the window as she pulled the Glock from her bag. She watched Kare walk all the way to the back door. If she saw anything amiss, Millanie knew she'd fire one shot in the ground and have the deputy running toward her. On a night like this, one shot would sound an alarm for blocks.

Chapter 46

WINTER'S INN

BEAU YATES SET DOWN HIS GUITAR AND STEPPED OUT ONTO the little balcony of his room. He'd spent the day talking to Lark and making plans. For now, he hoped to visit as often as he could and stay at the bed-and-breakfast. He didn't want to rush her. He loved her so much his insides ached. The only good thing about her not spending the night was that songs of missing her danced in his head.

As he looked into the darkness, he noticed the Blue Moon Diner sign with its faded painted blue moon. Through the trees he could see the back of the bookstore and a glimpse of the clock tower on Main. He'd had so many memories here, but none would ever hold a candle to yesterday when he'd walked out of the diner twice with Lark's hand in his. He wouldn't be surprised if the owner didn't bar him from the place.

A pickup turned into the back lot just across the creek. It was a little late to stop by the bookstore, but maybe someone just wanted to sleep off the drinking he'd done at

Buffalo's, or maybe it was someone picking up Rick Matheson. The lawyer's light was still on upstairs. If he decided to take on Max Dewy's case, he'd be working late every night. Rick was a good lawyer who took the hard cases. He was running for district attorney. If he got it, folks said he'd never have time for a wife and family. He'd grow old single like the last DA did.

Beau continued to watch the night, lost in his own thoughts of settling down.

The minute Kare Cunningham stepped from a truck, Beau made her out through the gaps in the tree branches. Even in the night he could see her scarves flying as she ran toward the back door. Too late for her to be at the bookstore, but maybe she'd forgotten something.

An instant later, he saw a shadow rise like smoke from the landing on the back stairs. A thin figure, dressed in black and wearing a hood. No one had opened the upstairs door to the offices. Whoever had been there was waiting for Kare.

Beau swung off the balcony into Martha Q's flower bed and started running. Kare was in trouble. Maybe the same guy who'd mugged him was planning to attack her.

He hit the creek bed at a full run and tumbled into the dried branches and leaves, then crawled up the other side and started toward the back door of the bookstore. The shadow was almost to her. Kare looked like she was frantically trying to get her key to open the door.

A shot, close, shattered the silent night.

For a moment the world froze. No one moved. Not Beau, or the shadow, or Kare.

Chapter 47

MILLANIE RAISED HER WEAPON, PREPARING TO FIRE AGAIN, but the shadow grabbed Kare just as she opened the door and he shoved her into the bookstore. They vanished, out of range. The girl Millanie thought she had covered had disappeared.

With her Glock in one hand and her cane in the other, Millanie struggled from the cab of the pickup just as she heard footsteps behind her.

"Captain. It's Beau." A voice came out of the night before she saw his figure. "What's happening?"

"He's got Kare," was all Millanie had time to say before yelling came from the bookstore. Pounding sounded from the open door as books began to fly out like missiles.

To Millanie's shock, the shadow of a man backed out, dodging not bullets, but books. Kare was yelling from inside. "Get away from me!"

When the man turned to run, Millanie raised her weapon and he froze.

She didn't move as Beau circled the guy and grabbed his arms from behind. The bar fights he'd probably had to stop during his career came in handy now. A deputy pulled his cruiser into the parking lot, lights flashing. He jumped out of his car, trying to draw his weapon at the same time.

Kare stepped to the doorway of the bookstore. She flipped on the back light Mr. Hatcher had finally put a bulb in after Beau was mugged. A circle of bright light shone like a stage and now there was no problem seeing who the criminal was among them.

"That's him," Kare said calmly. "That's the man who stood between me and my car."

"What do we do with him, Captain?" Beau asked. "This is my first capture."

Millanie smiled. She'd been working with total amateurs tonight, not a trained man in sight, including the new deputy, who was looking for his handcuffs. "Just hold him, Beau, so I don't have to shoot him."

Before Millanie could stop Kare, the fairy stood on her toes and slammed a book into the shadow's head. "That's for scaring me and for hurting Beau."

"I didn't hurt Beau," the man growled as he turned back to glare at Kare. When he did, his hood slid off and Beau jerked hard on the man's arms.

"I know who this guy is. He works at the bank. Lark told me he disappeared a few days ago. He's been embezzling money."

"People are innocent until proven guilty," Kare announced as she raised the book again. "Make a move, mister, and I'll clobber you."

"Take him away, Deputy," Millanie ordered, "before you have to arrest them all."

The young deputy had found his handcuffs and had no trouble doing his duty.

Kare hugged Beau for saving her life.

Beau claimed she'd saved her own life by tossing books. "You've got quite an arm," he complimented.

Kare grinned. "When I was mad as a kid I used to throw all my schoolbooks out the window. I got mad often."

"We have to get back," Millanie said, wondering if she'd be

able to explain how it was possible that a fortune-teller, a singer, and a crippled captain had captured a major criminal.

Kare had no trouble going over, in detail, everything that had happened.

When they finally made it back to the homestead, she ran right straight into Johnny's arms and he swung her around as if he hadn't seen her in years.

Millanie slid from the pickup and saw Drew standing, his feet wide apart, his fists on his hips. He didn't offer to help her. He didn't say a word; he just stared at her as if he weren't sure he'd ever seen her before in his life. She didn't miss the fact that the men were dressed. The truck must have awakened them when Kare drove away. They'd had no choice but to wait and worry.

When she was almost to the house, he said, "I thought we agreed on total honesty, Millanie."

She didn't have to answer. He'd used her real name. They were no longer together. In going along with Kare. In doing her job. She'd lost him, the one man she might have loved forever.

Straightening, she told herself she'd take it like a soldier. She'd be strong. She'd always been alone and she would survive alone again. She'd tasted real passion, what caring and being cared about might feel like. Since she'd met him she hadn't trusted Drew and now, at the end, it hadn't been him, but her who'd broken trust.

"I'm sorry," she whispered. A hundred reasons came to mind. She knew she could protect Kare alone. He or Johnny might have gotten hurt. It was Kare's idea.

None of it mattered. Trust was the most important thing between people and she'd broken his.

The light from the lantern in the house was behind him. She couldn't see his face. She wasn't sure she wanted to. The frame of the old house closed in around him. For as long as she lived here, she'd see him standing there. Cold. Withdrawn. No longer caring about her.

Finally, he turned and went inside, where Johnny and Kare were dancing around the kitchen.

A moment later he returned and walked straight to Millanie. Without a word he lifted her up and carried her to the truck.

"Hey, where you going, Professor?" Johnny yelled.

"I'm borrowing your truck to take Millanie back to town. There's no danger. We can all go back. I'm sure Martha Q won't mind if we wake her up and all stay there tonight."

Kare slid under Johnny's arm. "No thanks," he said. "I think I'd rather stay here with the bugs than go back to a fancy bed-and-breakfast with my brother-in-law."

Drew waved. "See you in the morning."

"Bring food when you come and make it closer to noon."

Drew drove away. He didn't say a word on the ride back to town. She decided that he was being what he'd always been, a nice guy. As he had the first night, he was seeing that she got home safely.

When they pulled up to the inn, he helped her down and they walked together to the porch. She wasn't surprised the lock code hadn't changed so there was no need to wake Martha Q. They let themselves in.

He walked her all the way to her door and opened it. She limped in and turned to face him. One last look. One quick good-bye.

"Thank you." She straightened, knowing that she'd ruined any chance of ever being with him. She was an expert at knowing people, but she hadn't trusted the one man she'd met worth trusting. She'd been too slow to care, too slow to love. "Good-bye, Drew."

He frowned at her, obviously still angry. Finally, he let out a long breath and said, "I'm not leaving, Millie, so stop saying good-bye."

He stepped into her room and closed the door. "I'm angry. I'm hurt, but I'm not leaving, and if you want me to, you'll have to use that weapon you've been hiding in your purse for days."

She set the bag down and waited.

"We agreed to trust—" he started as he began unbuttoning her dirt-covered blouse.

"We did," she agreed. "And I thought about telling you but—"

He knelt and unstrapped her brace, then slid off her trousers as she held his shoulder and balanced on one foot. "You need a shower, and then we'll talk. But get one thing straight, Millie, we will talk this out. I'm not leaving."

"I'll need a crutch for the shower," she began, too exhausted to complain about being almost nude in front of him. Her thoughts were circling so fast in her mind she wasn't sure she could think, much less talk things out.

"No, you won't need the crutch. You can lean on me."

Millanie fought back tears as he stripped off his clothes.

When he looked up he smiled. "I'm pretty beat up and scarred, Millie, but I'm here and I'm not going anywhere. I'm through running and hiding. You can lean on me from now on. You don't have to be a soldier anymore."

He lifted her in his arms and moved to the shower. As the warm water washed over them, they held each other without saying a word. Finally, he turned off the water and wrapped a towel around her.

When he carried her to bed and began drying her, she closed her eyes and smiled. As he strapped on her brace, she whispered, "Can we talk tomorrow? I'd like to sleep with the man I love tonight."

He bunkered her leg with pillows. "Honest, Millie?"

"Honest."

Without a word he moved beside her, holding her body against him as they listened to Beau a floor above.

A gentle melody of a lonely man finally finding one true heart.

Read on for a sneak peek of the
new Harmony novella from Jodi Thomas

MIDNIGHT BET

*Appearing in the anthology ASK ME WHY,
coming July 2015 from Jove!*

Chapter 1

RICK MATHESON DROPPED OFF THE SIDE OF THE WIDE porch of his cousin's home and walked toward a stand of cottonwood trees that were old when he'd played among their low branches as a kid twenty years ago.

Summer Sundays in the South, he thought. Everyone still dressed in their church best and stuffed on a potluck meal that was better than any restaurant could serve. He heard laughter from the under-forty crowd scattered in folding chairs on the front lawn and porch. They were supposed to be watching the little Mathesons play in the afternoon shade but the kids pretty much ran free range on the wide lawn.

The half dozen teenagers, who usually had the babysitting job, were over in the corral saddling a few of Hank's horses so they could ride. In an hour the shade in the canyon behind his headquarters would be perfect for an afternoon gallop.

Mathesons lived on farms and ranches for fifty miles

around Harmony, Texas. A few, like him, even lived in town, but Rick knew all considered this old place as the family home. It wasn't the original homestead. That had burned generations ago. But, Hank Matheson's ranch had been built on the first small acreage the family settled on. It was home base. Rick had grown up chasing fireflies in the front yard and racing his cousins on horseback across the open land. At thirty, he'd always thought he'd be married by now and have joined the kid watchers on the porch.

Only life and his apparent dangerous career choice had derailed his plan.

He looked back at his family and swore he could feel his heart turning to lead. He was in trouble this time, bad trouble and he had to keep it from them for as long as possible.

Rick was four years out of law school and, for the second time, someone wanted to kill him. He had no proof, just a feeling. Hang-ups on his phone. His old office had been broken into twice. A car, with the brights on, almost ran him off the road last week. Trouble was stalking him.

When revenge came after him this time, murder might succeed. If Rick told his family, they'd protect him, but he couldn't allow that. One of them might get caught in the crossfire. So he had to go on living his life exactly as always and pretend a storm wasn't blowing full out toward him.

Rick tried to shake his mood. Maybe he was overreacting? Hell, maybe he should change careers. Being a lawyer didn't seem to be working out. He thought of himself as good-looking, came from an upstanding family, well-educated, had all his own teeth. But, the last woman he'd asked out had simply smiled and said that she didn't date lawyers.

Maybe he should have made an objection to her rejection, but he hadn't been that into her to start with. She'd simply been someone he might go to dinner with or maybe move into a casual relationship with eventually. He didn't see love and off-spring with the lawyer-hater, or with any woman he met. He didn't see passion either, which bothered him. He was working far too hard. Monks had more of a social life than he did.

Rick turned and walked back toward the house. When he stepped inside the kitchen door, he heard his old Aunt Fat telling one of her favorite stories to the new bride of his second cousin.

"There's an old bridge near downtown that runs across a dried up creek bed where water used to flow wild." Aunt Fat, like the teacher she'd been for forty years, paused, making sure she had everyone's attention. "The bridge doesn't look like much now, it being old and all, but there's a legend about the spot. Word is if a couple kiss while standing in the exact middle of the bridge, they'll never stop loving each other."

The bride winked at her new husband and he nodded. Everyone in the kitchen laughed knowing exactly where the newlyweds would be heading as soon as the family dinner broke up.

Rick smiled. Aunt Fat had told that story for as long as he could remember and it always had the same effect on brides.

"You all right, Rick?" his mother asked as he passed her. She was one of those magic moms who could look at any one of her children and know their mood or temperature or if they needed to eat something.

"I'm fine, Mom," he lied. "I just got a lot of work waiting for me at the office. I think I'll head on in."

"You work too hard, Rick." She patted his back. "You're just like your father was." When her arm circled around his waist, she added, "And you need to eat something. You're thin as a fence post."

"I know," he answered, "but the work has to get done. I forget to eat." He'd moved into a bigger office last month and hadn't had time to unpack before he went to work. Now he felt like a prisoner barred in by boxes every time he showed up at the office. "I really need to leave," he said, knowing he'd have to say it at least one more time before he made it out the door.

Only tonight his mother surprised him. She simply kissed his cheek and whispered, "Offer Lizzie a ride back to town. She wrecked another car."

Rick might be tapping thirty but he knew a direct order from his mother when he heard it.

Looking over her head, he spotted Lizzie dressed like a hooker in mourning. Black fishnet hose. Black, almost see-through dress with one shoulder cut out to show off her tattoo. Platform sandals that could have doubled as stilts. The only color she wore lately was the green streaks in her hair. Elizabeth Lee Matheson. The only nut to ever fall off the Matheson tree. She'd gotten every wild, weird gene in the family and she'd always been a bother. She was a few years younger so he'd had to play with her when none of the other cousins would and teach her to ride when she didn't want to learn, and drive her to high school when she wrecked three cars her sophomore year. Her hardship license was hard on cars.

Rick could continue, but the list was too long and too painful. He didn't bother to argue with his mom now. "Sure. Glad to drive her home," he lied again.

Walking over to the long bar that separated the kitchen from the den, Rick tapped Lizzie on her bare shoulder. "You about ready to go, Lizzie Lee? I could give you a lift."

She looked up from trying to pop the top on her latest beer. "I'm sooooo ready to leave." As always, she'd brought a six pack to the potluck and drank most of it herself.

Rick helped her off the stool thinking that the high-heeled shoes almost made her normal size. For a woman who didn't tip five feet or a hundred pounds, four or five beers must make her dead drunk.

Lizzie waved goodnight to everyone while he tugged her around the crowd. Almost every family gathering, someone had to take her home and this must be his time.

He poured her into his new car and prayed she wouldn't throw up on the way to town.

"Hey, Ricky, you want to stop for a drink on the way home?" She giggled. "Oh, it's Sunday, I forgot. Every place is closed. Guess you'll just have to give me a rain check."

"I couldn't tonight anyway, Lizzie, I have work to do at my office." Another thing he hated about Lizzie, she called him Ricky when she'd been drinking. No one called him Ricky. Plus, if his dating life wasn't already dead, showing up with his wacky cousin in public would probably do the trick. She seemed to always say the wrong thing in a crowd or accidently spill something. His favorite flaw of his cousin's, if anyone can have a favorite flaw, was the way she always mixed up peoples' names. She called his cousin Hank "Hunk" and the preacher's second wife "Two" instead of Lou. Since birth she'd called the Leary twins, "Pete and Repeat."

"Could we stop at the bridge Aunt Fat was talking about?"

"No," he answered, starting the engine.

"I'd really like to see it. A legend in Harmony. Too bad my parents hadn't kissed on the bridge. I think my dad took every deployment he could sign up for to get away from mom. My first memories are of them yelling in the middle of the night."

He drove under the ranch arch and headed toward Harmony on the Farm to Market road everyone called Lone Oak Road. "All right. We'll stop. Five minutes."

She leaned back and closed her eyes. "Thanks for offering to take me home. You're the only one in the family I can stand to talk to or who wants to talk to me."

Rick tossed his jacket over her bare shoulder and cranked up the air conditioning even though the afternoon hadn't reached ninety degrees. Maybe the circulation would help clear her perfume from the air. "You're not so bad, Lizzie." In truth, she'd had it rough. Her dad had been in the Navy. When he was listed as missing in action, her mother couldn't stand the pressure and sent Lizzie, about eight-years-old, to live with her Matheson grandmother. He'd heard her mother cracked up completely when her husband was moved from missing to killed in action. Granny always said Lizzie's mother just went to sleep, but Rick thought a bottle of pills may have helped the process. Anyway, Granny and Little Lizzie grieved and the money they inherited from her parents helped keep food on the table.

Granny loved Lizzie, but she never let the girl out of her

sight. Rick remembered Granny even made Lizzie go every-where with her. Quilting. Widows' Sunday class. She had to sit in the beauty shop while Granny got her hair curled and sprayed every week. Rick remembered Lizzie called her grandmother's Sunday school class the "Nearest to Heaven" class and the all day quilting bees "Stitch and complain."

From grade school on she'd never fit in. Somewhere in middle school, she'd given up trying. Lizzie seemed to go out of her way to be unique. Half her outfits looked like they'd been on the Halloween close-out special rack. Granny always told people Lizzie simply marched to a different drummer, but if so Rick had never heard the beat.

"The whole family just tolerates me and I feel the same way about them," Lizzie said as she fought with her seatbelt. "They're all nice folks, but I feel like I've been assigned to the wrong family, you know?"

He didn't know, but he answered, "They all love you, honey." Lies were starting to dribble out of his mouth. At this rate he'd need a bib before long.

"That must be why they all want to change me into some-one else. I swear if they thought they could get away with it, half of them would vote to have me stretched so I'd at least look more Matheson." She poked her head beneath his coat like a turtle retreating into a shell. "I just want to find my people, you know? Somewhere, someplace probably far away, there are people just like me waiting supper, wonder-ing where I am."

"Right," Rick answered, thinking that if anyone ever found that place, it would take about a second to collect the money to send her there.

Ten minutes later, they pulled up to the bridge and climbed out of the car. She leaned against the fender pulling his jacket around her as if it were cold. "I'm never going to fall in love," she whispered. "This is probably the one time I'll ever stand on this bridge and I'm here with my cousin."

He agreed. "I almost fell once. Met a woman I thought was perfect but it turns out she didn't want commitment, she only wanted my body."

"Yeah, I played that game a few times in high school."

Rick didn't comment that he'd heard all about it from some of his friends.

She straightened. "I think I'd better head home. I don't feel so good. Beer and pot roast seem to be fighting in my stomach."

He reached for the handle on his side as she did the same.

Something sounding very much like a shot whistled through the still air. Rick ducked inside his car as if the glass would somehow protect him.

Lizzie, with less skill, did the same. As she leaned out to close the door on her side, his coat tumbled off her shoulders and into the dirt. She reached down, grabbed it and tugged it over her.

For a few heartbeats they were both silent, listening for another shot.

Without a word to Lizzie, he gunned the engine and threw the car into drive. They flew off the bridge and headed toward Lizzie's place on the other side of town.

Rick's mind raced. The shot could be another attempt on his life? One of these days whoever was out there wanting him dead might get lucky.

Lizzie didn't say a word as he drove down sleepy streets, past the tiny mall and bounced over railroad tracks. Nothing much had been built beyond the tracks in fifty years. A few grain elevators spotted the horizon. A dozen houses were scattered out along the winding road, not close enough to be town streets, or far apart enough to be called in the country. Half a mile farther Lizzie's house hid behind one of the town's veterinary clinics. Corrals and trailers scattered around the vet's office almost hid her place from view.

Rick bumped along a dirt lane to her property as he circled the corral to get to her house. An adobe fence, overgrown with morning glories, separated her land from the vet's. Rick didn't breathe until he neared her back door.

"You really should get this road paved, Lizzie. One day a car is going to disappear in a rut."

"Why, if it rains I can park in Dr. McCall's lot. He doesn't

mind and there's a path from my front door to his place."
She stepped out as if there was nothing else to talk about
and tossed his coat back to him.

"Thanks," she called without looking back.

"You're welcome," he answered too low for her to hear.

Rick tried to decide if gunfire in her world didn't seem
strange or if she was too drunk to have noticed.

Watching her hug herself as if it were cold and stagger
toward the porch, he wondered if she was really that drunk
or the ridiculous shoes simply weren't made for cobble-
stones. He didn't care. All he wanted to do was drop her off
and head back to his office. The federal prosecutor had asked
for his help on an old case, and Rick had a feeling that
somewhere in his files might be the clue needed to send a
really bad guy to jail. Only problem was, he had to get to it
before the bad guys got to him.

He'd call the sheriff and tell her about the shot, if it was
a shot. Then, he'd be careful about standing around looking
like an easy target. The idea of someone following him
didn't make sense. Harmony was a small town; folks still
noticed strangers and license plates that weren't local. If the
shot had been directed at him, it was probably meant to scare
him off and the guy just caught a lucky chance when Rick
was dumb enough to stop on the bridge.

Lizzie almost made it to her home, but she missed a step
two feet from the porch and sank her high heels into the
mud. Shaking off mud, she climbed onto the first step and
turned to wave good-bye. As if just remembering what had
happened, she yelled back at him, "You going to call that
gunfire in?"

He shook his head. "Probably only a backfire."

"Want to tell me why that might not be the truth?" She
glanced at him with those big eyes of hers. "You know,
Ricky, if you ever need me, I'll come running."

"No. Don't worry about me, Lizzie Lee." The last thing
he wanted to talk about with her was his problems. Shifting
the car into reverse, he offered a quick wave.

As he drove away, he remembered her house had once

been owned by the veterinarian who built the clinic. Years ago the clinic, Lizzie's house and the small shop across the road had all been one property. The last vet lived in the house, ran the clinic and rented out the shop. Now, Lizzie owned the house and the shop. She did pet grooming on Wednesdays and Fridays at the shop. Who knows what she did the other days but he didn't want her worrying about him.

Rick thought about asking where the new vet lived, but he really didn't care. With no pets he wasn't likely to use either of their services. "Good night, Lizzie," he yelled as he glanced back and saw her entering her house.

He tossed his jacket into the backseat knowing that it would need cleaning. Between her perfume and her dropping it on the bridge, he doubted he could wear it now.

Rick couldn't help wondering just how few friends she must have if she counted him among them. He thought of yelling, "Don't call me, Ricky, and for God's sake please don't ever try to save me," but she was already inside.

Rick laughed. The last person on this planet he'd ever call for help was his nutty cousin.